Book One of the Chronicles of Reality
Reality
<u>And So It Begins</u>...

Ruby —

Thanks for being such a wonderful friend, "mother", and teacher.

You are a wonderful woman. I'm so glad you are a part of my life.

Your friend,
Kris

Book One of the Chronicles of Reality
And So It Begins...

by

K.M. Outten

ISBN 1-58500-242-9

About the Book

There are those people who wake up in their dreary lives at the same time, eat the same breakfast, go to the same job, and watch the same television shows everyday. For them, the world is fine as long as no one "rocks the boat." Roxanne Black is *not* one of those people. In a world of mindless and spineless drones, there are those people who crave something more; a life with purpose, meaning and excitement. Roxanne Black *is* that person.

Roxanne Black is an extraordinary person living in an ordinary world. Her life of work and college is pushing her slowly closer to the end of a deep chasm. To escape the pain of the mundane, she buries herself in fantasy novels and movies, dreaming that life to be her own. Careful what you wish for...

Across a foggy reality gap, the kind that just might exist, there exists a world in turmoil. Another reality that is on the verge of a chasm of its own. Here, the people crave a savior. They are searching for the last of three Chosen souls to save them, hoping the last to be the best. The first Chosen One is an angry warrior, the second, a theif, and the third... Through the strong magic of a possessed pendant, they reach out and discover Roxanne, dreaming she may be their hero. Careful what you wish for...

When the two sides come together, all hell breaks loose. Lords falter, Fairies deceive, Heros fall, Shadows reign, and Roxanne learns to live again. This novel is an alternate reality story with a twist, a turn, then a total leap. Its a quest to save a world, create a willing but untrained hero, and save some dark souls... and those are just the good guys. If you've ever hated your job, your life, your relationship, or just plain cried out for something more in life, <u>And So It Begins...</u> Book One of the Chronicles of Reality will give you that brief moment of escape with the hope that there could be more.

This book is dedicated to my parents who gave me life, and then let me live it. And, to my husband who gave me the precious gift of time.

Chapter 1

I hate these fucking things. Roxanne swerved to avoid one of the pathetic booths adorned with oddities that resembled clothing from the sixties. She would be late to class again, that was a given, and having to manipulate her way around the "mall-dealers" was not improving her disposition.

"How about a nice jade necklace to go with your deep green eyes?" prompted a sleazy looking dealer.

Howz about a nice jade necklace crammed into your deep, dark, and disgusting orifice of a mouth? "No thanks, I'm late for class."

One of these days I'm going to learn to be more expressive, she thought. *My problem is I can always think of what to do, or say, but I seldom have the balls to say it. Actually I can't have balls...*

Roxanne was so deep in her usual ramble of thoughts that she didn't see the next booth; she didn't miss it either.

"Shit! I'm really sorry about that," she said as she stooped to pick up the numerous earrings and assorted necklaces she had managed to knock to the ground. "You see, it's just that..."

She stopped in mid-sentence as she came eye to eye with a very twisted old man. He was exactly that, twisted. His skin gave the appearance of having been wrapped around his face like a piece of old, wrinkled cloth, and his hands looked like twigs coated in the same mess of swaddling wrap. As for the rest of him she could only guess for he was covered from head to toe in a dusty black robe of sorts. Only his hands and face escaped the enclosed garment.

"It is quite all right my lovely young child, as you will find that I am as well," the man nearly whispered the words, yet his voice was oddly comforting.

Damn, I must have been staring!

The old man must have read her mind, "Most people do my child, most people do."

Roxanne was taken aback. Unable to think of a way to redeem herself she hurriedly picked up the remaining merchandise and started on her way. However, the old man was not as content for her to leave as she was at leaving. She had taken no more than three steps when he called to her to return. The strange thing was he never raised his voice beyond that soothing whisper, yet she heard him as clearly as though he were standing at her side. Reluctantly, she returned to his rag-tag booth.

"Before you rush off into the world never to return, might I inquire your name my child?"

"Roxanne," tripped off her tongue before she had time to consider that she was giving her name out to some complete stranger, who was weirder than she.

"Oh, it's quite all right. You will suffer no harm at my hands." He was doing it again. "Roxanne. That is a beautiful yet powerful name. Roxanne, would you like a piece of my jewelry?"

She knew it! He was just another swindler, an extremely talented one, but a swindler nonetheless. "Thanks, but no thanks. I'm busted."

For the first time he looked confused. "That you are my child," his gnarled face reddened, "but I fail to see what bearing that has on this situation."

Now it was Roxanne's turn to be embarrassed. "I mean I don't have any money."

"Please, I did not inquire as to whether or not you wished to purchase an item. I merely questioned as to your desire. At the least, gaze upon these objects of my labor and inform me which one you would choose."

"I really have to get to class..."

The old man's eyes pleaded with her soul. With a heavy sigh she looked over the jewelry. It was the most unusual collection of creations she had ever seen. All of the pendants had a life of their own. Each seemed to reach toward the gazer's eyes and hold them there with a force. The first was a depiction of a minute damsel chained to a tree as the fire of the pewter dragon lapped against her face. Roxanne thought she could hear her scream. She shuddered and forced herself to look away. The next magnificent piece displayed a gallant young knight in the midst of three tiny beasts. The beasts had evil eyes, blood dripping from their horribly detailed fangs, and crouched as though they might spring upon the hero at any moment.

Roxanne soon found herself lost in an endless maze of hundreds of tormented figures, each so detailed that it could start moving and existing at any second. Just when she thought she could take no more of the morbid little demons, a single, simple figure grabbed her attention. Gingerly she lifted it in her trembling hand. It seemed to burn with energy; it actually generated some heat. *And why not,* she thought. *After all, it is a dragon.* It was a perfectly formed dragon with crystal eyes, treacherous teeth, and a single flame shooting from its mouth. However, as with all his creations, this one too had its own weird twist. The perfectly reptilian body curved into a hideous claw, in which was held a shimmering crystal ball. Roxanne marveled at its powerful simplicity.

"I desire this one," she breathed.

"That is because it also desires you. Don't be afraid my child, take it."

"I really can't. It is too magnificent, and someone will surely pay you a great deal for it. Besides I..." This time his soothing voice left no room for argument. "You must accept my gift to you. No one else will pay me for that piece, for no one else can see it as do you. I will not suffer a refusal of my graciousness. Now take the pendant and go. I can tary with you no longer."

Without ever understanding why, she slipped the cord that held the lovely beast around her neck and turned toward her class. She had covered nearly half the distance before she turned to take a final look at her mysterious old man. He was nowhere in sight. It was as though he and his booth had vanished. With a shudder, she ran to class.

****

"How nice of you to join us today Miss Black. And so early too."

Roxanne had tried, as usual, to slip in through the back door unnoticed. She had also failed, as usual.

"Always my pleasure to brighten this dull class with my beaming presence Dr. Jameson." *Drop off the face of the planet into a fiery pit of hell.*

"I don't suppose you have your term paper to brighten my grade book."

"As a matter of fact I did manage to buy a decent one before class," she tossed the heavy binder, full of what she considered bull-shit, on his desk. But that's what philosophy was, bull-shit.

She took her usual seat next to Rick Nelson. He was a nice enough guy, with a body that could send a girl into spasms with one ripple of his numerous muscles. His firm, square jaw and dark blue eyes, together with his jet black hair made him easily the best looking Ken-doll she'd seen. The problem was his looks were all he had upstairs. He had the mental capacity of a fence post."What'd I miss?"

"Something about that Socrates guy. I guess he couldn't handle his booze, 'cause he died from just one drink. Guess he'd be boring at parties, huh?"

So much for that avenue of information. It appeared as though she would have to resort to listening to Dr. Jameson. The lecture turned out to be boring as usual, and soon Roxanne found herself wondering about that strange old man who had given her the fantastic necklace that hung around her neck. He had, she realized, exercised complete control over her. She had nearly been powerless against him. *Now you sound like one of those fantasy novels you are always reading, Roxie. It's just your unnaturally over-active imagination playing with your senses. So where'd the guy go?*

That question plagued her mind unrelentlessly for the rest of the class. Maybe he had had enough time to pack his belongings and move on. Perhaps she had been looking in the wrong place. None of these answers satisfied her. She leaned back in her chair and began to concentrate. *He went...He went... He went.. He went nowhere because he was never there!*

"Ouch!" A sudden burning in her chest pulled Roxanne abruptly back to the here and now.

"What is it Miss Black?"

Roxanne ignored the question. She lifted the collar of her shirt and looked at her chest. The dragon's flame was red with heat. As she stared at it, it slowly returned to cold metal. But on her chest was a tiny burn mark that hurt like hell.

"Miss Black? Miss Black? Are you okay?"

Slowly she looked up at Dr. Jameson,"I'm fine,"she mumbled. "Just fine."

Reluctantly Dr. Jameson accepted her response and returned to his lecture, and she returned to her own private thoughts. She was sure of one thing now, her mind was not playing tricks on her. The burn on her chest was real, there was no disputing that. She knew now that she had to find that old man again. She had to know what exactly he had done to her.

Almost as an afterthought, she tried to take the necklace off, but it was suddenly too heavy. *What the hell is this?* She tried again to remove the demonic thing, no such luck. *I've got to find that old bastard and make him take this damn thing off!* She grabbed her books and bolted from the classroom, not even lingering long enough to hear her professor's cries to return.

She ran straight for the mall, plowing through the crowds without hesitation, hoping against fate that he would be there. She reached the mall panting, out of breath, and pissed as hell. He, of course, was nowhere to be found. *That's because he was never here to begin with.* Frantically she searched the crowd of dealers.

"Did you see where the old man that was right here went?" she asked the nearest dealer.

"Do you want to buy a nice leather purse?"

"I haven't fucking got time for that bull-shit right now! Did you see the old man that was here leave?" Roxanne knew she was getting hysterical, but she couldn't calm down.

"For your information bitch, there was never anyone else here. I've been here all day!"

Roxanne fell to the ground. Somehow she had known that would be the answer. All she could do was shake her head. *What have you done to me? What the hell have you done?*

****

The shimmering figure of the beautiful young girl danced upon the mystic's cauldron. Her long brown hair danced on her broad shoulders, confusion tormented her deep green eyes, her tan face was bent in a frown, and her shapely body shivered in exhaustion. An ominous specter glared into the water, the girl shook as though suddenly chilled. A terrifying chuckle echoed from the black robes.

"This is the one?" queried a sinister voice from the blackness.

"Yes, yes. She's the one. She's the only one who saw me, and she's the only one who saw the pendant. I'm sure she..."

A spectral arm silenced the twisted old mystic. "Will she come?"

"It is fated now. The Protectors will call her here to save them."

"Are you positive she means doom?"

"Yes, Master. I am sure of it."

A spectral arm passed over the cauldron and the figure vanished. "So it begins."

****

Roxanne pounded on the apartment door. She could have saved time by hunting through her bag for her keys but she was too tired. Eventually her roommate's boyfriend answered the door.

"Where are your keys?"

"In the bottom of my bag. I thought I'd save time by knocking on the door; I didn't realize it would take a military effort to get someone to answer it," she pushed her way into the apartment. As usual, her less than pleasing roommate was sitting on the living room floor, surrounded by dirty dishes, painting her nails. *How I'd love to toss her off the balcony. Too bad she weighs a ton.* An evil grin crossed her face as she walked to her bedroom. Dropping her bag on her bed, she returned to the kitchen to get a drink. Plastered on the wall above the sink was another of Victoria's infernal notes. This one read: There is no ghost living here, but there are always unclaimed dishes in the sink. Once again, if you use a dish, wash a dish. Also, clean the stove and counter when you cook. Give a hoot, don't pollute. She almost threw-up. Every week there was a new note, and every day it was Victoria's dishes that were left in the sink, and her mess in the kitchen. And once a week she would wash them, all the while bitching about the mess, and that day a new note would appear on the wall. Roxanne had already disposed of her share of the annoying things.

"Did you see my note?" asked a whiny voice from the living room.

"Couldn't miss it Vic," *I'd like to cut her vocal cords with a chain saw.*

"I'm not saying it was you, but there were a lot of dirty dishes. I had to wash them all, and I think..."

"Save it Vic! I honestly don't give a shit. We all know they were yours anyway."

Before Victoria could respond, Roxanne stormed out of the kitchen, down the hall, and into the bedroom. *God that felt good.* She couldn't believe she had actually said something. It had bothered her all semester, but she had always quietly accepted it. Maybe there was a good side to this necklace thing after all. *Oh, that's right, I've still got to figure out what to do about this evil thing.* In the excitement of finally having the balls to say something to Victoria she had nearly forgotten the demonic dragon that held her captive. What she needed to do was get the thing off.

First she tried cutting through the cord, nothing. The scissors didn't even fray the rope. In a flash of genius, or not, she tried untying the cord. *No shit it didn't work, Roxie.* Beginning to become slightly frustrated, she attempted burning through the cord. All that did was heat up the dragon, threatening to add to her burn. She tried, once again, to lift it over her head. It instantly gained weight. *Just like Vic. Okay, now I'm loosing it.* For a moment she considered trying to melt the dragon, but only for a moment. *Well, it's not coming off, so now what?* Then it came to her, an idea so bizarre it might actually work. Grabbing her purse she headed out the door.

****

The streets of the drab little city she called home passed outside her truck window. How often she had seen these streets; how often she had wished she were looking at some other streets, anywhere else. All she saw in these streets was the here and now she had lived in for so long. *Life is endless,* she thought. *I wish I didn't want it to be over. Shit!* She slammed on her brakes and swivered to the left, just missing the idiot who decided it was necessary to stop completely before turning. Justifiable homicide. *Sorry officer, but he stopped before turning...*

Roxanne turned down Fourth Avenue and began scanning the roadside for the little shop she knew existed, she just wasn't sure where. She drove past a florist, a dentist, and three mortuaries. *This town is trying to tell us something and we aren't paying attention.* All the buildings, if you could call them that, where old and leaning. They resembled little old ladies who were hunched over threatening to die at any moment. Every structure looked like every other structure.Soon, all was a blur and Roxie wasn't even sure why she was here. But then she found what she had been searching for, or it found her.

Roxie hadn't even been looking anymore. She was content with driving in a nearly hypnotized state, and almost missed the black cat that ran across the road directly in front of her. Abruptly, she halted her truck, and that's when she saw the tiny shop. It was scarcely different from the rest. It seemed to slump against the building next to it, but she couldn't be sure of whether or not it was leaning on it or holding it up. The red brick chipped and fell as she marveled at it's age. One window faced the outer world, and she wasn't sure but she thought more light shone from inside the building than from without. The door looked as though it was at least a hundred years old. Hanging just above the door was a black sign with silver letters that read: Diana's Book Store. Roxanne parked her truck and went inside.

The interior of the store smelled of a thousand different fragrances. It failed to be a dark and musty place with shriveled-up old people working behind a barely standing counter. Much to her amazement, the store was brightly lit, the shelves of books were all new and sparkling, and the lady behind the counter appeared to be in her late twenties. She wore a kind grin and greeted Roxanne with a friendly nod. Roxanne gazed with open wonderment at the countless volumes of books, cards, spices, and candles that sat upon the glimmering shelves. Would she be able to find what she needed?

"May I be of service?" Roxanne turned to come face to face with the lady from behind the counter. "Are you looking for something in particular?"

"I...that is yes, well, sort of. You see I'm not really sure...It's just that my necklace..."

The counter lady smiled sweetly at Roxanne's apparent lack of control of her own mouth. "Do you need to know the value of your necklace?"

"No, not really. I was just curious as to whether or not there were any others like it. You see the man I purchased it from told me it was one of a kind. I just want to make sure I wasn't taken too badly," Roxanne cringed at the lie. She had never been any good at lying, but what else could she say. *Hi, I was just wondering if you could take this bewitched necklace from around my neck.*

"Wouldn't a jeweler be better suited for such a task?" inquired the lady.

Good question. "Well, it's just the nature of the pendant made me think that this type of store would know more." Roxanne removed the dragon from within the confines of her shirt.

"I see," said the clerk,"You felt a Pagan book store would have a better grasp on dragons. Oh, don't worry, I'm not really offended. This is the kind of reaction I always receive."

"No, it really isn't what you think," stumbled Roxanne,"The pendant has... well, it has a different design. It's unique."

The lady lifted the little demon and began examining it. Roxanne half expected it to bite her. The clerk turned it over in her hand several times, paying special attention to the flame and the crystal. After a few minutes she asked Roxanne to remove it from around her neck. Roxanne simply mumbled something about preferring not to until she knew if it was worth anything. The lady didn't seem to like that answer, but she accepted it. After a time, the lady went to a shelf and pulled a huge volume entitled <u>Ancient Jewels</u>.

"It appears to me that your necklace is very old. I can only estimate that its age is hundreds of years. It's not made of precious materials, but it certainly isn't worthless. If there is any written history of the pendant it would be contained in this book."

Roxanne looked at the book for a moment wondering if it might actually contain the information she needed. "How much for the book?"

"You may take it for fifteen dollars, or in return you promise to tell me the story of how you manage to get the damned thing off your neck. Please don't look so surprised, or I'll be forced to believe you underestimated my intelligence."

Roxanne humbly accepted the book, nodded a good-bye, and nearly bolted for the door. *Why do I feel as though I'm in a cheap Twilight Zone episode? I wonder if Dr. Jameson would accept that as an excuse for leaving his class. Excuse me for running out the other day, but you see I was caught in this Twilight Zone...* She shook her head and pulled herself back to her faltering reality. She stared at the volume in her hands. It was time to go home and try again.

****

This time she had her keys in her hand when she reached her apartment, but this time the door was unlocked. Roxanne looked at her watch, 12:37 a.m. She knew instinctively that her roommates were already in bed, and that, like the morons they were, had managed to leave the door unlocked yet again. *One of these nights someone's going to sneak in and slit their throats, and I'm going to let him do it.* She slipped through the door and locked it behind her. Quietly she walked down the hall to her bedroom. Without turning on any lights, she undressed and slipped into bed, a trick Victoria had never learned. Vic would have turned on all the lights, thrown things around, and started talking to her. *Oh well, shit happens.*

Roxanne laid in bed unable to fall asleep. Her mind was ablaze with the events of the day. Gingerly she fingered the miniature dragon that had started all these odd events. What was the answer? Was it contained in the book that was hidden under the seat of her truck? She had left it there for reasons she couldn't even explain to herself. At best she knew the book frightened her, and that made no sense whatsoever. But, nevertheless, she was scared. She had even been afraid of opening the ominous volume. She had driven around for hours before she finally stopped at a Village Inn. The book had remained unopened on the table infront of her for four hours. All she could muster the courage to do was lift it in her hands, turn it over, examine the binding, and then place it back on the table. She was really afraid that it wouldn't tell her a damn thing, and so she chose to wait. But for what?

****

Roxanne jumped out of bed, torn from her hideous nightmares by the screaming of her roommate's alarm clock. She looked at her clock, 5 a.m. Viciously she pounded the off button on Vic's clock. "Wake-up!"

"Did my alarm go off?"

"Yes Sleeping Beauty, now get up!"

Vic looked at her clock, and reset the alarm. From that point on, Roxanne was forced awake every ten minutes by the shrilling alarm until six thirty. *I'm going to find the person whose bright idea it was to create a snooze button and kill him slowly.* Victoria finally got out of bed at six forty-five; Roxanne pulled her covers over her head and slept 'till noon, after all, it was a Saturday.

By the time Roxanne was a functioning member of society, Vic had left to go home for the weekend. No big loss. Roxanne wandered out into the living room and said good morning to Jennette, her other roommate. Jennette wasn't nearly as annoying as Vic, but boy was she denser than brick.

"Do you want to see the new pictures of Andy?" Jennette asked as she brought the pictures over to Roxanne. "I took them over Spring Break."

Roxanne interjected the correct number of ooh's and ahh's as the all too familiar face of Jennette's boyfriend flashed infront of her. But her mind was most definitely elsewhere. She grasped her pendant and thought of the book that lay hidden in her truck. She knew she had to go get it and search for the information she needed. She knew she had to do it soon. She was already beginning to develop some sort of warped dependance on her bewitched dragon. She found its presence oddly comforting. Pictures scattered everywhere as Roxanne jumped up off the couch, ran into her bedroom for her keys, and then down to her truck.

Her hands were shaking so badly it took her a good five minutes to get the key into the keyhole. She climbed into her truck, shutting and locking the door behind her. *If I'm going to do this I'd better be alone.* She fumbled under the seat for the book she knew to be stored away there in secrecy. Finally, her trembling fingers touched the cold, hard surface of the book. She pulled it out and gazed at it for several long minutes. After a great length, she drew a deep breath and opened the book.

Nothing happened. *What did you think would happen, stupid? Did you expect it to explode?* Slowly she began turning the pages of the book that had terrified her all night. Pictures of exotic jewels danced before her eyes. Artists' renditions of countless pendants and earrings, bracelets and broaches, and even timepieces. The pages stood filled with every treasure imaginable, and right in the middle of it all was her necklace. She drew several short breaths in an effort to calm herself. It's just words in a book, it can't hurt you. *Neither can a normal necklace.* With a stubborn determination, she stilled the pounding of her heart and read.

> There exist in all the known worlds only three such
> amulets. No being is certain as to the forging of
> these brilliantly crafted designs. All that is known
> of them is legend. It is said they were forged in the
> fires of hell by three sister witches who longed to

remain joined for all eternity. Alas, the sisters failed to leave the hell to which they had journeyed. Thus, it is there they remain. The pendants, however, were soon transported to places within the known worlds by ways unknown. It is said that, once placed upon a lost soul, the necklace is irremovable. They are also said to join kindred spirits.

Roxanne slammed the book shut. *Irremovable!* There had to be a way to take the fucking thing off. She threw the book on the floor. *Liar!* She kicked the evil thing repeatedly before she calmed down enough to realize that it wasn't her book. *Shit!* She reached down and lifted the volume in her hands, examining it for signs of damage. The book appeared untouched. *Great, I don't even have the power to hurt paper.*

As she handled the book, a piece of parchment slid from between the covers onto the floor of her truck. *I spend more time picking things up off the floor of my truck...* Strange symbols covered the parchment. Roxie had taken French, Arabic, German, Russian, and a few African languages but she didn't recognize anything infront of her. *It's probably some language from another reality. Yeah, whatever, beam me up Scotty.* She slipped the parchment into the book, and went back upstairs.

****

"Why did you take off like that?"

Roxie cringed at the sound of Jennette's whining. "I thought I heard my truck's alarm go off."

"Oh, I hope nothing got damaged."

"It was a false alarm."

"I'm glad everything is okay."

And I'm glad you don't realize that I've never had an alarm on my truck. "Thanks Jennette."

Tired of dealing with morons, Roxie retreated to her room. She plopped onto her bed that she never made because it annoyed Victoria and Jennette so badly. Letting out a heavy sigh, she flipped open her philosophy book and pretended to read it. It only took twenty minutes for her to fall asleep.

When she opened her eyes she found herself surrounded by a grey mist, suspended just above the ground in a room that resembled something from the Middle Ages. Standing on the floor directly in front of her were thirteen robed figures. Each of the figures held their arms in the air, and the center figure was drawing images in the air with a wooden staff. Slowly he opened his eyes and began to speak. His lips were moving but Roxanne couldn't hear him.

"What? I can't hear you, " she shouted.

The man in the center stopped abruptly at the sound of her voice. He began to dissipate. Urgently he waved his staff around his head. Sensing his desperation, Roxanne tried to cling to the air around her, but another force seemed to be pulling her in another direction. She could not remain where she was. Yet the desperate man before her begged her to stay. A sudden, wild look crossed his face and he thrust his staff toward her. She lunged forward... and woke up on the floor of her bedroom.

"Holy nightmare, Batman."

"Huh? Did you say something?"

Roxanne lifted her head and found herself staring at Jennette's bony legs, it wasn't a pretty sight.

"Why is it I am always faced with unpleasant awakenings? Just once I'd like some gorgeous hunk leaning over me with a rose or something even more appropriate."

"I know. I heard you fall off the bed."

Jennette had misunderstood, big surprise. Roxie let out a heavy sigh, pulled her arms under her chest, and pushed. She managed to execute a beautiful "I'm tired and miserable and don't you wish the world would end" push-up. *Hooray for our side*. Now all she had to do was stand up, an act which had somehow surpassed her abilities.

"What time is it?"

Jennette looked at Roxie's clock, "Seven twenty three."

"No, you're looking at my clock so subtract fifteen minutes."

She always set her clock fifteen minutes fast to fool herself into getting up on time. Trouble was, however, she always remembered that fact.

"Seven o eight. Why do you do that?"

14

"Why do I do what?"

"Set your clock ahead. It doesn't seem to accomplish anything."

"Actually, it does. It keeps me entertained because Vic doesn't know it, so she's never entirely sure what time it is."

"You guys don't get along do you."

"Let's just say we'd be happier on separate planets."

"Why?"

"Look, I know you want to help me sort things out, and that's sweet, as always. However, I don't want to sort it out. I just want to get up, eat something, watch a little television...You can join me if you'd like, and we'll talk about Andy."

****

The aged man fell helplessly to the ground, his hands trying to retain their grasp on his staff. The impact sent twinges of pain through his worn body. He lowered his head as though to weep.

"Lord Brennen? Lord Brennen, are you injured?"

Brennen lifted his eyes to meet the piercing green eyes of young Lord Earin, "Three days. Three days of preparing. Three days of incantations. For three days I have attempted to bring the last of The Chosen to us. But I failed just when she was in our grasp."

"No Lord Brennen, you did not fail. She has felt us now; next time she will not resist."

"Next time...Ah Lord Earin, you are indeed so young and spirited. Perhaps with your energy it could be done. But come, lift me so that I may rest before it begins."

"It has already begun."

Both Lords turned to face the red-headed Lord Anjalina. Her green eyes were empty as though she were looking inside herself. Her pale skin glimmered with the sweat of the days efforts. Her jaw was locked against her teeth. Such a powerful woman.

"The Betrayer's troops are gathering. He summons thousands more with each breath. I have seen the preparations he makes. He no longer hides his movements; we are no longer threatening.

He will attack soon," Anjalina closed her eyes and concentration furrowed her brow. "One more thing... Mongrel has visited the other side. The Betrayer sent him to The Last Chosen One."

All was silent in the hall.

****

"It's the same old, same old situation. It's the same old, same old ball and chain..." Poison pulsated from Roxie's radio. She sang along and attempted to dance as well. *I have all the grace of an elephant on roller skates, check that, roller blades.* She whirled around, sending her long dark hair flying. How she loved her hair. She gazed at herself in the mirror. *Damn, I look good.* She had squeezed into her tightest pair of jeans, slid into her emerald silk shirt, and pulled her black leather boots up her legs. As always, she left her hair alone. It sparkled with soft luster.

"Are you going to Rocky tonight?"

Roxie smiled at Jennette's stupidity," I go every Saturday night. Why break a trend?"

"Why?"

"Beats going to some frat party, getting drunk, and waking up with Biff on top of me. Not to mention I enjoy it."

"Why?"

Roxie gritted her teeth, "I like it for the reason my ex hated it. He said it was nothing but a bunch of people fucking with their clothes on. Don't wait up." With that, Roxie grabbed her jacket and ran out the door to freedom.

Roxie pulled into the crowded theater parking lot. *What the... Wonder why it's so crowded tonight?* She circled the lot for a second time and finally found one space. *This space isn't big enough to park a Tonka truck in, my truck will never make it.* Maneuvering her three-quarter ton truck back and forth a dozen times, while pictures of demolition derbies danced in her head, Roxie managed to successfully park in the space. As she squeezed out of her truck, her spirits brightened with the knowledge that the person parked next to her would have to go through hell and back to get into his car. She smiled.

"Roxie! Baby! Thought you weren't gonna make it."

The hairy arms of Joe encircled Roxie from behind. He lifted her off the ground and twirled her around.

"Set me down you big buffoon. What are ya tryin' to break my back?" Roxie's lips parted in a smile as she turned to face Joe's wild grin.

Joe dropped to one knee, "Will you marry me?"

"I'm afraid not sweetie. I promised my mother I'd marry someone from my own species."

"Our love cannot be stopped by something as trivial as a mother. I shall wait for you inside, my love."

Joe kissed her hand and literally fluttered away. Roxie laughed. Now there goes the queen of the fairy kingdom. Joe was so gay he left ashes in his tracks. He was one of the best people in the world; one of the few real human beings left. If it weren't for him, some days she would never smile. Roxie walked up to the entrance of the theater, through the throngs of groupies, and in the front door.

"Good evening Daren. Howz it hangin'?"

"Same as always. You playin' a part tonight?" Daren only let cast in free.

"Not tonight. I'm just an observer."

"Cool. Head on inside." Cast and Roxie that is.

Once inside, Roxie relaxed. These were the people she trusted the most, the Rocky cast. They were quite the arrangement of low-life scum, but she loved them. And they loved her despite all of her many faults. Tonight everyone had already arrived.

"Excuse me, I'm looking for the Rocky cast," they all turned to face her. "You know that group of pathetic losers who are always late..."

"Ha, ha, Rox. We love you too," Mark stuck his tongue out at her.

"Don't stick it out unless you're gonna use it." Roxie slid up against Mark, allowing a sly grin to run across her lips.

Mark shifted uneasily. *God, you take my breath away,* he thought. Roxie's eyes widened, she had definitely heard what he just thought.

"What did you say?"

"When?"

"Just then."

"Nothing."

"Are you sure?"

"Of course I'm sure. What's wrong with you?"

"Nothing. I just thought I heard you say something."

Mark brought his hand up her back and began rubbing the back of her neck. His hand brushed against the cord that held her cursed necklace firmly in place. He lifted it up and gazed at it.

"Cool. Where did you get this?"

Roxie grabbed the pendant out of his hand and dropped it back beneath her shirt. "On the mall, from some guy."

"Sorry, I didn't realize it was so precious. What is with you tonight?"

Roxie flinched at his sarcasm. Unable to think of anything to say, she shot him a look that could have killed him, buried him, and held a funeral. Then she turned and walked outside.

What is my problem tonight. I just had the desire to stake one of my best friends through the heart. And he's far too good looking to die. Roxie walked around to the back of the theater where she fell to the ground to think. While she sat in the shadow of the ominous building contemplating herself, it started to rain. At first it was a light drizzle, but it was quickly becoming a torrential downpour. Soaked, tired, and pissed, Roxie decided to head for shelter. She had taken only a few steps before she was surrounded by a thick fog. Her heart began pounding audibly against her chest. She attempted to calm herself by inhaling deeply. But this only made her dizzy. *Calm down Roxanne. It's only a little fog. The worst that can happen is you will ram your face against the theater. Or it could suck the life right out of you. Stop that! I need to think. It's just fog. I'll just feel for the building...* She leaned toward the theater, misjudged the distance, and seemed to be falling. Just when she should have impacted the ground, all the world went black and reality existed no more.

****

Chapter 2

Slowly, the chaotic whirling of the world around her subsided. A cool breeze drifted across her neck, causing the hair on it to stand on end. When she dared, she cautiously opened her eyes. Everything was engulfed in an emerald haze that appeared to be a trick of light on the mist that surrounded her. For just a moment she thought she was seeing a stoplight through a foggy windshield, but only for a moment.

She was standing now; a feat she found most impressive considering her previous condition. The floor beneath her was hard and cold, as though it were carved from ice. She began searching for the source of the emerald light, but her eyes ached with the strain. Now she was getting pissed. Her head started throbbing and her feet felt like ice cubes.

"Great. I get sent to hell on the day they decide to turn off the heat!" she mumbled.

"This is scarcely hell," a calm voice replied. Roxanne jerked at the voice, a stunt that sent her reeling to her knees.

"Jesus! If I were a cat I'd only have one life left. You scared the hell out of me. Wait a minute, who are you?"

Mustering all the false bravado she could, Roxie climbed back to her feet and attempted to put the intruder on the defensive.

"I am Lord Earin. I was not attempting to startle you. I merely wanted to assure you that you are in safe keeping."

As Lord Earin moved closer, the emerald light grew brighter until Roxie could barely keep her eyes open.

"You think you could dim that light, doc?"

Lord Earin looked at Roxie with a puzzled expression. "What do you mean "doc"? I'm afraid I don't understand."

She brought her hand up to shield her eyes against the blinding glow. "You know, doc, doctor, medic, the guy who heals the sick!"

"Oh, you mean a healer. I am not a healer. Do you require

19

one?"

This is like an incredibly bad comedy routine. "Who's on first?" "No, I need the electric company."

"Pardon my ignorance, but I simply do not understand..." Lord Earin's voice wavered like that of a child faced with an adult problem.

By this time, Roxie's eyes were tearing from the strain of keeping them closed and the pounding of her temples. Feeling her last nerve being stretched to the breaking point, she inhaled deeply, lowered her voice pitch, and softly said, "Please dim that extremly bright light. It is making me very ill."

Lord Earin responded with relaxed recognition, "Ahh, my staff. I can see that it has caused you discomfort but I cannot dim it at this moment. Please understand, I am but one minor Lord, I am not capable of holding you on my own. I have called for assistance. I beg you to forgive me and use all your strength until they arrive."

Roxie took a deep breath and relaxed the tight clenching of her eyes.I should have brought my sunglasses. She sat down to save her strength and waited. She felt a warming in the ground when Lord Earin sat down directly across from her. She never opened her eyes, but somehow she knew exactly where he sat. This was going to be a long night.

****

Lord Brennen's eyes scanned the parchment unfolded before him upon his desk. He shuddered in horror at the size of the preparations being taken by the Betrayer. His evil would soon fill the already blighted land, and Brennen was unprepared and weakening with each passing day. But there existed no one else who could take his place. Only he had studied the texts of the previous Lords, only he knew the role to be played by the Chosen, and only he had faced the Betrayer before. As he starred at the movements of the enemy, he cursed himself for not being strong enough to hold the last of the Chosen. She had just been so far away....

"Lord Brennen! Lord Brennen! Please open your door. There

is an emergency."

The cries of Lord Anjalina broke the High Lord out of

his self- abusive trace. He set the parchment aside and opened his chamber door only to be face to face with the wild eyes of Anjalina.

"What is it Lord Anjalina that can cause you to appear so?"

"It is the young Lord Earin. He requires our immediate help. I'm afraid he has extended himself well past the powers of his practiced lore. Lord Brennen, he has summoned the last of the Chosen."

Lord Brennen closed his eyes in an effort to calm himself. His heart raced at the news, and at once he knew the danger in which Lord Earin had placed himself. It would be impossible for him to hold her for very long. Lord Brennen re-entered his chamber, gathered his staff, mustered all of his power, and followed Lord Anjalina to the Conference Hall.

Upon opening the door of the Hall, both Lords were momentarily blinded by the pulsating light of Lord Earin's staff. Lord Brennen muttered a protection spell and entered with Lord Anjalina close beside him. The brightness of the light around them was growing dimmer. They both knew it would not be long before Lord Earin's strength would fail and the Chosen would be lost again. They walked directly into the center of the emerald sea where they found the Lord and his gift on the floor. Lord Earin sat cross-legged on the ground, sweat pouring down his face, his staff in one hand while the other gently stroked the hair of the Chosen who appeared to be sleeping in his lap. As they approached he looked up at them and smiled softly.

"Her pain was so great I'm afraid I had to put her to sleep. Perhaps it was a mistake, for now I can feel my powers lessening."

Lord Brennen returned Earin's smile. "No, it was not wrong of you to ease her suffering. How long have you held her here?"

"I know not High Lord. I am so tired."

"You must hold her a little longer so that I can perform the spell that will bring her completely to this side. Lord Anjalina, give him your strength."

Anjalina knelt down next to Earin and placed her hand on his staff. Then, she let go of herself. She emptied her mind of all her personal desires and allowed her energy to flow from her body into the staff. At once the light brightened. The glow ceased pulsating and became a fixed source of power. After several moments she began to weaken. She had given too much too soon. She relaxed her grip on the staff, and Lord Earin slumped over. She had not given too much, her power had been taken by two sources. At once she tightened her grip. Now she alone held the Chosen to this world. Her head started throbbing and her hands burned from the heat of her powers. *Hold on! Be strong! I. Am. Not. Going. To. Fail.*

Suddenly, the pressure vanished. Lord Brennen removed her hands from the staff, and the room went dark. She pulled her hands to her chest, breathing quickly from the strain, and attempted to calm herself. Brennen took her hands in his and cooled the burning. Slowly she opened her eyes. The Hall was dimly lit by the candles on the walls. Lord Brennen knelt before her, holding her hands gently and smiling. She looked to her side and saw Lord Earin lying on the ground; he was alive. Next to him laid a young woman who appeared to be sleeping peacefully. Anjalina looked up at Lord Brennen.

"It is done," he said, "The last of the Chosen is here."

****

Roxanne felt the warmth of the sun on her face and cringed. She had never been thrilled with mornings and today was no exception. She felt herself slipping out of sleep and into reality, she didn't like it. She flopped over onto her stomach, pulled her pillow over her head, and realized that there was no window in her bedroom at the dorm. She threw the pillow and sat straight up in bed. The room around immediately started spinning. *Yes, stupid. But it is spinning out of focus, so it is doubly painful. Sometimes I'm so brilliant I amaze myself.* She closed her eyes and grasped her head firmly.

When she opened them again, she found herself in a rather large, but well furnished room. She sat in a huge white bed against the far wall of this chamber. Across the room sat a beautiful emerald couch. *Is the whole world turning green, or am I just seasick?* Infront of the couch there was a solid oak table. Numerous tapestries covered

the walls, each more brilliant than the one before it. Next to the bed she found a chair, much like an old antique rocking chair, with clothes laid upon it. At that moment Roxanne realized that she was completely nude. *Okay, time to think. How the hell did I get into this one?!* A gentle tapping at the door sent her diving under the covers.

"Are you awake, Chosen One?" A familiar face peered into the chamber.

"Don't you mean am I decent?"

Lord Earin let out a heavy sigh, once again her logic was beyond him. "I do not wish to engage in that again. And, I can see that you are awake at last." Lord Earin entered the room and crossed to the bed.

"Okay, I'll try to keep it simple. What do you mean by "at last"?"

"My sleep spell has lasted for three days. I never could get that one correct. All have been anxiously awaiting your awakening."

Roxanne suddenly realized that she was naked in a strange bed, having a conversation with a strange man, confused, and very hungry.

"Who has been waiting? Where the hell am I? Who the hell are you? Where are my clothes? And, is there such a thing as food here?"

"Your constant reference to hell disturbs me. Have you already heard of the dangers facing our land?"

Roxanne sighed,"Listen Doc, I'm not even sure which land I'm in, asshole."

Once again she had confused the Lord, she could tell by the strained expression on his face.

"What do you mean by this last word?"

"Nothing personal. It's just a way to keep from ending a sentence with a preposition. Never mind, only my English professor really cares."

Lord Earin smiled a dazzling smile, "You are a very interesting person, young Chosen One. Someday perhaps you will tell me all about yourself and where you come from, but for now there are more immediate needs to attend to. Are you hungry?"

"Food. Now there's something I can sink my teeth into," Roxie cringed," No pun intended of course."

"Of course." With that Lord Earin tapped his staff twice against the ground. The door immediately opened and in came a young boy of perhaps twelve carrying a huge platter of breads, fruits, meats, and cakes. Roxie could feel herself drooling. This was as magical as all of her favorite fantasy novels. *Wait a minute! Reality check. This is too good to be true.*

"Okay, fun's over. Time to wake up. This is all just... just, what? It's all a mass hallucination brought on by stress and reading one too many books. I'm not really here and this isn't really happening. In a few minutes I'll wake up behind the theater, soaked, confused, and tired. This is all a rather confusing and somewhat vivid dream, right?"

Lord Earin appeared calm. His eyes looked directly into her own and further until they reached her soul. He did not blink nor did he raise his voice above a whisper, but with unbending resolve he said, "Whatever you have believed in the past is now false. Truth will appear strange. But, as sure as that necklace that binds you will not be removed, this is real."Roxanne shuddered. His eyes let go of hers. She closed them and took a deep breath.

"You are telling me that my life is now false and all that I have learned to be fairy tales is true. You want me to forget the reality I know, clap my hands, and believe in fairies."

Lord Earin smiled ever so slightly,"Yes Chosen One, that is the truth."

"Give up the world I was forced to live in for so long. A world I despised. A world that I never felt a part of, for the world I dreamt of night after night?...... I can do that."

Lord Earin sighed, "Chosen One you have never truly existed until this moment. Now will you eat?"

Roxanne smiled, "As long as I'm here I might as well enjoy myself."

The young boy, who had not moved since he entered the room, carried the tray of food to her bed. Instantly, she was ravenous. Food of every kind passed her lips. The sweet juices of the fruits replenished her. The breads filled her empty stomach. After awhile she slowed down and began enjoying her food. She felt stronger with every bite, more alive and refreshed. She relaxed and scanned the room. Lord Earin was still standing beside the bed.

"Sit down Doc, take a load off," Roxanne gestured to the chair beside the bed.

"Thank you, Chosen One."

"If we are going to have any sort of relationship the first thing you are going to have to learn is my name. Roxanne. No more of this Chosen One shit, okay?"

Once again Lord Earin looked bewildered, "Do you not approve of your title?"

"No. As titles go, it's a great one to have. However, you need to learn to relax around me. Just call me Roxanne and there will be much rejoicing." Roxanne saw that infamous confused look flash across Lord Earin's face. "Sorry, inside joke."

"Indeed you are a strange one, Roxanne. If you do not mind me pointing that out to you."

"Mind? I'll take that as a compliment. Now if you don't mind Doc, I need to get cleaned and dressed. So..."

A red flush came across Lord Earin's face as he realized what Roxanne meant. He nearly leaped from his chair. Tapping his staff on the floor, he again summoned the young boy.

"This is Sage. He is our most promising apprentice. He will attend to your needs. Now I must meet with the other Lords to discuss disturbing matters. I shall return, Roxanne." Lord Earin left the room in an almost dramatic movement, leaving Roxanne naked and alone with a kid. *We could qualify as the typical family of the nineties.*

"Sage?"

"Yes, Chosen One?"

Not this again. I'll have to hold a press conference or something. "I need a hot bath, fresh clothes, and a sharp knife."

Sage looked confused and Roxie started to believe that

confusion was merely the permanent state of the people in this world. "What's wrong? Are you out of hot water?"

"Oh no Chosen One, we have abundant hot water. I don't understand your request for a weapon. "

Oh boy, this one could be a real riot. "I'm not going to use the knife to kill anyone, I'm going to use it to shave."

"Forgive my ignorance Chosen One, but you are not a man."

"Well I see they've taught you the essentials. I'm not shaving my face. I need to shave the hair off my legs. Great, now you are confused. Come here." Sage moved to the bedside and Roxanne stuck her leg out from underneath the covers.

"Now, rub the bottom of my leg. Doesn't that feel nasty? I need a knife to remove that, okay?"

"Yes Chosen One. I shall return with the things you have requested. The bath chamber is through that door. You shall find the water has already been prepared. Is there anything else you require?"

"How about a nice stiff drink? Never mind. Cancel that last order. Just bring the stuff and call me Roxanne."

Sage nodded and quickly departed. Roxanne sat in bed and stared at the room around her. Oddly enough, she wasn't bothered by the fact that reality had taken a hundred and eighty degree turn. As she sat staring at nothing, her greatest concern was for Sage. She forgot to tell him not to run while carrying a knife. "Guess he'll figure it out. Now it's time for a bath."

Roxanne staggered into the bath chamber, slid into the steaming hot water, and, for the first time in years, relaxed. Reality wasn't going to be so bad after all.

****

High Lord Brennen looked out across the Meeting Chamber at all the anxious faces seated around the table. He recognized each face. Some were aging friends, those sat closest to him. Others were young and unafraid. Those were the poor fools who would never be the same.

Some met his eyes as he gazed at them, others were too afraid of the power behind those eyes. All were joined in a common feeling of unease as the Betrayer grew louder and bolder in his movements. All but one.

Lord Brennen moved his gaze to the one source of calm in the room and found himself looking into the defiant glare of Commander Gabriel, the leader of the strongest fighting force on this side of the war. Lord Brennen attempted to probe the thoughts of this over confident fighter. Commander Gabriel grinned a sly grin. *You'll never know more than I want you to you old bastard.* Lord Brennen pulled his mind away. He knew that was as warm as the man would be.

The chamber door suddenly flew open and Lord Earin rushed in to join the others.

"Greetings Lord Earin. I trust you are well."

"My apologies High Lord, but I was detained by Rox... the Chosen One. She is awake at last."

"That is fortunate. She is needed, " the old lord sighed heavily. "Time is no longer an ally. She must be prepared to fight for that which we believe in."

Perhaps he was the only one who heard the emphasis on the word "we", or perhaps he had imagined it, not that it mattered she would fight for their beliefs, she had no choice. Commander Gabriel shifted uneasily at his thoughts. He resented the way she would be trapped and he didn't even know who she was, nor did he care. He was trapped himself, for the second time in his life. He felt his hand tighten its grip on the hilt of his sword. *Bastards! I'll win this war for you, but not for your damned beliefs.*

"... to the east. "Commander Gabriel brought himself back to reality. Lord Anjalina stood before the Lords and leaders. "Our scouts have reported movement from the Fire River to the base of the Shattered Peak Mountains in the west. In effect we are nearly surrounded. If we do not act soon, if we allow the Betrayer to continue his preparations..."

"We will all get an up close look at certain doom, " Commander Gabriel's interruption sounded almost nonchalant. "Unless we can get to him first."

All eyes in the chamber stared unbelievably at Gabriel. *Great, they all think I've lost my mind. Guess I've got the advantage.* He met each gaze with his "I'm feeling particularly clever today" face. Lord Brennen sat back with his eyes closed against the world. Gabriel knew what he was searching for so he gave it to him. For just a moment he allowed Brennen to glimpse the thoughts running through his twisted mind. He nearly laughed at the mental gasp of disbelief that entered his thoughts. *I told you, never more than I want you to know.*

Lord Anjalina stood defiantly facing Gabriel. Only a slight flare in her eyes betrayed the mental conversation she held with Brennen. She leaned across the conference table and nearly whispered, "Do you mean to suggest that we mount an offensive against him and all the demonic forces of hell."

"I'm not suggesting anything. I'm telling you if we don't attack him soon he'll destroy us at his leisure."

"What you are suggesting, " growled Anjalina," is insane."

"We will be at battle with his forces soon anyway. That cannot be stopped. So why not face him on our terms. We need to take any advantage we can."

"You don't honestly believe marching into his army of our own will to be an advantage do you? Even the Betrayer would call you mad."

"That, dear Lord, is precisely the point." All heads turned to face the voice that had jumped to Commander Gabriel's aid. Even the Commander was shocked to find himself staring at General Sabastian. Shock soon turned to satisfaction. General Sabastian commanded the respect of the entire army and all of the lords. He had lead them to victory in all of the Great Wars, and he was High Lord Brennen's oldest and dearest friend. With this man on his side the lords would have no choice but to follow his advice. Gabriel smiled.

General Sabastian explained, "The greatest advantage of all is the unexpected. The Betrayer will never believe that we would attack him. We are out numbered, he has better tactical position, and we have never thrown the first stone in the past. He has no reason to suspect us. The insanity of this plan may be what allows it to work."

Lord Anjalina opened her mouth to issue a protest but a soft yet stern voice interrupted her. "That may well be, but we cannot move until the last Chosen One is ready. We know not her skills nor her willingness to help us. All we know is that she must, and that, dear friends, could take more time than we have."

"I will train her."

All eyes turned toward the rear of the chamber only to discover they couldn't even see the bearer of the whispered voice. Slowly she leaned forward out of the shadows in which she had concealed herself and grinned at the shocked faces of the lords. Her ice-blue eyes seemed to burn with a hellish fire, her long golden hair sparkled in the candlelight of the room, and, for just a brief moment, she was the most beautiful creature any of them had ever seen. But, the grin disappeared from her visage and she moved further into the light allowing them to see the left side of her face where she wore her namesake, a deep-purple scar that resembled a coiled snake.

Lord Earin shifted with obvious unease, "Do you think it is really such a good idea for someone as... "

"Disturbed," she interjected.

"... important as you are to waste time with training a new recruit?"

"If I'm as important as you say, and she is so necessary it seems it is not only a good idea but the best idea."

Lord Earin looked to each of his fellow lords with mental pleading for support. They all returned indecision as their answer.He felt as though he were lost. This woman could not give Roxanne sufficient training, he had to prevent it. Lord Brennen spoke.

"Whether or not I agree as to the assumptions of this being a good idea, I believe that, under the circumstances, it is necessary to have Snake give the Chosen One her physical training. Lord Earin will train her in the ways and history of our world. Now go, all of you to your respective duties. We must prepare for battle."

That should have ended the meeting. That always ended the meeting. Not this time. Commander Gabriel stood, drew his sword, and swung at Snake's hidden figure. She was ready, somehow she was ready.She dodged to one side, slid back in the opposite direction, and came up in between Gabriel and his sword with a dagger poised to slit his throat. No one else in the room had time to react. The fight ended.

"What is the meaning of such behavior?!" boomed Lord Brennen.

"The meaning? Isn't it painfully obvious? Just my dramatic way of proving Snake is the best for this job. Why do you have to debate it? Why do you even worry? Let her be the best. Accept it. And, let me do my job. You may have made some mental connection, but I missed the decision. Do we attack or do I prepare my men for defeat?"

Lord Anjalina's staff came to life with green fire. Her gaze tried to burn right through the Commander's soul, but he resisted. Her fire burned brighter. She took a step toward the defiant man and stopped. For a moment she appeared to fight with herself, then the fire died as she dropped back into her seat. Snake fought back her desire to throw a knife through the High Lord's throat. She'd seen his control quench that fire. *You bastard. You have no right to that kind of control. She was defending you!* She turned on the High Lord, her ice blue eyes on fire from within. Her hand inched with the longing for violence. *I could kill you right now,* she thought. *But you won't,* came a muffled reply. Realizing what he was attempting, Snake closed her mind and turned her back to the aging Lord. She felt like vomiting.

Commander Gabriel shifted his gaze from Snake's rigid form to the old Lord. Somehow he thought he should do something, so he stepped between them. "So far I see all I have is your attention. What I need is an answer. What am I to do with my men?"

The High Lord never moved. No sign of life could be detected from his body. Yet Gabriel sat sweating in a chair as though he'd just come from a lost battle. He found himself gasping and could scarcely hear over the pounding of his heart. He gawked at the High Lord. The corner of his mouth twitched slightly.

"We fight." And then he was gone.

One by one the lords followed. Soon he sat alone with the shadows.

"What did he do to me. What the hell did he do?"

Now this I can handle. Roxanne stood infront of what resembled a mirror in her room admiring the way she looked in the outfit these people had provided. She guessed her own clothes had been incinerated. But, that too was just fine with her. Even if this turned out to be a dream, even if she had lost all mental control, she still wanted as few ties with "reality" as possible. She gazed at herself for a little longer then slide the knife she had used to shave into one of the long, black boots provided. *No sense in being too trusting.* Just the there came a gentle rapping at the door.

"Chosen One? Are you prepared?" Roxanne recognized Sage's voice.

"Prepared for what?"

Sage pushed open the door hesitantly and stared at Roxanne with a child's innocence. "For your training. Lord Earin requests your presence in the main garden."

For some reason the phrase "requests your presence" sounded more like a command then a request, but Roxie decided not to fight it. She

smiled at the young apprentice and took his hand. For a moment he appeared to want to run and hide, but only for a moment.

"Let's go, but let's go slowly." Sage nodded. Roxie knew that if she ever wanted to have some sort of control she had to know where she was, so off she walked soaking in every detail.

****

Snake sat on the stone fence surrounding the main garden. She hated being closed in, it left her without options. She leaned against one of the many grotesque statues that were placed along the wall and she sighed. She had no idea why she had volunteered to train this person, for the most part she hated people. She usually found ways to avoid them and she never sought out their company. Yet, she had somehow been drawn to this unknown person, the last of the Chosen. Perhaps it was because she had also been unwillingly chosen. The fire that burned within her soul flared, she glanced at the young lord pacing the garden below.

Lord Earin resembled an overanxious child. He paced the distance between two large vale trees for the thousandth time. Every few moments he would stop and listen for some sound of approach. Soon, however, he would return to that annoying pacing. All those years of training and he still hasn't learned the patience of the Lords. *Good. At least he remains human. Still...*

"She will come." Lord Earin jumped at the sound of Snake's voice. "She won't refuse your summons. She really has no choice."

Lord Earin seemed disturbed by Snake's words. "Oh but she does have a choice. We all have a choice," He shot a defiant glare toward Snake.

As Snake sat contemplating the *choice* of sending a dagger flying into the Lord's skull he suddenly stopped his pacing and nearly darted to the garden's entrance. Snake pushed her violent thoughts aside and dropped down from the wall. *Time to meet the infamous last of the Chosen. What joy.*

Lord Earin entered the garden accompanied by a young woman with long brown hair and a young apprentice. Snake scanned the Chosen One looking for signs that would indicate her importance. But the woman before her appeared to merely be a healthy, beautiful person. *Well, what did you expect? Did you want her to be wearing wings and a halo?* Snake thought about moving toward the group but then her defensive nature took over and she stood her ground.

When the group stood before her Lord Earin spoke, "This is Snake. She will be training you in the arts of battle. Snake, this is the Chosen called Roxanne."

Neither of the women moved. They stood locked in a powerful gaze, and for a split second Lord Earin felt as though he were standing in the presence of a power greater than that of the Betrayer. The moment soon passed.

"Why am I being trained in the arts of battle?" The question caught Lord Earin by surprise.

"I'm sorry I haven't had a chance to explain... Things will be made clear... I will tell you. For now I ask that you accept some things on faith and allow Snake to train you." Lord Earin realized at once how desperate he sounded and knew he was asking too much.

"I don't know if you've thought about this from my point of view or not, but I'm accepting a whole hell of a lot on faith right now, starting with the very existence of you people."

A sly smile found its way to Snake's lips at the sight of a Lord being cowered by the strange woman, but she removed it at once. "Train or don't, it makes no difference to me."

Roxanne turned to face Snake. "That's a hell of an attitude to take. Shouldn't you be saying something inspirational to convince me how important it is that I learn all that you know?!"

"I did."

Roxanne stood frozen. She glared at this stoic woman for a moment. She was beautiful even with the coiled scar that must have given her that name, but she was as cool as Han Solo had been in <u>Star Wars</u>. *I wonder what it takes to shake someone like her.* Roxie smiled. There was only one way to find out.

"Okay Doc, I'll take a rain check on the explanation, for now."

"That means you will train?" questioned Earin.

Once again she had managed to confuse him. *I have got to stop doing that. It's getting downright painful.* "Yes, I will train."

Lord Earin was visibly relieved. "Sage will remain here to help you with whatever you require. As for myself, I must join Commander Gabriel and the other Lords to plan for the upcoming...," he paused and shot a nervous glance at Roxanne, "...battle, on which I will brief you later."

"I hope you plan on being more than brief. After all, she will be fighting for your beloved way of life."

Roxanne could feel the distaste that dripped off of Snake's statement; she thought about saying something smart-ass to alleviate the obvious tension but she couldn't think of anything particularly witty. *Oh well, it's probably for the best. With my luck I'd end up with a sword through my throat.* Lord Earin felt the tension as well. He glanced at Roxanne, glared at Snake, opened his mouth, closed it, and then bowed out of the garden. Turning to face the cold figure of Snake "Solo," Roxanne was sure she had made a bad decision somewhere along the line, she just wasn't sure where.

Snake stood silent for a moment, contemplating exactly what it was she was planning to teach this new woman. She was alarmed to discover that she had no clue. *Great. Here I am face to face with another human being and clueless. Guess I could let her stand there feeling confused for a few minutes... while I figure out what the hell to do.* She decided not to try that for too long.

Roxanne studied Snake's unmoving face. She could see that Snake was pondering something, *yeah, probably how to humiliate or murder me. Oh, that's nice and morbid, Roxie.* Whatever thoughts ran through her mind, Roxanne knew, without a doubt, that she stood face to face with a pro.

"So "Last of the Chosen," sarcasm oozed from Snake's mouth, "do you have any idea how to use a sword?"

"Well "Snake," Roxanne tried to respond with an equal amount of bad attitude, "I don't really know." She failed.

"Don't really know. That's helpful. And do you keep your memory with you at all times?"

Roxie felt like slapping the shit out of Snake, not because she was being a total bitch, but because that was a better come-back than she would have thought of using. Suddenly she found herself smiling. She knew she must be grinning from ear to ear due to the look of complete confusion on Snake's face."Try to understand. My memory isn't doing me much good at this point. Too much has changed too fast. But, on the lighter side... I've read enough of these novels to know that I should be able to just pick up a sword and kill an entire army, in fifteen seconds or less."

"I don't know what it is you've been studying, but I'm relatively sure you have been lied to. You say a lot has changed, I'm telling you life is as stable as it's going to be for a long time. Get use to it."

Despite the bite in her voice, Roxie felt that this hard lady was being as kind to her as she could be. *Someday I will find out what permanently pissed you off, and then you will definitely have to kill me.*

Roxie quit grinning and sighed, "Well hand me a sword so I can learn how to use it."

Now it was Snake's turn to grin. *So you're just going to pick up a sword and* use *it, I don't think so Chosen one.* She slid back over to the stone fence she had been sitting on and tapped it twice with the dagger that seemed to just appear in her hand. Instantly Sage appeared with two large broad swords. *Sage? That boy was so damn quiet Roxanne forgot he was anywhere in the vicinity.*

Sage handed the swords to Snake. She bowed slightly to show that he deserved respect too. Then she turned to face another of the Chosen. *Let's see how good your memory really is.* Taking one of the swords by the blade, she extended it infront of Roxanne. Roxie grasped it firmly by the hilt. *This isn't so bad.* Then Snake let go. She was never really sure whether the sword or the Chosen One hit the ground first, but she remained convinced that this would be harder than she thought.

****

Lord Earin lifted his head to the gentle rapping on the library door, "Enter."

The door swung open and Sage walked through followed by Roxanne's limping form. Earin leaped to her side and offered assistance; Sage flinched at the remark he knew would be coming.

"Back off, Doc! I'm a big girl. I can walk by myself!"

Earin bit down hard on his lower lip, swallowed the resentment that was flowing up his throat, and calmly said, "It would not appear so."

Keeping a firm grip on her arm, he motioned for Sage to help him lift her to one of the cushioned chairs that adorned the grand library. If she hadn't been so completely exhausted, Roxanne might have actually fought the aide so freely given to her. As it was, she merely had the energy to sigh with relief when her feet were propped up off the hard ground.

"Sorry, Doc. I know I can be a bitch with a nasty attitude sometimes."

At least he understood the intent behind her words this time. "All is well with me. Rough training session with Snake?"

Roxie noticed the contempt dripping off Snake's name. There's that lovely tension again. "You can say that again."

"Why?"

I have got to stop doing that! "Let's just say this had better be a really good tale of intrigue and romance." *Shit! I'm doing it again.*

The confused Lord shook his head, opened his mouth as if to say something, thought better of it, and ended up retreating to the safety of his desk. He pulled out a large volume and thumbed through, apparently looking for something. But, soon he changed his mind, replaced the book, and began his story.

"I know this history far too well. Sometimes I think it would consume me. Yet, I know it only half as well as High Lord Brennen... Still, I digress. In the beginning there were fairies. Fairies, elves, and pixies; all the higher life-forms. They... how should I put this? They... understood. Life made sense to them and all the workings of life. All three lived in harmony with each other and the world around them. They possessed powerful magic which they used to maintain all the beauty and harmony around them. They remained content creating.

But it would not always remain so. Some of the elves moved farther and farther out on the fringe of the land. The farther away they traveled the more magic they lost, until they became as we are today and thus the human race was born. For many hundreds of years all four races lived in harmony... Eventually, some of the wisest humans journeyed into the center of the land to learn all they could from the fairies, elves, and pixies. They hoped to learn all the secrets of the magics which preserved the beauty around them all. They studied all they could, there were thirteen in all, and returned years later with their lore.

Having a deeper understanding of the great scheme of existence, these thirteen were dubbed the lords and protectors of the human race. They used all their knowledge to help further the development of all people. Among the thirteen were three sisters.

These sisters studied every piece of lore they could, until they had learned it all. However, that wasn't enough to assuage their intense curiosity.Soon they started experimenting with new magic; magic they, themselves, created out of existing lore.

But, there was danger in this new magic. It grew out of greed and desire; it was not pure. The more the sisters played with their new found powers the more dangerous it became. Soon the other lords noticed a change in the sisters. They were consumed with their black magic. When the other lords confronted the three they laughed and said that they had discovered a magic too powerful for even the fairies to contain; a magic that would destroy all petty creatures and render unto them complete control of all the known universe. The lords, wrought with panic, banished the three to the outer fringes.

Then He came. Slowly at first. At first he came in small, undetectable ways, slowly working his way into the land. The Betrayer, born out of the depths of the fringe and the magic of the sister witches. He crawled into the roots of the trees, the tops of the mountains, the water of the streams, and into the minds of the lesser creatures. He even got so bold as to create legions out of the sacred dead. Then he declared war.

The war lasted so many years. Somehow, it seems as though it may never have actually ended... There was at the time a very young lord with an extreme talent for the mystical ways of the fairies. He had spent many years among them, many more than were required for his learning as a lord. He, for a time, thought he might dwell in the center forever. But, when the sisters were banished there was a great call for three new lords to enter the fold, and so it remained from that time forward. Three lords would leave and three new would come. This worked for many years. It was followed closely until one year when a fourth lord died mysteriously. That was the year this lord had finished the last of his training. Thus, the young lord felt he must join the ranks of the lords.

As I said, he had a particularly powerful magic. It was him, in fact, who finally put an end to the terrible war. He took it upon himself to locate and study the texts used by the sisters. He believed that it might be possible to turn their own magic against them. So for months he battled the forces of the Betrayer by day and searched the texts for the source of the power behind him by night. One night, when he thought he could search no farther, he stumbled upon the answer. The sisters had created for themselves three amulets which joined their kindred souls and increased their individual power. It was these amulets that allowed the deep joining which made it possible for them to create more power than ever before imagined. It was these amulets that would be their undoing.

According to the text, the amulets joined kindred souls, so the young lord gathered all the other lords together and created the most powerful summoning spell. They cast the spell for three days before they were able to bring the sisters before them in the lords fortress. This young lord then took a banishment spell from the text studied by the sisters and aimed it directly into the amulets. The fight was intense; the young lord nearly died; but, in the end, the sisters were gone and the blight of the Betrayer removed from the land. Unfortunately, so much damage was done that all that remains of the fairy lands is the center, the Silver Forest which is still protected by fairies, pixies, and elves. No one but the training lords have been allowed within the forest for years.

However, the amulets remained. The young lord, knowing the power these foul things possessed, took it upon himself to either destroy them or change their mystical properties. Unable to destroy them, he altered them to join the kindred spirits of those who could save the land in its time of need. There exist those still who believe the amulets still possess dark powers...Anyway, that young lord is our own High Lord Brennen. And those amulets are the ones that you Snake, and the Commander wear around your necks."

Spell-bound until that moment Roxanne nearly fell out of her chair at that last statement, "Snake is one of the Chosen!?"

"You did not know," the look of confusion crossed his face and then disappeared. "Ahh, but then, who would have told you. Certainly not Snake. She does not share much of who she is, not even when she should."

"I can't believe I was taking abuse from her all day and she didn't even bother to tell me that she too was Chosen. I mean in the very least... Wait a minute. Who's the last one?"

"Commander Gabriel. He leads the strongest fighting force in the army. He seldom takes orders from anyone but General Sabastian himself. His disposition is less than charming. You will probably like him."

Roxie's burst of laughter startled the young lord.

"Don't look so upset Earin. Whether you realize it or not, you just made a joke." Roxie kept laughing.

"You amaze me Ch... Roxanne. It is the middle of a crisis and you can find humor in the mere speech around you."

"It's called a defense mechanism."

"Defense from what?"

"Clinical depression."

"I really do not understand you Roxanne."

For a moment Roxie sobered up. "Look Earin, I don't really understand you either. Hell, I don't even understand what is happening in my own life right now. All I do know is that I am trying, but I can only go so far by myself. Just try to understand me. That's all I ask."

Lord Earin smiled a soft smile. "I will try. I promise you at least that much from me. I will try."

****

Dark shadows moved across the dimly lit cavern and air that had not moved in centuries stirred the thick dust on the cavern floor. Mongrel shuddered. Even he felt anxiety here. No one could feel comfort in this chamber.

"Ahh, home." Mongrel turned to face the elated face of his master. No one except him.

This really was his home. It had been in this very room hundreds of years ago that he was created by the three sister witches. It was here that all of the planning and plotting had taken place. Here the magic had been created, and here it had been taken away. So, it was here that the Betrayer decided to take his revenge. This dark, evil cave would be his new abode. From here he would destroy the lord protectors of the land.

Mongrel interrupted the intense thoughts of his commander, "Shall I bring all of your things to this chamber?"

"This is a powerful place isn't it?" His voice filled all the space in the chamber. Mongrel did not answer; he wasn't expected to. "This is my new throne room. I want all the power of my mothers to aid me now. Bring my things."

"As you wish."

Mongrel humbly and hurriedly bowed out of the room. The Betrayer circled the cold chamber absorbing all the traces of his creation that remained. Slowly he became aware of a sort of presence in the cavern with him; a living presence that, somehow, was not alive. He found himself drawn to the center of the room where, upon a stone dias, sat a stone cauldron. As he approached the cauldron, smoke started to flow over the sides, heat began to radiate from within, and a low rumbling shook the ground slightly. He hesitated. The cauldron drew him forward. He looked inside.

Murky water swirled and bubbled inside the cauldron. He waved his hand across the top of the demonic thing. Suddenly a scene appeared. He stood in the same cavern before Mongrel who had with him a young woman with flowing black hair and deep emerald green eyes; the last Chosen. She said something to his figure which he could not hear. His figure laughed as she moved to his side. Then the image was gone.

The sound of feet shuffling on stone aroused the Betrayer. He looked up to see Mongrel had returned with his things. An evil grin found its way to his face.

"My dear Mongrel, it would appear that you are correct. The last of the Chosen will betray the protectors; she will come to us."

****

Chapter 3

"You have all the mental capacity of a very dull stick."

"And you, my dear, are as pleasing as one."

Commander Gabriel ducked just in time to miss the retort Lord Anjalina chose, which was apparently to take his head off with her staff. He had pushed her too far again. *So what else is new? If she didn't try to kill me at least once a day I'd think she didn't love me.* He admired her passion, even though it was usually aimed at him in a negative manner. She could be moved to action for what she believed in. Problem was, her beliefs always <u>collided</u> with his. "Nice try Lord Anjalina. Next time don't lead the swing with your shoulders, it practically shouts "I'm going to hit you.""

Solid wood connected with his abdomen. "Like that?"

Returning to a standing position the Commander managed to cough, "Sarcasm hardly becomes you."

"Enough!"

The two combatants turned to face General Sabastian, who, from the look of things, was none too impressed with their little tiff.

"We are here to discuss our plans for this war, not to start our own among the leading officers. I cannot afford for you to kill each other now. If you hate each other so much you can fight to the death after the war... if you both survive!"

Lord Anjalina and Commander Gabriel exchanged a glance of panic. *That man before us is not to be messed with, is he?* Anjalina grinned in response to Gabriel's unspoken message.

"And stop holding those infernal mental conversations!"

"We apologize," they stated in perfect unison. The General groaned with disapproval. *At least they've stopped fighting... for now.*

"Time to get back to the plan of attack," said General Sabastian, wasting no minute of the truce. "Our scouts tell us that the Betrayer has moved his throne room from the dark towers of

41

the Shattered Peak mountains to the depths of the Fringe Plains. It appears as though our enemy has gone home. This definitely changes the plan of attack..."

"Wait." The General flinched at Commander Gabriel's interruption. "Has he moved all his troops from the Peaks to protect the new base?"   "No. Several of the troops remain at the old base. Probably as a decoy so we fail to notice the move."

"But that doesn't make any sense either." Now it was Anjalina's turn to interrupt. "The move he made was too obvious. You don't just move a major power and most of his troops without somebody noticing. He had to know the move would draw attention."

General Sabastian nodded, "Then, why did he leave those troops behind?"

A new voice entered the debate, "There needs to be no mystery here..." Everyone turned to face Snake's shadowy figure. *Why do I always fill like I just snuck up on these people.* "Old evil one wants to split our forces. He knows that where he goes we have to follow. His destruction is our main concern. At the same time..."

"...we can't afford to ignore the other group of troops because they may be preparing the major onslaught of the war," finished the Commander. *Bastard!*

General Sabastian sat rubbing his forehead. Protests and debates filled the room as all the lords and army leaders started to panic. He let them fight. Right now he needed to think. His hand moved from his forehead to his long, red beard and began a rythemetic tugging. All these people depended on him to have the answers; he wasn't sure he had them. He closed his eyes, silently searching for some inner guidance or strength. When he opened his eyes again he knew what must be done... and he hated it.

"My fellow leaders," his voice was scarcely louder than normal yet it drew the attention of everyone in the room, "I know what we need to do. It would be nearly impossible for us to split troops again, and that bastard knows it. We are spreading our forces entirely too thin as things stand now; one more time would break us. Therefore, I am now taking volunteers for an additional assignment. A small group, to leave in the next week, will journey to the fortress in the Peaks and destroy it."

The intense humming noise of just moments before returned as all the people in the room began protesting in shock. What the General was suggesting was pure insanity. The very idea that they were going to run an offensive in the first place had been hard enough to accept, but this? To run a secret first strike? The General must be loosing his mind. Didn't he realize how incredibly dangerous that would be? The Betrayer would retaliate with a vengeance. Slowly the protests began to subside until complete silence filled the chamber. General Sabastian looked up to see the face of his oldest dearest friend smiling down at him.

"Lord Brennen," he sighed. "Thank you for coming."

"My dear, old friend, I would never leave you alone with the lions in your time of need." He turned to face the rest of the faces in the room, "Friends, I understand your concerns... I share them with you. However, this is our most desperate hour. If we fail to act now, if we fail to take every advantage we can, we are lost."

"But destroying the fortress..."

The High Lord cut off the interruption, "... is the only thing left for us to do. Never call the improbable impossible, and never call the inspired insane. General Sabastian is a brilliant military leader and a great man. Follow him."

With that the High Lord took a seat next to his friend. General Sabastian placed a thankful hand upon his shoulder. For a few moments they held a mental conversation which visibly relieved many of the pressures on the General's head. After a few minutes had passed, they embraced, High Lord Brennen left the room, and the General stood to face his adoring public.

"Now, this mission is strictly volunteer. I, myself, will lead the attack. Who will come with me?"

Commander Gabriel stood. "I'm not sure that is entirely the best idea. What if something goes wrong and we loose our top military man? Although you are probably the best man for the job, I think you should remain behind." *Never put all your ranking officers in one shuttle craft.*

"Thank you for expressing your concern, but, I am indeed

the best man for the job so I'm going. Besides, I'm not sending anyone on a suicide mission without my protection."

"Fine. Then I'm going with you to watch your back."

"Oh really?" Lord Anjalina broke in, "And just who, exactly, is going to watch yours?"

"I am." Once again, all eyes in the room turned to stare at Snake. *Stop staring at me like I just materialized out of thin air.*

Lord Anjalina seemed taken aback. Who would have guessed Snake to be the one to voluntarily risk herself for another human being, especially a man.

"Aren't you needed for the training of the Last Chosen One?" Anjalina asked.

"I will finish her training. We leave in a week. That gives me plenty of time to bring her to a level in her training where she can train herself until I return."

"That settles it then," boomed General Sabastian, "Assemble a strike team of ten of your best <u>volunteers</u>. We begin planning in the morning."

****

Roxanne felt the heat of the morning sun on her face. *Not another goddamn morning already?!* She rolled over and pulled the blankets over her head. *One, two, three.* Like clockwork a staff struck the bed where she should have been lying. Should have been was the operative phrase here; she had rolled out from under the sheets, grabbed her broad sword, and come to a full standing position on the floor next to the bed.

"Your reaction time is getting better," Snake sat in one of the huge chairs on the opposite side of the room grinning smugly. "Next time, though, I won't give you so much time to prepare yourself.

It drove Roxie insane that Snake always managed to look so relaxed. It was almost as if she hadn't moved from that spot all morning.

"Didn't want to make you look bad, so I decided to take it slow and easy this morning. How goes the war plans?" Roxie tried always to divert Snake's attention with questions. It kept her

44

from playing the smart-ass come-back game all morning.

"Better than I thought considering who's in charge. I just hope this strike doesn't take any longer than planned because I have more pressing matters to attend to this week. Grab you gear. Let's get some real training in today," with that Snake slid out of the room.

Roxanne immediately hit the bath. She knew if she wasn't on the training ground in five minutes Snake would invent a new more painful way to train her. *Better get a move on, but I really need to shave today. You could always save time by repelling down the castle wall. The garden is right underneath you...* She decided to shave.

Snake paced the garden. There was no possible way Roxanne was going to make it in time. She only had about a minute left and Sage had just arrived to tell her that the "beloved" Chosen was just now putting on her clothes. *Why does she insist on making her life as difficult as possible.* Just once she could be predictable. Suddenly Snake felt something hit her head. It was a pebble. She looked up. Or maybe not.

"Hey boss! Howz it hangin'?" Roxanne could hardly suppress a smug grin as she hit the ground. Snake changed that.

"Next time try not to loosen any of the building and let it fall on people. It only alerts them to your presence."

"Have you ever had a nice thing to say in your life?"

"Can't. I'm a cynic, remember? It would be totally out of character."

Roxie couldn't help but laugh. For a split second she thought she saw a smile creep across Snake's face, but only for a second. Snake immediately proceeded to start the warm-up which Roxie followed with religious dedication. Since she had started her training with Snake every muscle in her body had become tone and strong. She had the agility of a cat and the ability to handle any sword and some knives. *Bet I could market this workout back home. You too can learn to kill your neighbor with your bare hands... Only eight hours a day, seven days a week...* Bare metal connected with her torso. *Back to life, back to reality.*

"Keep your mind here!" shouted Snake.

This had been the number one problem in training Roxanne.

She had this incredibly nasty habit of letting her mind wander.

"Sorry."

"Sorry will not stop some crazed enemy soldier from opening up your throat."

"Well you're no enemy soldier, are you? I can't help it. My mind has always had this nasty habit of working faster than my body, especially when it gets use to what my body is doing."

"Are you saying the usual training I've put together for you is getting boring?"

Careful Roxie, you are definitely walking into a trap here. "More or less." *What the hell did you do that for stupid?!*

"Well, I can most assuredly fix that little problem."

Snake walked over to the wall and tapped twice. Sage appeared. Snake leaned down and gave him a very secretive message that sent shivers down Roxie's spine, mostly because Sage flinched at whatever the idea was. Sage nodded his recognition of the duty laid upon him and bolted out of the garden. Smiling a truly evil smile, Snake leaned against the stone wall and waited. *That woman is entirely too pleased with herself. I'm in very deep shit.*

A few minutes later Sage returned. He gave the appearance of being totally dismayed, the reason for which became readily apparent when the most beautiful man Roxie had ever seen sauntered into the garden. He must have been six feet something tall with flowing brown hair, deep hazel eyes, broad shoulders, and the most incredible arms that ended in the most muscular hands. This was a man of presence who was use to getting what he wanted.

"Thank you for coming Commander." Roxie thought she detected almost a hint of civility in Snake's voice.

"You left me precious little choice, didn't you? You know I'm always up for a challenge."

"Excuse me," Roxie found her voice, "Exactly what challenge are we talking about? Because if it involves me in any way shape or form I think maybe I should be let in on it. What do ya think?"

The Commander turned to face Roxanne for the first time. "So you are the Last of the Chosen. Nice to be trapped with you.

Don't look so confused. I'm Commander Gabriel, one of the Chosen."

Somehow she had known that. *No shit Dick Tracy. Could have seen this same pattern developing in one of those novels you are always reading.*

"What?" Asked both Snake and Gabriel.

"What what?" Returned Roxie.

"Who the hell is Dick Tracy?" Demanded Snake.

"What the hell? How did you know I was thinking..."

"We heard you," responded Gabriel in his nonchalant tone. "This is scary... Probably another great gift bestowed upon the lucky three of us wearing these goddamn necklaces. Oh well."

"Oh well? We have just discovered that we can read minds and you say oh well."

"No my dear Roxanne, we have discovered that Snake and I can hear you think smart-ass remarks. So far that's it." *I hope. Last thing I need is to have to put up more walls.*

"Walls against what?" Roxie said smugly.

The Commander turned with fire in his eyes. It was a look that burned straight through her eyes, down into her soul. Dropping his voice to a dangerous depth he began to speak, but an outburst from Snake stopped him cold.

"Stop! It is my mind! My thoughts are my own! I'm not sharing my life with anyone!"

"Whoa babe, calm down. Look, none of us want to be inside each others' heads so I suggest we learn to signal mental thought."

"What exactly do you suggest Commander, a secret knock?"

"Why not Miss Roxie? A mental sort of "let me in." Snake, are ya wit' me?"

"Am I what?"

"With him. Do you agree?" *Where did you pick up a phrase like that Commander? That sounded like something I might say.* Either he wasn't listening or he chose to ignore her question completely.

"Okay. If you want in ask for in and wait for a yes response to start listening."

"That only works if you trust us Snake."

He hit her soft spot. "No. I don't have to let you in."

"Then you'll have to know we're coming," added Roxie. "However, since none of us really want the others poking around we can expect a mutual respect for mental privacy. Agreed?"

"We have no choice," muttered Snake.

Commander Gabriel clapped his hands together, "Good. I'm glad we are all becoming such great pals. But, we do have other things to attend to, and I'm really not a friend of serious contemplation so..."

Snake bowed a mocking bow and pointed for the Commander to lead them out of the garden. Gabriel returned her bow with a simple nod of the head and then started out of the garden. Snake indicated that Roxanne should follow. She just shook her head and obeyed, knowing full well that it was useless to resist.

****

"You want me to do what?!"

Roxanne searched the crowd of soldiers to find one that was under six feet tall, she couldn't. She looked toward the Commander for some sign of compassion, she found none. *The little bastard probably thinks its funny.* So, she turned on Snake ready to duel to the death in a battle of wits just to get out of this one. Snake wasn't playing games.

"You said the training was boring and unchallenging. Here's your chance at a bit of spice."

"I never said boring is bad. Besides, this is more like dumping a load of jalapenos in tomato soup to give it some pizzazz."

"If you can't do it..."

Roxanne turned on the Commander, "It's not a question of "can't," I just don't want to injure any of your men, or their prides."

Snake grinned. She had known Roxie would do it, she loved a challenge, or, at least, she hated being told she couldn't do something. And, somehow the Commander always knew the right buttons to push with everyone, absolutely everyone. It was one of his many annoying habits that managed to keep him estranged from the lords. *Wish I could be so lucky. Oh well, there is only so much that can be accomplished in one lifetime.*

"Listen up soldiers," boomed the Commander, "Snake, as you all well know, has been training our newest recruit in the art of battle. Somehow, she has gotten it into her head that she is a better teacher than I. I disagree. In order to settle this small discrepancy we are holding a challenge. Snake has said that Roxanne can beat ten of you in a given day. Today is that day. All I need are ten volunteers."

Roxie turned to glare at Snake. *Ding-fucking-dong boss lady. Ten? What are we on drugs?!* Snake shrugged her shoulders. *It's a nice round number.*

"I'd like to volunteer Commander."

Gabriel looked at the soldier who first stepped forward. It was Smanson, his leading broadsword fighter. This might be a better fight than he had thought. His move triggered the rest and nine other volunteers appeared in the blink of an eye. They were a tough looking crew, most over six feet and all trained experts. Gabriel almost felt sorry for Snake's little victim.

"Here are the rules and regulations. The fights will be held in this clearing and will begin hand to hand. A practice sword will be placed at each end of the clearing. Combatants can only pick up the sword at the opposite end of the clearing after the initial fight has begun. In the event that Roxanne defeats the first challenger the next will immediately step in to replace him. If Roxanne has already picked up a sword the challenger will automatically given one. Hits in fatal areas count you out as well as actual knock-outs. These are real fights people. This is to be treated as a battle situation! Understood?"

Everyone nodded. Roxie shuddered. She thought back to the morning and wished she had at one time or another learned to keep her big mouth shut.

Snake took her aside. "Don't let yourself think, just do. This stuff should be in your blood and running through you. These guys will probably take it easy on you at first because you are a woman. Use that; let it work for you. You'll beat the first five without even breaking a sweat." Snake smiled the closest thing to a warm smile Roxie had ever seen. For the first time she thought they might be friends.

With grim determination Roxie took her place at the end of the clearing and sized up the competition. He was a tall man with broad muscular shoulders, veins running down his arms, and rough callused hands. Something tugged on Roxie's mind. What about this particular man bothered her? Too late to think the start signal was given.

Immediately he lunged for her. She ducked low right as he should have wrapped her and pulled her down. As he went over her head she reached up, grasped his legs firmly and plucked him out of the air. He hit the ground hard. Roxie started to let go of his legs to head for the sword but was stopped by sudden recognition. His legs were disproportionately small for his upper body. This man was a seasoned sword fighter; one she couldn't afford to sword fight with. In a split- second change of plans, she bent his legs as far backwards as she could, mounted his back, and proceeded to knock his head against the ground and a very large rock. Challenger number one was unconscious.

Realizing she hand no time to celebrate her victory, Roxie jumped up and turned to face the next challenger. He was a shorter man of stockier build. This man was definitely a fighter. He looked like a man that could out bear-hug a bear. Now was the time to go for the sword. Roxanne pulled one out of Terrel Davis' play book. Running straight for her opponent, she faked left and went right. He tripped her. *Always said no one could run like Davis.* It was her turn to hit the ground hard. He reached down and tried to grab her by the back of the neck, but she moved so fast that he could only get a grip on her shirt, and what a grip it was. Unable to break his hold on her shirt she decided to let him have it. She untucked it from her pants and slid down. Without ever stopping to look back, Roxie dove for the sword, whirled on her challenger, and landed a solid blow right on the center of his chest. Apparently he had been too shocked by her previous idea to move. Laughing at his own stupidity he went down like a good corpse should. *Two down and I'm sure as hell not sweating.*

She was debating whether or not to attempt putting her shirt back on when something inside her told her she shouldn't be standing exactly where she was standing, so she stepped left. A sword sliced the air next to her. Working on improvisations, she hit the ground and crawled between the legs of the man behind her. That drew a small chuckle from the crowd of spectators. Shit. *Get your mind off the crowd, Roxie. This is no time for stage fright.* She stood and turned to face the new challenger. He came at her full speed with sword swinging. The two swords collided in the air. This man had extreme power behind his swing; power she couldn't match. Two, three, four more collisions. She had to think of something fast. She couldn't hold him off forever. She didn't have to. He dealt a blow that knocked her sword out of her hands and sent it flying. *Fuck this is going to hurt without a shirt. That's it!* She went down two seconds ahead of his death-blow, rolled, and grabbed her shirt out of challenger number two's "dead" hand. Before the new guy had even turned around Roxie wrapped her shirt around his head, ripped the sword from his startled hands, and dealt him a death-blow to the back. Snake had been wrong because now she was definitely sweating.

Challenger number four wasted no time in making his attack run. Before number three had hit the ground number four knocked Roxie flat on her ass, jarring the sword from her hands. She couldn't breathe. He pinned her to the ground and proceeded to choke the life out of her, in a manner of speaking. Panic seized her mind. For the first time in her life Roxie thought she might die of something other than boredom. The world started to get fuzzy. *This guy is actually going to kill me!* She wasn't ready to die. This time she pulled one out of her own play book; she nailed this determined asshole right in the balls.

He reacted as all males should, he cringed in pain and let go of her throat. She rolled out from under him and went for the nearest sword, but he managed to get a firm grip on one of her ankles, preventing her from moving close enough to the sword to grab it. *Fair enough.* She kicked him in the head. He let go. Determined to get out of this as quickly as possible, she picked up the sword, turned, and hurled it like a javelin right at his heart. A move which drew a slight applause from the crowd.

Come on guys... If I have to pretend this is a real fight you think you can pretend you're not here? The applause died quickly, so Roxie poised herself to face the next of her many challengers.

But he never came. Wondering what was taking so long, Roxie turned and found herself face to face with Lord Earin. He did not look pleased with the situation. She glanced behind him to see Snake leaning nonchalantly against a nearby tree and Gabriel giving a "wasn't it clever for the universe to include me" grin. She felt like she was sixteen and had just been caught sneaking out of her bedroom window. *Oh hell. Dad's home.*

"Snake. Commander. High Lord Brennen and General Sabastian request your presence in the plan room. They wish to finalize plans for the first strike." His eyes never left Roxie's. Somehow he merely directed his voice back over his shoulders toward the pair.

Roxie felt a tugging at her mind. She opened it up. It was Gabriel. *Got to go babe. Dad wants us home before dark.*

Have fun darling. Call me when you can come out and play.

Snake decided to add her two cents. *That could be awhile. We're in big trouble. They'll probably make us go on a secret mission or something.*

That sucks. And I was winning, too.

The Commander decided to ignore that last comment. "Tell me Lord Earin, who has been assembled in the plan room?"

"Just the strike team and the High Lord. They feel that the less people who know the details the safer it will be."

"Wait a minute," Roxie burst into the conversation. "The General, Snake, and you are all going on this strike?!"

The Commander smiled smugly, "So what's your point?"

Roxie backed down a little, "Nothing. Just something they use to say back home. Never put all your ranking officers in one shuttle craft. But they always did, so I guess I shouldn't be surprised that it works that way elsewhere as well."

"I guess there are some universal truths, aren't there?"

There was something disturbing in the Commander's smile as he made that last statement. Roxie knocked at his mental door. *Just wanted to let you know that I'm going to figure you out eventually. Sleep well.*

Snake raised an eyebrow. She herself had tried to figure the Commander out a thousand times and she kept coming up with the same answer; that man didn't want to be figured out. She could respect that and so she left him alone. The standing around was getting to her so she turned and headed back to the main part of the castle. Taking her cue, Commander Gabriel followed. Almost as an afterthought Snake stopped and said over her shoulder, "You would have beat them all Roxanne." And then she walked away. Roxie smiled.

****

"Jesus, Doc. Hard on people much?"

Lord Earin sighed. He had known since he lead Roxanne out of the clearing this morning that she was upset with him. If she only understood the pressures laid upon his shoulders. There had been a time when he would have made side bets on the winner, but those times had long since passed. He smiled a weak smile at Roxanne.

"I was not trying to be harsh. I just do not think it is the best idea for our best soldiers and one of the Chosen to risk killing each other or injuring themselves right before we enter a major war. Believe it or not, we might just need you for this war."

"Point taken. But, consider this; that was the closest I've ever come to an actual combat situation. Without that I might have walked right into a sword in the middle of a battle. I know it was dangerous, but it's all I've ever had, Doc."

"I know." He sounded almost defeated.

"Okay, Doc. Tell me what is really getting you down. A small fight in the garden didn't drain the life out of you."

Once again he sighed. How could she know him so well so soon? Hardly a moment passed that he didn't contemplate this lady, yet he still couldn't figure her out, but she could look at him and all but read his mind. *You are an intriguing one, my dear, and perhaps someday I will understand you.*

"Just the normal everyday strain placed on a lord and protector of the land right before a major war. We must protect all that we hold sacred; our way of existence. Yet, all the power we possess is nothing when laid next to that of the Betrayer. We need something more..."

"Hey Doc, that's what us lucky Chosen are for, remember? Aren't we suppose to ride in on our horses wearing shiny white armor and all that fun stuff?"

"That, my dear, is exactly the problem. Don't look at me with that perplexed look on your face, you know what I mean."

"Your wrong. I only think I know; enlighten me."

Earin lost his patience, "Goddamn it Roxanne! No one knows for sure how or even if those fucking necklaces work! Not me, not you, not even the High Lord himself! I've done nothing but search and study for the past few weeks, desperately seeking an answer! I've read everything, but still no answer in sight. I'm suppose to guide and train you; give you insight to the workings of our world and your role here and I can't even tell you exactly why you are here! Don't you get it? Don't you see? I can not help. I feel so lost. Yet here you sit, so proud, strong, and determined... ready to fight against God knows what for no reason at all..."

"No, there is a reason; you. If someone as pure as you is willing to give his entire life for a cause then there must be something worthwhile about it. I've never had your kind of will or dedication before. Now, for the first time in my life, I have a chance to <u>accomplish</u> something and that's precisely what I am going to do."

"But I..."

"Jesus Doc, no one is perfect. So now you've discovered that you are fallible, so what? Get over it and get on with it. You can't possibly know everything. And to tell you a little secret, I don't really care how or even if these fucking necklaces work. I'm going to fight my hardest with or without them."

"What if they are all that can save us?"

"Then we'll learn as we go. That's all we can do. Now give me another history book to read and prepare to answer a whole shitload of questions."

Lord Earin looked on Roxanne's face in amazed awe. A slight smile invaded the corners of his mouth. *You just might save us all, lady. You will definitely save me.* He handed her a book and began the history lesson.

****

Snake shot a severe glance at Commander Gabriel. *This man may just be crazy enough to get us all killed.*

Gabriel responded with one of his "gee, aren't I clever for knowing it all" grins. *Yeah, wouldn't that be a relief. I thought we might actually have to fight in this damn war.*

Snake looked back toward General Sabastian. He was staring hard and fast at the map before him. For a split second he looked like he might actually be able to stare right into the soul of the Betrayer, but it passed and he looked up to resume his speech.

"Don't think I can't sense your extreme dislike of my plan, but it's all we've got. If any of you has a better plan I'm listening." He paused to let them exchange glances. They didn't. So he gave them time to add some smart-ass remark. They didn't. Mentally, he sighed. "So, it remains thus. I don't have to tell you how important this strike is to our attack. We have no choice but to win."

"And to get back alive." The General nodded at Commander Gabriel. "I mean, let's face it, these troops couldn't fight their way out of bed in the morning without us there to pull the covers off their heads."

"Oh, so that's your secret weapon. Getting them out of bed? Now I'm sure we'll win this war."

The Commander grinned yet another insufferable grin at Snake. "Can't win the war in a bedroom."

Snake leaned in across the table and said ever so slyly, "Well then, I guess you're not doing it right."

That was it for the General. "Okay children, get some rest. We leave before sunrise. With or without covers over our heads."

Still grinning, Snake and the Commander left the room followed close on the heels by their strike team. The General glanced at the completely silent form of the High Lord. He appeared to be in deep meditation. The General thought about saying something to his dear friend, then decided against bothering the poor man. He knew the burdens that weighed on his shoulders. Instead, he rose to make his exit. The calm, powerful voice of his friend halted him.

"No, I don't think you are insane. You possess the greatest military mind I've ever known. You've saved us all before, and if anyone can save us now it will be you."

General Sabastian smiled, "I remember a different story, my friend. It was a lone, young lord that saved us all before. This time I only hope I can share that burden."

"You already are."

"Do you think my team will come back alive?"

The High Lord hesitated and then sighed, "I honestly don't know. But, all my faith and strength go with you, my friend."

"That will be enough." The General started out the door and then stopped. Without turning he muttered, "We will return, I promise."

As he left the room, Lord Brennen found himself grinning from ear to ear as a tear rolled down his cheek. In all the many years that he had known the General the man had never once broken a promise. He'd come back or die trying.

****

A murky dampness filled the early morning air in the courtyard. Twelve figures sat silhouetted against the darkness upon their majestic horses. They were waiting. A horse snorted and pawed at the ground with its front hoof. The rider shifted in his saddle. A couple of the others looked back toward the castle. The silence was getting too eerie.

Suddenly, out of the darkness, appeared the last rider. He sat tall and proud in the saddle; a magnificent man with an awesome purpose. Determined, he rode to the front of the waiting warriors.Never saying a word, he motioned them forward. There was no turning back now. Riding in personal silences, each individual knew that that first step forward had just started The War. They all donned their own personal guilt and rode on into bloody battle.

Chapter 4

"Mongrel."

The shadowy figure never raised his voice above a whisper, yet, somehow, it echoed down every corridor of the caverns. He turned and waited for the miserable little creature to appear out of the walls. He did.

"At your beck and call my master."

The Betrayer smiled ever so slightly at his complete control over this pathetic worm.

"They have left the castle and she is not with them."

Mongrel felt the very real threat living inside his master's statement. He slinked over to the stone cauldron and muttered some magic words that were instantly forgotten. He was pleased by what he saw.

"She will come master, but she will come alone. They will not know, nor will any come with her. So shows the cauldron."

Mongrel shot a nervous glance toward the forbodding figure that commanded him. Two fiery eyes dimmed and the overwhelming presence disappeared. Mongrel sighed with relief. And so he would be spared another day.

****

Snake jumped down from her horse and circled around to the base of the Shattered Peaks. As always, she was the "point man," as Gabriel called it. *If the job is point "man," then why are they always giving the honor to me.*

Because you are the only one of us with enough stealth to handle the job gorgeous.

Flattery will get you nowhere. Now, get out! I'm trying to concentrate.

There was no response so Snake moved on. The semi-abandoned Fortress sat on the highest possible peak of the mountains. From where she crouched all she could see were shear cliffs with absolutely no pathways leading to the fortress. She ascended the cliffs and slowly began to circle the peak. She searched every single approach, from every last side, but there was <u>no</u> direct path to that fortress. All the cliffs surrounding it where shear for at least a hundred feet. Sitting in dark seclusion, Snake pulled her bottom lip between her teeth and pondered. She knew the answer, but she hated it. *Exactly how much harder could this get.* Unknown voices came out of the darkness directly behind her. *Answer: a lot fucking harder.*

Positioned as she was in a cluster of boulders surrounded by high vegetation, Snake knew she could be safe for hours. She didn't have hours. She waited for the voices to move past her hiding spot. Instead, they stopped directly infront of her hidden grove. *Fuck! Like I need this tonight. Well, maybe their friendlies.* Snake raised her head ever so slightly above the boulders only to see three of the ugliest trolls she'd ever seen. Considering the facial quality of trolls, that was pretty fucking ugly. *So much for that idea.*

Knock, knock doll-face. Where are you? Camp's kinda lonely with eleven other men as the only source of entertainment.

Small problem here. I'm stuck in a grove of boulders about a league north of you. Three ugly trolls have camped outside my front door.

Isn't "ugly troll" redundant?

Get a little serious Commander... They are severely ugly.

So, what exactly did you have in mind?

I'm thinking I should just slide right out the front door. I'm probably going to have to crawl. Might take awhile.

How long is awhile?

If I haven't made contact with you by the deepest dark of midnight come get my horse. I'm going now. Don't call me, I can't afford distraction.

Good luck and may the force be with you.

The what?

Nothing.

You sound more like Roxanne every day.

Good luck.

Snake shook her head. She'd work on figuring him out much

later, right now she had urgent business to attend to. She crouched low to the ground and felt for loose dirt. Slowly, she removed her jug of water and poured some into her pile. She mixed it and applied the mud liberally to her face. Making sure none of her long, blonde hair had escaped her soft, black helmet, she pulled herself to the ground and started forward like a snake.

Time stopped the second she left the closed-in safety of the rocks. She could hear her breathing echoing in her ears. Calmly she reminded herself that she was the only one who could hear it. Still,

she reduced her breathing to a necessary minimum. Almost a part of the ground, she moved toward the outer edge of the camp. Although she was totally concealed in shadow, Snake felt exposed by the light from the camp fire. *Remain in control. You are the only one who knows you are here. Pull that grand ego of yours out of your ass and relax. Just a walk in the park.* Mentally she allowed herself a Commander Gabriel "wasn't the universe clever to create a specimen like me" grin. Somehow she felt better.

She was nearly half way across the perimeter of the campsite now, and the trolls were occupied with consuming whatever poor creature they had managed to bash in the head just before dinner time. A bone came flying her direction, bounced off her head, and landed on the ground beside her. She never even flinched. Slowly she pulled herself forward, closer to her goal. *Keep it slow and steady. Don't get anxious.* One of the trolls got up and started walking toward her motionless figure. Her reflexes took over where panic should have seized her.

Just as he was about to step on her, and definitely discover her, she rolled away from the campsite, stood, slit his throat, and laid his dead form down. The whole thing took only seconds. Snake crouched and stared back at the dead troll's companions. They were still eating. *Thank any deity for small favors.* Seizing the opportunity, Snake began grumbling in a low tone and dragged her package into the brush, making certain to make as much noise as possible. However, she knew it was merely a matter of time before his body was found and the whole mountain alerted to their presence. *Think!...*

She leaned over and, using the jagged edge of her knife, cut three more gashes into his throat. She tore his shirt and covered his

body with dirt. Then she howled like a mad dog, tore through the bushes, and bolted into the wilderness. ... *If all else fails, pass the blame.*

****

Gabriel paced the darkness just outside the campsite. *Where the hell was Snake?* He knew damn well not enough time had passed for him to panic, but he slowly was. She had asked him to wait for the deepest dark of the night, it wasn't time yet. So on he paced. Occasionally, he glanced back toward the fire to take a body count. Everyone was always there. *I'm acting like a second grade teacher on field trip.* He kept pacing. A gruff voice behind him stopped him cold.

"Snake can handle herself. She's twice as evil as they could hope to be."

The Commander turned to face General Sabastian, "I know. But her information is so important. Besides, she's more icy than evil."

The General smiled a knowing smile, "Yes, I can see how concerned you are about the information she has acquired. If she can't handle herself there is little to nothing you can do for her."

The Commander sighed, "I feel like an over-protective mother. I need to know where every member of my force is and exactly what they are doing."

"That, my dear Commander, is why you are so successful." The General cocked an ear toward the dense forest. "Her horse is coming. Try not to look too frazzled it will kill her confidence."

The General headed back to camp. Just as Gabriel could make out

the approaching horse and rider he heard from behind him, "Icy more than evil? I guess you could be right."

Snake rode her mount right up to Commander Gabriel's face and leapt off. Her face was covered in mud, her hands with blood, and she was breathing heavy.

60

"Must have been one hell of a fight. Either that or you're just glad to see me."

Snake's eyes flared for a moment, then turned to ice. "It was one hell of a fight."

"Care to tell us how many of them will be showing up here tomorrow to return the favor?"

Snake grinned and moved into the camp. Sitting next to the fire, she grabbed the water bucket and began washing her hands and face. "None of them."

The Commander shook his head. *Must you always be so goddamn secretive? Somebody has to know something about you. Guess I'll try for that honor.* He stared at Snake. She pulled out her knife and sharpened it. For some reason he was glad he had shielded that from her.

"Bad news General. I circled the entire peak. It's all shear cliffs. There is no direct entrance to that fortress."

The General poured himself a cup of ale and positioned himself just across from Snake. "What exactly are you saying?"

"I'm saying, there is no direct way in. The only way in..."

"... is a secret passage," finished the General.

"Looks like we're going hunting tomorrow," offered one of the recruits.

Snake grinned a sly grin that sent chills down the young soldiers spin.

"Not unless you are one hell of a hunter Vic," responded Commander Gabriel. "You see, the one thing we don't have is time. We don't have time to spend playing hide-and-seek with the bad guys. If we aren't in that fortress by tomorrow evening we can kiss this war good-bye."

"Why?"

This time the General decided to enlighten him. "I don't want to shock anyone, but the Betrayer knows we're here. Don't look so confused. He has more magic and more spies than you can ever possibly imagine. If we don't strike quickly, we'll find ourselves in a full-scale battle right here on the mountainside within a day."

Vic started to panic. "What the hell are we going to do?"

Snake leaned forward bringing her scar into the light. "We

play follow-the-leader instead. I just left two very ugly trolls without their buddy. When daylight breaks, I'm betting they head straight for home. They're big and mean but not too brave, or smart."

General Sabastian nodded. "Do you remember where to pick up their trail?"

Snake responded with an evil glare.

"Sorry." He raised his voice, "We head-out at daybreak. Snake will lead the way. Now get some rest. You will need every alert sense you have." With that, the General headed for bed.

"Rotate watches as usual. Vic, you and Slovosky take the first turn." Snake stood and moved to the far edge of the camp. "Good-night gentlemen." Gabriel finished giving the orders and followed her form.

Snake had disappeared into the darkness. *So what else is new.*

"Someone following me."

Gabriel looked up into the tree where her voice had come from. She sat like a panther, poised and ready to strike.

"Nice trick. I didn't even hear a leaf rustle."

"You weren't listening, you were looking. You'll have to learn to do both." Snake leaned back against the tree trunk and pulled her bottom lip between her teeth.

"I was distracted."

"So I noticed. Why did you follow me then?"

Gabriel started to make a smart-ass remark, then he changed his mind and decided to attempt honesty. "Because you've been on my mind for a long time now. Your presence disrupts all my senses. And I want to know why."

Snake leaned forward, once again exposing her scar. "At last, the man is honest. Guess you aren't all mystery and surprises."

"I never said that."

Gabriel leaped into the air, grabbed Snake by the legs, and pulled her down into his arms. She opened her mouth to protest but was stopped by his warm lips pushed passionately against hers.

As he started to remove her shirt, she muttered, "The

General told us to get some rest."

Running his hand across her firm breasts, he replied, "And you told me to practice using more of my senses in unison..."

Hitting the ground, absorbed in animalistic passion, the last true words she uttered were, "I said both."

****

Lord Anjalina stretched. She had been looking over maps and battle plans all night. A golden beam of sunlight shone upon the parchments scattered across the conference room table. She stood and walked around the table, eyeing everything as she circled. Just one advantage. That's all she wanted to find. Just one way in which they weren't beat.

Lord Earin spoke softly, "It's hard, isn't it?"

Anjalina lifted her eyes to his. "We are out-numbered, out-positioned, out-powered, out-magicked, out everything. I fear I'm loosing hope."

Her eyes were red, her face haggard, and her voice weak. Yet, somewhere inside she possessed immeasurable strength. He just had to find a way to trigger her passion.

"I found myself expressing the same fears some days ago to the last of the Chosen. She gave me a new sense of hope and desire. She possesses so much faith in us. She called me pure and said anything we believe in is worth fighting for. Hold on to that belief. We are fighting for our way of life; we are fighting for all that we hold sacred; it's all we have. Let it be enough."

"I'm so drained. I'm afraid it won't be enough. How will we survive if our desire fails us."

"If our faith fails us... perhaps, then, we deserve to fail."

Lord Earin left the room as silently as he had entered. Tears began to roll down the lady Lord's cheeks. Somehow she had to find a source of strength. She had to rediscover her faith. She had to find hope. She turned toward the parchments strewn on the table. It wouldn't be there. She moved to the window and stared into the

daylight. A gleam of silver from below her perch caught her eye. It was the sunlight reflecting off the sword being expertly wielded by the last of the Chosen. *Perhaps there.* She left the war plans behind and headed for the garden.

She was greeted by the grunts of a warrior as she entered. She walked toward the center of the garden where she discovered the powerful form of the Chosen One engaged in strenuous exercises. She appeared to be doing battle with an imaginary foe that she could somehow see and feel. She thrust with all her might then jerked back as if counter-attacked. Her sword went flying from her hand, she dove for it, turned and thrust upward. When she rolled to her side to stand she saw the Lord watching and stopped. She stood and dusted herself off.

"That was quite an impressive show. Must have been a powerful enemy."

Roxanne smiled, "Yeah, but I always win, for now anyway."

"I must say I'm amazed that you have continued your training with such an intensity, considering your trainer isn't around, Chosen One."

Roxanne flinched. *I really am going to have to hold that press conference.* "First of all, my name is Roxanne. You can even call me Roxie, but please do not call me "Chosen One." Secondly, my trainer is gone not my reason for training."

"And why do you train, Roxanne." Lord Anjalina seemed to almost choke on her name. *Oh well, she'll get use to it.*

Roxie grinned from ear to ear, "So I don't have to fight." Anjalina looked at her with that infamous confused Lord look she had seen so often on Earin's face.

"Sorry. I keep forgetting you haven't seen the movie. You honestly don't know why I train?"

"I honestly don't know."

"Because this is real. All my life I wanted this to be real, and all of a sudden it is. But, just when I get the chance to really live, somebody wants to take it all away. I can't let that happen. Right now I have a chance to accomplish something worthwhile. Whether or not I can win I'm going to go down in a blaze of glory. I'm going to go down saying I <u>acted</u> on what I believed in, and it will be enough... end of soap-box."

For the first time in weeks, maybe months, Lord Anjalina smiled. "I don't know what a "soap-box" is, or a "movie." All I do know is you are very strong-willed, Roxanne. And, you have given me a glimpse of what I am seeking. Perhaps now I will rest and be able to find the remainder inside myself."

The beauteous red-headed Lord turned and exited the garden, taking all her strength with her. Roxanne smiled.

"Okay, so I'll just wait here then. We really must talk like this more often. Nice lady. Not all together upstairs, though." She laughed. *Well I think I'm funny.*

She picked up her sword and tapped it twice on the nearest tree. Sage appeared only a few seconds later. *Gee, what kept ya'.* She was feeling particularly hot and sweaty today.

"Sage old buddy, what do you say to a nice cold dip in the moat."

Wrapping her arm around his smiling figure, Roxanne walked out of the garden a little more self-assured today. They just might win this war yet.

****

Commander Gabriel slipped. Just a little, but it was enough to send loose rocks and the entire company sliding to the ground. Snake shot an ice-cold glare back at him. He shrugged an apologetic shrug, but it didn't do much for improving her disposition. Becoming almost one with the ground, Snake slide silently forward. Silently? He tried but couldn't hear a sound. As he thought about her many skills he found himself grinning. *You are truly an amazing lady, whether you're made of ice or fire.*

Snake reappeared and motioned for everyone to fall back and regroup. They moved back. She pulled everyone so close they felt like they were sharing breaths.

She began to whisper, "They haven't seen us, despite all the noise we're making," she shot a deadly glare at Gabriel, "They are moving through a small mountain path just ahead. The entrance has to be there."

Slovosky developed the balls to interrupt, "How can you be sure?"

The Commander cringed and ducked to miss the fire that had to be coming from her eyes. *One day they'll learn not to question her, I hope.*

"Physics. It's a small mountain path. They are large, ugly trolls carrying supplies. They can't go very far unless they are planning on spending the evening wedged in between the peaks. Soooooo... I say we wait for them to get inside and settled before we strike."

"Wrong."

Snake spun on the General. "You have a better plan?"

General Sabastian grinned, "They don't call me the greatest tactical genius of all times for no reason. We wait long enough for them to get through the door, then we strike. Catch them before they can reach a better position and before they can join the others. We need those forces as split as possible because we are smaller than possible and surprise is our only advantage."

Snake nodded. *You are a genius, but you'll never know that.* He looked at her and motioned forward. Taking the hint, she slid through the surrounding vegetation and into the mountain passes ahead. Gabriel counted to twenty. No Snake. He followed Snake's trail with the rest of the men close behind and General Sabastian bringing up the rear. It wasn't long before they were crossing the open mountain ground into a perfect bottleneck passage. *Babe, I hope you know what you're doing.* No response. All of his senses came alive and he slowed the forward movement.

The entrance wasn't hard to find, as someone had been kind enough to leave it wide open. Halting his men, the Commander drew his sword and entered. He nearly tripped over the first corpse lying directly inside the mouth of the entrance, but Snake's hand came out of the darkness to steady him.

Do you always make this much noise on secret missions?

What noise? The body of the other troll would have muffled my fall. And where the hell have you been, young lady?

Killing bad guys. I wasn't about to break my concentration to chat with you.

A furious whisper broke their mental conversation, "Would somebody please tell me exactly why my strike force is standing and not striking?"

Gabriel cocked an eyebrow and let loose with an infamous

"gosh aren't I about to be so clever" grin. "Just admirering Snake's handy work, boss."

The General lowered his eyes to the two dead bodies lying at his feet and then brought them up to meet Snake's. They were burning with a fire that came from a secret, dark place inside her soul. *You little vixen. You won't be controlled, will you?*

"You said you wanted them dead as soon as they got inside..."

"Correct. I'm just not sure you let them get inside, Snake."

Snake lifted one brow, and Gabriel knew that she'd only let the trolls put the key in the lock. Anything to make a point.

The General glanced around the chamber they had entered, actually it was more of a hallway leading to a long set of stone steps that wound upward into disturbing darkness. The only light came from the small door that they were all now crowded around. He looked at his men. Two or three of them copied their notorious leader and leaned nonchalantly against a nearby wall, a couple examined the chamber, and the rest would look from the dead bodies to Snake back to the dead bodies. *They really need to get use to her, she is definitely going to save their lives some day.* For a split second he questioned the choice of certain members of the party... but he couldn't, this mission was <u>strictly</u> volunteer.

"Well kids, time to light a torch and move on into the wild blue yonder."

The General chuckled at Gabriel's attempt to lighten the tension, "Sorry dad, no torches. We wouldn't want anyone to see us sneaking in the window, now would we?"

As usual, one of the recruits panicked.

"No torches!! I don't know if any of the rest of you have noticed or not but it is completely black past this point. If we don't take torches how are we suppose to find our way, touch and feel?!!"

The General's eyes became slits, his bushy red brows attempted to become one in the center of his forehead, and his voice dropped below a whisper, "If you don't lower your voice I will take you out myself. What possibly made you believe that a secret strike volunteer mission would be easy? Act like the soldier you are and pull out a rope."

The silenced soldier closed his own mouth against another protest and obeyed the command. The General began to believe that there may be hope for this one.

"Snake? You take the lead. We'll tie this rope around waists so we don't loose you."

Snake shrugged, "Whatever works. Just keep up and, this is for all you calm and collected characters, at the first sign of confrontation, cut the rope first and then do battle, okay? I'm not going down with any of you."

Commander Gabriel smiled a sly little smile at the image of "Joe Cool" standing alone with the rope still clinging to his waist. He took his position mid-group and handed the rope back through the line of victims. The General anchored the rear as always and they started slowly forward.

Remind me to thank you later for telling the General about my ability to find my way in the dark.

Why don't you just thank me now and save yourself some time?

I really do hate you.

I know, I hate you too.

****

Snake slammed against the wall, immediately pursued by her opponent's burly hands. She slid her aching back down the cold stone, avoiding his grasp, and stabbed a long-knife into his crotch. Hot blood covered her arm as she forced the blade upwards into an entire series of vital organs. His muffled screams echoed in her ears as she pushed him off and turned to face the next attacker.

Across the circular chamber the General confronted two trolls wielding battle axes. The biggest, ugliest troll lunged forward and attempted to severe the General's sword arm while the second swung for his neck. With a look of near disinterest and very little effort, the General simply ducked and let the trolls deal each other bone crushing blows. Seeing that they hadn't managed to kill each other he neatly slit their throats with one fluid pass of his sword. Staying in a crouch he turned to face his next attacker.

When it became apparent that none were coming the General turned his gaze to Snake who sat across the chamber staring at him with mutual realization on her face. This attack was over, but where were all the others. Snake stood and cut the remains of the rope from around her waist. Sabastian had forgotten his was there until that moment. Mimicking Snake he pulled his off, hoping the blood that coated it belonged to one of his victims and not a friend.

A noise from the dark hall behind them sent them both flying against a wall with swords poised. They prepared to strike but were halted by a familiar voice.

"Anybody home?"

The General breathed a sigh of relief at the appearance of the Commander and, for the first time, realized how important this man was to him.

"Nobody here but us trolls," said General Sabastian.

Snake sheathed her sword and casually leaned against the wall, "Did you manage to bring anybody else through this battle, or do we settle for just you?" *Nice to see you're still alive.* Somehow she had known he was.

The Commander grinned an almost gentle grin, "It seems that some of the boys had a sudden stomach flu and they're out in the hall pulling themselves together. The rest are stashing corpses so as not to draw unwanted attention." *Nice to still be alive, gorgeous.*

"Did we loose anybody?"

Gabriel turned his attention back to the General, "No, but a couple of the boys aren't going to far. Vic's leg is broken. Seems one of the bigger trolls stepped on it after bouncing him off a wall. Unfortunately for the troll he got a knife stuck in his kidney and died of kidney failure. Keagan took a knife in the shoulder and just managed to avoid loosing an arm to an ax, so I gave them the medical supplies and told them to head back and guard our escape route."

Snake pulled her bottom lip between her teeth in silent contemplation while the fine leaders of the war discussed details of the battle and the remaining mission. Finding what she had run a mental search for she folded her arms, took a deep breath and said, "Correct me if I'm wrong, but wasn't Keagan our arrow man?"

The two men turned to face her. The General spoke.

"'Aint that a bitch. Commander, we don't happen to have anyone else with his accuracy lying around here somewhere do we?"

Snake didn't like the mocking tone of voice the General was using. She liked it even less coming from Gabe.

"I'm not entirely sure there General. Perhaps I could ask among the men and see... Oh, wait a minute," he said giving himself a slap on the forehead, "What about me?"

Both men laughed until a stoney glance and an icy grin from Snake silenced them. At that moment they were quite sure she was capable of slitting their throats with a smile. Gabriel made a mental note: *It's not wise to upset a Wookie, or a snake.*

At the sound of the approaching troops General Sabastian ceased all joking and slide back into the character of a cold, calculating military man. When the men entered the chamber they were faced with their same uncompromising leader who allowed no weakness. Commander Gabriel was once again leaning nonchalantly against a wall and Snake was removing her knives from several of the corpses strewn throughout the room. The smell of blood and sweat permeated the stale air. It was all rather comforting.

The General seized command. "We have no time to rest. Keagan and Vic have been sent to cover our exit. Despite what has befallen us we will proceed as planned with Commander Gabriel taking over as the arrow man. I don't have to tell you how dangerous this is becoming, you can see that. I will, however tell you that time is running out for us. If the Betrayer knows we are here, as I'm sure he does, he is either sending reinforcements or pulling his troops. We have to take as many out here as we can, so let's move."

Without uttering a word, the tiny force gathered their weapons and their courage and marched forward into destiny.

****

A very harried Lord Brennen closed his eyes and leaned his heavy head into his hands. Hands that had one time seemed so sure and strong, but, that now shook with increasing weakness. He sucked in a deep breath of stale castle air and nearly fainted with the exertion of returning it to the chamber. *I'm not going to survive this war.* That assertion was shocking yet almost comforting. Gently lifting his head, the High Lord scanned the all too familiar library. He had locked himself in this room without human contact for what felt like an eternity hoping to find a miraculous answer. *What a foolish person I am... Did I really expect to be that lucky more than once?* Still, he kept searching for something. A light rapping on the chamber door brought him around to reality.

"You are free to enter; this is not a private place."

The face of Lord Ambrose peeped through the now open door. "I was concerned... I did not wish to interrupt you as you were obviously in deep thought."

Brennen smiled at the timid man before him. His eyes, which spent many a minute being averted, were a soft silver and full of unknown kindness. The few tufts of hair that remained attached to his head were snowy white, and he had reached only half the height of normal men. Yet, for all the warmth that flowed from within, he was one of the oldest and most powerful Lords.

"Not really. I was just resting from my search."

The aging Lord allowed himself a warm grin, "Then it would appear that Lord Anjalina was right when she expressed fear that you were shutting us out of your pain. She has tried to reach your mind for hours now and you have not answered her. She asked me to look in on you."

Warm tears began to roll down the High Lord's tired face, "I just can't concentrate. Everything is so hard. I keep looking but feel that even if I found what I was searching for I wouldn't even realize it. I seem to be failing."

The last words were barely spoken but Lord Ambrose felt them more acutely than any of the others. The poor gentle man infront of him was indeed failing, but only in his physical strength.

"High Lord you must get some rest or..."

Something in the High Lord snapped, "I don't have time to rest! There is too much undone. Can't you see that I have to find something; do something; help somehow... Yet, here I sit as helpless as a baby with so much unanswered. I can't help in training. I can't fight. All I can do is prepare, and I can't even do that."

All the pain of his dear friend welled-up in Lord Ambrose's heart. He reached out to this great figure of a man the only way he had left.

"Brennen, oh my dear friend, if it had not been for your strength and guidance there would be no land now left to defend. It was your strength that brought us through the last time and it is your knowledge that will bring us through this time. But you are killing yourself and leaving us deserted before the battle has even begun. We need you now. The troops look for you to smile upon them and, not seeing you, they wonder what is wrong. The other lords need your guidance. And you, my friend, you need to rest."

The two eyes locked eyes for a few precious moments. The High Lord's stoic stare could not overcome the concerned smile of his friend. Smiling a relaxed smile he closed the book that had sat unread infront of him and stood to follow his friend from the chamber. The young apprentice standing outside the library door caught them both by surprise. In obvious tension, the young man greeted the Lords with a bow.

"Rox... The Chosen One has asked me to extend an invitation to the High Lord to join her in her chamber for a "much needed meal before a well deserved nap." She also has a pressing question to ask of you."

Upon ending his message, the young apprentice appeared anxious to bolt from the area and return to a safer realm. The High Lord placed a warm hand on the young man's shoulder and tried to imitate one of Lord Ambrose's smiles.

"Why are you so worried Sage? Do I not know you? Did I not bring you here to serve? Am I not your mentor and your friend?" Sage nodded. "Then why the sudden fear?"

"My Lord," Sage paused a glanced with pleading eyes into the face of Lord Brennen, "There is just so much that I can't understand... She just knew that I should meet you here, now. She just knew."

The High Lord shared in the anxiety of the apprentice before him. How did she just know? There would be another time to discuss this. Not now and not with the skittish youth.

"You forget, she is Chosen and possesses a magic that not even she understands. It is this that will save us." *Or doom us all.* "Now go and tell her that I will indeed join her for a meal."

Sage disappeared as quickly as he had appeared. The two Lords grasped each other mentally and then parted, each feeling a little more ready to face the world than before. And, as Lord Ambrose watched his life-long friend slowly limp off he felt sure that the man before him would save them all. A tear rolled off his cheek as he turned and headed in the other direction. *Just one more time.*

****

Roxanne paced the confines of her room. She had walked every last inch of her bed chamber a thousand times, in fact, she was developing an intimate relationship with the cracks in the walls and ceiling. At first, after the strike party had left, she had had no problem finding ways to occupy all the minutes of her waking life. She continued her training, read history books and maps of the land, and explored all the passages of the castle. But weeks had passed. Her training was becoming routine, all the books were read, all the maps memorized, and all the castle mazes strung with string. No doubts about it, she was starting to feel useless. She hated feeling useless.

But it was more than the useless feeling that was bothering her now. It was those horrible dreams. How could they feel so real? Why couldn't she stop them? They started as mere images; simple and haunting at first. And then... Roxanne dashed the vivid images from her mind. *Get a grip Roxie. This isn't the land of Freddy. Dreams aren't _real_. That's what I said about worlds like this too. Okay! That's enough... I'm so confused.* A knock at the door brought her back to her senses, sort of. She reached out with her mind for a second.

"Come on in High Lord."

She turned to face the door as it opened and what she saw was not the man she remembered. The man she remembered had been strong enough to tie her to this world, make life and death decisions, and to send evil witches to hell. The man before her now stood like a helpless kitten trapped on a tree branch clinging desperately without the strength to hold on. She hesitated for just a moment and then took his hand and lead him to the couch. Grateful for her comforting touch, the High Lord smiled and allowed himself to be lead like a child. The table before him was laden with all kinds of fruits, meats, and breads. Roxanne motioned for him to eat.

"I knew you were neglecting yourself, but this is ridiculous. You have to take better care of yourself, Lord Brennen. There will come a time when you will be called to the battlefield; for that we will need you alive."

The High Lord paused in between bites of much needed food, "So the other Lords have informed me. I'm afraid that everyone else thinks about my health more than I do myself."

Roxanne smiled, "That's not exactly a good thing now is it?"

"So tell me Chosen One..."

"Roxanne."

"What?"

"Look, a long time ago, in a galaxy far far away, I was given the name Roxanne and I'd really like people to use it. This "Chosen One" shh...stuff is too much for a sane gal to handle."

The High Lord gave Roxanne that now infamous confused look she was so use to seeing when she dared open her mouth. *One day I really am going to hold that press conference.* But the look was soon replaced by a calm gaze directed into her soul. She felt a small ting of probing. She closed off a part of her mind and let is pass.

"So tell me Roxanne, why did you send for me?"

She shifted in her seat, uncertain as to whether or not she should unleash the burdens of her mind on this tired and essential man.

"Oh, I'm not as tired as you think. In the past I have found that working through others problems has often helped me conquer my own. So, please tell me why you called on me."

Trying to appear undisturbed by his ability to read her thoughts, Roxanne revealed her fears to him. "Do you ever dream? I don't mean those scattered thoughts of random events that cloud our minds. I'm talking about dreams that are so real you wake up still locked in mortal combat?" She paused to look into his comforting eyes. *At least I'm still here, in reality.* She resumed her speech in a low almost conspiring tone, "Those are the kind of dreams I've been having. So real that they touch my mind during the day. Always the same. I'm standing in some dark stone chamber, alone and cold. But somehow I'm not alone. There is this other presence that surrounds me and chills me. Then a deep voice speaks, not so much out loud as in my head. It says, 'I knew you would come. You have condemned them and now belong to me.'" Her voice was mounting in tension, her breathing quickened, "I try to scream at the voice but nothing comes out. I search everywhere for a tangible form; for something I can fight against and conquer, but there is nothing. The voice laughs viciously in my head; I want to stop it but I can't. It has complete control over me. I can't get out and then..." She stopped realizing that she was nearly screaming. She glanced at the High Lord, wiped her sweaty hands on her pants, "... and then I wake up in a cold sweat feeling more like I've done battle than slept."

Suddenly she realized that she had just bared her soul to the High Lord of the land she was somehow expected to save because she and two other saps happened to be wearing matching necklaces and there wasn't really anything he could do about dreams anyway so the whole thing was really rather silly. She felt like laughing hysterically. Lord Brennen saw things differently.

Sitting before this possible savior of the land, with his stomach full of good food, the High Lord felt a new sense of energy. Distracted from his own suffering by the plight of another he felt a renewed feeling of power and compassion. Here was something he could "fix." He was coming back to life. Ever so gently he smiled, allowing this strength to flow through his tired frame.

Looking into the searching eyes of the Chosen One he said, "Dreams are not reality, but they can be extensions of it. Tell me, what are your greatest fears?"

Just like that I'm suppose to tell you what I'm most afraid of. I don't think so. "Being alone and out of control. I need something I can control." *Way to go Roxie. Great job of defending your innermost secrets. It's a good thing you're not revealing too much of yourself or anything.*

"That is exactly what haunts you in your dreams. You are being forced into your greatest fears."

"That's the whole point, boss. I'm being forced. These thoughts aren't coming from me. These thoughts were formed by someone else. Someone who can invade my mind."

It was as the High Lord had feared. The Betrayer had found her weakest point. What could he do to stop it?

"There is a distinct possibility that the Betrayer has found a link, a path into your mind."

Roxanne bolted from her chair. "Are you telling me that fucking bastard has a way into my private fears?!"

Lord Brennen slowly nodded. "I know that prospect is frightening but..."

"Frightening? He can talk to me when I am sleeping and you call that frightening?! No shit Dick Tracey."

Lord Brennen grabbed Roxanne's hands and forced her to look into his eyes. "You must calm down. This is a scary thing but it can be handled. He has found your weakest point and can send you messages in your dreams, but they remain his messages, not yours. He can't read your thoughts. He must be guessing at your fears as they are quite common. If he can reach you, we can read him. And we can block him."

Roxanne fell into a seat. She had this overpowering desire to run a sword through something, she just wasn't sure what that something was. She fought with her anger for a few minutes and then sighed.

"Okay, boss, how do we fix it?"

The High Lord muttered something unrecognizable, waved his staff over Roxie's head, and smiled.

"That was a protection spell. It should block him out, I hope. As for your feeling of uselessness... Please don't look so shocked. I only have to look at you to see that you need to "do" something. I will have Lord Earin put you in charge of special training for some of our top soldiers."

"Thank you for the mental block, and I appreciate the other, but do you really think groups of grown men are going to want me telling them what to do? Something tells me I might be treading on some toes."

"When it comes to the good of the land, all differences mean nothing. Besides, Lord Earin is convinced that you could have beaten all ten." The High Lord grinned for the first time in months.

As he left her chamber, heading for much needed sleep, Roxanne grinned too.

****

Chapter 5

General Sabastian glanced back over his shoulder at the disappearing corridor; the way out just got further and further away. *How the hell are we ever going to get back out in time?!* He counted his steps. *Twenty-one, twenty-two, twenty... Fuck!* Too many steps in too little a time span. Some of the men were going to have to go out ahead, which meant a bigger delay in getting this strike over with, and Gabriel was going to be cutting things far too close. For a split-second the General thought about switching positions with his trusted Commander, but only for a second. He couldn't hit a target that size at that distance every time. *Besides, my old body isn't as fast as it use to be.* All that amounted to was he could no longer keep up with his horse. Then Snake was there.

General Sabastian suppressed an urge to throttle her. One second she had been leading the men down a dark winding staircase to doom; the next she was standing directly infront of him without warning. *God, she was good.*

She placed her mouth on his ear and scarcely whispered, "We are at the entrance to a large meeting chamber. We should do it dead center."

Placing his mouth next to her ear he asked, "Are we at the center of the fortress?"

"Close enough. Any further and we might not be getting out, at all."

The General nodded at his fears echoed, "How many inside?"

"Ten. But they aren't the problem. The real challenge comes from the three other unbarred entrances to the chamber."

Fire flashed in the General's eyes. *This should be more fun than I thought.* Yet, it had to be done. He motioned for Commander Gabriel to bring the rest of the men into a fall back position. As he started explaining the situation to the men, Gabriel smirked at the mental conversation he'd had with Snake in which they already discussed all this. *Connections; it's all in who you know, and can mind-read with.*

"I need a man at each entrance; Dawson take the north, Jennin take the south, and Roogin on the west. Whatever happens <u>do</u> <u>not</u> leave your posts and <u>do</u> <u>not</u> let anything past you! We need to set-up and get out with as little trouble as possible."

The men nodded in understanding. Snake suppressed an evil grin, noticed a couple of the men were looking at her, and then changed her mind. Grin accomplished, the men turned and left her to her private thoughts. *God, I've gotten good at that.* Assuming the standard positions, the strike force moved forward to the edge of the entrance. The General motioned to Snake. She moved into the chamber and disappeared. Taking positions on either side of the entrance, the General and the Commander strained their eyes for any indication of Snake's whereabouts. The didn't strain long.

One, two, and now three guards fell; all of them clutching desperately at the daggers protruding from their throats. The other seven rushed toward the hidden assailant, and the strike force rushed the other seven. Somewhere in the back of his mind the Commander had the thought that a collision like this would be a very effective slap-stick routine. But he had no time for distracting images; three of the trolls had reached Snake. Pulling out her broad-sword, she caught the battle ax of one troll and thrust a small dagger into the knee of a second. Commander Gabriel ignored the first two and went straight for the third.

Lunging forward, he felt his battle worn blade connect with solid flesh. He finished the swipe, pulled his sword back, and then finished by slicing through the soft, exposed throat of his opponent. Arms wrapped around him from behind. *Oops! Forgot about the other four.* The war-torn Commander, with all his tactical genius, sat down. The bulky troll couldn't bend his torso that far and was forced to let go of his prey. Suddenly, the edge of a battle ax cut through his unexpecting throat. Gabriel leaped up and brought his sword to bear on the calm face of his commanding officer. The two exchanged understanding glances and turned to face another attack.

While the rest of the force had been playing with the few trolls left, Snake found herself locked in mortal combat. When she blocked the ax of the first attacker to reach her, he pulled back and both weapons went flying. Fortunately, that only left him weaponless. She slammed a dagger into the knee of the second troll. Blood oozed onto her hand, making it hard to grasp the hilt. She left it there. Her first friend reached over his buddy and wrapped her up against his smelly body. She let him slam her into the wall. Mustering all her strength, Snake pulled her feet up and pushed. The strain made her legs ache. Her back felt like it was about to break. She could feel her legs giving out. They did. He slammed back into position, and a dagger hit him square in the neck. Snake removed it, thrust it into his heart for good measure, and then slid to the ground.

The hilt of this dagger sat with perfect weight in her hand. It was hers. *I guess that evil bastard didn't like where I left it.* She looked up to see him limping towards her, battle ax in hand. With the ease of a seasoned fighter she planted the dagger deep in his chest.

Keep it this time. She moved out from under the standing corpse and turned to face the next attacker. She found herself face-to-face with the rest of the strike force.

"Was that it? Is it over?"

Snake glared at the over-confident young man.

"Hardly," she hissed.

As though her words were their battle cry, a small army of trolls swarmed Dawson's entrance. The General was first to reach his side.

"Don't let them through. Make them fight in that tunnel!" he boomed as he thrust his broad sword through a tangle of torsos.

Gabriel knew he was right. If they kept them bottled up in the corridor they would only have to fight a couple at a time. They couldn't afford to take on all of them at once. Taking position behind the General, he ordered the men to form a fall back circle for support. Jennin moved into the circle; Gabriel slammed him against the nearest wall.

Flashing his ever-famous "gee wasn't the world clever to include me" grin he breathed into the confused soldier's face, "I

81

do believe the General told you not to leave your post."

The abashed man's face went from fury to blank. He came to attention and moved back to his entrance.

"A little hard on the kids today, weren't you, dad?"

Gabriel suppressed the urge to slap Snake. "Someone has to be the disciplinarian."

Snake allowed a sly smile to cross her lips at the twitching of the Commander's hand. *Try it, and we'll see who leaves alive.*

"Jennin is not the only one having a mental slip. Isn't it just possible that these ugly fuckers will eventually figure out how to move around to the other entrances."

Gabe cocked an eyebrow, "You thinkin' we should close them in first?"

Snake raised an eyebrow and bowed slightly. The Commander ordered the second group to move forward as the General and the first line fell back to rest. Blood was dripping off the arms of the General.

Gabriel motioned to the General's arms, "Your's or their's?"

"Mostly their's."

"Can you hold things here for awhile? Snake and I thought we might sneak out back so as to keep everyone where we want them."

For a moment Sabastian thought about offering them some of the force for help, but only for a moment. Instead, he simply nodded and then moved forward in the ranks to take control of things from this side. Snake and Gabriel moved past Jennin and down the dark winding hallway. Jennin stood firm at his post.

****

Dust swirled through the air of the confining cavern. Small unspeakables skittered along the stone floor. A small servant sighed with undying faithfulness. Mongrel was tired, but he could not rest. The darpresencese of his master loomed ominously over his shoulders. Stooping over the smoke-fillecauldronen, he muttered a few undistinguishable words, threw in a few disgusting things, and stirred it all together with a few strokes. It started to bubble and foam. Forms appeared on the surface. Then He materialized from deep inside the shadows.

Never above a whisper, but always unbearably loud, his voice rattled through Mongrel's ears, "Ah, more troops loyal to me. Send these to join those blocking the Silver Forest."

Then He was gone. Each time a brief appearance, and then nothing. Arms reached out over the sides of thcauldronen. One by one evil beings in various forms crawled from the depths of hell into this world. Mongrel sighed again.

****

Roxie leaned against one of the larger trees in the garden. Her shoulders ached, her back was killing her, and one of her knees was swollen to the size of a softball. It had been a great training session. Sage appeared with cold water and a wet rag, followed closely by Lord Earin. Sage handed Roxie the rag drenched in cold water. She applied it to her knee. *God, this feels good.*

"What's on your mind, Doc?"

It still drove him insane when she did that. Glancing at her knee, he said, "You have been injured."

"I'll live. You should see the truck that hit me, though," she added with a grin. He responded with a look of confusion. *Score!*

"At this point I'm not even going to ask for an explanation. I merely came to see how the preparations are going."

"So far, so good. Mind you, this is based on the opinion of someone who has never been in a battle, is lost in an alternate reality, and has a very over-inflated opinion of herself. I'd say we're perfect."

The Lord laughed.

Roxanne grinned from ear to ear. "My dear Earin, I do believe you are lightening up."

"I guess I just can't help it with you around." He joined her under the shade of the tree. "At times like these I can imagine that our world is what it once was; we are not preparing for war; and you and I are friends, not comrades in arms."

Roxanne took his hand in hers, "We are friends. And I'll meet you back under this tree when this is all over and done."

The two friends sat under the tree, holding hands and gazing into each others eyes. The moment intensified. All sound stopped. And, for a split second, Roxie felt the urge to lean over and kiss the timid Lord passionately. *Okay, now things are definitely far too serious.* She didn't.

"So, any word from the strike force." She knew there hadn't been. If they were anywhere nearby, Snake and Gabriel would have contacted her.

Lord Earin was both relieved and disappointed that Roxie had broken the magic of that moment. Fighting back his desires, the Lord shook his head.

"I thought as much. You know, not that I'm looking forward to it or anything but, I'd really like to get this whole war thing started before I'm too old to hack evil demons in two."

"This war will start soon enough. The Betrayer still prepares and moves forward. His troops keep growing like worms cut in two. He is effectively surrounding us. My concern is not whether or not the fighting will begin, but whether or not we will be ready for it." Earin paused. Staring at Roxanne with pleading eyes, he said, "I can't lead these men."

Don't even look at me, Doc. "You will if you must. Trust me. But, don't stress too much, Commander Gabriel will make it back; he doesn't seem to think the world can run without him." *Sad thing is, he's probably got a point.*

"High Lord Brennen believes that General Sabastian will return by whatever means possible. He looked me straight in the eyes and said, 'Dead or alive, he will return.' I pray it's alive."

Roxanne stared at a blade of grass she had decided to play with. Lord Earin gazed through a hawk-like bird circling above. They were each absorbed in their own private wondering; neither of them moved. They simply sat like statues. Sage hesitated to approach, but duty, as always, propelled him forward.

"Excuse me Lord Earin, but the High Lord has requested both your's and Roxanne's...the Chosen One's presence in the library."

Roxanne sighed, "Well, looks like the fun never ends. Do me a favor will ya'? Run ahead and tell him I'm on my way. I have got to take a quick dip in the moat first."

Once again Lord Earin looked extraordinarily confused. "But we don't have a moat."

Sage grinned triumphantly as he watched Roxanne sprint off toward the small lake at the end of the garden. For a moment he considered telling Lord Earin where she was headed, but, instead, he clung to his own private knowledge of the Chosen One like a forbidden lover.

Looking up at the bemused Lord, Sage simply smiled. "Come. The High Lord awaits."

****

Snake slid her body along the cold, stone wall. Every little pebble seemed to stab through her skin; she was impossibly close to the barrier of rocks. *Better a lot paranoid than a little dead... if there is such a thing.* Behind her, Commander Gabriel leaned his body into the stone and wondered how the hell Snake managed to disappear into the wall even when he knew exactly where she was. He tried to mimic her; he couldn't. There is only so close a human being can get to another solid surface. *Hey, that's it. Maybe she ain't human.* The grin that had crept across his face died suddenly. Snake's beautiful, yet sinister face appeared in the darkness.

Do you hear what I hear?

Gabriel listened to the heavy grunts traveling through the darkness. *If you are talking about the noises of a minor battle, yes. If you are receiving alien messages, no.*

Snake's eyes narrowed to slits, then reopened with a flash. *There's a battle raging somewhere?*

Cross my heart and hope to... never mind. How many are we talking about?

Hold one.

Snake's dark figure moved off quickly. Gabe counted. *One-one thousand, two- one thousand, three- one thousand...* A familiar face returned as abruptly as it left.

Looks like twenty-three or four. I can't be sure with as many corpses as are scattered throughout.

Look, if you can't even get more accurate than that, I don't

85

want you counting. Paranoid much there, Snake?

She let that one slide. More accurately, she stored it in memory vowing revenge at a later date.

None of them are guarding from the rear. I can take three with daggers in seconds.

I have four extra shots with the bow.

Time lost to re-cocking the bow?

I can launch two arrows at a time, accurately.

Good. That only leaves sixteen or seventeen others to kill with swords or hand-to-hand. Not the best odds.

Gabe grinned from ear to ear. *You think, maybe, we should spot them a man?*

"Contain them! They are breaking through! Goddammit, hold them!"

The command voice of their General sent the two assassins darting down the corridor, pulling out weapons as they ran. The first seven trolls fell hard to the ground. Snake and Gabe switched to swords and charged forward at full speed. They managed to finish off a couple more from behind before the others woke-up enough to turn around. Then the real fighting began.

The trolls could stand four abreast in the hall, and they knew it. The first four turned, each wielding a battle ax. Snake dropped low and dragged her broad sword across four pairs of kneecaps. Commander Gabriel came from high and sliced through two necks. Wasting no time, Snake met him in the middle after running through the other two. And, miraculously, thirteen trolls were dead. Unfortunately, the rest of the trolls didn't think very highly of what had just happened. Four more charged.

Snake blocked two battle axes against her battered blade. Letting them move in closer, she brought her knee up into the groin of one and planted her elbow in the other troll's face. At that same instant, Gabe nailed one troll with a standing drop-kick that sent him flying back into the mangled mess of his fellow trolls. Landing, he brought his blade up just in time to block the death-blow of his second friend. Snake slid a dagger through the shoulder blades of the bent over troll. The other returned her elbow to the face and sent her reeling to the ground. He jumped on top of her and found a sword protruding from his back. Snake pushed the heavy body off her and moved into a crouch.

The Commander blocked another battle axe blow and followed the blade of his sword with the hilt. Blood spurted from the trolls ugly face. He moved one of his hands to clear his eyes. Gabriel lunged; and one more troll fell dead. Looking across the hall he saw Snake come out of a crouch to trade blows with a hideous troll. *Well, looks like there really is no rest for the weary.* Swinging his sword above his head he charged forward. *Duck!* Snake ducked; Gabriel swung; one more troll lost his life, and his head. More trolls rushed toward them.

Shit! They're behind us.

Snake moved in behind the Commander. Standing back to back, the two warriors fought with all their might. But they were closed in and knew they couldn't hold it forever.

Snake called out to Gabriel. *We are going to be crushed unless we can get some more room and some help.*

Gabriel hacked an arm off one of the many bodies in front of him. *What did you have in mind, gorgeous?*

Just this.

Snake maneuvered herself around until she was facing the chamber entrance. "General! Let them in!"

General Sabastian blocked yet another body from moving forward. He was covered in sweat and blood; most of it his. He tried to ignore the gash in his thigh. *Come on Gabe. Don't you fail me now.* Then a familiar voice broke through the darkness. It was Snake telling him to move the trolls inside. Hesitating for seconds only, he ordered the men to form a fall back ring at the center of the chamber.

"We are bringing them in. Be prepared for a surge. Everyone on the line drop back behind those in fall back."

Then the General stepped back from the entrance and the trolls rushed forward. The strike force managed to catch them in the crescent of swords they had formed; the fighting intensified. As soon as the trolls moved forward, Snake and Gabriel worked their way out of the death trap and began forcing the last trolls forward into the waiting circle in the chamber. The General was waiting for them on the other side.

Trolls fell left and right. The strike force fought with a renewed vengeance at the sight of the Suicide Duo pushing their victims to the slaughter. The circle tightened. Bodies fell. And then there were none. The grunting had stopped, and all around there was no sound but that of heavy breathing and no movement but that of chests heaving up and down in painful breaths.

Snake began walking the newly formed graveyard. Her movements seemed to awaken the rest of the team.

Roogin's eyes followed Snake's shadowy figure. "Commander? What's she doing?"

Gabe glanced toward the dark lady. "Retrieving her knives, no doubt." *God knows she spread them around freely enough.*

General Sabastian's powerful voice broke through the somber silence. "Jennin, Erikson, and Gyric, sweep the hall. I want every piece of every dead troll in here, now. No need advertising ourselves. The rest of you start piling pieces against the north wall. Commander, set up the device."

Gabriel prepared a jovial retort to the General's order, but changed his mind when he noticed the blood rushing down his leg. He was at the General's side in an instant.

"Well this was smart now, wasn't it?" he said, applying pressure to the cut.

General Sabastian brushed his hands aside. "Yeah, well, it's an attention thing. Now get to work assembling the device. I can dress my own wounds."

The Commander cocked his head to one side, "Hie Hitler! Just don't bleed to death, 'cause I'm not dragging your body home with me." With that Gabriel left General Sabastian in his own care.

The old veteran slid to the ground and stretched his leg out in front of him. Glancing at the men around him, he calculated just how funny it would be to ask Snake to bandage his gash. He shook his head. He didn't want to die today. Instead, he pulled out his cantina and poured water over the slash. It was a nice clean cut; there weren't any jagged edges. A thought tugged at the corner of his mind. *Now let's see, who had the medical supplies? That would be Keagan and Vic. And they are... back at the entrance. Not to worry. I am prepared.* Reaching into a pouch that he always kept at his side, he produced bandages and a needle and thread. This was not the first time he had sewn himself together, and it sure as hell wouldn't be the last. *Here goes something.*

Snake leaned against the wall, bringing one leg up so that the sole of her boot rested on the wall.

"Nice patchwork."

General Sabastian tried to sound nonchalant, "Practice, and lots of it." She didn't move, so he asked, "What's on your mind, Snake?"

"Howz the leg feel?"

Why was it she refused to come directly to the point? "It hurts. So what's on your mind?"

"I was just thinking about how far it is from here to the entrance; how fast the trip is; and, how long it will take that thing to destroy this fortress and anything stuck in it."

Fire surged through the General's body, "I will not leave my men to die."

"And they will never leave you. If you can't keep up, you will condemn them to death." Then she was gone.

He wanted to lash out at something; instead, he pulled in all of his energy and calmed his outward self with all the skill of a seasoned officer. His mind raced for options as he pulled the thread through his skin one last time. By the time he had finished closing the hole in his leg, he had reached a tactical decision. He glanced at Snake; she wasn't gonna like this one. *Oh hell, time to piss off the troops.* He pushed himself off the ground and into a nice stance.

"All right, listen up 'cause here's what we are going to do."

****

Lord Earin closed his eyes and slowed his breathing. The other Lords were all assembled inside the chamber; he could feel them. He opened his eyes, took a deep breath, and pushed open the door with an excuse for Roxanne sitting on his lips. None was needed. Standing in the far corner, arms folded, hair dripping, and face beaming was the Last of the Chosen. He didn't

89

know whether to laugh or cry. So, he simply bowed in greeting to the other Lords and placed himself at the table directly in front of Roxanne.

"You did that one purpose, didn't you?" he mumbled as he slipped past her.

She answered with a grin, "Me? Can I help it if you walk slow?"

High Lord Brennen motioned to Roxanne. "Please, sit."

She shook her head, "Thanks but no thanks, I'd rather stand." The leader of the land looked confused, but asked no questions. Lord Anjalina looked as though she was about to burst. Roxanne grinned. *They can hide every emotion but that one. The need to know might kill her.* For a short moment, Roxanne considered letting her off the hook... She changed her mind. Without uttering a syllable, the High Lord drew the attention of everyone in the room. All eyes faced the man of rock as he spoke.

"I wish this were to be a meeting of inspiration and hope... but, it is not. The situation is this; there is a large force of demons moving towards us even as we speak. If they are not upon us tonight, they will be by dawn."

Roxanne scanned the room for reactions. None of the Lords seemed to have heard; they all sat motionless. *Snake was right. They aren't human anymore.* If this had been the army leaders, someone would be outraged by now. Instead, they sat like stone walls. It was as if this were an everyday occurrence. *They can't really be this calm. They aren't all riding with Wookies.* Roxanne closed her eyes and concentrated. There was a source of unease directly before her; it was Lord Earin. Somehow that failed to surprise her. He had always been the most human of the bunch. Apparently it didn't surprise the High Lord either.

"Lord Earin? You have a concern?"

"Yes, High Lord. Who will lead our own attack force? Both of the higher commanding officers are gone and the individual squad leaders don't carry that kind of power."

Lord Anjalina broke in, "I find it hard to believe that an army of trained soldiers can not act without their Commander to hold them by the hand. Most of them have fought in wars before. They know where to stand, what weapons to use, how to use them, and what to defend."

Lord Earin flinched at the fiery Lord's words. "I am well aware of all that. I am not questioning their ability to fight or to defend us. I _am_, however, questioning our ability to lead them in unexpected situations. Who among us will make those decisions? Who will be responsible for those lives?"

Roxanne stepped forward, "I have an idea. How about I be responsible for your life, you be responsible for Anjalina's, she can be responsible for... let's see, Ambrose, and so on down the line. Come on Doc, are you really that afraid that someone might die due to a decision you make or an order you give? I've got news for you, people are going to die no matter what the decision. How about we all watch each other's backs and see if we can't prevent it for awhile?"

"She's right, you know." They both turned to face the High Lord. "This is going to be a long hard war. We have no choice but to fight it, even if we don't feel properly prepared." He paused, allowing the rest of the Lords time to respond. No one did. "Now, start rotating shifts on the watch. I need one of you among the troops at all times. Chosen One, gather your force and move to the front gate. We need you and your men ready to move first at any moment. Understood?"

"Yes, sir." _My men, huh? There has to be an unnecessary sexual reference in there somewhere._

"Lord Anjalina, I need you to stay and discuss future plans with me. Lord Grant, report to the training field and brief the troops. Lord Earin, help him set up a defense strategy. The rest of you please get some rest before this all starts. Dismissed."

As they left the room, Roxanne pulled Lord Earin to one side. "Look Doc, I didn't mean to come down so hard on you in there. I just got the feeling that you were wigging out on me."

The Lord sighed, "What do you mean by "wigging out"?"

"Oh shit, I'm sorry. I meant I thought you were loosing control of yourself. You were letting your fears dominate your actions."

"Do you really believe that is why I am so concerned? I know that I will be unable to prevent everyone from dying. I understand it so well that it keeps me up nights. The thought of all those deaths... anyway, my real concern is whether or not the men will listen."

Roxanne grinned. *This guy's smarter than I thought.* "Of course they'll listen to you, Doc. After all, you guys are the Lord Protectors of the Land."

Lord Earin recognized her tone of voice. "No. We are the Lords; they are the Protectors, and they know it."

As he turned to walk away, Roxanne felt a sudden and deep sympathy for this struggling soul. She also realized that he hadn't always been a Lord. *One day you'll have to tell me all about it.*

The Lord turned suddenly.

"?Did you say something?"

Roxie grinned and shook her head. The familiar look of confusion settled on Earin's face as he continued on his way. *Nothing of importance anyway.* Still grinning at the discovery of something new, Roxanne headed off to round up her men for battle.

****

Snake glared at the path in front of her. *The old bastard did this to purposely piss me off. I should have slit his wrinkled, old throat.* She smiled at the visions of death and dismemberment that danced through her head. *What the hell kind of plan is this anyway?*

Gabe's cocky mental voice filled her head. *It's the kind of plan that gets the highest number of players out alive. Anyway, you can't do those kind of things to a ranking officer; it's illegal, not to mention anti-social.*

Yeah, but it's lots of fun at parties. Now leave me alone while I "strategically withdraw" and leave a nice little trail of bread crumbs for you hero-types to follow.

As you wish my bitter little bitch.

Hey asshole, I'm neither your's nor little. Try and remember that.

Snake turned her concentration back to the task at hand. It had been decreed from on high that she would take the rest of the strike force back to the mountain entrance to meet up with

Keagan and Vic, stringing the rope along the walls behind them to facilitate the exit of the General, the Commander, and Jennin. *So I get to babysit while the men play war. Good plan.* She took a few more steps forward, stopped, pegged more rope to the wall, and then moved the force again. Behind her, she heard a man trip. *Why is it that I seemed to be surrounded by clutzes and morons? Do I possess the only brain here?* Rolling her eyes, she stopped and allowed him to regain his footing before moving forward.

Under normal circumstances she would have taken great joy in demoralizing the little twirp; but, these were not normal circumstances. It just wasn't worth it anymore. The rest of the world was just going to keep on being ignorant and annoying no matter what she did, and she just didn't give a fuck anymore. Grabbing her rope, she moved forward.

****

Gabe unwrapped his homemade bomb and examined it carefully. All the parts were properly in place. *Good. I'd hate to have the party spoiled because someone forgot the candles.* He placed it in the center of the cavern and began securing it to the floor. If this didn't work nothing would.

General Sabastian stood above him watching the chamber entrances. He scanned for any hostile activity; none. He remained tense. They could not afford to botch this job. He tried to think of something inspirational to say, but changed his mind. This was not a time for words.

Jennin tried to look as composed as his commanding officers; a task that was harder than it looked. The Commander looked like he could have been adjusting any piece of furniture in the comfort of his own home, and the General looked bored enough to fall asleep where he was standing. These men were made of steal. What was he compared to them? *Not a whole hell of a lot, that's what.* The Commander's voice broke the tension filled silence and nearly sent Jennin through the roof.

"Well, she's ready. How 'bout youz guyz? What do you say we blow this joint?"

General Sabastian chose to ignore the Commander's pun. "Ready whenever you are. Well, gentlemen, shall we leave this soiree?"

Jennin laughed a nervous laugh, but found himself unable to speak, so he simply nodded.

"What's your maximum distance?"

Gabe intently examined the target he had left for himself. "If I can see it, I can hit it."

The General nodded. "Let's get moving then. I don't want to over-stay our welcome."

That seemed to be all the conversation they were capable of as not another syllable passed their lips. In dead silence, they made their way back down the dark corridor, each man consumed by his own private contemplations. This was truly the do or die moment. All things were about to begin; they could feel it. And, for a fleeting second, each man questioned his desire to be there.

Jennin grasped that thought and held on to it in desperation. *I should not be here. This should be someone else. I should be back at the entrance. We'll never make it out. What the hell am I doing here?* He began to breath heavily. Sweat filled the palms of his hands. Then this man who had killed hundreds of foe and survived many a battle began to panic. Panic seized him out of nowhere and blinded him. He couldn't focus. *Remain calm. Remain calm. It's almost over. It's almost over.*

The Commander signaled a stop. This was as far as he could see. He motioned the other two closer and whispered, "This is it. Once I ignite it we have a thirty second delay before the explosion. After the initial explosion, this place is going to start falling down around our heads." He glanced at the General's leg. "I suggest the two of you move further on ahead."

The General shook his head and Jennin mimicked the movement. Gabe shrugged and dropped into a firing crouch. He pulled out the torch and started to ignite it. A shadow crossed his field of vision. A lone troll had entered the chamber and was heading with definite interest toward the bomb. *Damn!* Gabriel knew he had to stop him before he got to close and fucked with the trigger. He went for another arrow. None. *Fuck!* He had used all his extras earlier. Instead he reached for a dagger, knowing his accuracy wasn't that great. All of a sudden he really missed Snake. The troll was dangerously close to the bomb. He hefted the dagger and prepared to throw. He never got the chance.

For some unknown reason, Jennin snapped. Swinging his sword above his head and screaming with all his might, he charged back down the hall and head-on into the grasp of the troll. For a few scattered seconds the two combatants exchanged blows. But then, almost as though it had been choreographed, the troll brought his battle ax to bare on Jennin's throat at the same second that Jennin lunged forward and slid his sword into it's evil heart. Both warriors dropped motionless to the floor. The battle ended.

The General and the Commander stood with heaving chests at the chamber door. Neither one could believe what had just happened. There had been no need for Jennin's actions; none at all. What had just happened? Gabriel started into the chamber, but the General's hand on his arm stopped him.

"Someone had to have heard that scream."

The Commander part of him understood and nodded. Quickly as they had arrived, the two men returned to the point of no return. This time there would be no reprieve. Commander Gabriel crouched in the dark corridor, ignited the arrow, and sent it flying into history. He waited only to see the flash of the fire connecting with the tail end of the special powder that would light the bomb. Then the two men were gone.

They raced down the hall, hands sliding along the top of the rope left by Snake and company. Both men counted. Fifteen, sixteen, seventeen... They rounded another corner and prayed with each passing step that the damn thing would work. Twenty-three, twenty-four, twenty-five... Yet another turn passed and still they seemed to be going nowhere. The General's leg called out in agony, but he ran on. The Commander's lungs ached with the strain of breathing, but he moved forward. Twenty-nine, thirty.

They were never really sure whether it was the sound of the explosion or the force of the tremor that ran through the fortress that knocked them flat; all they knew was one minute they were running at top speed and the next they were picking themselves up off the ground. However, it was definitely the sound of the building collapsing behind them that sent them scrabbling to their feet. They knew it was only a matter of seconds before the whole place came down around their ears, but they had no idea how close they were to the entrance.

The running was harder now. Each step sent pain shooting up the General's leg. The fortress shook all around them, making their footing more and more unsure. The inward collapse was moving closer. The Commander found himself dodging falling rocks. The men turned corner after corner. The hall behind them filled with debris. The ceiling over their heads cracked. Things were definitely coming to a hard end. And then they were at the top of a long familiar set of stone stairs. Glancing at each other, the two men started down at a dead run.

The light of the entrance started to penetrate the darkness. A huge chunk of the ceiling landed just a couple of stairs behind them. The light got brighter. A boulder shattered between them. Shooting glances above them, the two men did what had to be done. They closed their eyes and dove for the door.

Thunderous roars filled their ears and dust clogged their throats, but they were alive. Gabriel rolled over onto his back and slowly opened his eyes. *Yep! Sky's still blue; clouds are still fluffy; and Snake is still pissed.* He grabbed the boot that was tapping next to his head and looked up into her angelic face.

"Could you please stop tapping? You see, I have a fucking headache."

Snake sneered down at him, "And who's fault is that? By the way, you look like shit."

"Thanks, bitch."

An evil grin crossed her lips, "Anytime, dragon-breath."

"Would the two of you just shut up?! Some of us are trying to die in peace, here."

Gabe rolled up on his side and stared at his boss. The man looked like he had already danced with the reaper. Dried blood covered his arms and torso, fresh blood gushed from his leg, and dust mixed with sweat to form a nice little mud mask on any skin that was exposed.

"Good morning, darling. Time to wake-up."

The General slowly unsheathed his sword and dropped it next to his smart-ass companion. "Do me a favor and run this through your guts for me; I'm too tired."

"Much as it does my heart good to see you boys fighting, I really must insist that we get the hell out of here. In case you missed it, we just demolished the bad guys' fortress, and I seriously doubt that will make them happy. So... "

General Sabastian forced himself to his feet. *Why is it that this bitch is always right and always feels the need to share it with me?* Reaching down, he helped Commander Gabriel to his feet. Both men leaned on each other for a couple of seconds, but that was all they could afford. Taking command of the situation, General Sabastian ordered the men into a full retreat. Without a word of protest, Snake took point.

****

Mongrel flinched as, before his eyes, the fortress crumbled to the ground. It would be his fault. He knew that somehow it would be his fault. He braced himself for whatever attack his lord and master would choose. None came. Slowly, he opened his eyes and raised them to face pure evil. The piercing red orbs of the Betrayer were locked on the scene that played out in the cauldron, and, for a moment, Mongrel thought he detected a smile. Then those forceful eyes were upon him. He flinched.

"They destroyed my house... But, it is no matter; they cannot destroy my home. They have only weakened themselves. Look, there stands all of their military leaders... Still, they destroyed my fortress... Make them pay."

The hissing of his master's voice died and was replaced by the silence of death. Mongrel knew what he had to do. With the glee of a child who has escaped punishment, he ordered the attack. Today, Mongrel smiled.

****

General Sabastian stretched his legs closer to the campfire

and allowed himself a sigh of relief. For him, the hard part was over just as the war was about to begin. What lay ahead were all the things he knew. He understood war and was unnaturally comfortable fighting in one. *At least, this secret strike shit is over. What the hell was I thinking? I should have stayed at home and let the kids handle it.* He shrugged his shoulders. It was far too late to change any of it now. He decided to catch up on some much needed sleep, but the Commander interrupted that idea.

"How goes it, boss?"

"Just wishing things were different and chastising myself for worrying about things I can't change. How 'bout yourself?"

Gabriel laughed a half-hearted laugh. Then silence filled his face. He stared at the ground as though he were desperately searching for something lost.

"Tell me, General... Tell me what the hell happened back there."

General Sabastian felt a pain deep in his chest as he let himself remember what he had been trying so hard to block-out. He shook his head. "I really don't know."

"It's just so odd. I mean, one minute I'm standing there with two very composed war veterans, and the next I'm standing over a severed head. What the hell happened? Jennin was better and smarter than that."

Pain coursed through General Sabastian's body. He wanted to let it out somehow, but he couldn't. A man as hard as he knew no release but violence.

The voice of his friend drew him toward reality. "Maybe it was too much for him. Maybe he felt trapped. Maybe..."

"Maybe, my friend, you should cut it the fuck loose before it kills you. There is no real reason for what he did; none that we will ever know, anyway. He's gone. There was nothing we could have done differently to stop him. We couldn't have run faster, or fought harder, or been any smarter than we were." The General's voice had become a harsh whisper and sweat rolled down his face. "It's over. Find a way out and move on, okay?"

The Commander seemed to be staring right through him and into the soul of the dead man he cared so much about. There was a fierce struggle in his eyes; a fire burned so deep. To the

General, he looked like a caged animal. Then, as fast and ferrous as it had come, the battle was gone. He opened his mouth, but no words passed his lips. Instead, he grasped the hand of the greatest man he had ever known and gave it a hardy shake. Then the Commander was gone, leaving General Sabastian to toy with his own thoughts.

He had no idea why, all Gabriel knew was he had to search out Snake. The mental link between them was stronger now, making it easy for him to place her position in the camp. He moved away from the fire and further into the darkness. Snake sat perched in a tree. Maybe a better name for her would be Panther.

I'm quite content with my identity, now fuck-off.

Such language for such a pretty girl.

Snake dropped out of the tree directly infront of Gabriel and held a knife to his balls.

"Don't patronize me, EVER! And leave me alone."

Gabriel felt the fire in her voice and it ignited all the fury in him. He grabbed the dagger and sunk it into the nearest tree.

"Look you evil, soul-less wench, if I wanted to be treated like a spineless rat I'd get married, again. I only came over here to talk to you like a friend. So take whatever it is that is crammed up your ass out, and try treating me like a human being."

They stood locked in a ferrous stare; each breathing heavily into the face of the other. Then Snake moved. Without a sound, she was back in her perch, biting on her lower lip. Gabriel refused to move. Finally, she spoke.

"I don't want to talk about it. I just want to be left alone with it. I have a lot on my mind. Things I don't care to share with anyone, okay? And you are dangerous because you can get in there. Get it?"

Gabriel shook his head. "No, I don't get it. But, you don't want to explain it to me either. So, I guess that means I ignore it. However, that doesn't mean I ignore you." With that, he joined her in her spot of surveillance.

Snake sifted uneasily. "Look, I will tell you this much: there is something I have to take care of; some part of my past that I can't escape. And, every time I think about it I hate the world a little more. No matter how hard I try to escape it, no matter how much I grasp for control, it always consumes me in the end."

Gabriel tried to move closer to her but her foot against his chest held him at bay. "You aren't making any sense. What the hell are you talking about?"

"There is something I have to do, by myself. But, I will be back."

"Be back? From where?"

"My past."

Gabriel tried to gaze into her eyes, but they were walled over with an inward gaze. Whatever it was that she was thinking about was definitely consuming her. He wanted to help her. He also knew he couldn't. So, he did the only thing he could think of; he kissed her.

At first, her lips remained cold and uncaring. But, the rage inside her private hell ignited into animalistic passion and filled her with fury. They made ferrous love long into the night; their bodies pounding out their aggressions against each other's sweaty flesh. When it was over, they had both lost something of the human part of themselves. In the darkness, Gabe shivered.

The next morning she was gone.

****

Roxanne stretched a leisurely stretch and rolled out of bed. The sun sprinkled some rays of light about her room; she cringed. *Never could figure that "joy of sunrise" thing out.* She moved to the table where Sage had left her some food. She often wondered whether he ever slept or just spent every moment anticipating her every move. Picking up steaming hot ale and nicely chilled fruits she decided he was a cyborg. She munched on something very similar to a peach and tried to talk her eyes into focusing, but it was no use. She just wasn't a morning person. It didn't help that she had been up all night on one of the guard routes. *You'd never see that in any books I ever read. I guess alternate reality is tough, too.*

A knock at the door rudely interrupted her thoughts. Sage poked his head in the door.

100

"Roxie? Lord Earin wishes to see you," he whispered.

"Tell him I'll be 'round in a minute."

"Actually, he is standing behind me in the hall. I merely wanted to make sure you were awake and..." a smirk worked it's way to his lips, "descent."

Roxanne laughed at the shared joke. *I'll make a cynic out of you yet.* "Well, I'm awake, anyway."

Sage moved and allowed Lord Earin to enter. It crossed Roxie's mind that Sage was becoming more and more of a guard-dog, but she ignored the thought. Lord Earin looked exhausted. He seemed to drag himself into the room with his staff. Roxie jumped from her seat and helped him to the couch. Now she was awake.

"What the hell happened to you? What did you do, start the war without me?"

Lord Earin smiled. "I felt it would be best if I stayed on guard throughout the night. Besides, I could not sleep."

"Martyr yourself much, Doc? Did it ever occur to you that you can't save the world single-handedly? You might, God forbid, need help. So why kill yourself? Are you trying to make it easier on them?"

This time he laughed. "And how about you? Are you always this subtle when making a point?"

"Only when talking to someone as thick-headed as you."

"Okay. Point taken. I will rest later..."

Roxie tilted her head and cocked an eyebrow.

"... er, I mean, immediately after I leave you."

"Better. Now, what brings you here so bright and early, Doc?"

The smile left his face and the unearned age returned. "The force we saw surrounded us on three sides in the night. Our back is literally against the cliff wall that covers the fourth side. I fear we are in grave danger. They will attack... it's just a question of when."

Roxanne sat in calm silence. Suddenly, a single thought pulsed in her brain. "Has the fortress been destroyed?"

Instead of the puzzled look that so often responded to her questions, a look of complete understanding crossed his face. "It was reported destroyed only moments ago."

Roxanne nearly ran to her bed and began throwing on her clothes and weapons. "Then take a rain-check on your nap and down a hand-full of No-Doze 'cause it looks like we are about to rock-and-roll."

Lord Earin managed to stand and started muttering an energy spell. Roxie watched as color flashed in his cheeks and his hands stopped shaking. *Medieval No-Doze... Pretty effective.* As she sheathed the last of her daggers, screams arose from outside and Sage appeared out of nowhere.

Gasping for breath, he exclaimed, "To arms! To arms! They are attacking! We must hurry to the gates!"

Earin and Roxanne exchanged troubled glances. Then they were running down the twisted corridors at full speed. They had to reach those gates. With each step, the screams grew louder and sounds of battle hummed in their ears. Lord Earin was becoming desperate to be at his comrades' sides. They needed him.

As the battle got closer, Roxanne started to feel nauseous. This was the real thing she was running toward. She had never done this before and was becoming less and less sure that she could do it now. These weren't training games anymore. This was actual death. Her hands started to shake and she really missed Snake. *Okay. What would Snake say? Probably something really cynical and harsh like: Well, here's your chance to not get killed. Good luck. Which would be followed by: Don't think about it; just do it. Let the training work for you. Just another drill. Great. Good. I feel better. Not.* Her chest tightened and she found she could hardly breath. *Great, I'm going to die before the battle.*

All at once, they were there. Lord Anjalina was standing in front of them barking orders and firing arrows. She never stood still and never wasted a second. Injured men were pulled off the wall and replaced by healthy ones, who were often replaced by those who had been taped back together. Arrows and stones lay everywhere. The smell of sweat and blood filled the air. Things that had been gray were now red. All around her, Roxanne saw death.

Lord Earin ran to the side of his companion. "Where is the High Lord?"

The red-headed warrior spun to see who she was talking to. "He's on the main wall." She looked at Roxanne. "And he needs you, now."

The blood in her veins ran ice cold. "How long have you been fighting?"

Lord Anjalina appeared disturbed by the question. "Since the screams went up."

With that, the lady Lord returned to her battle. Roxanne stared at all the blood around her. *Since the alarm. That couldn't have been more than two or three minutes. All this blood? Since the alarm?!* Her head started to spin. She found it hard to focus on Lord Earin's face infront of her.

"Are you alright Chosen One?"

That snapped her out of the state she was crashing into. "I told you, it's Roxanne."

He almost allowed himself a smile. "Sage will take you to Lord Brennen. I must stay here and help Lord Anjalina. Will you be alright?"

She couldn't think of anything to say, so she simply nodded and let Sage lead her to the High Lord. They found him in the middle of hell. What they had seen before was Disneyland compared to what they were seeing now. Dead men were being pulled off the wall and being replaced with the least injured. The rocks were slick with blood. Men were pulling arrows from their dead comrades bodies, and sometimes from their own, to fire back at the enemies. Everyone was crouched beneath the top of the wall. Arrows and rocks whizzed past their heads. Occasionally, flames would fall from the sky. And the entire gate shook as the trolls and demons attempted to break it down.

Standing in the middle of all the carnage, the High Lord calmly shouted orders, blessed the dead, and healed the wounded. Roxanne found courage in him. He seemed relieved at her approach.

"Things are not going very well, are they? We must turn the tide of this attack." The High Lord spoke quickly like a man who would soon be uttering his last word. "The gates will not hold through much more of this battering. They are going to force their way in in moments if we don't do something."

Roxanne shook her head. "But what's that something?"

"Let them in, of course."

Roxanne turned to find herself facing a tall blonde soldier. He was probably six feet tall with broad shoulders and bright blue eyes. *Yeah Aryan Nation.* His body was covered with sweat and his face was covered with a cocky grin. This had to be one of the Commander's men.

"Chosen One, this is Major Elway, one of the Commander's best men. Major Elway, this is the last of the Chosen."

Roxanne flinched. "I was planning on calling a press conference about that. Call me Roxanne and I'll call you crazy. Let me get this straight. Your plan is to let them in? Who's the Commander's worst man?"

"The plan is tactically simple and mortally dangerous, as all good plans should be. We fire a barrage of oil coated boulders, followed by flaming arrows in a half-circle just behind the team working the ram, thereby cutting them off. Then we open the doors, pull the rammers inside and ambush them."

"What about the rest of the army? Don't you think they'll risk a little fire for a chance at getting inside?"

Major Elway grinned a sly grin. "That is where you come in. A small band of soldiers, who are exceptionally well trained in hand to hand combat, will be lowered over the gate to hold off the attackers until the gate can be closed. They will then be pulled back up by the same ropes."

Roxanne shook her head. *Now who believes in fairies?* "Sounds like a charming little suicide mission for me and my men."

"I'll be right beside you."

"Oh, you'll be there. Then I'll take two."

****

Roxanne tugged nervously on the leather gloves she had donned. They were to protect her hands when she slid down the rope infront of her. *Yeah, but who's gonna protect my back?* She switched from her gloves to tugging on the rope. It seemed to be securely in place. Everything was prepared. All that was left was to wait. The gate rumbled as it took another hit from the ram below. Roxie held tight, sure each time that the gate would break; it didn't.

Down the line from Roxanne, Major Elway checked his own equipment for the hundredth time. It was still as secure as it had been two seconds ago. He was being paranoid; he knew it. Still... He pulled on the rope one more time. *Damn! What am I doing?! I'm going to drive myself crazy.* He looked around for the arrows. Everything was being loaded. It wouldn't be much longer now. He pushed his body flat against the stone as yet another crash of the battering ram rocked the gate. When the trembling subsided he checked the men down the line.

He found his scan stopped by the Last of the Chosen. She sat with her back to the gate and her gaze fixed on the arrows. *She's too beautiful to die.* The second that thought entered his head, Elway shook it loose. He couldn't afford to think that way. *This is not a suicide mission! She is a fellow soldier, not a buxom beauty.* She turned her head and caught his gaze. He held it for a minute and then turned away. Whatever thoughts she had in her head sent chills down his spine, and he knew that she would come back alive.

"Ready. Aim. Fire!"

Arrows soared over their heads and flames shot up from the ground below. Screams echoed over the battlements. Roxanne peaked at the scene. The archers had been dead-on; all the boulders were on fire. Trolls stood at the edge of the ring of fire and looked confused. It was at that moment that Roxanne realized these creatures were morons. *Hell, they probably don't even know what that hot stuff is. We may make it after all.* A signal from down the line caught her eye.

The Major called out, "Open the gates!"

Roxanne heard the creak of the solid iron doors. The ramming team rushed forward. She jumped.

Before she even realized that she had jumped, Roxanne was standing in the middle of the ring of fire, facing hundreds of demonic looking creatures, with only eleven men to help her.

She had a feeling that this was not a good thing. The flames in front of her burned hotter and hotter, singeing the air, and making breathing painful. The force on the other side of those flames pushed forward. *Are they complete idiots? Those flames will eat them alive.*

The creaking of the gates behind her awoke all of her senses. If they were going to get inside they would have to attack now, before the gates shut again. No campfire was about to stop them from obtaining their objective. Major Elway shouted a warning and the first group rushed forward.

Several of the hideous creatures were consumed by fire; never to make it past the boulders. Instead, they melted into nothingness. This gave Roxanne a sense of relief. But, it didn't last long. The thick-skinned trolls were barely scorched as they past through the fire wall. Seeing their buddies on the other side seemed to enrage the others to action. Only seconds after the first few had made it through, a swarm of trolls pushed forward to consume the small band of warriors.

As soon as the first body came out of the flames, Roxanne dropped into a cat-like crouch, holding her broad sword ready. A huge, smelly troll rushed her. She lunged forward, leaped into the air, and removed his head from his shoulders. As his severed head hit the ground, she felt her stomach turn to mush. Her head reeled. *Holy shit, he's dead! I just decapitated another living creature. Holy shit! Holy shit!* It seemed too hard to stand.

Just when she thought she might pass-out, an arm grabbed her and yanked her to the ground and a dagger flew past her head and into the chest of the troll that had almost ended her life. She turned to see Major Elway facing her with a fierce look on his face. He didn't stare long. He turned to run through two more trolls. Roxanne felt the hand let go of her arm. She looked at her savior. It was Karlis. He gave her a questioning glance. She answered his concern by standing and slicing through the troll baring down on him from behind. With that, they both returned to the battle.

Reaching deep down into a place inside her that she hated, Roxanne turned her emotions off and let the training take over. Ignoring the fights going on beside her, she concentrated on the three trolls that were running at her with battle axes ready. She knew she couldn't counter all of them at once, so she rushed the center troll. As he bore down upon her, she dropped and slid under his legs. Being the bright fellow he was, he leaned over and tried to follow her. His friends turned, forgetting that they were swinging dangerous weapons, and sliced through each other's torsos. Roxanne came back into a stance and promptly ended the heart beat of the third troll who was laying flat on his back. She turned to face the next attack.

On the far side of the battlefield, Major Elway was deep in blood and bodies. He pulled his sword out of his latest victim's chest just in time to block the death blow of a new attacker. While he traded blows with this troll, another charged him from the side. Dropping one hand from his sword, he reached across his body and pulled out his rapier just in time to block the charge of the second troll. Now, he was locked in mortal combat on two sides. He knew he couldn't hold this fight for long.

Roxanne yanked her sword out of the heart she had just stuck it into and stole a glance down the battlefield. What she saw amazed her. Major Elway was facing down two trolls at once with a sword in each hand. A blow from one side sent him to his knees. The two attackers bore down on him. There was no way he could hold them both for much longer. She sheathed her sword, pulled out two daggers and charged.

Jumping over corpses and dodging blows, she made her way to the scene fixed before her. Praying that her timing was on, she leapt. As the troll brought his ax up and prepared to strike, she landed on his back and stuck a dagger into his eye. Blood oozed out, covering her arm up to the elbow. She let the second dagger fly into the arm of the second troll. And then, she and her dead stead hit the ground. She rolled free and came up with her sword in hand. Major Elway sliced the second attacker from groin to temple, then turned to face Roxanne.

She smiled. "Even?"

He smirked. "Even."

They both turned to face the next wave of attackers, but there were none. All of the creatures stood on the other side of the flames. They seemed anxious; almost as if they were anticipating a great release. The twelve member team pulled in closer together. Roxanne scanned the enemy for even a hint of what was about to happen. Then she saw what they already knew. The fire was going out.

The gate door slammed behind them. Roxanne turned to her men.

"The fire's going out! Hit your ropes, now! Get back over the gate!"

As though her words held prophetic force, the fire subsided to a dull glow and what seemed like the entire demonic force rushed forward. Every member of the team hit their ropes and started to climb. On the gate above, soldiers started pulling the ropes up to keep any unfriedlies from following the team. As each man reached the top, he moved down the line to help yank up the rest of the team. Next to her, Roxanne heard Karlis cry out.

"Cut it loose! Just cut it loose!"

The men up top refused to cooperate. Roxie looked down at Karlis. Two very hideous demons had managed to attach themselves to his rope, and one had wrapped some sort of tentacle around his body. He couldn't move. Everyone seemed to freeze. Roxanne knew what had to be done.

"Stop pulling!"

The men looked over the stone, but kept pulling.

"Goddammit! Stop!"

The rope stopped and Major Elway's face appeared above. "Have you gone crazy?"

"No more than you. Tell the men to hold on tight. I'm going to swing over and grab Karlis. Once I have him, cut that damn rope loose."

The Major nodded his understanding. *Damn bitch is really trying to die today, isn't she.* He relayed the orders and grabbed hold of the rope. He wasn't about to let her go easily.

What the hell am I doing? Am I trying to get myself killed? Arrows whizzed past her head. *Great. Not like this was hard enough already.* The castle archers returned fire. Roxanne prayed for a miracle. Reaching down, she tied her legs firmly into the rope, pulled out her sword, let go of the rope, and started swinging. It seemed like forever had come and gone before she grabbed a hold of his rope, but she finally caught it.

"What the hell are you doing?" yelled Karlis. "Just cut it loose."

Her calves began to ache. "Stop whining and let me save you. Grab my arm." He hesitated. "Do it!"

He reached up and firmly grasped her wrist. Swinging with all her might, she severed the tentacle and pulled Karlis off the rope. The force of the men pulling on her rope sent Roxanne and Karlis flying into the wall. She cracked her back against it, but his grasp went limp. Letting her sword fall, she reached down with both hands and held tight. Blood was gushing from his head.

"Pull them up. Pull! Pull!"

The Major's voice echoed over the battlements. Roxie turned to see what had happened to the other rope. It was no more. Looking down, she smiled to see that her abandoned sword had landed in the skull of one of the tenacious demons. This pleasure only lasted a few seconds as the muscles in her arms and calves started to burn. Karlis' limp body seemed to gain weight. She felt her hands slipping. Where the hell was the rest of the team?

Like a savior out of the blue Major Elway reached down over the battlements and grabbed ahold of Roxie's calves. *Not quite the romantic fondling I'd hoped for, but it will have to do.* Sweat rolled down his arms like raindrops. She hoped to hell that he could hold them both because she knew she couldn't anymore. Then a second pair of hands wrapped around her thighs. They moved further. Then another set around her waist. Then her feet hit the ground, followed promptly by her ass, and the weight of Karlis' limp figure was taken away from her. Blood rushed out of her head and back into her body causing the world to spin. She buried her head in her hands.

A comforting voice came through the darkness. "You are a crazy bitch, you know?"

Still holding her head firmly in her hands, she mumbled, "Anything for a little excitement."

"Death can't possibly be that exciting."

"You're right; but I am still alive. So stick that in your pipe and smoke it."

The Major chuckled. Then all playfulness left his voice. "You ready? We have to leave the combat zone- all hell is about to break loose."

Roxanne looked into the still slightly fuzzy face of the Major. "I thought it already had."

Grabbing her arm and pulling her back down the scaffles he murmured, "You 'aint seen nothin' yet."

Roxanne was only mildly surprised to see all of the soldiers crouched on the ground behind the stone gates. She scanned the area for the Lords, but all she saw were soldiers, enemy corpses, and one very used battering ram. She placed her mouth next to the Major's ear.

"Where are all the Lords?"

He appeared irritated by the question. "Watch and learn, Chosen One."

Despite her natural urge to throttle people for so calling her, Roxie turned her attentions back to the battlements. Like the Phoenix from its ashes, all thirteen Lords rose from behind the stone blockades. They all seemed to be glowing with an emerald light as they lifted their arms skyward. Arrows flew past their heads, but never came near them. A dull chanting sound filled the air, starting very low but slowly rising in pitch and volume. The Lords were pouring sweat; the sky whirled above their heads; and the dull chanting became an unbearable screech.

Suddenly, and without warning, a blast sprang forth from the arms of the Lords. Every living thing before them was instantly reduced to dust. Not a tree, not a blade of grass, not a demon or troll was left alive. A single thought crossed Roxie's stunned mind. Ashes to ashes, dust to dust. As unexpectedly as they arose, all thirteen Lords collapsed. One minute they stood like stone protectors of the fortress; the next, they fell like puppets with cut strings.

Major Elway and his men rushed to the aid of the fallen Lords. They were alive, but unconscious. Slowly, the men carried them off to their chambers. Just as slowly, Roxanne climbed to the top of the battlements and looked out across the now barren land. Nothing. She scanned for the remotest sign of life but found only dust. She strained her eyes. At the very edge of the horizon she spied the green of growing grass. *Nice to know that wasn't complete devastation.*

Standing on the battlements, wind rushing through her hair, staring at utter destruction, Roxie realized that this battle was over, but the war had just begun.

****

Mongrel stared with disbelief into the cauldron as everything before him disappeared. Frantically he moved the view from side to side. Nothing. He could not believe the entire force had just been wiped from existence. He had to find a sign. A shadowy hand moved across the water. Mongrel's blood ran ice cold.

"Let us look at the castle."

Mongrel bowed his head and obeyed his Master's command. Slowly, and with intense fear, he focused on the castle. All thirteen Lords had collapsed to the ground and men were moving them. That was as far as they could see. The magic prevented further viewing. Mongrel looked at the form of his great controller.

"Are they dead?"

His voice was almost warm as he answered, "Close enough."

Then he was gone, again. Alone and confused, Mongrel controlled the urge to laugh like a madman.

****

Chapter 6

Lord Earin felt himself returning to consciousness. A small groan escaped his throat as he attempted to fight the inevitable. He didn't want to wake up, not really. He wanted to be able to sleep though the rest of this God-forsaken war, but he couldn't. Reluctantly, he opened his eyes and tried to focus on the wall infront of him. Surprisingly, he found that he could.

In fact, his bed chamber did not spin the way he had expected it to. Instead, he found that he was wide awake and well rested. He also found that he was starving. *I feel like I've been asleep for years.* He pushed that thought to the back of his mind and turned immediately to food. He stretched a huge stretch and slid out of bed. Perhaps he shouldn't have been, but he was slightly surprised to see plates of food and hot cider waiting for him on his bed chamber table. He smiled and started to eat. A small knock at his door interrupted him.

"Enter."

Sage's innocent face peered into Lord Earin's chamber. "Greetings Lord Earin. It is good to see you awake, again."

Earin gave the young page a puzzled smile. "Why? How long have I been asleep?"

"Two days."

"Two days? I've lost so much time. There is so much still to do. Why didn't someone wake me?"

"The Chosen One would not allow any of the Lords to be disturbed. She said that if blowing themselves up was the only way to get the Lords to rest, then she was going to make it count."

Lord Earin smiled. He knew that there was no fighting with that woman when she wanted something. For a moment he tried to be angry with her, but only for a moment. She had done what she believed best. And, as he moved his well-rested body, Lord Earin was forced to concede that she had been right.

After a small pause, Sage continued, "She also said she

wanted to see you when you were awake."

The Lord stood to go. "Okay. Where is she?"

Sage grinned and shook his head. "I'm not allowed to tell you until you eat something and take a bath. Roxanne's orders."

"Why does that fail to surprise me?" murmured the Lord.

With no other real, or intelligent option before him, Lord Earin sat at the table and began to feast. Each morsel that passed his lips reminded him that he hadn't eaten in two days, or more, and so he continued to eat. Sage waited patiently.

After a few minutes of inhaling food, Lord Earin's attention was drawn back to the perfect figure of a waiting attendant in his room. Questions began whirling through his mind. Questions that he knew the young apprentice could answer. *Unless he has other 'orders,' of course.*

In a measured voice, he began his questioning. "How many of the other Lords are awake?"

"None," responded Sage, sounding nonchalant.

Earin tried to respond with the same amount of composure. "The Chosen One's orders, again?"

"Yes," came the curt reply.

"And exactly when does she plan on waking them up?"

Sage grinned. *...waking them up, asshole?* "After she talks to you."

"What?"

"She told me that since you would probably be the first to awaken, she would like to talk to you and then you could wake the rest of the Lords and brief them."

"Did it not strike you as odd that she knew I would wake up first?"

"No."

I knew he was going to say that. So much for that line of questioning. He tried another approach. "I assume that we won this battle, then."

Once again Sage gave one of his in-depth replies. "Yes."

"How many men died?"

This time Sage's voice faltered. He lowered his eyes and whispered, "Fifty-seven."

Fifty-seven!? Lord Earin felt the earth spinning under his

114

feet and the food in his stomach wanting to come back out. *Fifty-seven? How could we loose so many men? Why!?* He looked up at the pain in the young man's face and knew there was no mistake; fifty-seven men had indeed died, and this war hadn't even started yet. As he rose to enter his bath chamber, he made a silent vow. *Never again.*

****

Roxanne sat under her favorite tree in the garden and rubbed her sore muscles. Despite everything, she still found pleasure in training. After that first battle she became obsessed with perfecting her skills. She was never going to be caught off guard again. This was a place where she really could die; and die horribly for that matter. But, she wasn't the only one capable of dying. She let her mind run through all those faces she had seen staring into the empty air. Some peaceful, others twisted in pain. A cold breeze caused her to shiver. She decided to empty those thoughts from her mind.

A soft voice from behind yanked her into the here and now. "Remembering?"

She shook her head, "Growing up." She paused and soaked in the silence. "How do you feel, Doc?"

Somehow it was very comforting to hear himself called "Doc" again. "Rested, thanks to you."

Roxanne smiled. "Anytime."

Lord Earin moved to face Roxanne. He was shocked by what he saw. Her eyes were red and swollen and her cheeks were moist. She looked haggard and worn. This was not the face of the beautiful carefree lady that had entered this land. This was the face of an aging woman with great weights upon her shoulders. With sudden and intense guilt, he realized that he and the other Lords were responsible for this change. His heart broke.

Roxanne looked up into his face and allowed her eyes to smile at him. This gave him a sense of relief and hope.

"Sit down, Doc. Take a load off."

He obeyed her pleading eyes. "When was the last time you

slept?"

She smiled. "Looks like we switched roles this time. I will rest as soon as I'm done talking to you."

"Speak swiftly then."

For the first time in a long while she laughed out loud. "Now, my dear Lord Earin, that was funny."

Lord Earin smiled. She always did have a habit of finding humor at strange times. It was good to hear that laugh; it always pushed a little of the darkness away for a little while. Somehow, he smiled in response.

"Now, Chosen One," he let sarcasm drip off the title, "I followed your orders for rest and food..."

"You had very little choice."

"... So, tell me what it is you need for me to know."

Roxanne stretched her arms overhead, trying to loosen the muscles. There was too much on her mind. She had gone over questions a thousand times; she had had this conversation over and over in her mind, but the pieces were thrown out of order and she couldn't find up. Bringing her hands to her head, she tried massaging knowledge in through her temples.

Attempting to maintain composure, she began, "I guess the first thing you should know is that stunt you and the other Lords pulled worked. You completely wiped-out the bad guys, and every living thing near the castle for miles." She studied his face for a reaction. His eyes were closed in deep concentration. She continued. "Fifty-seven of our own men are dead. Jesus, Doc. Fifty-seven. I counted them myself. I looked into every single face... No, never mind. I won't deal with that ghost now." She stopped for a minute and tried to re-link her thoughts. "The Betrayer pulled most of his troops back toward himself after the fortress blew. Major Elway seems to believe he is regrouping. Anyway, none of our scouts have seen any movement past the Silver Forest. But, all movements made are made by huge forces. There are thousands upon thousands of them."

Lord Earin's eyes flew open. "What are they doing around the Silver Forest?"

"Come again?"

"Are they attempting to enter the Forest?"

116

"No. They won't even skirt the outer edges. They are avoiding it like the plague."

"Good."

"Why the sudden panic, Doc? I thought you said the fairies won't let anyone in but training Lords.?"

"I just had to know. If he had even tried to go near the forest, this war would be over. Any creature with the strength to overcome the fairies has already conquered this world."

"No such luck. It would appear we are going to have to fight this one."

"Where is the General?" He knew the answer to that one before the question was even finished.

Pain shot across Roxanne's face. "The strike team's not back, yet."

He wished he hadn't asked. "They will be."

She shook her head. "They better be."

The silence that followed was unbearable. Lord Earin knew that Roxanne had not finished. He knew the real question was still crashing against her mind. He wanted her to ask. He desperately wanted a chance to explain to her. But the question didn't come. Instead, she just sat there, staring at nothing. Finally, it was too much for him.

"What else is bothering you? What is it that you wish to know?"

Her eyes flared with life. So much life that he almost wished he hadn't spoken. She carefully studied his face.

"How long have you Lords known about that trick of your's?"

He didn't want to play this game, but he had no choice. "It's part of the lore we are taught."

"So, you've always known?"

"Yes."

Her voice became measured and venomous. "Then, tell me why. Why did I risk my life fighting behind a wall of fire? Why did Karlis almost sacrifice his life on that wall? Why did we use up energy and resources? And, why the fuck did fifty-seven men die?"

Now it was his turn to hold his head in his hands. "There are

so many things I need you to understand. So many reasons..."
His eyes pleaded with her's. "So much I fear you will never
forgive."

Her voice softened. "Try me."

Lord Earin closed his eyes and inhaled deeply. His whole
frame was shaking. He had known, from the second the decision
had been made, that they were going to have to answer to a lot of
people. He could have faced any of them without fear; any but
Roxanne. Staring at her unemotional face, he felt that somehow
the reasons weren't good enough. But, they had made the
decision, and she had every right to know why.

"The spell we performed is not part of the lore learned from
the fairies. That spell came out of the books of the three witch
sisters; Lord Brennen discovered it while searching for their
weakness. In the end, it was decided that instead of destroying
those texts we should keep them safely locked away in case the
need for them should ever arise. Slowly, bits and pieces of them
worked their way into some of the Lord training; pieces like that
spell. So, the decision was made to destroy the books so that no
more would be tempted by the dark lore." He paused to judge
Roxanne's reaction to this much of the story. She was simply
leaning against the tree with her arms folded across her chest. No
emotions crossed her face. He continued.

"It wasn't until after Major Elway suggested the basic suicide
mission you went on that we realized how truly desperate the
battle had become. And, at that point, Lord Anjalina suggested
we use the spell instead. The basic first reaction from most Lords
was no. You see, there is an inherent danger in using dark spells.
The power they allow you to wield can make you hungry for
more. They are addicting and dangerous. Every time you use
one, you loose a little more of what is good in you." Again, he
paused and stared at his silent student. Her eyes were closed
against the world but a tear glimmered on her cheek. He wanted
to reach out to her, but she was untouchable. He started again.

"Since this spell requires the power of all the Lords, it took
some time to finally persuade compliance. Even in the end there
was a great deal of hesitation. We all knew we were facing very
real danger. The amount of energy required would either knock

us unconscious or kill us, someone might become addicted to the promise of power, and we might kill more than we intended. And that, dear Roxanne is why."

All of his words whirled about inside her head. There was so much pain mixed with all he had said and all she had seen. They had made the choice the only way they could have, of course. She understood that now. But, that couldn't stop the pain, or the anger. It wasn't right for that many good people to die. And, she had taken another's life for the first time and now she understood how the Lords could be afraid of dark power. Slowly, she opened her eyes to face the trembling figure of her friend. Tears flowed down her cheeks.

"Don't look so scared, Doc. I will always stand behind you; you are my friend. All I wanted was an answer, and you gave it to me."

Relief rushed over his face followed closely by concern.

"Tell me, why do you cry so?"

Roxanne closed her eyes and took a deep breath. Opening them again she said, "Because I killed another being for the first time."

"That's why you cry? Because it hurts you to have been forced to take a life?"

She stood and placed her hand on his shoulder. "No. I cry because I enjoyed it."

With her confession still hanging in the air, she turned and left the garden. Lord Earin wept.

****

Sage paced impatiently outside Roxanne's chamber door. He knew that when she had finished talking to Lord Earin she would come here, but she wasn't back yet and the situation inside the chamber was unacceptable to him. *That man has no business with her. What does he want?* He continued pacing until he saw her turn the corner. He immediately assumed his position outside her door.

Roxanne smiled when she saw Sage standing dutiful as always. *What does that boy do when no one's around?* He broke

119

away from his post and met her in the hall.

"Major Elway is waiting to see you. I told him that you were talking to Lord Earin and that I would have you send for him later, but he insisted on waiting. He said it was important."

Roxanne smiled inwardly. Even if he had tried, Sage could not have hidden his obvious disgust for anyone who wanted any of her attention. He was acting like the son who didn't want his divorced mother to start dating again.

"I'm sure it must be, then. I just hope it's not that pressing. I'm beat."

"Do you want me to send him away?"

Easy, kid. You sound like Uncle Gwiddo. 'Do you want that I should take care of 'em?' "No. I will get rid of him after I hear what is so important. What I want you to do, kiddo is get some rest. Take the day off and sleep, 'cause that's exactly what I'm going to do."

Sage tried to stifle a yawn, "But, I'm really not tired."

"Sleep anyway. Consider it an order. I'll call for you when I wake up and then we can hit the "moat" for some relaxation, okay?"

He smiled at that. The "moat" was something that belonged to just them. She knew he really enjoyed having secrets that no one else understood. Without another protest, he turned and jetted off down the corridor. Suddenly, she realized that she was smiling. Somehow, that small person always managed to brighten her day. She shook her head. *And now for our mystery guest.*

Upon opening her chamber door, she found something she hadn't quite expected. Major Elway was there, but he wasn't patiently waiting as she had imagined. Instead, he was stretched out on the sofa fast asleep. *Oh yeah, this must be real pressing.* She debated whether or not to wake him or just ignore him and hit the sack herself. She decided she was exhausted.

She moved over to her bed and removed her weapons and boots. Leaving the rest of her clothes on, for obvious reasons, she climbed into bed. Just as her head hit the pillow, her sword hit the ground, and both her and the Major jumped to attention. The whole thing struck Roxanne as comical. She started laughing.

The Major shook off his sleep and confusion and sheathed his sword. "What's so funny?"

Roxanne grinned, "We are. Jumping around like a couple of kids in a haunted house."

"I'll let you know whether or not it's funny as soon as my heart makes it out of my throat. When did you get back?"

"Just long enough to create mass confusion trying to get into bed."

The Major cocked his head to the side. "You weren't planning on waking me up, were you?"

"You looked like you needed it."

This time he laughed. "Thanks, but I'm wide awake now."

"Well, as long as we're both completely wired, why don't you tell me what it is that is so important that it kept you up nights."

"Ha, ha, very funny."

"Okay, so what is it?"

He hesitated for a moment and stared at her as though he were trying to read her thoughts.

"Well?"

He shook his head. "Um, sorry. Well, I... The Lords are waking up."

"The Lords are waking up. I know."

"Yeah, well, I didn't know you knew when I came to tell you."

"Didn't Sage tell you I was talking to Lord Earin?"

"Yeah, well, I wasn't sure if you knew the other Lords were waking up, too."

"That's it then? You waited here, sleeping on my sofa, to tell me that? Okay. Thanks for the info."

His stare intensified and he stepped toward her. His voice was scarcely more than a whisper. "No. That isn't why I came here."

Her heart started to pound against her ribcage as she read the thoughts pulsing in his eyes. She found she could hardly speak. "Why did you come?"

He reached down and wrapped his muscular hand in her hair

and pulled her face close to his. "For this."

He placed his lips on hers and kissed her passionately. Her legs went weak and her entire being pulsated with heat. When the kiss stopped, she fell into his chest.

Timidly, she looked into his searching eyes. "A bit forward, aren't you?"

His smile beamed down at her. "You haven't slapped me yet. Besides, we could be dead tomorrow. There's no time to be shy."

She smiled a sly smile. "Valid point."

He swept her into his arms and carried her to the bed. Laying on top of her, he began to undress her. Suddenly he stopped and kissed her again as though it were the last thing he would ever do.

"What's wrong?"

He looked at her questioning face. "It's just that I promised myself I wasn't going to allow myself to do this; it could cause too much pain. But..." he faltered. "But, I can't die without making love to you."

As he uttered that last seemingly true, yet very corny statement, it occurred to Roxanne that he might just be a really talented player. *He's probably got women all over this land. Hell he's probably got them all over this castle.* But, as he moved his body into hers, it occurred to her that she really didn't care.

****

Knock, knock. Anybody home?

Roxanne rolled over and looked out the window. The sun was still blazing high in the sky. She rolled back over. Major Elway was still fast asleep in the bed next to her. *Good God.*

No, but close.

Roxanne shot straight up in bed; she should have known.

Good morning. Nice of you fellows to drop by.

Morning? Check your sundial, Roxie. It's way past high noon.

Gee thanks, Gabe. However, some of us just went to bed.

Well, your ma and I warned ya 'bout stayin' up too late.

Speaking of which, where's Snake?

122

Complete silence filled the mental connection. Roxanne's heart leapt into her throat.

Where. Is. Snake?

Beats the hell out of me. One minute she's there; the next she's gone. After the strike was over, she said she had something personal to take care of, and then she disappeared.

Did anybody go after her?

And follow what trail? She could disappear in a flat stretch of solid rock on a sunny day.

Do you think she'll come back?

She has to.

For a moment, Roxie detected something that sounded like desperation in the Commander's mental voice. Could it be that his interest in Snake wasn't strictly professional. She decided not to pry, for now.

Where are you now?

We're coming up on the main gate. What the hell happened here?

Big party.

Who won?

Who are you talking to?

Good point.

Okay. I guess I'll throw some clothes on...

Why?

... and find all the Lords so that you'll have an audience to tell war stories to.

Alright, Rox. See ya in a few.

With that, the mental connection went down, almost as though a phone connection had been cut. Roxanne looked, once again, at the sleeping figure next to her. His boss will probably want to see him. She slid out of bed, quietly so as not to wake the Major. Only after she had bathed and put on some fresh clothes did she kick him out of bed.

She laid down on the bed next to him, smiled, and started tapping on his chest repeatedly. It took a minute to register on any of his senses. But, when it did, he came around fast and hard. His eyes snapped open, he grabbed both of Roxie's wrists, and pinned her to the bed. She laughed. *I hate it when she does that.*

"Easy, Nitro. It's only me. No need for death."

"What the hell, Rox. Are you trying to give me a heart attack or get yourself killed?"

She put on her most innocent face. "Why, whatever do you mean?"

"Ha, ha."

"Actually, I just wanted to tell you that Commander Gabriel and General Sabastian are back, and I'm guessing they'll want to talk to you."

"Shit!" He rolled off the bed and started dressing hurriedly.

"No need to panic just yet. They aren't even inside the castle. They were only coming up on the gates a few minutes ago."

He stopped and stared at her. "How is it, then, that you know where they are and what they are doing?"

She sighed. "Look, for reasons beyond our control and understanding, the Commander, Snake, and I have some sort of mental connection. You're just going to have to trust me when I tell you that I know where the strike party is."

Elway sat down on the edge of the bed, cocked his head to the side and peered at her. "Are you a real woman or some kind of demon?"

She crossed to him, placed herself in between his legs, and whispered. "All woman... with certain demonic impulses."

He wrapped his arms around her waist. "I'd have to agree with you on that one."

"Why'd you ask, then?"

He pulled her in tighter. "Maybe I wanted you to refresh my memory."

She laughed and pulled away. Picking up her weapons, she dashed for the door, pausing only long enough to say, "See ya at the briefing."

And then she was gone. Major Elway sat alone on the bed contemplating this woman of mystery. She was unlike any of the many of women he had known. And, for a passing second, he felt guilt over his past. The thought scared him, so he brushed it aside and finished getting dressed. *I'll be damned if I'm going to let her get to me.* With that thought, he knew he damned himself to hell.

****

Lord Earin paced the length of the chamber like an expectant father. Roxanne followed his form with her eyes. *Does he have any idea how annoying that is?* He stopped, almost as if he were responding to her unvoiced question, and looked toward the door. When no one entered, he started his act once more. She rolled her eyes and looked at the faces around the room. All of the Lords looked rested and alive for a change. Lord Anjalina even appeared to be smiling, while Lord Ambrose was beaming.

In fact, there was only one person in the room who was tired. Roxie stared and the dozing figure of Major Elway. He had placed himself in a strategic corner of the room and immediately gone to sleep. She smiled. *Yeah, I'm just that good.... Those two days with no sleep couldn't have possibly had anything to do with it.*

A familiar voice entered her mind. *What are you babbling about, now?*

She was just about to respond with something really clever when the door flew open and in walked a very haggard looking strike team.

You're lucky. I was just going to shame you with something really clever.

Instead of answering, the Commander turned to her and gave a mock bow. "Guess who's back?"

She returned the gesture. "Well, if it 'aint the infamous legend in his own mind."

Commander Gabriel laughed. High Lord Brennen rose to embrace his dear friend General Sabastian. They held their embrace for a few moments, and, when it was over the High Lord's eyes shone with understanding and the General's with relief. The two friends took their place at the head of the table. The rest of the strike team had seated themselves. With a slight grin, Roxie watched the Commander slide right next to the newly awake Major.

High Lord Brennen began, "I will leave it to General

Sabastian and Commander Gabriel to inform their men about the strike later. The important thing is that it was indeed successful."

"Where are Jennin and Snake?"

Roxanne turned to face the Lord who had spoken. His grey eyes seemed to burn with some hidden pain as he ran his fingers through his shoulder length black hair.

"I'm sorry Lord Trenton, Jennin is dead." The High Lord knew the two men were dear friends. It broke his heart to see the tears in his fellow Lord's eyes.

"And Snake?" He asked hesitantly.

Here Gabriel piped up, "She had something she needed to take care of. She will meet with us when it is finished."

The tone in the Commander's voice silenced all discussion of the subject, and the High Lord continued.

"I know the last few days have been long and painful for everyone. I also know that most of you are exhausted and pushed beyond your limits; for your courage and strength I thank you. However, I must ask you to give to the land again. The main force of the Betrayer's troops is moving quickly toward us. They are within a week of the Silver Forest... We have to stop them. This is complicated by the fact that several smaller forces are scattered between us and the Silver Forest."

Major Elway stretched his arms in front of him. "So, when do we start marching?"

"Tomorrow," came the General's reply.

He surveyed the room before him, but no one even flinched. These people were all completely prepared to follow any order he made. He didn't know whether to be proud or sick.

"I know most of you need to get some rest immediately, so we will go through this briefing as quickly as possible..."

While she listened, Roxanne felt a distant mental tugging; she opened her mind.

Well, it's about time.

She nearly jumped out of her seat when she recognized the voice.

Snake?

Who else would be pounding on your mind like this?

Are you on your way in?

126

No. I'm just passing at my closest point to the castle.

Where the hell are you?

Look, it's nobody's business but my own, okay?

Okay.

I just wanted to tell you that I will be back. Count on it.

As long as you are planning on coming along, we are heading for the Silver Forest and we leave tomorrow.

Right. By the way, did you win?

Suddenly, Roxie realized that Snake had to be at least on the outskirts of the devastation. She controlled an urge to run out and join her.

Don't. I wouldn't want to have to kill you.

There was no laughter in her voice. Roxie knew that when she sounded like that, Snake could slit your throat with a smile.

Just a passing thought. Good luck and may the force be with you.

Have you been talking to the Commander?

What? Why?

Nothing really. He just said the same thing to me earlier. Sometimes I'd swear you share a brain. Actually, that would account for a lot...

Ha, ha. Now, be careful.

Hey, Roxanne. May that force thing be with you, too.

With that, her voice was gone. Roxanne's mind raced. Where was Snake going? Would she be back? And where the hell did the Commander pick up that phrase? She knew the answer to that before she even asked. Suddenly, she remembered she was in the middle of a military meeting. She tuned back in way too late.

"... and when we reach that point we will, hopefully, be in the position to move on to the Betrayer's new fortress.

Most of this rests on our military power and speed, so we need to be well rested." General Sabastian checked everyone's face for understanding. He found it. Even the Last of the Chosen seemed to be back from wherever she'd been. "Now, I want everyone to rest. Dismissed."

With that, the General turned and lead High Lord Brennen

out of the room. He was quickly followed by the rest of the Lords. A few of the military leaders gathered around their Commander and bombarded him with questions. Roxanne put her feet on the table, leaned back in her chair, and waited. Gabriel looked like a suave congressman surrounded by power-hungry reporters. He answered questions, told stories, and charmed audiences every which way. Roxanne smiled. *Alright, you cocky sonofabitch, just wait 'till you hear what I have to say.*

Slowly, the men started to leave the room, each satisfied with his understanding of the "truth." Soon, Commander and Major were left alone to pat each other on the back for jobs well done.

"Tactically simple and mortally dangerous? Just like all good plans should be, huh Major?"

"Just like you always say, Commander. Besides, pulling last minute victories out of loosing situations is my specialty."

Careful, Major. You're starting to sound as cocky as me.

He is.

Who asked for your opinion?

No one. You just sounded like you needed it.

I'll deal with you later.

"As long as you don't get yourself killed."

"Don't worry. I've never put myself in that dangerous of a situation."

Roxanne gave Gabriel a small flash of the thoughts that were running through her mind, and he used them wisely.

"Never underestimate the power of that woman, Major. It might kill you."

Major Elway allowed complete confusion to cross his face. Roxanne allowed a sly grin to cross hers. And the Commander stood as stoic as a statue.

Replacing confusion with assurance, Major Elway saluted. "Like you always say, learn from a pro. Goodnight, Commander."

Before he left the room, Elway walked over to Roxanne and kissed her hand. "I'll take care of you later."

Roxanne kept smiling. "If you're lucky."

The Major bowed and gracefully exited. The two Chosen

Ones were left alone.

"So, tell me Commander Skywalker, how did you get here?"

All the charm disappeared from Gabriel's face. His eyes flared and sweat rolled down his cheek. Roxie got the feeling that this might have been a bad idea. But, the man of steal would not be broken so easily. A grin swept across his face and he calmly brushed away the sweat from his brow.

"The same way I left, my dear. I rode my horse."

Suddenly, Roxanne had the feeling that she had just started a game of mental chess.

"Let's not play this game. For, you see, when last we met I was the student, but now I am the Master."

He stared long and hard into her eyes. She could see that images were playing against the back of his mind; images she had triggered. Somehow, she felt guilty. But, the images stopped moving and he stopped staring. Without warning, he spoke.

"Only a Master of evil, Darth."

She breathed a sigh of relief and answered his unspoken question. "May the force be with you. That little phrase gave you away."

"But you never heard me say that."

At this point, she knew someone was about to get in trouble; she proceeded anyway. "Well, you know that little meeting we just had? I sorta missed it."

"Why?"

"Well, Snake called, and..."

"Excuse me. You and Snake held a mental conversation during this meeting and no one bothered to tell me?!"

"I didn't think I should bother you during such an important meeting?"

"I'll take bullshit for a thousand, Alex."

"Look, I didn't think about it, okay? Anyway, I said to her, 'May the force be with you', and she said that you had said the same thing earlier. Now, it does not take a rocket scientist to figure out the rest of it."

For the first time ever since she had laid eyes on him, Commander Gabriel looked like a man with no control. He fell into a chair and stared at nothing. After a period of time that felt like forever, he spoke.

"I was in the Marine Corps on the other side, you know. I was there for many years and learned a lot of great tricks. That's why I'm so useful over here. I know so much. I've been here for years, incognito. Then, out of the blue, you walk in and find me out because I liked Star Wars. What are the odds?"

Roxanne smiled at the staggered man before her. "Pretty good, actually. Most people liked Star Wars."

That was all it took to pull the ego out of the man. His face filled with a shit eating grin and he let out a chuckle. She wanted to bombard him with questions; find out why and how he was here, but she didn't. There had been memories flashing through his mind earlier. Memories he didn't seem to like. So, she left it alone. She stood to leave, but his voice stopped her.

"Tell me something. Where did you get that necklace?"

She sat back down and stared into his eyes, searching for his motives. "From a little knarled man on the mall at my university." Remembering the event set the detective in her to work. She leaned forward like she was revealing a secret. "The funny thing was, he just gave it to me, then disappeared. It wasn't until I realized that the damn thing wouldn't come off that I attempted to find the little fiend. By then it was too late."

The Commander sat back in his chair and tugged at his chin. "Ever hear the Lords mention the name Mongrel."

"I don't know. Maybe. Why? Who is he?"

"He's the Betrayer's right hand man. Let me rephrase that: he is the Betrayer's little knarled right hand man."

Heat rushed through Roxanne's body. "But why..."

"...would he find you? I don't know. Maybe the Betrayer had thoughts of pulling you over himself."

"That only makes a little sense. Wouldn't he be better off if there were only two of us instead of three? And, if he had the necklace, why would he purposely give it to me?"

Commander Gabriel shook his head. "I really don't know. What's even more disturbing is the thought that he was actually in possession of the damn thing."

Thoughts rushed through her mind. "Okay. How did you get yours?"

His face grew somber and his voice got quiet. "It was a gift."

"From who?"

He hesitated. "From a beautiful little girl who knew that I liked dragons. She found it on her way home from school one day and made me promise to wear it always."

Roxie was getting impatient. "But <u>who</u> was the little girl?"

"My daughter," he whispered.

She nearly fell to the ground. *Daughter?! You have a damn daughter?* She had never stopped to consider that this man might have had a family. She never thought of his life outside of this place. *Of course he has a life, Roxie. What did you think, he was a robot?* She sat back into her chair and did nothing. She wasn't sure she wanted to know anything else. She closed her mind and concentrated on breathing. However, her mind would not be controlled. Images of this man as a father kept playing through her head. Something about the whole thing bothered her. *If you have a daughter, what the hell are you doing here?*

The Commander smiled. "Because I don't have a daughter anymore."

Roxie cringed. She hadn't meant to broadcast that particular question. "I'm sorry. I didn't mean..."

He shrugged. "It's okay. If I told you I hadn't thought about this for years I'd only be lying. Thoughts of her cross my mind every day."

Curiosity became too much for her to control. "What happened?"

Gabriel sank into his chair, put his feet on the table, and concentrated on thin air. Slowly he began to speak. "I married my high school sweet-heart and we moved into a house with a white picket fence and a German Shepard. Beautiful, huh? Can you imagine me with a white picket fence? Anyway, I went into the Marines and she became the dutiful house wife. I thought her life was pretty boring. I was wrong." The last phrase was just above a mutter, then he trailed off completely. Roxanne thought perhaps he had changed his mind. He hadn't.

"After awhile I started college and began investing some of that hard earned military money; a friend of mine was a brilliant stock broker. Pretty soon we had money and a daughter. That was the happiest day of my life. God, was she beautiful. She was my little angel. She grew into a spit-fire. Everything excited her and everything was her's to control. She was into trouble every two minutes..." His voice trailed off, again. This time she was sure he wouldn't finish. She was wrong.

"Anyway, to make this short and painful. I came home from school one day really early and found the wife in bed with my best friend. However, when I dragged him into the street, without his clothes, he informed me that he was only one of many. When I confronted her, she told me the same thing. So, being the intelligent man I am, I decided to leave her and take everything with me. Before I could file for divorce, she showed up with three of her friends who told me they would testify in a custody battle that I beat her and my daughter if I tried to leave. The bitch had me. She said if I left her penniless she take my baby away from me and I'd never see her again. So I stayed."

His voice dropped to a whisper, "A few months later, I got a call informing me that my wife and daughter were dead. They had died in a car accident. It seems that my 'better half' thought it would be a good idea to drink a half a bottle of vodka and then take a little joy ride. That fucking bitch ruined my life. Months later, when I woke up here, I decided that it didn't matter whether it was a dream or not, I was staying."

Roxanne stared at the strong man sitting across from her. Just days ago he had destroyed a fortress; years ago he put one up. She felt pain seeing him so exposed. She hadn't meant to bring him to this place, and she sure as hell was not about to leave him there.

"So I guess now all that's left is to figure out Snake and I'll have all the truly great mysteries taken care of." *Beautiful, Roxanne. This man has just poured out his heart to you and you are callous enough to make a very bad joke. So much for that sensitive and understanding crap you have been feeding everyone.*

"Ah, but you understand more than you realize." *Shit! I did it again.*

The Commander fixed a "what-would-the-world-do-without-me" grin to his face. "I wouldn't take it too hard. Nobody's perfect... except me, of course. And now, I must prepare for battle."

As he stood to leave the room, all of his walls back in place, a single question raced across her mind. "What was her name?"

The Commander never turned around and never spoke. His response was a distant mental impression. *Amber.* As he disappeared down the hall, Roxanne knew she would never see that side of him again. She wasn't convinced that that was a bad thing.

Chapter 7

The city gates loomed ominously in the distance, their shadow covering the world before them. Snake shuddered at the sight of them; Snake always shuddered at the sight of them. The first time she could remember seeing them she had been so young that just their massive size had been intimidating. The last time she'd seen them they had stood between her and freedom- that was exactly one year ago. She shook her head and pulled the dark cloak closer to her left cheek. The memories that attacked her would be dealt with soon, now, however, there were more important things to deal with.

Scanning the two guard towers on either side of the gate, Snake quickly picked out all seven of the "concealed" guards. They were strategically placed to keep all undesirables out of the city, especially now. Something clicked in her head. She halted her horse and jumped down. Pretending to check her saddlebags, she searched for the other guards she knew had to be around. Seven wasn't enough for the paranoid king. She soon found them. *Ah, clever devils.* Three more at the entrance, posing as beggars. *Most beggars I know try to avoid wearing new boots and carrying semi-concealed swords.*

Now came the challenging part. As each person entered the city the guards would examine their faces for her condemning scar. She knew the cloak that clung to her face was not enough to get her past. She had to find a better way in then straight through the front gate. She started searching the surroundings with her eyes. *Then again, maybe right through the front gate isn't such a bad idea after all.*

Snake walked her horse to a concealed area behind a grove of trees. She had spent many hours hiding in this spot and had a feeling she would probably spend many more doing the same thing. *I hate repeating myself.* She secured her stead next to a stream and then slipped back onto the main thoroughfare. The caravan she had spotted earlier was just moving past her.

Judging by the flowing curtains and the brightly dressed yet scantily clad women, Snake guessed this was traveling harem. *Guess some people will always have to pay for it.* She smiled. Even with her name-sake, she wasn't one of them.

There were four wagons and twenty or thirty women, but only two men. Choosing her mark, she stepped onto the third wagon, pulled her cloak over her face, and slid between the dark curtains that covered the back of the wagon. *Here goes nothing.* She disappeared into the scenery.

The wagons rolled forward for a short distance then stopped. She heard the grumbling of low voices as the guards questioned the two men. Snake strained to hear what they were saying.

"...for the King's birthday as requested," growled one man.

"How many women are in your group?"

"Twenty-seven."

"Check the wagons. Know this, if there is even one extra you will loose access and will forfeit half your property."

Snake cringed at the word "property." She knew that these women were owned, she just hated to hear it. There was no response from the leader. *Must be praying.* The distinct footsteps of soldiers reached her ears, and, judging by the timid protests of the women, they were searching every wagon. The curtains on the second wagon rustled. Snake slowed her breathing to non-existent and secured her grip on the overhead bar from which the curtains were hung. The voices ahead of her subsided and the footsteps approached. If she didn't time this perfectly some poor guards were going to die, blowing her chance to get through the gate.

The footsteps stopped. Her heart tried to beat loudly, but she held it in check. A gloved hand reached through the curtain and threw it open. At that same instant, Snake launched her body to the side and hooked her legs around the side of the wagon. She went completely still. The women inside started hurling insults at the soldier. *Shut the fuck up! The less talking you do the sooner he leaves.* Stupidity never failed to piss her off.

It seemed like an eternity passed before the guard decided to leave. Snake felt her grip slipping. She cringed and held on with all her will power. She could not afford to fail; too much depended on her getting inside; her sanity depended on it. Finally, a very young voice made the guard an offer he couldn't refuse.

"If you let us inside, I will meet you later this evening..."

"Yeah? Well I don't never pay for it," replied the proud soldier.

The young voice responded in a mother-like tone, "Now, did I say you would? I like your face, and I'd like your body. No charge, okay?"

That was enough for this particular soldier. He pulled the curtains shut and called the all clear. Snake slid back into place, letting her arms fall to her sides. *Wonder what they're smuggling? No lady of the night ever gave this product for free, ever.* It intrigued her for a moment, but she let it pass and smiled at the gullibility of the guard. *He'll definitely be getting fucked tonight, but he sure as hell won't enjoy it.* It served him right for being stupid.

The search went quickly now as the guard's head danced with the promise of a deceiver. It was only a couple of minutes before the wagons started rolling forward again. Snake closed her eyes and concentrated on those gates. She could feel the presence of evil in them, and her stomach tied itself in a knot as she emerged on the inside of the city walls. She was home.

****

The voices that had held her motionless for so long finally started to fade as the women moved away, each to their separate duties. It turned out that the harem was smuggling illegal magic; an extremely dangerous hobby, indeed. It had taken them forever and a day to unload the right spells to the right women with the proper instructions. *Why couldn't they be smuggling slaves or gold or something that is closer to their own intelligence level?* She wanted to jump out and scream, but she had learned patience years ago, and so she waited.

"Alright. When the rest of the girls take off, I need you three to head for the king's chambers. Get there quickly so he don't get mad and go lookin' for ya. We can't afford to have him snoopin' around the castle with his guards. We need him nice and content, okay?"

The women responded to the gruff voice with the proper amount of submissive oh's and ah's, then they all moved to their separate tasks. Snake knew she wouldn't have much time. Quickly, she slid into the wagon and traded her black cloak for colorful wraps and overpowering perfumes. Checking for any sounds or movements outside the wagon, she decided it was all clear and moved into the open. The group had vanished. Now she had to play things very carefully. Timing was of the essence. If she couldn't catch those women on their way to the king's bed chamber, she might have to talk to a guard. She couldn't afford to have anyone stare at her for too long because the thin veils that now covered her face could not effectively conceal the scar beneath. She began moving.

The twists and the turns of the castle felt like old friends to her. Despite what had happened behind these walls, this would always be home. She moved with ease down the corridors and, for the first time in years, felt a kind of remorse. That this place that had been her home and friend for years should forbidden and dangerous to her made her want to weep. It also increased her rage at the man who had made it so. She hurried her steps as the evil desires in her increased. She had to catch those women.

The light tinkling of bells and the soft coo of female voices suddenly filled her ears as she approached the hall that she knew contained his bed chamber. She stopped at the corner and peered around it at the group before her. The three women stood before the guards. *Flirting like a bunch of whores. Guess that is their job.* They seemed to be taking too long. Maybe they're lining up future work. Seems like highly unchallenging work.

One of the guards leaned over the leader and stroked her hair. "Why would you want to fuck the old man when you could have me instead?"

The whore responded with the proper amount of indignation and charm. "He pays well!" Her voice softened, "Besides, who says I can't have you later?"

The guard roared with laughter and the poor girl looked confused. "I don't need women like you, now get inside."

Fury welled-up in Snake's veins. She despised those who preyed on the weak. There had been no need for that. She made a mental note to make him pay for that, if it didn't interfere with her main goal.

The last of the girls disappeared into the room and the guard started to pull the door shut behind her. It was now or never. Putting on her daintiest expression, Snake ran around the corner and called out in a tiny voice.

"Wait! Please wait."

The guards turned and laughed as Snake executed a perfect trip allowing herself to fall to the ground. She picked herself up and feigned tears. The guards shook their heads.

Grabbing her by the arm and pulling her to her feet, the youngest one muttered, "Come on, girlie. We don't want you to get lost out here."

Snake lowered her head and mumbled an over-zealous thanks as she was escorted to the door. *Okay. This guy lives.* Before she could get inside, however, the laugher snagged her arm and yanked her to him. She turned her left cheek to the side and held her breath. *Shit! I want to kill you, but not now.*

"Not so fast. No one enters here without paying a toll first."

How about I cut your balls off and gift-wrap them for you, you slimy, filth-ridden bastard. "Let me pay it later, when we have more time to do it right," she cooed.

That was, apparently, the correct thing to say. He laughed in her face and pushed her through the door.

"Get inside, whore!"

His evil laughter echoed in her ears as she stumbled into the chamber. *This one dies. No matter what.*

With all the stealth of a panther on the prowl, Snake crept into the inner chamber. The women were piled into the bath chamber, busy applying face paints and fragrances. She knew she didn't have much time. She had to find a place to hide. But where? It had to be a place that no one would ever look for her. She knew the guards would do a thorough room search before the king ever went to sleep, and she had to be in there but completely undetected. She scanned the room. Everything was too obvious and far too open. The options were beginning to look slim. *Unless I tie myself to the ceiling or melt into the bed, I'm pretty much moat-bait.* That's when it hit her. *And, why not?*

Quickly, now, as her time was dwindling, Snake made her way to head of the bed. Several long, silky, covered pillows occupied that spot. She untied the end of the bottom pillow and slid in, hoping to hell she didn't develop a sudden fear of enclosed spaces. She pulled the open end in after her, re-tied it, and pushed it back out on itself. She knew it would be looser than the rest. She prayed that none of the guards were fashion experts. Cutting a tiny slit in the covering to breath through, she let out a sigh. Now it was time to wait. As the harem girls approached the bed, a single thought pulsated in her head. *I hope the king's not a moaner.*

****

A young and gentle princess wandered down the corridors of the castle. Her eyes were big, blue, and naive; her hair was long, blonde, and fluffy. She appeared as the perfect model of helplessness. Coming around the corner, she ran into an older version of herself. The family resemblance echoed in his dark blue eyes and solid high cheek bones, but it ended in his jet black hair and the gleam of evil in his eyes. Opening her trusting eyes as wide as they would go she spoke.

"Cousin, you startled me. I was just going to the library, would you care to join me?"

He leaned over her, like a dragon over its prey. "I had something else in mind."

Grabbing her by the shoulders, he forced her into a dark chamber. She cried out at him, "Gregor! What are you doing?!"

Her voice seemed to ignite a deep fury inside of him. He wrapped his hands in the front of her dress and ripped it open, exposing her bare young breasts. She cried out in terror. He began groping at her body and pushed her violently to the floor. She yelled for him to stop as tears rolled down her face, but he just kept coming.

"Please, no," she cried. "You're my cousin."

Striking her across the face with the back of his hand he

growled at her, "Shut-up and quit fighting. If you relax, you might just enjoy it."

Then he plunged himself into her young, virgin body. She exploded in pain and screamed with all her might. Footsteps reached her ears as the nearest guards responded to her scream. Realizing what was about to happen, her cousin cursed at her, spat in her face and pulled himself off her just as the guards entered the room. She lay on the ground, bare-chested and crying. The guards looked from the broken wreck to the prince. He stood in the corner with his chest heaving.

"Your Highness?"

The gleam of evil flashed in his eyes and spewed out of his mouth in the form of a life shattering lie. "I can't believe what has happened to me. My young cousin, whom I have loved so dearly, as though she were my own sister, has just tried to seduce me."

The young princess could not believe what she was hearing. "That's not true. It's not," she mumbled through her tears.

The prince did not falter. "She lead me to this dark chamber and pulled her top open and offered herself to me. I was in shock and tried to remind her that we were cousins. When I refused her, she became enraged and flew at me, prying at my clothes. To protect myself, I was forced to strike her and throw her to the ground. That is when you showed up. I'm so sorry that it had to be this way. I love my cousin and wanted to avoid seeing her punished."

The young girl pressed her face against the cold stone floor. Nothing she said now would alter the course of events. She might have been naive, but she was far from stupid. His father was the king and he was the pride and joy of the kingdom. No one would ever find fault with him. She knew she was doomed.

****

Now the young princess knelt before the king and his son, her accuser. Court had been called and all the noble eyes of the kingdom were on the scene before them. The young girl shivered at the cold. If she had had the strength to look around, she might have noticed the sympathy in the eyes of those around her. She would have known that she misjudged and that most believed the frail, young angel. But, she did not have the strength. She stared straight at the face of the king. He spoke.

"Young niece, it pains me that this should have happened. Still, it did occur and such an offence is unforgivable. Under normal circumstances, you would be imprisoned for life or even put to death. However, my son has begged for mercy in your case and so it shall be. You are hear by banished from this kingdom and stripped of all titles and possessions. Further, you are to be marked so that if you ever return, you will be known to all and immediately arrested and put to death."

Two of the guards in the room moved to her side and held her securely in place. In the midst of all her confusion, the princess noticed that they were the same guards who had come to her rescue, or so she had hoped. The prince pulled his dagger out of its sheath and moved towards her. *Just plunge it into my heart and finish the job you evil bastard.* One of the guards grabbed her head and turned her left cheek to her attacker. She saw him smile as he cut her.

The blade was cold but it seemed to burn her skin. She cried out on agony; the same cry that had failed to help her before. She muffled the sound and let the tears flow from her eyes. Then the prince stood back from his work and the guards released her. She fell to the ground in a trembling heap.

"Now," roared the king, "You are marked with a symbol that will let all know how deceitful you truly are. You are marked with the symbol of the snake."

The word "snake" echoed over and over in her ears. Suddenly she snapped back into complete consciousness and shook off the dream-like state she had slipped into. Sweat poured off her body as she tried to erase the stream of all too familiar memories from her mind. It was no use. Those memories haunted her constantly; playing with unrelenting realness at the back of her mind. She could never stop them. It was the memories that controlled her actions. It was the memories that had brought her here again as they did every year on the anniversary of her betrayal.

Snake touched the scar on her face and mentally shook her head. *There is no time for this. I can't afford to loose my chance*

142

to dreams. Giggles and moans came from the bed. She felt like wreching. *Maybe this time I should just kill him.* Visions of herself helplessly trapped beneath him flashed through her mind. She decided against death. *This evil demon needs to suffer.* There was one thing she realized she did owe this man, he had taught her to hate. And she loathed him with every inch of her being.

The disgusting sounds continued for quit some time, driving Snake to the brink of insanity, but she refused to slip out of consciousness again. There would be only one chance at this; she could not miss it. After what felt like forever and a day, the king finished his play and ordered the girls out of the room. Then silence. *Playing opossum? What? Do you think I'm stupid?*

Silence echoed in her ears for the rest of eternity before there was another sound, and she felt deep satisfaction at the fear she had instilled in him throughout the years. Finally, however, he called for the guards. Straining her senses, she picked up six distinct sets of footsteps.

"Search every inch of this room! I will not be taken again this year. This woman is a menace and must be stopped! Oh, and if you find her do not be concerned for her life. I WANT HER DEAD!"

Snake grinned. *Good luck with that one, asshole.* The sound of running water told her that the king had retired to the bath area. The sounds of furniture being over-turned told her that the guards were tearing the room apart. *All of this for me? Gosh, I'm flattered.* Suddenly, her mind snapped back to seriousness at the sound of the covers being yanked from the bed. She unsheathed one of her daggers. If the guards started throwing pillows off the bed she was fucked in a hard way. They didn't.

"What are you wasting your time over there for? Don't you think that if she was hiding under the blankets I might have noticed her in the course of things? Now get to your posts!"

Now this is funny. Saved by the king. I must remember to thank him properly. Snake listened intently as the guards moved off to their posts. Two of them made their way out the balcony door to stand watch over that entrance. Two others moved to the outer chamber door, closing it behind them. *Good.* The last two, however, did not go very far. They placed themselves at the foot of the bed. *Oh, now this could get challenging.* Then came the sounds of the ugly, smelly king crawling back into bed dragging the covers behind him.

Now came the hard part, the waiting. It took all of her resolve not to leap from her hiding place and plunge a dagger into his heart as soon as he had settled himself. But, she knew that would only bring temporary satisfaction and might even get her killed; she didn't really want to die. So she waited. She waited for the king to stop fidgeting. She waited for his snoring. She waited for the guards to start yawning. She waited for hell to freeze over. She waited forever.

A loud yawn from one of the guards, followed by the sound of him stretching, sent Snake into action. With the precision of a surgeon, she quietly and slowly cut through the pillow covering. When the incision was complete, she held her breath and waited for a reaction from the guards. None. Slowly, she slid from her cocoon and onto the floor at the head of the bed. The guards stared diligently forward; Snake looked down upon her prey. Just the sight of him sent hatred coursing through her veins. She clenched her jaw and forced control through her limbs.

Her first reaction was to kill him. Her first reaction was always to kill him. Lifting her dagger, she smiled. *You should be so lucky. Welcome to hell.* Instead of shoving it into his chest up to the hilt, she poised it above his cheek. A sudden snort from the king sent her to the floor. Listening with her entire body, she could hear the guards turning. She stopped breathing. Inaudible whispers and light laughter told her the guards had gone back to staring. The only problem with that was they had moved. They were no longer in that lulled state; they were awake and aware. She waited.

She knew it was getting close to daybreak, now. There was no time to wait. It was now or never. Sucking in a deep breath, she lifted herself back into a crouch and peered over the pillows. The guards were standing dutifully at their posts and the king was sleeping like a baby. *As he should be.* Her mind raced and ordered her to hurry, but her hands held fast to practice and moved methodically. Gently, she laid the tip of her dagger against the kings face and drew a line toward his ear. The razor sharp weapon opened the skin and blood oozed down his cheek. Sweat poured down her face. In all the years she'd pulled this night raid, the king had never woken up. She hoped this year would be the same.

His eyes twitched at the pressure, so Snake lifted the blade focusing her attention on the guards. If the king did wake up, she could slit his throat and silence him in seconds. The guards would be slightly more challenging, and so she watched over them with hawk-like eyes. Nothing. *It's a good thing you are such well-trained soldiers, you sons of lower life forms.* After a few moments, she dipped her finger into the pool of blood that had formed on the pillow as it rolled down the king's face and began to etch a message onto the wall. BOO!- again.

Snake grinned then shook her head. There was no time to admire her handiwork. If the guards turned around she would be finished. Quickly, she contemplated her next move. She had to get out of the room, tonight. If she hesitated, they would find her. Her mind raced through the options, then landed on a draw.

Digging through her pockets, Snake pulled out a gold piece and hurled it with all her might into the wall right next to the balcony. Instantly, the room came to life with guards. The two guards at the end of the bed bolted to the balcony and the two who'd been asleep outside ran in to meet them. Then someone shouted alarm, bringing in the guards at the door. The king sat up in bed, confused and panicked. Snake seized her opportunity.

She leaped onto the bed, kicked the king in the head, and sprinted towards the open door. As she passed the outer guards, she snagged a dagger from the belt of one and plunged it into the heart of the other. Without ever slowing down, she had silenced the laugher. *I told you, you die.* The other guards weren't that slow to react. As she passed through the door, a group of arrows whizzed past her head. She ducked and kept running. Suddenly, fire shot through her leg as an arrow landed in her thigh. *Fuck!* She stumbled but refused to go down. With a sweeping motion, she broke the shaft off to keep it from getting caught on anything and ran on.

Cold confidence started to give way to utter panic as she moved further into the castle. She could hear the shouts of soldiers behind her, and knew it was only a matter of seconds before the whole castle would be alerted to her presence. She ran on. Torches came to life around the castle and voices echoed down the corridors. Blackness filled her head. She had to find a way out of this mess. Then, a thought pushed its way out of the darkness to save her. Veering left, she ran straight for the library.

When she reached the door, she knew she was safe. As a child, she had spent many an hour exploring the castle, especially the library. It was always her favorite room, filled with books and privacy. When she wanted to be left undisturbed, she grabbed one of the many volumes and hid. It was to her favorite hiding place that she now turned. *I really need a moment alone.* Swiftly, as the guards pulled closer, she searched out the large statue of a previous king that occupied a corner of the room. It stood on a pedestal taller than any man she'd ever met. She moved behind the massive thing and disappeared.

Home at last. Sliding to the floor of the secret compartment, Snake let out a heavy sigh. She had discovered this place when reading an old diary she'd found lying around. Apparently, the old king had used this compartment to hide his most precious valuables. Thrilled with uncovering a mystery, she had searched out the chamber. But, when she found it, it was empty. Sitting in the total darkness of her marble box, she didn't mind so much anymore; she had other things to attend to.

Slowing down her breathing and listening with all her senses through the thick marble, she could hear the sounds of heavy search. Furniture was overturned, precious things hit the floor, and voices echoed throughout the castle. As muffled as the sounds were, she knew they must be in the library. She hesitated. The wound in her leg screamed at her for attention, but the outer world told her to remain still. Indecision crowded her mind. *If they find me still injured, I won't be going very far.... Fuck it.*

Quickly now, she pulled out a flint and went to work. She lit a small candle and placed it in the farthest corner of the box in which she sat. Though it scarcely produced enough light for even her eyes, she felt like it burned like a signal fire. Controlling an urge to snuff it, she hurried on with her work. She unsheathed one of her daggers and stuck it into the wound. Tears and sweat streamed down her face, but no sound escaped her lips. Carefully, she pried at the arrow head until it loosened its grasp. Slowly, because there really was no other way to do it, she worked the head back out of her thigh. Blood spurted out of the now open wound. Snake answered the immense pain with a snarled curse. She knew what had to be done next. She held the end of her dagger over the small flame and waited for it to glow red. Then, without the slightest hesitation, she shoved it hard against the hole in her leg.

Curses ran through her head, but none escaped her lips, at the sound of her own flesh burning. Still, she held the dagger in place until the pain was too much. She yanked the dagger back and let curse after curse slip past her lips. *There has to be an easier way to do this.* There wasn't. She looked down at her seared flesh. *That's gonna leave a mark.* She tore a piece off her cloak and wrapped it around her thigh. Medical problems aside, she returned to plans of escape.

She had to leave tonight, of that she was certain. By tomorrow, not even a flea would be leaving the castle. Her mind raced for options. There were no secret passages, no cunning disguises, and no magic tricks readily available. That left her one option. *Looks like I just walk right out the front door. Very stupid.* She paused to listen for movement. The room answered her with silence. She moved.

Slipping out into the chamber, she peered around the side of the statue cautiously. Complete darkness. She closed her eyes and listened for breathing, or any other signs of life. Nothing. Sinking into the floor, she slid across the room and eased herself into the door.

Listening at the door, she could hear at least seven distinct voices. That cut that exit off. Even if she managed to get past those seven before any of them sounded an alarm, she would probably run into a whole battalion down the next hall. She had reached her last option. That made her smile. A friend from her checkered past had once told her that only when you run out of options do you find a way out. She concentrated on the room that surrounded her, and found an exit.

****

A small pebble worked its way loose and fell to the ground beneath her. Snake cringed. *I'll bet Roxanne would find that pretty funny.* She held her position against the wall, waiting for a reaction from below. One of the four guards stretched and yawned. No one else moved. Snake continued down the wall. Voices from below froze her motion.

"I'm getting tired of doing this every year," muttered the stretcher.

"Yeah, I know," answered an older voice.

A third voice added its two cents. "Every year he calls out all the guards, and every year she escapes. Does he really think he can stop her?"

A low voice entered the conversation from the shadows, "I heard that she has mystical powers; that she can change shapes and make herself a shadow. They say she won't stop until she draws a drop of blood from him to match every drop he spilled of hers."

The first voice joined back in, "What happened? Why does she come like this? I mean, hey the King's a monster, but this is a little obsessive."

Realizing that the guards were only distracting themselves from their duty, Snake once again started her descent.

The older voice answered, "No one knows for sure what happened. She was a princess once, and he her cousin. For whatever reason, she was banished and scarred for life. Obviously, she felt it was unfair. A couple years after her banishment she started showing up on the anniversary of that day and tormenting the king."

"Where did she go?"

"There were rumors of her being connected with a band of thieves and such. But, they were only rumors. I don't know. Between you and me, I think the lady's justified, and whatever the vendetta is, I know I don't want to get in the middle of it."

The others mumbled their agreement as Snake hit the ground behind them. She stood in silence, waiting for the right moment to strike.

148

The youngest guard stood directly infront of her. "All I know is, after tonight, if I saw her, I'd probably just shake her hand."

Snake couldn't resist. She stepped out of the darkness. "Now's your chance."

All four guards turned, swords flying into attack positions. Nobody moved.

In a voice lower than a whisper Snake spoke and extended a hand. "I said, now is your chance. Shake it. I'll only bite you if you attack."

The young guard's sword trembled. He looked to the other soldiers for guidance. They all stood dumbfounded. She peered deeply into the face of the young man infront of her, knowing she would never kill him. If forced into action, she would only remove him from play. A voice from her left pulled her gaze.

"He was lying, wasn't he."

She focused the full force of her stare on the older guard. It took only seconds for her to remember the younger version of that face. One of her fallen heros.

"The Prince... er... the King was lying all those years ago, and no one stopped him."

Her voice came out as a growl. "Stop him? Hell, you fuckers helped him. You knew what happened the minute you entered that room, didn't you?"

His eyes fell. "I was young and afraid."

"You were a coward. Tell me why I shouldn't kill you where you stand."

The instant the threat was uttered, she knew she could not kill this man. One look into his eyes told her how he had spent his life. The guilt of his actions had tormented his every moment. His face was wrinkled and tired, and his eyes were old and beaten. She took pity on him. The feeling made her sick.

He sighed. "You should. You have every right; just as you have every right to murder that demon in his bed. I almost wish you would."

Another thought crossed her mind. "Call off the others. Make them throw down their weapons."

At his order, they reluctantly obeyed. Snake lunged forward and grabbed the soldier by his shoulders. Putting her mouth to his ear, she uttered a phrase she had never formed before. "I forgive you." Then she was gone into the night. Tears rolled down his face. And, the night returned to silence.

Inside the castle, the King sat alone on his bed and nursed his wound. He stared at the words above his bed. She would never kill him, of that he was certain. No, she had sentenced him to a fate worse than death. She was bitter. The thought of her reminded him of what he had done. A small twinkle of guilt pushed at his heart. He pushed it aside and ordered the execution of his chamber guards to dull the pain. Evil, after all, must go on.

Chapter 8

Roxanne stretched out on the hard ground next to the campfire; she was exhausted and every inch of her body ached. These battles followed by marches, followed by battles, followed by marches were getting harder and harder. She closed her eyes against the pain and death and attempted to sleep. The sound of softly approaching footsteps brought her back to consciousness; she opened her eyes.

"Sorry. I didn't mean to wake you."

"That's okay, Gabe. I would just get use to sleeping and then where would I be?"

The darkness filled with the sound of his laughter. "God forbid any of us have normal sleep habits."

This time she laughed.

"It wasn't that funny, Rox."

"I know," she eeked out in between bursts of laughter, "but I can't stop laughing. I think I'm just slap-happy."

The Commander shook his head. "Great. We're in the middle of the greatest military crisis of all time and one of the leaders has lost it."

Roxanne composed herself, "Just one of us... I don't think so."

Gabriel put one of his ever-famous smiles on his face. "Are you implying that I'm not altogether all together."

"No. I'm flat out telling you that you are lost."

Gabe's smile eased itself into a cunning grin. "Say anything you want but I know which direction the wind blows."

Roxanne pushed herself up onto her elbow and stared at the Commander. "If you are going to start quoting Shakespeare, I will be forced to raise my opinion of you, and neither of us wants that to happen."

The warning signal of the nearest sentry stopped all conversation and sent Gabe and Roxanne diving for their swords. Around them the entire camp had gone silent. Roxie felt her heart push against her chest. *One one-thousand. Two one-thousand.* She counted the beats and waited for the all clear as she feared an impending attack. Seconds turned into years; Gabe pulled in a deep breath and waited. Finally, a voice echoed throughout the dark. The all clear was sounded and the camp resumed normal operation.

"I guess I'd better go see what that was all about," muttered the Commander. "I swear, you can't even have a conversation without alarms sounding."

Roxanne grinned, "Well, you do say some pretty alarming things..."

"Ha, ha. Very funny."

With that he turned to leave the clearing. Roxie laid back down, closed her eyes and counted his footsteps. She wasn't even to twenty before the steps stopped cold. She felt a tugging at her mind. *Do you feel that?*

She rolled back onto one shoulder. *Feel what?*

A voice and a shadow stepped out of the darkness. "Feel me, stupid."

"Jesus, Snake!" she exclaimed as she leapt to meet her friend. Gabriel hadn't budged an inch. He simply nodded a greeting. Snake took the hint, but ignored it.

"Well, how was your vacation?"

Snake directed all of her attention towards Roxanne. "The weather was nice, the surroundings were bleak, and the company was distasteful. All in all, I had a pretty good time."

"Yeah, maybe sometime you'll tell us all about it."

Gabe's voice shot in from the side, "I wouldn't hold my breath. Now if you'll excuse me, I need to go see what spooked my sentry."

As Gabe watched Snake's face for a reaction, he sensed a mental tug from elsewhere. *Bitter much? At least try to be happy to see her.* Out of the corner of his eye, he caught a glimpse of the smile on Roxanne's face. It greatly resembled the one that spread across Snake's face.

"No need to check, Commander. I tripped the alarm when I came in."

Gabriel cocked an eyebrow. "Loosing your touch?"

152

The smile on her face slipped into sinister. "Not at all, Commander. I merely tapped him on the shoulder to ask directions and he jumped out of his skin and started sounding alarms."

"Great. You purposely scared the sentry to cause mass confusion."

"Exactly. But," she added before he could burst into a tirade, "if he was doing his job awake, he might have heard me coming."

Gabriel looked as though he was about to explode. Roxie saw most of the colors of the rainbow coarse through his cheeks before he settled back on a nice neutral tan. Which was quickly followed by a cocky grin and a snide remark.

"Oh shit! I knew there was a part of the training I forgot. What the hell would I do without you?"

Jack-off.

Fuck you.

I can hear you.

They both turned to face Roxanne, who was grinning from ear to ear.

"Look guys, I don't want to know."

That was all it took for the laughing to begin.

"So we're back to this again, are we?" asked Gabe.

"Now who's slap-happy?"

Snake looked from one friend to the next in a small state of confusion. *They are both completely insane. Reminder to myself: next time stay gone.*

"I hate to interrupt happy-time, guys, but there is this small war going on and I'd really like to be brought up to speed."

Gabe sobered up. "Oh, you'd like to be briefed. Check her out Rox. She disappears for days, no one has any idea where she might be, and when she returns we are suppose to jump because she wants to know what we've been doing. Well, that's just great."

Roxanne cringed at the response she knew had to be coming; and it did. Before he had pulled it half-way out of the scabbard, Snake had his knife up against his throat.

Her voice was scarcely a whisper, "I answer to no one, nor

do I owe anybody anything. What I did was my business and mine alone. You are lucky to have me back here, so why don't you quit fucking with me and tell me what the hell is going on!"

Snake leaned against the nearest tree, Gabriel leaned over his sword, and Roxanne laid back own next to the fire. *This is getting ridiculous. If the two most relied upon members of this force could not be relied upon, they were screwed.*

"Okay. Which one of you are coming with me?"

Snake crossed her arms against her chest, "Going with you where?"

Roxanne smirked, "To hand over our necklaces and lives to Lord Shit-for-brains, of course."

Gabe dug his sword a little further into the ground. "What the hell are you babbling about, now?"

"If you guys want to kill each other do it after the war, but right now we need you alive and working together. Whatever happened out there stays out there and we get on with it, okay? But, you are acting like infants. Neither one of you are being the cold, heartless, unfeeling cynics I've come to love." *I think I liked you better when you weren't in love.*

She wasn't sure whether or not they had heard her last thought. Frankly, she didn't really care either. All they could do was deny what was painfully obvious to even the blind. She waited for some kind of response. She didn't wait long.

"Are you implying that I'm a nice guy?"

"No. I'm merely saying that you aren't cold and heartless."

Snake decided to join in, "Sounds to me like she's accusing us of caring about more than ourselves."

The Commander nodded, "That's what it sounds like to me."

"Hey, I calls 'em like I sees 'em."

"Shows what you know. Just for that, you can just go help my troubled sentry stay awake while I brief yon slithery serpent." *So there you overly insightful little bitch.*

It occurred to Roxanne that she was being punished for something that was in no way her fault. *Good.* At last, things were getting back to normal. *Whatever that might be in a place that shouldn't exist, where good and evil are battling for control, and magic necklaces control the fate of men.* With a sigh and a bow, she turned and trotted off to find one very awake guard.

The Commander and *the* Snake faced each other. Each could feel a bitter chill in the air. Neither one spoke; it was all they could do to just stare at one another. Gabriel examined Snake's icy blue eyes and her life-long namesake. *She's right, this is ridiculous.* Snake had said there was a part of her past that had to be dealt with, a part she didn't want to share. That was something he could understand. There exists in the deep, dark corners of every mind something too precious or too painful to share. *You win. It's your life. You keep it.*

"So, you want to know what's been happenin'?"

Snake carefully examined Gabe's tone, listening for his well-noted sarcasm. *What are you up to?* She didn't hear any.

"It'd be nice to know who to bet on before the next battle."

"It all depends on what kind of odds your getting. So far, we've managed to make forward progress towards the new home of Old High Lord Evil One. However, we never go more than a couple of days before we run into a large number of his hordes. At which point, we fight for hours until we win. They haven't overwhelmed us with numbers, yet, and they aren't that bright. At the most, they keep us from getting a good nights sleep."

Snake raised an eyebrow, "So he's purposely wearing us down until he has his main force ready."

Gabe squatted infront of the fire. "Yeah, that's how it seems. Our scouts report larger numbers of demons and other uglies than we are seeing..."

Snake watched as the Commander's eyes focused on some thought in the darkness of his mind. She'd seen that look before and knew it meant trouble.

"What's on your mind?"

Gabe snapped himself back into focus. "What if Old Smelly One is doing more than building up his force?"

Snake didn't need a guide dog to see where he was heading. "You suspect he wants us closer?"

He nodded and stared into the fire. *God, I hate being so smart.* He had long known that the Betrayer was fully aware of every move they made, what he hadn't known was the fact that the Lord of all evil was controlling those moves as well. Gabe stood and stretched.

"Well, my dear, looks like it's time to brief some Lords and stuff." *Friends?*

"Right behind you. The fun never ends around you guys does it?"

Friends. Now there was a word she hadn't used in a lifetime. And, with that unspoken apology in the air, the two most calculating members of this army retained their reputations and each other.

****

Roxanne leaned against the trunk of the tree she had climbed into and let her feet dangle from the branch. *Sentry duty 'aint so bad.* She stifled a yawn. *Except for the boring part.* Nothing to do, combined with lack of sleep was killing her. She truly understood the other sentry's pain. *Great. I feel like a twelve step program. Hi. My name is Roxie, and I'm a recovering sentry.* The sound of approaching feet pulled her out of her personal musing. She opened her mind and listened.

"What's up, Doc?"

Lord Earin smiled a gentle smile. *How does she always know?* "Greetings Roxanne. What are you doing up in that tree?"

"Sentry duty."

Confusion and something close to anger swept across the aging Lord's face. "Who has you pulling sentry duty? You should be resting, not doing grunt work."

Grunt work? Sentry duty? Where ever did you pick up such phrases? The feeling that Lord Earin hadn't always been a Lord flooded through her senses again.

She smiled, "Well, even the grunts need a nap. I told the tired boy to take a nap; he looked like he needed it."

So do you. "Once again, you make the attempt to be super-human."

This time, Roxanne chuckled. "If I didn't know any better, I'd say you are developing a full-fledged sense of humor, Doc."

"Perhaps I am."

"So, what's on your mind?"

He knew it was senseless to play any games with her. *Best to just get to the point.* "Tell me what your world is like."

"Why?"

"Simple curiosity, Roxanne. Simple curiosity."

Roxie shrugged her shoulders. "I don't know what to tell you. I'm not really sure what you want to hear."

"I want to know what your world was like. What kind of things did you see? What kind of a world did you come from?"

She pulled her dangling legs into her chest and rested her weary head on her knees. For the first time since she had left it, she seriously contemplated home. Oddly enough, she discovered she did miss it. After a few minutes had passed, she tapped the branch in gesture to Lord Earin and began.

"Might as well take a load off, Doc. This could take awhile. Where I come from things are dying, or, at least that's the way I feel. It seems like things are fading away and no one can stop it. Rain forests, ozone, or so they say. But that is all superficial. Trees and air don't worry me. More important things are slipping away. People... Where I come from we don't need a Betrayer; we've got ourselves.

Instead of playing games, watching cartoons, and dreaming about the future, kids are slashing each other with razors, killing each other for reasons they can't explain, and hoping to make it through the next day alive. The desire to be the toughest has replaced the desire to be the brightest. It's as though their brains are malfunctioning. They don't talk or create; they simple fight and destroy. Adults say they worry what kind of a world will be left for today's youth. I tell them not to worry, there won't be enough of them left to worry about.

It's as though they've become disenchanted with life. When I was young I played dress-up and pretended to be anything I wanted. I've always been a dreamer, always looked to the future, and I always believed in magic. Kids today don't have that. Magic has been reduced to cheap stage magic where rabbits are made to appear out of hats on a regular basis."

"What of the Protectors of the land? What do they do?"

"Well, that's the real trick, you see. There isn't a group of thirteen Lords who possess magic and supreme knowledge.

There are no fairies to learn from and no texts of lore. Instead, there are hundreds of different groups of leaders, thousands of people "in charge", and even more definitions of the truth. One group in power over a certain area and it's people has no control over the others. So leaders negotiate."

Confusion leapt to the Lord's face as it had so many times. "What do you mean?"

Roxanne sighed. "It would be like High Lord Brennen promising to bring peace by talking to the Betrayer. Then, he goes to the Fortress 'o doom and talks. One promises to do this, the other gives up that, until they agree to live side by side with each controlling an area of the Land. The High Lord would agree to overlook anything the Betrayer does on his side of the imaginerary line they have drawn. Then, they lie, cheat, and steal for all time and eternity, occasionally going to war, and always ending in compromise."

"So they promise to take care of those around them, but betray you for no reason?"

"Oh, they have reasons. It's a crazy little thing called greed. My dad told me that in politics, as in life, it is your best friend who makes your worst enemy. It's those you trust the most who can hurt you the worst."

"Doesn't sound like a very pleasant place."

Roxanne stared out at the leaves infront of her until she found one she liked; she focused all of her energy on it. Her mind opened and her memory came alive. First it was her old bedroom with Snoopy curtains, then came snow forts in the backyard in Utah, next it was horseback riding, followed by long drives in her beat-up old truck. Her mind raced around until it settled on a familiar face; the face of her little brother. They had spent hours, days, years together playing games that no one else knew how to play. For the first time since she arrived in this new land, she thought of him. *My God, what if I never see him again?* She hurriedly brushed that thought from her mind and smiled a weak smile at Lord Earin.

"Listen, Doc, it isn't all that bad. I'm just being bitter. No, it isn't perfect... but there are a lot of good things back there too. A lot of good things that I miss."

After such a statement, Lord Earin was painfully aware that he shouldn't go any further with that line of questions. However, since he didn't have a clue as to what else to say he just stared into the folds of his white robe and waited. Roxanne broke the uncomfortable silence.

"So, tell me, why the sudden interest in my home town?"

With nothing but the truth as an answer, Lord Earin knew he had no choice. He stared further into one particular fold of his robe. "I wanted to know what you have waiting for you. I wanted to know what I had taken you away from and whether or not..."

Roxanne stared firmly at his face until she managed to pull his gazed upward.

"Whether or not what?"

Earin let out a heavy sigh, "Whether or not you want to go back."

She cocked an eyebrow at the ever-serious Lord. "It sounds suspiciously like you don't want me to go?" *That's a good question, Roxie. Do you want to go back?*

"No... I mean, yes... I mean, whatever you desire," stammered her frazzled friend.

Roxanne stretched her legs back out, watching the muscles she had acquired ripple under her leggings. She wondered if she would still have this body if she went back. *I should hope so. I busted my ass for it... Actually, Snake busted my ass, but that's another story entirely.* She looked into the perplexed face of her newest and closest friend.

"Look, Doc, there's a lot going on now that we can't control; a lot that needs our immediate and total attention. What do you say we deal with that now and this other stuff later," she paused for effect, "much later, okay?"

Earin smiled a gentle smile at his friend, "Okay."

"Good!" she exclaimed with a hearty pat on his leg. "Now, let's move on to a more interesting subject."

"What could *possibly* be more interesting than that?"

Roxanne leaned forward and whispered like a child asking for more ice cream before bedtime, "Why don't you tell me what you did before you pulled this Lord slash Protector gig?"

Where are you, my dear?

Gabriel's mental voice filled her head.

"Hold one, Doc. I've got an incoming message."

She ignored the confusion on his face and responded to the Commander.

I'm right in the middle of something, Ray. Could you come back in say an hour, hour and a half?

Cute, but this is important. Get over to the High Lord's tent. We are having a pow-wow.

We never have any fun anymore.

ROX-ANNE!

I'm coming, I'm coming.

"Well, come on then," she said as she jumped out of the tree.

"Exactly where are we going?" asked Earin as he followed her.

"Commander Gabriel has called some sort of meeting of the minds. He's got all the important people in the High Lord's tent."

With an obvious sigh of relief, Lord Earin jumped out of the tree and followed the radiant form infront of him. He felt as though he'd had a narrow brush with death and escaped; he smiled. *Saved by the Commander. I might even thank him.*

"Oh, and, Doc?" came Roxie's voice over her shoulder, "Don't think this little interruption lets you off the hook. I will ask again."

Then again, maybe I won't.

****

Some small unknown creature scurried across the cold cavern floor, chripping as it ran for the familiar cover of darkness. Dust swirled around its tiny feet and minute pebbles chinked back down against the ground. Somewhere down the dank corridor a dull chanting bounced off the walls and echoed throughout the fortress. And, for a moment, all was right with *His* world.

But, soon, He grew tired of the chanting, and the waiting began to bore Him. He wanted something more. He needed something more. So, He slipped down the corridor, scarcely noticing the small creature who tremored at His presence, toward the continual hum of chanting. At the end of His journey, He pulled within himself and, then, slowly let His presence be known. Mongrel, who had been hunched over the cauldron chanting, stopped and pulled himself into a full standing position. The twisted old wizard knew something was coming; he braced himself.

A specter-like hand floated through the air and stirred the contents of the bubbling cauldron.

"Our forces have grown quite large. It seems that we are poised and ready to condemn the land. Yet, I hesitate. Do you know why that is?"

The Betrayer paused and shot a glowing glance at the squirming figure beside him. He allowed him only a moment to think; no time to venture an answer.

"I wait," He boomed, "because she has not taken the steps **you** assured me she would."

Mongrel shivered but held his ground and responded in a trembling voice, "She will, she will. Patience..."

"Patience," snarled the form of evil. "You are telling me to have patience. I have waited centuries for my time. You were not even alive when I began waiting, and you are telling me to have patience."

He didn't raise His voice above a whisper; He never did. He didn't have to. Yet, his words echoed with such a force that the ground trembled and dust fell from the walls. The bent magician nearly lost his courage, but he continued anyway.

"I have seen it. All that has happened, I have seen. All that will happen, I have seen. She will come."

He knew the miserable creature before him had not the strength to lie- he was too possessed by fear. "We will wait."

He began to ooze back down the hall. "She had better come."

As He disappeared, Mongrel knew that she had indeed better come.

****

The Commander looked around the room and tried to see past the dismayed faces; he couldn't. Something close to despair had settled over the leaders of the right. And he had nothing to hold against them. Their greatest fears had just been made true; the Betrayer was not only ready and waiting for them, he was willing for them to come as well.

A small, gentle voice floated up from the back of the tent and broke the unbearable silence, "So tell me what has changed?"

Lord Anjalina turned to face the ever-jolly form of Lord Ambrose, "What do you mean? Everything has changed. Didn't you hear? We are walking into a cleverly laid trap."

The hopeful Lord smiled, "Yes, so I heard. But, does that really change things?"

"What are you getting at?" asked Major Elway.

"What I am saying is, we have always known He can see us, yet we move forward. We have always known the bulk of his force lies waiting, yet we move on. And," smiled the gentle Lord, "we have always known this to be a crazy attempt at victory, yet we move on. So I ask again, what has changed?"

General Sabastian took command of the situation. "Absolutely nothing has changed! We continue with our mission. We have come this far without being overcome, we might as well finish the job. Who knows? We might even have a couple of surprises left for the old King of Doom. Perhaps we **can** get there before He is ready."

"Well, you're right about one thing," heads turned to face the woman of ice, "nothing has changed. We must move on. But, make no mistake, Foul One is ready."

Must you always be so cheery?
Must you always be a smart-ass?
Must you ladies quibble?
Must you be so nosey?

"So what you are saying is, we take all of our men, all of the Lords, and all three of the Chosen One's and march directly into a trap. Then what do you suggest? Should we slit our own throats and lay down to die?"

Major Elway's comment set all of Roxanne's nerves on edge. *Big baby.* "What choice have we?"

"We could march back to the castle. Make him come to us.

Force him to fight us on our own ground."

"That would accomplish nothing!" roared General Sabastian. "If He can see us, and if He wants us to come, do you really think he's going to let us go? The second we turn around, all of those troops the scouts have been reporting are going to fall on us with the full vengeance of hell. As long as we move forward, we can protect ourselves that much longer."

"What's a little while amount to when you're marching to your death?" said the Major sullenly.

Until now, the High Lord had let the military leaders handle this meeting. He let them hurl insults and ideas. He let them try to work things out. Apparently, this was not going to happen. So he decided to intervene and put an end to this, here and now.

"That is enough!" All shouting stopped and all eyes turned to face High Lord Brennen. "As bleak as things may seem, they have been darker before. The Major has a legitimate claim to fear. It is a scary thing to face your own mortality. But, we truly have no choice but to move forward. Only now, we move faster, and hope to take the enemy with some surprise. I know we are all frightened. However, we have one thing on our side that we cannot forget. We have the three Chosen and the force of the magic amulets."

"Which nobody really knows anything about," mumbled the Major under his breath. He nearly fell out of his seat when the ancient Lord responded.

"No. That is not the case, young Major. Plenty is known about the amulets; it's their bearers that will take you by surprise." With that, the aging yet powerful man folded his arms across his chest and took his seat.

General Sabastian tugged at his red beard for a moment, glanced at the strong face of his robed friend, and then into the tender, smiling eyes of Lord Ambrose. He knew they had no choice but to move on; he knew that was their only chance at success; but, he knew that Major Elway was right in more ways than one. He stopped tugging, assumed his commanding stance, and stood.

"What remains, folks, is this: The Betrayer knows we are coming. He is ready for us," he shot a brief glance toward Snake who acknowledged with an abrupt nod, "and waits patiently. However, the scum-bag does not know that we have figured this all out."

... all out, asshole.

What the hell is that all about, Roxie?

Relax, Gabe. It's just a little something between me and my old English Professor.

Must you relay it so loudly then?

Yes, I must if I intend to teach you anything.

Hello, hate to interrupt and all, but we are having an important meeting that you two should pay attention to, asshole.

Sorry. echoed in Snake's mind in both mental voices as she returned her attention to the meeting. And, Roxanne smiled at an English lesson well learned by her icy friend.

"...so we can still assume a small element of surprise." finished General Sabastian.

As the General took his seat, Roxanne cringed at having missed more of the important stuff because she couldn't keep her mind from wandering. *It's a curse.*

"What do you have to say about all of this, Commander?"

I should have known the red-headed bitch would start something. She must have guessed he had been otherwise distracted. "Well, Lord Anjalina, I agree with Lord Ambrose. This new knowledge changes nothing. We move on just as swiftly and carefully as before. All that has come of this is our own awareness of Old Ugly One's true power. Only now do we really see what we are up against."

The Lady Lord nodded her head, "Perhaps, then, you should prepare your troops."

"They are already prepared."

"You alerted them before you came to us."

The Commander sensed then irritation rising in her voice. "Lady, we alerted them before this war ever started. They have been trained from the beginning to spot traps. In fact, they've probably seen this coming for days."

One day someone is going to remove that smug little grin from your disrespectful face. Lord Anjalina suppressed the urge to whack the Commander over the head with her staff. Instead,

164

she turned to the High Lord for a conference. Gabe watched the mental chat with his "'aint-it-hard-being- perfect" grin firmly attached to his face. He knew he had pissed her off again, he suspected it was dangerous, but he loved living on the edge. The mind-lock between the Lords ended.

"Quite right Lord Anjalina," announced the High Lord, "it is late and we all need our rest. Tomorrow we continue as planned."

With that, the meeting was over and the decision to move forward was made. As they left the hall, each leader seemed to carry with them the knowledge that tomorrow was coming, and there is absolutely nothing the could do about it. The only non-somber face in the crowd was Commander Gabriel's. In fact, he grinned a flamboyant good-night to the ever-serious Lord Anjalina. She turned away, pulled her flowing robes closer to her well-formed figure, and walked defiantly away. Watching her walk off, her red hair wisping around her face, Gabe had a thought he seldom did about her. *She'd be downright pretty, if she were human that is.*

Roxanne's voice snapped him back to attention. "You know, it's not wise to upset a Wookie."

"But, ma'am, no one worries about upsetting a droid."

"That's because droids don't rip your arms off when they loose, she looks like she could do that."

Gabe cocked an eyebrow, "No fair changing a movie quote."

Roxanne returned the look, "I'm just warning you. Be careful or she *will* wipe that grin off your face."

"You heard that, too?"

Now she grinned, "Are you kidding? I think people back home heard that one. Why do you piss her off like that?"

He shrugged, "Because I can."

"Yeah, well I can swim through shark infested waters, but that doesn't mean I would do it at all, let alone on a regular basis."

Gabe patted her on the shoulder, "Well, you see, that's the difference between us Roxie. You are cautious and I am..."

"...stupid?"

"... adventurous."

"Well, whatever you are, I'm tired and I'm going to get some rest."

This time a sly grin crept across Gabriel's face. He too had seen Major Elway come out of the tent. He would have had to been blind to miss the look that passed between the two. And, he would have to really be stupid not to realize where Roxanne was heading. *Oh well, no rest for the weary. Scratch that. Make it, no rest for the horny.* He decided to let it pass without comment; not so much out of kindness as out of self-preservation. He had every intention of hunting Snake down and giving her a proper apology.

"Good night then."

"Yeah, same to you." She turned to follow Elway's fading figure. "Oh, and Gabe?" she called over her shoulder.

"What?"

"She went west young man. Good night."

He started to reply, couldn't think of anything clever to say, so he shrugged his shoulders and followed his lead.

****

Roxanne sat at the edge of the tent and stared into the darkness. Behind her, the Major stirred in his covers. It had been an exhausting night, but still she could not sleep. She focused on a small shadow in the night; a shadow she knew belonged to the ever-faithful Sage. He was never more than a few feet away, a trait that once was annoying, but now was comforting. His little figure beside her gave her a sense of warmth. She knew he wasn't happy with where she was right now. She smiled a small smile as she pictured the look of disgust that must be on his face right now. No, he most certainly was not happy.

Major Elway moved again, drawing Roxanne's gaze into the tent for a moment. He was beautiful in the moonlight. The beams danced perfectly across his muscular chest and played with the highlights in his soft blonde hair. He was yet another comforting figure in her life, though she knew she did not love him. No, he was a great friend, a strong partner, and a wonderful lover, but not the man of her dreams.

She turned her restless gaze back to the outside world. *What is wrong with me? Why can't I sleep?* She had been ready to pass-out earlier, but now she couldn't even close her eyes. There was something cold in her soul; almost something evil. She felt hollow, but didn't know why. *What the hell is wrong?* She shook her head and laid back down. *I've got to sleep. Tomorrow is another day of... another day of what? Maybe I've got it wrong. Maybe tomorrow is just another day.* With that she closed her eyes, wished Sage a mental goodnight, and attempted to sleep.

****

Snake watched the leaves of her perch rustle in the night breeze, and wondered what was beyond them. She strained her ears to hear movement that might be disguised by the sounds of the wind and the night. She heard nothing. She probed the darkness with her eyes, searching for unknown movement. She saw nothing. So, she allowed herself to lean back and close her eyes for a night of light sleeping. But, she couldn't sleep.

Instead, her mind drifted to the figure asleep down below; a figure she had disentangled herself from only to run and hide in this tree above. She concentrated on the sound of his breathing. It calmed her for a moment- but only for a moment. The calming effect was precisely why she was hiding. He was getting too close, way too close. She didn't know what to tell herself. She was attempting to keep the physical separate from the rest of her, but he was not making it easy.

She had spent a lifetime first learning to fear, then learning to despise men. She was good at it. For close to twenty years she had kept them away from the part of her that needed the most attention. But, now, he was trying to sneak into that place. She could feel him pushing; constantly worrying and caring about her... it made her sick. *Let him worry. He's the only one getting hurt.* She knew she was lying to herself, but it felt better than the truth. *Besides, he has no idea who I really am. The only thing I've shared with him is my bed.*

That statement stabbed her in her most protected area. She glanced down at his sleeping form. *How can he just sleep like there isn't a problem in the world. Does he really think it will all just go away if he closes his eyes?* Apparently so. She decided to follow his lead and let the problems of the world go away for now. She pulled her cloak tightly around her body and squeezed her arms close against her heart- hoping it was still safe.

****

Chapter 9

High Lord Brennen inhaled the cold morning air outside his tent and waited for the sun to break through the canopy of tree branches overhead. He let his mind search out the twelve other Lords while he stared into the new day. He found each presence alert, alive, and uneasy. He attempted to send a feeling of calm comfort in return. The force of the effort shook his aged form, for he too felt a strange sense of foreboding. It was as though the very air around him held an evil chill. *Don't let your mind play tricks on you, old man.*

But, the High Lord knew it wasn't just a trick of his age. There was something evil in the air, and he feared it to be the source of all evil; he feared it to be the Betrayer. As he had so many times of late, he was struck by the feeling that he would not survive this war.

The sun peeked through the trees, bringing the High Lord back to the here and now. All around him the camp was coming to life. Soldiers packed and stowed their gear. Cooks brought around food and water. Lords performed morning rituals. Animals ate. And, Lord Brennen wept silently. *How many of these people will die?* They were all so alive and innocent just then... he almost couldn't bear it. But, he had to, and, so, for him the day began.

****

"To-day!" Roxanne smiled as the pillow she had thrown landed with a solid thud on Elway's head. The smile vanished when he didn't even move.

"You know, for a trained killer, you sure are a heavy sleeper."

"And for such a pretty lady, you sure are a pain in the ass," came the muffled reply.

Roxanne lifted the pillow off Elway's head with her foot and peeped at the boy-wonder. "Oh, so you are awake."

"Come a little closer and I'll show you just how awake I am," he smirked.

She smirked right back, "No thanks. Been there. Done that. Bought the T-shirt. Now...," she leaned closer to his ear, "**GET UP!**"

The Major groaned and lifted the pillow from his head. It felt like a ton of stone to his tired form. *This woman is going to be the death of me.* He knew better than to spend the night with Roxie before a day of marching, but he couldn't help himself. As he slowly pulled himself into a sitting position, he watched her strap on the last of her many knives and step outside the tent. *God, she is gorgeous.*

"Whenever you are ready, I'll be packing my gear and checking the team. Anytime you want to help, you can."

He could feel the sarcasm dripping off her words. "Yeah, if you're lucky."

She tossed her long, brown hair over her shoulder and disappeared into the day. The Major wiped his hands across his eyes while letting out a small groan. *Why is it this never gets any easier?*

"Well, here goes yet another day of fun and excitement."

Mustering what was left of his energy, Elway pushed himself up and slid into his clothes. As he reached for his sword, a sudden eerie and evil chill ran down his spine. And, all at once, the almighty Major was afraid. *Calm down, boy. Your imagination is starting to get the best of you. Still...* He crept to the entrance of his tent and peered out into the daylight. The whole world was just as it should be. People were packing, Lords were praying, and soldiers were practicing.

"I must be going crazy. See, here's proof. I'm talking to myself."

He turned back into the tent and finished getting ready for the long march, all the while painfully aware that he was not crazy.

****

Mongrel checked the air behind him for the hundredth time, but there was still nothing there. Yet, he knew, that suddenly, and without explanation, He would be there. He would be ready to judge; ready to threaten; and, ready to destroy. So, Mongrel inhaled another deep breath of musty air and looked over his shoulder one more time.   Still nothing. He was driving himself crazy. So, he turned his attention back to the cauldron infront of him. Many dark and dangerous figures danced upon the water before him; the last of the dark forces.

"Is everything ready?"

Mongrel nearly jumped out of his skin. He found himself shaking so hard that his teeth trembled. "Yes, Master," eeked out of his startled form.

Mongrel could feel the red eyes behind him close in contemplation. "Then send the troops."

"Yes, Master," managed to slip past his lips once more.

"Oh, and Mongrel?"

"Yes, Master?"

"She had better come."

With that, He was gone just as quickly as He had arrived. *How I hate that phrase.* With every utterance of that phrase, Mongrel knew he was getting closer and closer to destruction. If, by chance, his visions were wrong, and she did not come, he would find himself floating in oblivion. Of that, he was certain. Quickly, he ran his hand over the murky waters of the cauldron, erasing all the figures before him. Now, he called up the future. What he saw sent a smile across his face. She would come. Of that, he was certain as well.

****

Lord Anjalina pulled her robes closer to her body, but that did not stop the cold. She was well aware that the chill that now sent shivers up and down her spine was coming somewhere from within and not from an early morning breeze. Yes, she knew the source of the cold, but she clung to her robes anyway. There was something very wrong with this day. She felt a deep sense of sadness and wondered how many she would mourn before this day came to a close. Shaking those thoughts from her head, she started forth on her self-imposed mission to find General Sabastian.

Finding, the stout man would not be a hard task. He would be wedged in the middle of all the preparations; seeing to it that every little detail was covered. *If he keeps on like this, the war won't have a chance to kill him.* She moved toward the center of the camp where several of the teams were preparing for the unavoidable battle. The grunts of combat and the smell of sweat filled the air around her as she closed in on the center of camp. And, for some reason, the chill in her body ran deeper. *Something terrible will happen today, I am sure.*

Calm yourself, dear Lord Anjalina. She immediately recognized the soothing voice and reached out for it like a scared child grasping her parent's hand.

But, High Lord, I can feel there is something wrong.

We are at war and very near to the Betrayer now. That is enough to put us all in agitated states.

Then you feel it as well.

Yes. But, we are the Protector's of the land. We must curb our fears and help those around us.

How can I protect them from a force I cannot see?

With your heart, dear Lord. With your heart.

Just as quickly as he had come, the High Lord vanished from her mind. Although she felt empty and alone, she was not angry for she knew that he must be needed elsewhere. *After all, there are eleven other Lords out there who are probably just as scared as I am.*

"Hello. Is there anybody in there?"

She had been so deep in her own thoughts that she had managed to walk into the middle of battle preparations without even realizing it. She smiled the warmest smile she could muster and greeted the Chosen One.

"Greetings Cho...er...Roxanne. I hope all is well with you this day."

Suppressing the urge to tell her how nothing was well because she couldn't shake the feeling that all hell was about to break loose and there was probably no stopping it, she smiled and replied, "Fine. And you?"

"As well as they can be when all around you there is war."

My, my. And I thought I was the Grim Reaper today. Guess she forgot to take her happy pills. "What's on your mind, Lord Anjalina? What brings you to this neck of the woods?"

The Lord pulled her robes closer to her body. *Easy, Nitro. If you pull those robes any tighter, you'll loose circulation. Mental note: Find out why Anjalina has gone off her rocker.*

"I am looking for General Sabastian. Have you seen him?"

Roxanne sheathed the sword she had been leaning on. "He's just beyond that cluster of trees going over some last minute plans with the Commander."

"He would be."

Roxanne couldn't help herself, she burst out laughing.

"What is so humorous?"

"You. I swear, just when I thought there was no chance of it, you Lords seem to have developed a sense of humor."

A small, barely detectable grin made its way to the fiery Lord's lips. "Perhaps I just can't bring myself to take certain people seriously."

"It's better if you don't. Just like my father use to say: Life's too short to take it seriously."

"That's what I'm afraid of."

The momentary warmness that had covered her left with the red-headed Lord who had sparked it. Watching her walk away, Roxanne was once again covered in a cold and lonely feeling. *I have got to shake this deep, blue funk.* It crossed her mind to warn Gabriel that his friend was on the way, but she let the thought keep right on moving. *I gotta have some fun today. Besides, he just loooves surprises.*

As she left the side of the Chosen, the chill in Anjalina's heart returned in full force. For some inexplicable reason, she had felt a fleeting moment of warmth and calm while in Roxanne's presence. *Perhaps Lord Earin is correct. Perhaps she does have the power to save us.* However, with the distance between them increasing, and the cold returning, the fiery female Lord began to wonder if anything could save them. She shook her head to clear it and stepped defiantly through the trees before her.

"Well, well. Invading the enemy camp, Lord Anjalina?"

As always the Commander knew just what to say to make her feel at home. She glared into his soft brown eyes and fumed at his clever grin. *Why is it he always looks so calm and rested? Doesn't this ever get to him?*

As she spoke, a gust of wind swept past them, picking her red hair up and tossing it about her face. She looked like an angry angel, and, for the Commander, her words held prophetic force.

"I have come to see the General."

Apparently, he was alone in his revelation for the General hardly seemed impressed. He merely placed his plans aside for the time being, leaned his massive body against the nearest tree, and responded.

"What can I do for you, Lord Anjalina?"

For a second, almost as though she were questioning her own purpose, she hesitated. But, she quickly recovered and stepped forward, taking the General into her confidence.

"General?"

"Yes?"

"I am very concerned about High Lord Brennen."

General Sabastian came to life at the mention of his friend's name, "Why?! Is there something wrong?"

Lord Anjalina held up her hands in a calming motion. "No, no, no. There's nothing wrong. That is to say nothing now...I mean concrete...I mean... I don't know what I mean for sure."

Confusion added to the millions of other emotions already etched into the General's tired and aging face. "Calmly tell me what it is you are trying to talk about."

"Do you want me to leave?"

Anjalina spun toward the Commander. Was that true compassion in his voice?

"Really. If you would be more comfortable in private, I will go."

Perhaps you aren't completely heartless after all. She must have let her thoughts show upon her face, for the Commander quickly regained control of his "coolness."

174

"I mean, it's not as though I have a ton of stuff more important to do than stand around with you trading secrets. I've got battles to plan, people to train, and bad guys to kill. So if you two sweethearts will excuse me..."

Just like that, the Commander had taken the pressure off both situations and managed to leave everyone's dignity intacked as he left the clearing.

The General's voice called Anjalina back to the task at hand. "Are you shocked to find that he is actually human? He really can be nice, given a chance and the desire to do so. However, it seems he's much happier letting people believe he's an asshole."

The stunned Lord let out a long and heavy sigh, "Why is he like that?"

"Don't know. And, even if I did, I'd probably never tell."

"He'd kill you if you did. He's not a man to cross."

"Lady, you speak truer than you know. Now, back to the business of High Lord Brennen..."

The deep, sorrowful gaze that she came with returned to the lady Lord's face. "There is something terribly wrong in the Land today; something more than the Betrayer, and I fear the High Lord may somehow in the middle."

"My dear Lord Anjalina, what are you talking about?"

"It is no secret to the rest of the Lords that Lord Brennen fears he will not survive this war. It is in his every thought and gesture. We all feel his fear, no matter how hard he attempts to hide it."

The General tugged at his beard as he listened to the frightful words of Lord Anjalina. He wanted so much to argue; so much to call out to the forces of evil that it was not true, but he could not. He knew as well as the rest of them that Lord Brennen moved and acted as a man already defeated.

With a heavy sigh he asked, "What can we do about it?"

A distant gaze filled Anjalina's eyes, "About how he feels? Nothing. About him surviving this war? Anything and everything possible. I'm not ready to loose the High Lord, and neither is the Land."

The General tugged even harder at his rough red beard. He, too, had felt an evil chill in the air. It seemed to be all around him. He knew there was something deathly wrong, but couldn't place it. All he did know was he was a man afraid.

"I will increase the guard around Lord Brennen."

The Lady Lord shook her head, an action that sent her hair cascading over her shoulders, "That won't do. He will send them away at the first hint of battle, and he can be very persuasive."

She had a point.

"Okay. So, then what do you suggest I do about it. I am kinda limited on options."

He had a point.

"Who, of you're very best men, can you spare?"

The General contemplated the options. *My best, huh? Lady, you're hallucinating.* There really wasn't a spare running around. Everyone with any ability at all was running a position of command; this war had cut them short of everything.

"The thing is, we are spread pretty thin as it stands. I've got pages wielding swords and people under the age of twenty leading battalions. I was about to hand the horses swords and see if they're any good."

An icy chill ran down the desperate Lord's spine. Something between panic and despair seized her heart. *Why does this have to be so hard? Are we really doomed to failure? What will become of the Land if we fail?* Her body began to shake and her lips trembled with the threat of tears. And, for just a moment, she thought she was about to loose the last of all her strength.... But, somehow she held on.

"All I'm asking is one man. I'd do it myself if he'd let me, but we both know he would never let that happen. Just one man."

The General could see desperation flowing through her entire body. He knew something had to be done. He hefted a dagger and sank it hilt deep into a tree at the far end of the clearing. In response, a very tiny person appeared at his side.

"Malcolm, find Major Elway and bring him here at once. Tell him it's extremely urgent."

As they watched the page disappear, there was only silence. And, they both seemed to realize that their hope went with him. Lord Anjalina looked to the sky and shuddered, and the thunder rolled.

****

"Are you trying to be an idiot, or is this something you do naturally?"

Roxanne ducked just in time to miss the rather large stone the Major chucked her way.

"Easy, Nitro. What if that had hit me?"

He stopped in mid throw, "Then I would have felt terrible."

As the second rock cleared her head, Roxie called out, "Hey, we are suppose to be training here."

"I am. I'm practicing taking out gorgeous yet annoying enemy types."

"Look, all I was trying to say is, if you try to sneak up on the enemy like that, you'll be dead in a matter of seconds."

"Oh, and I suppose you have a better idea?"

"As a matter of fact, I do. Stay as close to the ground as possible. I'm talking dirt eating close. That way, whether there are bushes and trees or not, you will still be a part of the scenery."

Elway raised an eyebrow, "Why don't we ask the resident expert?"

"Where is Snake anyway? I haven't seen her all day."

"I spotted her briefly this morning. Looked like she was heading North, with a purpose. I thought it best not to bother her."

"Good idea, Karlis." If that lady didn't want to be bothered, it was best to leave things that way.

Roxanne shrugged her shoulders and turned back to the business at hand.

"Well, since we have no "resident expert" running around, I guess you'll just have to believe her prodigy and that would be... Oh, who could that be? Wait! That would be me. My, my. Looks like I win."

About the time she had really started to tighten Elway's nerves, a page by the name of Malcolm appeared in between them. *Do they all do that?* He had a message from General Sabastian.

"The General requires your immediate presence on a matter of extreme urgency, Major," blurted out the frazzled young man. *I think the lack of rest is getting to him.*

The Major nodded in response. Turning to face Roxanne, he sheathed his sword and mouthed a smart-ass comment. *Ah, the love*, she thought. She responded with a wave.

"Have a nice time, dear. Don't stay out too late."

"See ya when I see ya, darling."

And then he was gone and she was once again all alone with the troops. Alone. Alone and free to teach them anything she wanted. *Sometimes life is goooood.* So, she tied her long, flowing hair back out of the way, dropped to the ground, and began her lesson in how to sneak.

****

When he reached the clearing where General Sabastian was waiting, the Major was a little shocked by what he found. Not only was the General there and pacing, but Lord Anjalina was there as well, looking like a mouse on an open field at midnight. *What the hell has gotten into these two? They look like death just walked by and whispered "You're next."*

"Major Elway reporting as ordered, General."

The man of stone appeared where only moments ago a child had stood as soon as he heard the Major's voice. *Nice trick.* The General moved beside the lady Lord. And, there they stood; two immoveable forces, their matching red hair shimmering as the wind tossed it to and fro. They appeared majestic, powerful, and dangerous. For a moment, Elway felt like a man summoned before the executioner.

But, that all changed with the sound of the General's voice, "My friend, we need your assistance."

"Whatever you need, just ask. I am always ready to serve and protect."

Glancing at the fierce Lord beside him, the General continued, "Lord Anjalina has brought a matter of great importance to my attention. The High Lord may be in very grave danger over the next several days due to his proximity to the

178

Betrayer. It it obvious that someone of his importance and skills will undoubtedly be the target of attack. That is why we feel it is necessary to increase his personal security."

"Of course, General. I'll get some of my best men right on it."

"Not so fast there, Major. It's not that simple. You see, the High Lord does not consider his personal safety to be an issue of importance. He would rather die than "waste" people on his protection. He thinks he does just fine himself. So, when I say we are going to increase the security around him, I mean from none to one. You."

The General stopped and let his words sink into the Major's head. The blonde haired, blue eyed man before him stood as cool as ice. *Kinda reminds me of someone else I know.* Whatever he was thinking, he was keeping it to himself. They locked eyes for a few more seconds before a voice bordering on desperate broke in.

"I hope you understand how important this really is. This man represents all our hope and strength. Without him, I fear all would be lost."

Major Elway turned to face the Lady of our Faltering Hope, "Yes, I do realize how important this is. However, I think that there is something you fail to realize that the High Lord, himself, must know. He is not the last and only hope for our Land, we are."

The perplexed look of shock remained firmly fixed to Lord Anjalina's face as Major Elway exited the clearing in search of his ward. As he tugged at his beard in contemplation, one thought ran through the General's mind, *He has a point.*

****

Roxanne leaned against the trunk of the tree that she was sitting under and looked up at the cloudy sky. As she massaged her tired muscles, the wind kicked up blowing dust into her eyes. *Great. Even Mother Nature is trying to pick a fight.* It was going to rain. She knew that. Hell, she could have told you that without a cloud in the sky. This was just the kind of day for a downpour.

Everyone was on edge, the Betrayer was only hours away, and they were about to start another of those lovely marches. It was definitely going to rain.

"Why is it that I always come across you in this position?"

Roxie looked up at her friend's curious face.

"Well, Doc, it's probably just luck. Sit down. Take a load off."

Lord Earin smiled as he always did when she was near. He placed himself on the ground directly infront of her and stared at her lovely face. What he saw ate at his heart. God, how she had aged. The youthful naivety had long since vanished, and was replaced with a look of strong determination. And, when he looked closely, he could see sparkles of grey in her hair. There was one thing that had not changed, though; the light in her eyes still shone with amazing force. She was still alive.

"How goes the preparations for the upcoming battle?" he asked.

"Same old, same old."

Then there was silence. Not a comfortable silence like that shared by lovers in the aftermath of love, but an awkward silence like the first time your parents find a used condom in the trash, and it's not theirs. *Now this is strange.* Roxanne struggled to find a reason for the discomfort. They had never had this problem before. The relationship she shared with Lord Earin had always been an easy, free flowing one filled with conversations of every kind. There was no reason for the silence. *Unless it's that silence before the storm type thing kicking in.* She decided to find out.

"So, tell me, Doc, how do you feel today?"

As always, honesty poured from his lips, "I feel as though the world is not right today. It is as though a darkness is hanging right above us but we can't see it and we can't touch it. It's like He's laughing at us."

Well put there, Freud. And tell me about your mother. "I know. There is something wrong with everyone and everything today. I mean, Lord Anjalina has taken it upon herself to be the Grim Reaper."

The ever-famous and much requested look of confusion leapt to Lord Earin's face.

"The who?"

"The messenger of death," said Roxanne with a smile.

"If that is the case, why are you smiling?"

"I'm smiling because no matter what, no matter when, and no matter where, we always end up where we started; me making smart remarks and you failing to understand them."

Earin shook his perplexed little head, "I don't think I will ever understand you, Roxanne."

She smiled an even bigger smile, "I know. 'Aint it great?"

Cocking his head slightly to one side, he responded, "That entirely depends on your definition of great."

Then it hit her. There was some unfinished business between the two of them. *No wonder he's been so quiet. He's probably hoping I forgot. No such luck.* She decided to hit him without warning.

"So, Doc, tell me what you did before you became a Lord."

The look on his already haggard face told her she had hit her mark dead on. Thoughts flashed across his eyes and answers formed themselves on his lips, but no sounds came. For a split second, Roxanne thought her honest little Lord might actually lie. Not today.

With a sigh, he gave in, "I was a soldier. More to the point, I was a member of Prince Jordan's personal guard."

Roxanne was stunned. Not by what he had said, but by the fact that he had been so reluctant to say it. Now it was her turn for the confused look.

"And this is shocking because...?"

Lord Earin shrugged, "It's not, at least, not for you. However, it is something that would send chills down your spine if you were, say, one of the Lords or the General or something."

"Okay. I give. Why is this news so damn spine-tingling?"

The nervous Lord shifted uneasily, "Well, Prince Jordan is an infamous character..."

Without warning the movie *The Three Amigos* jumped into Roxie's head. *Oh, the in- famous.*

"... You see, when the Betrayer was banished for the first time, He, unfortunately, did not take all the evil in the world with Him. Evil, after all, is eternal. Evil was also what controlled a group of people who worshiped the Betrayer. They believed that one day He would return and they did everything they could to make the Land ready for Him. They devastated forests, slaughtered people, and hunted down and murdered several Lords. They were sinister and maniacal; their leader was the worst of them all."

"Let me guess, Prince Jordan."

"Exactly."

"No studying," mumbled Roxanne under her breath.

A sick look covered Lord Earin's face, "He was untouchable. A smile for everyone and kindness and generosity oozing from his pores. He was the epitome of goodness on the outside. But, on the inside, he was filled with the fires of Hell.

He held secret meetings to plot against the Land, and I protected him. He sheltered assassins, and I protected them. He captured and murdered Lords and leaders, and I protected him." Here the distraught Lord stopped to gulp some air as the tears and the sweat flowed down his tortured face.

"I was so blind that even when the other guards turned I shunned them and laughed at their weakness. I believed the Prince's every word and gesture. Dammit! I was a great fucking soldier!"

Roxanne reached out and took her fearful friend's hand. He was trembling beyond control. With everything in her soul, she reached out to him. She took in his pain and tried to make it her own so that she might lessen the burden on his heart. The jolt of his pain stopped her heart. When it started again, she found herself gasping for air. Lord Earin stared forward through glazed eyes; he never even saw what had just happened.

"Then, one day, my stupidity hit me in the face. I walked in on the sacrifice of a young child to the spirit of darkness being lead by the prince I had sworn to Protect. I stood, dumbfounded. My entire life came crashing down around my head, and I just stood there like a scared child."

Once again, there was silence between them. It was all she could do to keep from crying. She wanted to help him, comfort him, but she didn't have a clue how to do it.

"Anyway," he sighed, "I vowed to right my wrongs, and, so,

became a Lord. The rest of the Lords don't know why I'm here. For that matter, they never even ask. I just do everything I can to fulfill my promise to the land."

Roxanne shook her head slightly to clear it. *Does everyone in this place have some deep, dark secret they're hiding from? The worst thing I ever did was cheat on that geometry test in seventh grade, and that was a hard test.* She looked into the face of the gentle man before her. His eyes were cold and withdrawn. He was a man searching his soul, and finding all the ghosts.

"So now what?"

The distant Lord looked at Roxanne through confused eyes, "What do you mean?"

"Well, I can't decide whether to go in search of the Betrayer or to hunt down Snake and find out what part of her past she's hiding. Although, I suspect it would be safer to go after the Betrayer."

"What are you talking about?"

The newly formed war veteran stood and stretched her tight muscles, "Just that everyone seems to be so busy fighting personal demons that it's hard to believe anyone has any energy left for this war. And, I've figured everyone out except Snake, sooo, I was thinking why not."

Lord Earin smiled a meek smile, "I guess we all make ourselves and our problems too important."

She shook her head, "Listen, Doc. I'm not saying our problems aren't important. I'm just saying there are other things to deal with right now. If I wanted, I could spend all day wondering whether or not I'll ever see my little brother again," that thought pierced her heart like a fiery blade. She pushed it aside. "But, I don't have time. If we all work together, trust each other, and deal with these problems later, we might just win this war."

"Okay, we deal with them later. But, Roxanne? There are two things you need to remember. One, it's the ghosts we carry that make us who we are. And, two, I didn't want to deal with this at all."

Hello. Would somebody please get that knife out of my back. Several comebacks played across Roxanne's startled mind, but she ignored them all. It wouldn't achieve anything to argue with him now. Not to mention the fact that he had a point. *So, what do I say?* Fortunately, she didn't have to say anything; the Commander came to her rescue.

"Hey, Roxie, Earin. Either of you seen yon slithery bitch around?"

Lord Earin grinned a smug little grin. It was painfully obvious that the Commander was in love with Snake, but was attempting to hide it from everyone, including himself. *Oh well, it's fun to watch anyway.* "You know, I was just wonderin' the same thing myself," said the auburn-haired beauty. "I haven't seen her all day, but Karlis said he saw her this morning."

"Did he say where?"

Roxie grinned, "He said she was heading North with a purpose. He felt it would have been unwise to ask questions."

The ever-present smug look disappeared from the Commander's handsome face, "Let's hope she's not pulling another of her famous disappearing acts."

I'm not! came the panic-filled mental voice.

Where the hell are you and what the hell is wrong?! broadcasted the Commander.

Snake's mental voice was getting closer, but no less panicked.

I'm on my way in from a self-imposed scouting mission. Now, sound the alarm, grab all the shit, and run like hell for the Silver Forest.

What are you talking about?

Look! There is no time. The Betrayer is coming and all of hell is coming with him! In about five minutes, his entire army will be crashing down on us.

That's impossible. Where are the sentries and scouts?

Dead.

Her one word reply echoed in their minds. Commander Gabriel moved into immediate action.

"Earin, get all the Lords together and tell them to high-tail it toward the Silver Forest. We need them to get us inside."

"That's next to impossible. The fairies won't let anyone in."

Grabbing him by the collar of his robes, the Commander

pulled Lord Earin as close to his face as possible in order to get his point across, "The entire army of darkness is headed this way. All of my scouts and sentries are dead. And, Snake is scared shitless. Now, does that tell you anything?"

Confusion and indignation left the Lord's face and were quickly replaced by panic and understanding, "Yes, Commander. That tells me you had better let go of me so that my fellow Lords and I can get to the Silver Forest and find a way inside."

"Good," replied Gabriel. As Lord Earin scampered off, Commander Gabriel turned his attention to his fellow Chosen One. "Get 'em together and get 'em moving now."

"I'm gone."

With that, Roxanne disappeared, the alarm went up, and the Commander went in search of the General. *God help us, this war is finally starting.*

A figure came crashing through the trees, causing the Commander to wheel around, sword in hand. The icy blue eyes of that familiar face stopped him dead in his tracks.

"Yeah, it's started. But let's not kill the messenger."

With nothing else to say, the Suicide Duo turned and headed into history.

****

Chapter 10

Dark clouds covered the sky, lightening danced from cloud to cloud, raindrops fell like stones, and a deep mist engulfed the whole of the forest before them. However, despite the weather and the knowledge of the impending doom baring down on them, the thirteen Lords stood firm in their task. They had no choice, really. There was no where else for them to go. The Betrayer's forces were moving in on them from all other directions. The small company of hope was surrounded, and, once the fighting started, they would be grossly out-numbered.

Lord Ambrose looked on his colleagues with a warm smile. He knew it wasn't much, but it was the only show of hope and faith he had. Besides, he still believed in the forces of good. Deep in his heart he knew they would triumph. They had been blessed so far. They had all three Chosen, they had made it this far alive, and Snake's warning had given them time to reach the Silver Forest and prepare for battle. In fact, the optimistic Lord only had one source of sadness in his life, and that was his friend Lord Brennen.

He glanced down the line of Lords at his aged friend and felt, once again, his desperation. He knew the High Lord had prepared himself for death, but he refused to let him go so easily. Ambrose's smile turned into a look of fierce determination. *That war isn't over either, dear friend.*

The sounds of thunder and pouring rain blended with the sounds of General Sabastian and company setting up for bloody battle until they faded into nothingness. The damp air became meaningless and reality ceased to exist as High Lord Brennen moved between his friends and the forest and began his spell.

It was a communication spell of epic proportion; a communication spell designed to get the Lords an audience with the fairies and a chance at access to the forbidden forest. The High Lord uttered a few indistinguishable syllables, then raised his staff into the air. Following his lead, the twelve other robed saviors raised their staffs high into the air. Green light burst forth, engulfing all of the Lords and the spell began.

Major Elway threw his hands up to shield his eyes against the blinding light. *How the hell am I suppose to keep an eye on the High Lord if I'm blind?* He turned his head from his ward for a moment and faced his fellow fighters. They were all staring past him, eyes wide, and jaws drooping. *What the...?* He spun around to find out what was so damned interesting.

What he saw nearly knocked him to his knees. All thirteen Lords were glowing green with power; not their staffs, but the Lords themselves. However, that paled in comparison to the shock value of what the forest was doing. The trees had come to life with an equally eerie silver glow, which, in and of itself, was not all that wondrous. What was amazing, however, was what the trees contained.

"Fairies," muttered several people behind him.

The Major shook his head to clear it. *Fairies?* But of course. That's what they had to be, Fairies. Small, angelic faces suspended in an awe inspiring fog that appeared and disappeared; there one second and a dream-like impression the next. Thriving in the sanctity of their magic, the Fairies danced across the trees before the glowing Lords, who somehow appeared pathetic now in comparison. *Well, we got their attention. Now, let's see if they will listen.* With that thought, the Major turned back towards the troops. Not a soul stirred.

"Hey! Prepare troops!" All around men shook their heads. "Might I remind you that hell is coming up fast on our heels! Let's move it!"

The General pulled his gaze from the vision before him and nearly slapped himself for allowing himself distracted. *Years of military training, gone to waste.* Instead, he focused his frustration on his troops.

"You heard the Major, times a'wastin! Move it! I want totally fortified defenses set-up and ready to go, now! You've got less than a minute to build me a fortress I could raise a family in!"

The sound of the General's voice sent a spasm of movement through the stunned soldiers. Quickly, and with embarrassment still hot on their faces, the men barricaded themselves in. The General searched the defenses for any short-comings. None. *The only way that evil bastard is going to get in here is to materialize behind us.* As soon as the thought crossed his mind, he wished it hadn't. There was no telling just what that being was capable of; popping up behind them wasn't entirely out of the question.

"Malcolm!" bellowed General Sabastian.

The shaking young man appeared where once there was no one. *How the hell do they do that?*

"Find Snake now."

Despite the despair he obviously felt at the size of such a task, the heroic young page ran off to do his duty. He flew past soldiers and horses. He ran past packs and weapons. He leaped over bushes and rocks. But, he could not find her. This did not surprise him. Although he was still a child, he knew that if Snake did not want to be found, she wouldn't be. With a heavy heart, Malcolm turned back toward the General.

"Need any help?" came a small voice from behind.

Malcolm turned to face Sage, who held the coveted position as page to the Last of the Chosen.

"I've been sent by General Sabastian to find Snake."

Sage cringed at the cruelty of such a task, but only for a moment. A sudden jolt of inspiration changed the pain into a smile.

"Perhaps I can help. Return to the General and tell him she is on her way."

"I-I don't understand."

Sage attempted one of Roxanne's smug grins, "Just trust me."

As Malcolm turned to go, Sage couldn't help but laugh a small laugh. *Not bad for an amateur.* With the grin still plastered on his face, he turned and headed to Roxie's side. He didn't understand how or why, all he knew was that she could communicate with Snake and the Commander anytime she wanted. He knew that if anyone could find Snake, it would be her.

While Sage was returning to Roxanne with his message, Malcolm was returning to the General with one of his own; one he hoped would be correct.

"General, Snake is on her way," reported Malcolm in a timid voice.

"Guess again. She's here."

Both Malcolm and General Sabastian turned in surprise to face the dangerous beauty who had slide in behind them unnoticed. Once again, Snake felt like she had just materialized out of thin air. *Come on, guys. I know I'm good, but this is getting ridiculous.*

"Good. I have a task for you," said the General once he recovered. "It would appear that our position is well fortified, and that the only way the Betrayer's troops are getting in here is right over the top of us."

Snake quickly scanned the area. "So it would seem, General."

He nodded. "As a matter of fact, I was just thinking the only way he could sneak up on us would be to magically pop in behind us..."

Snake hardly needed to be escorted to where the General was heading. "Gotcha. I'll head out immediately and find out if they are still coming straight for us. I'll report back through the Major."

Before he could even tell her to be careful, she was gone. *She's even more insane than the rest of us.* With that thought lingering, and the knowledge that he was the one who had sent her, the stoic soldier swallowed his guilt and turned to deal with his duties.

****

Silence. That was all that existed in the caverns of his new home. The chanting had finally come to an end. All the troops had been summoned and sent. There was nothing left but to watch and wait. And, silence. The Betrayer moved slowly through the passageways of his home, taking in the wonderful lack of noise, and feeling all powerful.

But, suddenly there was a change in the air. The calmness began to dissipate, and a lesser emotion made its way through the air and right into his very black heart. Fear. It was becoming more and more pressing with each inch he floated across the floor. Strong, unaltering fear. It was an old feeling, as well; one that the source was all too familiar with. And, that source was all but upon him.

Calmly, the Betrayer turned the corner and approached his faithful servant. He was hunched over his cauldron as usual.

The Betrayer spoke quietly, "Well?"

Mongrel jumped as though He had bellowed the question. Turning, Mongrel recovered himself and spoke, "Tonight. She comes to us tonight."

The impressions of an evil grin flickered across what could have been a face. The shadowy figure made a small movement that resembled a bow. Then He was gone. As always, Mongrel sighed a sigh of relief.

****

Sweat poured into the High Lord's eyes. He could feel the pressure of his heart pounding against his chest. All around him was a sea of green, and nothing else. Desperation and anguish pushed into his thoughts, but he pushed them back. He had to remain calm, lest he panic the other Lords. Yet, for a brief second, a single thought entered his mind, *This, too, will fail.* With all the effort he could muster, he cleared his mind and held fast to the images in the forest before him.

Soon, it seemed as though time had stopped and he alone stood in the cold, green mists facing the impenetrable forest before him. Yet he held on. From somewhere in the nothingness behind him, he imagined he could hear the sounds of battle, but he was not sure. So, he held on. Faint bursts of noise and shocks of blows came at him from the darkness, but they meant nothing. All that mattered was the forest and those shimmering images of the fairies he had once been so closely joined to.

Then, when his faith and strength had nearly failed him, all of the world stopped pulsing. The shimmering faces infront of him became solid and all of his pain and desperation melted into an immense calmness. Somewhere in the back of his mind, he was vaguely aware of an intense battle being fought, but it was too far away to matter. Instead, he let himself be taken into the calm.

Welcome, Brennen. It has been a long time.

The High Lord instantly recognized the voice of his mentor.

Greetings, Shylark. It has indeed.

I see that you are now the High Lord. That is as it should be. You always were the strong one.

Ah, but my strength is leaving me.

What is your distress, old friend?

The land is in danger again, and those who are with me represent the final hope of all the land. We are strong of heart and will, but few in number.

What is it that you require?

Admittance.

Then there was silence. The High Lord felt the presence of his mentor lessen, although he did not completely withdraw. Some time passed before the tired Lord received a response.

For you all. The words were more of a statement than a question.

Brennen drew a deep breath. *For us all. There is no other choice for us, my friend.*

After a pregnant pause, Shylark's voice returned filled with the sorrow of his burden. *We shall have to consult. Know this, in opening the forest to all those, we risk contaminating the purity of its soul, for you Lords have made use of the dark magic.*

That is true. But, know this, Shylark, in closing it, you may seal the fate of the rest of the land.

This time, the mentor withdrew. But, before he was completely gone, and the spell completely broken, High Lord Brennen thought he heard the fading voice say, *He has a point.*

And, then, the High Lord turned to face the other Lords, reality, and the fury of hell that had come down on his small band. But, only when he looked down at the crumbled form of Major Elway at his feet, did he feel the awesome shock of reality.

"Dear God," escaped from his lips, and that was all.

Snake silently slithered through the overgrown foliage of the dark forest. Her eyes raced back and forth, quickly scanning the world around her for any signs of disturbance. So far, there were none. *Hooray for our side. Now, if this damn rain would just let up for a second, life would be just peachy.* The rain that had been pouring down all morning had turned the world into a morbid swampland and Snake into a soaked serpent with an attitude. Her clothes clung to her body like a desperate child clinging to its mother. Her hair was plastered to her head and face. And, her boots came dangerously close to sloshing with each step. All in all it was not turning into a good morning.

How goes it?

The Commander's voice threatened to break her extreme concentration.

Much better when I'm left alone.

Touchy. I'd just like to know when we are going to be hopelessly slaughtered; I do have a schedule to keep.

In a hurry to die?

Not particularly. I'd just like to know when things are going down.

Then perhaps you'd like to be on recon detail next time.

Perhaps I would.

Well, great. Why don't you relay that to our illustrious leader?

And why don't you just kiss...

A sudden sound vibrated through the forest, sending Snake to the ground, and pulling all of her attention into the here and now. With all of her skill, she concentrated on the world around her. The air was strangely warm, as though thousands of people were breathing in a small, cold area. Not a single animal stirred; even the rain seemed to have lessened in response to some unknown disruption. Snake strained to hear the throngs of evil she knew had to be close.

Snake! Dammit! What the hell is going on?

Back off, okay? I'm checking on something.

There was no smart-ass reply, so she guessed that, for once, the stubborn Commander had listened to her. *Will miracles never cease.* Slowly, Snake removed herself from the ground and began to creep up the nearest tree for a better look. As she climbed, the noise that had caught her off guard earlier repeated itself. This time, however, she knew exactly what it was; the crack of a rather large whip. Small amounts of panic seized her heart. This was not a good thing; she wasn't even close to the morning's campsite.

With the speed of a panther, she covered the rest of the distance to the top of the tree in which she was perched. Peeking over the leaves, she looked down on a scene of mass destruction. *Oh my God...*

It was worse than she originally thought. Only a short distance from the base of the tree she now clung to, the front scouts of the legion of doom were busy clearing a path by demolishing everything. But, the immediate danger her life was in paled in comparison to the danger she knew the small band at the silver forest was about to encounter. As far as she could see, the land was covered in a sea of black and grey bodies. Now, the panic was complete.

Gabe! Roxie!

The response from them both was immediate.

What the hell is wrong? boomed Gabriel's voice.

Where the hell are you? came Roxanne's concerned reply.

Snake mustered all the suave she had left in her soul and tried to remain calm. *Get in that forest, now! I don't care if you have to kill a few fairies to do it. Just get in.*

Roxanne came back calmly. *What if that's not possible?*

Snake's stomach sank. *Then we are going to have to find a miraculous use for these necklaces, because nothing else we have is going to come close.*

At that exact moment, with all of their concentration at its peak, and all of their emotions alive, all three of the Chosen grasped the amulets around their necks, and saw. In a burst of power, unlike anything in the known worlds, they all saw through the minds of each other and those who had come before. Images of the past, of the evils done, the powers felt, and the salvation. And, images of the present; glimpses into the lair of the Betrayer, where he sat smiling, visions of the fairies debating whether or not to respond to the summons of the Lords, and a long hard look at the enemy that was upon them.

In a flash, they saw it all.

Snake, get out of there, NOW!!!

Roxanne's mental voice came across as softly as a whisper, but the force was clear. Snake immediately started to descend.

You get back here in one piece, or I'm coming after you.

As much as she couldn't afford a distraction from him now, Snake called out to the Commander.

The hell you are. We can't win this thing without you, and you've got much bigger problems than me coming your way.

A small, uncomfortable pause filled the air, but then the "cool" Commander responded. *Hardly.*

As she ran back to the battle zone, Snake felt reassured.

****

The intensity of all that she had just seen ran back and forth across Roxanne's mind. She shook her head in an effort to clear it; she couldn't afford to loose her edge now. She had to pull it together and lead her troops in a battle with the devil himself. But how? She had looked into the eyes of the demon, and evil was all that was there.

"Roxanne! Come on, babe. Snap the fuck out of it! Don't go mental on me now."

Roxanne snapped her head up and stared into Gabriel's pleading eyes. It wasn't until that moment that she realized that she had been staring into her hands at her demonic necklace ever since the world of darkness had been opened to the Chosen. She shook her head in embarrassment at her weakness.

Smiling, she responded to her friend, "I'm okay. Now, let's get to work."

The stunningly calm Commander grinned back, "Right. Let's rock and roll."

With that, they were immediately in action. Gabriel went straight for the General, and Roxie went straight for her men. Without ever speaking, the two Chosen knew exactly what had to be done.

The red-headed hero was easy to find. As always, he stood like a rock in a sea of chaos, head held high, and gruff voice barking orders to all those around him. No matter how many people there were, no matter how much confusion, he never missed a detail. He was a man firmly in control. As he approached with his message, Gabe feared that this might be the one time General Sabastian would end-up proving that he is, in fact, human.

Taking a deep breath, Commander Gabriel dropped the bomb on his friend. "General, Snake has reported in. The good news is, the army is still coming straight for us."

The General didn't like the sound of things, "If that's the good news, I'm not sure I want to hear the bad."

"The bad news is all of them are coming."

"How many is that?"

"All of them. A sea of thousands. Boss, we are severely screwed."

Looking at his friend's face, Sabastian found the traces of fear and knew he was telling the truth. He turned to look at the Lords. They stood motionless, glowing like a small beacon of hope in the increasingly dark world. *They have to get us in there.* Once again, as soon as the thought entered his head, he wished it hadn't. There weren't enough men for the task he was about to assign, but he had to.

"Commander, I need a line of well trained soldiers protecting the Lords, now. They must not be touched, or the spell will fail. Go."

Without an argument, or a question, the Commander was gone. As desperate as the situation had become, he felt a strange sense of hope in the General's calmness. Even now, he was solid as a rock. *Now we know why he's the boss.* With that very itsy, bitsy amount of hope in his seemingly cold heart, the Commander began to round up troops to protect the Lords at all cost.

The General didn't bother following the Commander's movements; he knew the job would be done. The Commander only ever disobeyed him when it was only his own life at stake.

Instead, he turned his attention in search of Roxanne. He didn't have to look far. The powerful beauty was walking towards him, tucking her long, auburn hair up under her helmet. For a brief second, the General let pleasant emotions course through his body. *She could touch the heart of the Betrayer with those looks.* But, he senses soon returned. *That is if the devil had a heart.*

"Reporting as ordered, General," smiled Roxie.

General Sabastian couldn't help but grin, "I should summon all my people mentally."

"Just a little anticipation to aid preparation."

That was enough pleasantness for the man of stone. "Get your men and get them to the front of the barricades. They will be the first line of hand to hand defense. The archers will be in the trees to both sides of you, so watch the arrows from above."

"Gotcha."

Then she, too, was gone. Her men close behind her. Guilt and panic made an attempt to seize the stoic man's heart; he fought them back. *One thousand and one... that's all this is. You've one it a thousand times before.*

The thought had barely left his head, when the alarms went up. He looked out at the sea of black approaching, and his heart began to pound. *Good God.* He may have done it a thousand times, but never like this. He glanced around him as his men set themselves for battle. Fear and determination mixed in their eyes. He removed the fear from his and stepped forward to join the ranks just behind Roxanne's men. Shooting one final glance over his shoulder to make sure the guard was in place around the Lords, he yelled "FIRE!", and started the war.

On command, the archers released their arrows in perfect unison. Screams went up from the enemy throng, as several ghoulish creatures hit the ground, only to be trampled over by the hundreds more behind them. It didn't even slow them down; in fact, it seemed to enrage them. They rushed forward now with greater momentum.

"FIRE!" rang out again. And, again, the archers responded with skill. And, again, more creatures fell, only to be beat into the ground by those coming behind them. This quickly became a frightening pattern, that the General saw as hopeless. So, he made a snap decision that he prayed would do some good. Looking down, he saw the panicked face he had so often taken for granted.

"Malcolm! Get all the pages, animals, and any non-combatants to the edge of the forest, right beside the Lords, now!"

The young man hesitated for a mere split second, held back by his training that told him to stand, always, beside the General. However, an order is an order, and it would be unwise to disobey. In a matter of seconds, Malcolm was gone and all the other pages were close behind him. General Sabastian turned all his attention back to the battle at hand. *If we don't all make it, maybe there is hope for the young...*

Roxanne held her ground, even though all of her senses told her to turn tail and run. The mass of black that was the enemy surged forward toward them, promising to over-take and over-whelm them. Time was almost up. She stole a glance toward the forest; the Lords remained motionless, stuck in a glowing green limbo. *So much for that idea.* A line of troops had taken watch over the Lords, with Gabe at one end and Elway at the other. That was enough of that. She moved all of her attention forward.

The first wave of the enemy was upon them. The archers were still firing as fast as they could load their bows, but they could not slow the demons down. Roxanne brought her sword up to bear, and all of her men followed suit. Remaining as calm as possible, she stood firm and kept all of her men beside her. The ugly horde was only a few feet away. She could smell their breath. Still, she waited. She could sense the anticipation from her men. Still, she waited. Only inches remained...

The Last of the Chosen reared her head back and yelled with all her might, "ATTACK!"

On that one word, eleven of the bravest and best soldiers in the Land jumped over the barricades and into the horrific fury of war. As she leapt, a calming voice entered Roxie's head, *May the force be with you, always.* She didn't bother responding to Gabe, she didn't need to. Besides, she was surrounded by a few thousand smelly monsters, and kinda busy.

The first onslaught swarmed over and all around her. This

was not even close to a one on one. She needed some fighting room, now. Pulling one of her long knives from it's sheath, she stood, sword and knife in hand, and extended both arms. *God, I hope this works.* Then, she pulled a Wonder Woman. As fast as she could, she spun in circles, slicing through everything she came into contact with.

Within seconds, the brazen beauty's arms began to burn. With each cut, she thought her arms would be ripped out of the sockets. The thick skins and armor of the creatures she was fighting seemed almost too much for her weapons, but she kept turning. Fortunately, these disgusting demons weren't very bright, so they just kept charging instead of stopping to fight. Limbs, heads, and chunks of flesh cluttered the ground all around her. The strain was beginning to overcome her strength. Sweat poured down her face and into her eyes, threatening to blind her. That was all she wrote; Roxie couldn't take it any more.

As skillfully as the woman that had trained her, the newly formed war veteran sheathed her long knife, wiped her face, grasped her sword with both hands, and came to a stop. Dropping into a crouch, she prepared to do battle with the rest of the army. And, she wasn't disappointed.

The first three trolls that bore down on her were easily dispatched. Roxie merely dropped, sliced through all of their exposed stomachs, then she let the archers finish off the stumbling corpses. All too quickly, however, she was engulfed in bloody battle. She tried to see what the rest of her men were facing, but her view was blocked by charging bodies and she couldn't afford the time to stop and look. All she had time for was block, thrust, and slice.

A sharp pain in her thigh sent Roxanne spinning around to counter yet another attack. All she could see were enemy soldiers. She began to feel isolated, out-numbered, and just plain scared. Then, just when her sanity was about to give away, she reached out mentally.

Gabe! What the hell is happening? I can't see a thing.

The Commander's voice came through like an oasis in the desert.

Keep doing whatever it is you are doing. You're men have contained the first wave.

As she stuck a knife in the groin of whatever ghoul stood infront of her and looked around, she found that impossible to believe.

Contained? We have been consumed.

Wrong. When you pulled that Wonder Woman thing, the rest of your team followed suit. It was like a defensive line of blenders. Behind you.

Roxie spun, sliced, and returned to those troops infront of her.

Thanks. But we can't keep going like this. There's eleven of us and about ten billion of them.

The sound of bodies hitting the ground behind her sent Roxanne spinning again. Three trolls lay dead at her feet, each with a familiar knife protruding from their backs.

Make that twelve.

She couldn't see Snake, but she didn't need to. Snake had a way of making her presence felt.

Okay. Twelve. Thanks.

Snake silently accepted her soul-mate's thanks. The sneaky assassin didn't have the time to chat. She was temple deep in ugliness. *What else is new?* She had managed to make it most of the way back to the Silver Forest without being spotted. However, it wasn't long before the only thing left to hide behind was an enemy soldier. When she saw this, and tapped into the conversation between Gabe and Roxie, she knew it was time to act. Now, she was committed.

Diving under the legs of the nearest troll, she made her way forward. Instinctively she rolled onto her back and stuck her sword through the creature above her. As he came crashing down, she rolled to the side and continued forward. She knew that was where she had to be. That's where the enemy was headed and that's where help was needed. So, on she fought.

Gabe let out a small sigh at the sound of Snake's voice. For a second he thought about calling out to her, but then decided against it. The last thing she needed was any distraction; she was so buried in the devastating sea of monsters that he couldn't even see her. What she really needed was some help. The lover in him wanted to run to her rescue, but the Commander in him knew better. *If she needs help, there's nothing I can do.* He looked over his shoulder at the glowing Lords behind him. Everything depended on them; he couldn't move.

General Sabastian held his ground and watched the battle before him. Arrows flew, swords flashed, and bodies fell. So far, none of the bodies were theirs, but that would change. This he knew, and hated. It was all he could do to stand back and wait. But, tactically, nothing else made sense. They were too small to rush the enemy horde, and they were trapped. They needed to conserve as many of their resources as possible. So, until the fierce army of evil broke through the first line, all the General could do was wait. He knew he wouldn't have to wait long. Quickly, he glanced back at the Lords and prayed.

Roxie was beginning to tire, but they just kept coming; an endless stream of smelly, ugly, evil demons. *At least all they're really doing is marching. It's not like they're fighting very hard...* She let that thought trail off into a grand sense of realization. Immediately she reached out to the Commander.

We have a problem, boss.

That's obvious.

I mean another one.

That's just what we need.

These guys are headed straight for the Lords; they aren't even stopping for prisoners.

The Commander stared even more intently at the battlefield and realized she was right. Although swords were flashing, they were only the swords that belonged to Roxie's team. The fight looked more like chopping through a jungle than an actual battle. And, the ghouls kept coming.

Okay, here's the plan. I'll have the General send forward some reinforcements...

No good. We can't hold them at this position. They will eventually overrun us.

Then fall back behind the General. Reinforce his men and run a block as long as you can. But get the hell out of Dodge before you are swallowed up.

Right. I'll get my men to fall back in unison if you find a way to let the General in on things.

Suddenly, where there once had been only trolls, Snake appeared. She was covered in blood and sweating; a rare condition for the ice-lady. But, she was still in control.

I've got the General.

With that, she was gone again, and both Roxie and the Commander knew the situation was handled. So, Roxie reached down into her diaphragm and commanded her team.

"On my command, move!"

Every last member of the tightly formed unit responded with a resounding "Gotcha!"

At least they're all alive.

Still hacking away, the tired defender waited for a signal from her mentor. She didn't wait long. For, as soon as Snake reached the General with the news, he ordered the pull-back and protection. Looking over the battlefield, he cursed himself for not having seen it sooner.

After only seconds, that seemed to last an eternity, Snake's voice entered Roxanne's head.

Jump on it!

Coming back at ya!

"Move!"

That one word sent a rumble through the battlefield. The eleven soldiers jumped back. At top speed, they turned and dodged their way back to the barricades. In only a matter of seconds, the amazing fighting force was standing behind the rest of the army, breathless and tired. Unfortunately, they weren't going to have any time to rest. Roxie took a deep breath, stretched her arms, and joined the General and Snake back at the front lines. Her heart swelled with pride when the rest of her team moved their way back to the front as well. *They're crazy.*

Looks like they learned everything from you.

She ignored the Commander, because there was fighting to do.

The General stood majestically in the center of hell, barking orders and hacking apart ghouls of every shape and description. As always, he appeared calm and completely in control.

Roxanne slid in next to him and picked up where she had left off.

"Archers, fire on the rear troops. I don't want to see their ugly faces near me! Jordan, Bonam, and Verish, gather any arrows you can and resupply the archers! Now!"

The red-headed giant never missed a slice or a thrust as he directed his army, or what was left of it. Snake admired his strength. He controlled all that was going on around him with a cool hand, never letting any advantage go the enemy, and never accepting defeat. *I wonder if he is human?*

People often ask the same of you. The Commander took care not to broadcast that thought to the ferocious fighter. Instead, he held it inside along with all of his other feelings for her, and concentrated on the battle. He ached to join his comrades. He felt so useless merely standing and watching. He felt like a newscaster covering a train wreck, but he had to remain in position. For the millionth time, he looked back at the Lords and attempted to will them into being finished. Nothing.

The Major's voice pulled him back to reality. "You can't force the spell to work, boss."

"Bet me. Besides, I've got to do something. I can't just stand here."

The seemingly calm Major shook his head, "I never thought I'd get to say this to you but... You can and you will."

The Commander pulled back in mock shock, then nodded. The Major was right. No matter how hard it was to watch what was happening, he could not leave his post. The Lords needed protection more than the soldiers who were trained in the art of battle. So, with a heavy heart, he returned to his watching and waiting.

Even after throwing duty in the face of his Commander and friend, it was all the Major could do to return to his post. He knew he belonged in battle. He belonged right beside Roxie; leading the attack, and, yes, watching her back. It seemed, no matter how hard he tried, he couldn't shake the feeling of doom that had come over him in the wee hours of the morning. Watching his friends in battle, he had a sense that the worst was yet to come. And it was.

So far, the courageous troops had managed to contain the

enemy. Not even a single troll had crossed the barricades. But, the troops were tiring and the onslaught was never-ending. They couldn't hold out forever, and the Lords hadn't budged. Then, the tide turned, and a horrible situation became a real-life terror. The marching marauders, as if on some unheard cue, pulled out their weapons and started to actually fight.

At the first glimmer of steel, Snake shouted out a warning to the small army of defenders. "Weapons! They've got 'em!"

Suddenly, the General and his men found themselves face to face with more than just bodies. Swords and battle axes came at them in a wild fury. However, thanks, again, to warning from Snake, they weren't totally unprepared. They were, however, panicked. Now they were forced into a battle of epic proportion.

It was a mere matter of seconds before the grotesque army managed to break through the barricades. There was just not enough defenders to enter into hand to hand combat with all the creatures surging forward. They found themselves being run into the ground by the opposing force. And, now, some of the men began to fall. The General knew a move had to be made.

As he cut through the torso of the nearest troll, he barked out a fall-back. "Everyone fall-back to a defensive position directly infront of the Lords, now!"

Like the well-trained soldiers they were, the small army began a perfect and orderly retreat. Each line fell in behind those behind them until they had backed up to the point just infront of the defensive line already held by the Commander and the Major. Once in place, they secured themselves for the battle.

Commander Gabriel had watched anxiously as the battle progressed into a war. As soon as weapons appeared on the other side, he knew he wouldn't have to join the battle because it would soon be on its way to him. Now, with the entire army standing directly before him, he knew how right he'd been. His heart began to race, but he controlled it. With all the cool confidence of a trained leader, he stepped forward to take control of his men. *Time to earn my pay.*

Meanwhile, back on the other side of the battlefield, the General grabbed Snake and Roxie for an important task.

"We need to get those archers out of those trees and back to the forest where they stand a chance. And, we need to get them before they are completely cut off."

Roxie glanced up at the trees. "It's gonna be tough. They are on two different sides of this battle. We can't cover them both at the same time."

The General didn't hesitate. "Snake, can you get to the archers on the left and tell them to cover for the archers on the right?"

"No problem." Then she was gone in the crowd.

General Sabastian turned to Roxanne, "Now, we have to clear some space at the bottom of those trees so the archers can come down, safely."

Roxanne nodded, both to the General, and to her team. On her cue, they started across the battlefield and to her side.

"Alright, we are going to get the archers out of danger. We need a space at the bottom of the trees, now."

That was the only order the men needed. Without the slightest hesitation, they chopped their way to the base of the trees. Within seconds, the ground below the trees stood clear. Roxanne and her men formed a half circle around the base of the trees and entered into mortal combat with any trolls that came near them. Looking out into the sea of creatures, however, she realized that this was not going to work for long. They were quickly being overrun and cut-off from the rest of the troops.

"General!"

The General, who was standing directly beneath the trees to assist with the evacuation, turned to face Roxie. What he saw stunned him. She was covered in blood and sweat, a huge gash ran all the way down the side of her thigh, she had long ago lost her helmet, and she was fighting with both her sword and her knives. To him, she was the perfect picture of a hero. *God, please, don't make her a martyr.*

"What's on your mind, lady?"

"We have got to move this show. We are going to be cut-off, like yesterday."

One glance around him, told the General she was right. There wasn't much time left, and they still had to reach the other archers. Immediately, his mind raced for options. There had to be a way out of this with his people intact. His brain began to pound against the side of his skull. It seemed that they were going to have to sacrifice one group to save the other. *I do not accept the options!* He had to find a way out.

****

Slicing through what must have been the thousandth troll he'd fought, the Commander attempted to find his missing friends in the crowd. But, Roxie's team, the General, and Snake were nowhere to be seen. This was not a good thing. As the battle intensified, so did his need to know where the other leaders were, and not just on a personal level. If the opportunity did present itself for escape, he was going to need all the assistance in leading this army that he could get. He knew what he had to do.

Stepping back, he called out to Major Elway, "Major! Take command."

Although he was torn between duties, the Major immediately assumed command. Whatever the Commander had on his mind had to be important. Still...

"Keagan! Take-up guard for the High Lord. No one gets past you, understood?"

"Yes, sir!" replied the dutiful warrior as he moved into his spot.

Standing beside the Lords, Gabriel reached out to Snake and Roxie.

Okay, ladies. Someone want to let me know what's going on?

Snake's voice entered his head. *It seems little miss Roxie has managed to get herself stuck.*

Bite me.

Now, now, Roxanne, that's no way to talk to your superior.

I know. But, I was only talking to Snake.

Instead of carrying this charming conversation to its disastrous end, Snake decided to move to more important issues.

You guys aren't going to be able to get over here before we all get isolated.

Looks like. Have any suggestions?

Now Gabe was confused. *Will someone please tell me what's going on?!*

Look, we are trying to get the archers to safety, but we are running out of time. Roxie and the General are pulling the first set down, while I cover them from this side.

The truth of the matter is, we need a new way to get Snake and the other archers out of trouble, 'cause we can't protect both.

Instead of panicking, the cool Commander turned to assess the situation. His eyes rapidly scanned the treeline for answers. He looked up and down the trees, from the point where the archers were stationed all the way back to the line of battle. *All the way back...* Suddenly, the tactically simple, but mortally dangerous answer jumped into his head.

Snake, how talented are you?

Better than most.

That's what I thought. What are the odds of you getting those archers to the battle line via the treetops?

There was a moment of mental silence. Then, Snake's response.

It's doable. But, Commander, you had better be there to bring us down. None of these guys has a sword.

Not a problem.

Roxanne's voice jumped in. *Okay. The General and I will bring these guys in, and wait for you. Oh, and, Snake?*

Yes?

Don't die or anything.

Yeah, well, don't knock any stones loose.

And, both of you get your beautiful butts back here, 'cause I'm tired of carrying you.

Snake considered responding to that, but quickly decided against it. There just wasn't time for it. Instead, she turned to take on her dangerous task.

"Listen up guys. We are getting the hell out of here, now."

Sean, the head archer, looked to the other side of the battlefield where he could still see the General and the other men.

"And, just how are we suppose to do that? The support team

is on the other side of the world."

Because she needed everyone's full cooperation, and because she wanted everyone calm, Snake let that one slide. Actually, she stored it in memory to be dealt with at a more opportune time. However, being the loving person she was, she couldn't let it completely pass.

Smiling an evil smile, she said, "We're gonna fly."

Panic crossed Sean's face, "Excuse me?"

"Calm down. We are going to travel across the tops of the trees."

"That sounds a whole lot better," came the sarcastic reply.

Snake was reaching the point with this guy, but she maintained. "It's either that, or you can slide down the tree and try walking through the enemy below."

Sean had no response for that. So, Snake started across with the reluctant archers close behind.

****

When the mental pow-wow ended, Roxie wasted no time in moving out of the battle line and back to the General.

"Hey, boss!"

For a split second, General Sabastian thought he'd turn around to see Commander Gabriel standing there when he heard the word "boss". Of course, it was Roxanne facing him.

"What have you got for me this time?"

"Well, I just talked to Snake and Commander Gabriel..."

Confusion danced in his eyes for a moment. "How?"

"It's just a little trick we learned. Anyway, they've got the other archers covered. All we have to do is take care of our end of things."

The General stared into the messenger's eyes, as a feeling of relief and confusion covered him.

"Not that I'm questioning you, but, how are they getting them out of the trees?"

Roxie shrugged, "They're not."

General Sabastian never asked another question. He merely looked up into the trees, followed the same line that the

Commander had, and accepted the options.

"Okay. Let's move out."

As she lead the small band away from the trees, Roxie let a single thought enter her too often distracted mind, *They don't call him a military genius for nothing.*

****

Deep in the musty caverns, a dark shadow moved back and forth, methodically. His red eyes searching the room around him for answers to unvoiced questions. At his side, the knarled form of Mongrel stared intently into the large, stone cauldron.

"Have the Lords stopped glowing?"

Mongrel waved his hand frantically across the waters until he focused on the Lords. He cringed.

"No."

His master's voice responded calmly, "Have the troops broken their defense line?"

Once again, the terrified little man searched the waters. This time he was more confident.

"Yes."

"Is she still alive?"

"Yes."

"Good," was the final reply. The Lord of Darkness knew that the Lords had only one hope, and that was to enter the Silver Forest; as long as they were glowing, the fairies had not answered them. He grinned with the knowledge of the spell once used by the Lords; the spell that defeated his troops, but would keep them out of the forest.

Turning to leave, he simply stated, "Bring her to me when she arrives."

"Yes, Master."

****

Roxanne pulled a knife from the horrid body that lay at her feet and threw it back into the fray. She followed it only long enough to see it land in the torso of an enemy body; no time to pat herself on the back, there was fighting to be done. Hefting her sword with both hands, her arms were on fire with the pain of exertion, she started hacking off pieces of trolls as fast as she could. Beside her, the General was making a tossed salad out of enemy parts with his battle ax. Briefly, they made eye contact. And, for a split second, they gained strength.

Down the battlefield, Snake dodged in and out of enemy soldiers; removing knives from the dead ones and strategically placing them in the live ones. Karlis and a few other members of the strike team attempted to keep her covered as she ran her self-imposed suicide mission. They were the farthest from the Lords, and in the most danger. But, they kept on fighting.

Snake stabbed ghoul after grotesque ghoul, until she was covered in blood. Every inch of her body was soaked in it. *I wonder how much of it's hers?* That thought had crossed Karlis' mind hundreds of times as he watched her run through the enemy bodies as if they were trees. She moved with lightening fast reflexes, and never hesitated. As he stared at her, Karlis caught a glimpse of her eyes. What he saw nearly knocked him over. They were solid blue and soulless. *Now you're seeing things.* However, as he carried on the battle, he wasn't so sure.

****

Once again, the Commander found himself separated from the rest of the command crew. *Alone again.* He had returned to his post infront of the Lords, with the archers now stationed behind him. They were the final line of defense. If the enemy horde managed to get through the troops, they were all that was left. The Commander knew he couldn't let it get to that point. So, he fought on.

The battle had intensified around the group protecting the Lords, especially near Major Elway. There was no doubt that the trolls were trying to get to the High Lord and break the spell. His safety had become paramount. Commander Gabriel glanced down at his best man, hoping he would be able to hold.

Using all of his strength, Major Elway sliced through the neck of the nearest troll and shoved the body into the others that were close behind. He managed to knock a few down, but they'd get up with an attitude, and he knew it. Stepping forward, he pulled a knife from the nearest corpse and put it to good use in the throat of another assailant. But, ten more replaced that one. *This is getting ridiculous.*

He strength was beginning to wan. Mentally, he began begging the Lords to hurry. In the pit of his stomach, he knew his time was running out.

Then, Snake was infront of him. He shook his head to clear it, but it really was her; drenched in blood, but her. She had a sword in one hand and a couple of knives in the other.

"The Commander thought you could use some help."

Although his pride and sense of foul-play called for a sarcastic response to that, the Major kept quiet. With a simple nod, he silently accepted the much needed assistance. Besides, Snake could throw and resupply herself with knives in seconds flat. Which meant, she could take care of three soldiers to his one. Things seemed to be looking up, now.

But, as is with most battles, the tide would change yet again. Without warning, the enemy troops just stopped. They quit fighting and moved into a full retreat. The Major, suddenly, found himself fighting great amounts of air where there had once been mountains of monsters. He whirled around to face the only person left, Snake.

"What the hell is going on here?"

Snake shook her head, "I don't know, but I don't like it."

The Major joined in the head shaking, "I hate it. Why would you retreat when you're winning?"

That was the real problem. The Betrayer's forces had backed them into a corner and beat the hell out of them. There was no reason for the move they just made. The High Lord of darkness had to have something up his sleeve. Just what it was, was something they had to figure out, now.

Wiping the blood from her eyes, Snake turned to Elway, "Stay here. I'm going to find out what's next."

Before he could utter another syllable, she was gone. *God, that's unnerving.*

Snake went straight for the other Chosen, all the while

keeping an eye on the disappearing bad guys. She reached the General about the same time as the Commander.

"Come here often?"

Even now, he had to make jokes.

"Only when you're not around."

But, then again, so did she.

"Hey, children. Might I remind you that we are in the middle of a life and death situation?"

"You might," came the unisoned response to the General's question.

Breathing deeply and taking every advantage of this brief break from fighting, Roxanne intervened on the General's behalf. "Look, Han and Leia, as much as we all enjoy this mindless bantering of yours, I think it's best if we skip the lover's quarrel and get back to the situation at hand."

"Oh, check out the big brains on Roxie."

She smiled at the Commander, "Ya know ya love me."

"If the three of you are quite through, I'd like to say something."

Biting their tongues, and swallowing their smart-ass remarks, the three soldiers snapped to attention.

General Sabastian took a deep breath. These guys were going to be the death of him. *Or, maybe it's the other way around.* Despite their ability to be flippant, the all looked like they'd gone through hell. Roxanne and Snake were drenched in blood; the Commander was a mixture of blood, sweat, and dirt; and Roxanne had a huge gash down her thigh. *That one's gonna leave a mark.* Yet, here they stood, strong and ready to fight. And, even though he didn't want to, as their leader, he moved on.

"The main question here is , what the hell is going on? You don't retreat when you're winning. They must be planning something." By the looks on their tired faces, the General knew they were already contemplating that. "Thing is, we probably don't have the time, and we sure as hell don't have the resources to find out what that is."

The Commander piped in, "So, how are we going to prepare for what's coming next?"

Roxanne spoke up, in a voice that was somehow less sure of

itself than usual, "Well, they know we aren't going anywhere. They know that we will fight 'till the last man is standing. And, we know that they want to get to the Lords before the Lords get into the forest."

Snake let it slowly sink in, "So, what you're saying is, they are regrouping for a mass, quick attack on the Lords."

General Sabastian glanced toward the green glow and those that stood before it. Then, he focused on the dark line in the distance. What he saw stopped his heart.

"Dear God, archers."

Instantly, they sprang into action. The Commander and Snake headed for the Lords at a dead run; the General ordered the rest of what was left of the army to grab all shields and beat a path to the Lords; and, Roxanne cursed herself for being right as she ran to the aid of her friends. *This deal is getting worse by the minute.* And, it was about to increase ten-fold.

The Major had been watching intently as the others pow-wowed about the strange situation. He knew they were in for some trouble, but, it wasn't until he saw Snake and the Commander running towards him that he began to panic. At the rate they were moving, he knew he didn't have much time. He also knew where the problem had to be coming from. One look at the enemy horde, sent him into the same panic mode as those heading towards him.

But, all of them had reacted just a little too late. The archers had already taken aim, and, by the time the Major could get into motion, the arrows were in the air. With his shield lost somewhere on the battlefield, there was only one thing he could do...

All the world became a blur for Roxanne as she watched the scene unfolding infront of her. Arrows flew through the air, on the Commander's order, shields went up infront of the Lords, the Lords ceased to glow, and Elway threw himself, body and soul, infront of High Lord Brennen.

"Nooooo!" came screaming out of Roxanne's throat, as she tried to dive between Elway and the arrows with her shield high in the air. But, she was too late.

When she hit the ground, the Major was already lying there

with arrows protruding from his chest and legs. Blood oozed from his body and mixed with the dirt to form a hideous brown muck. Looking at his dead form, Roxanne filled with a rage she had never felt before. It was a fury that started in the pit of her soul, then burst outward in a furious fire of vengeance. Consumed with her new hatred, she leapt to her feet and charged the far-off enemy line, waving her sword frantically above her head.

Before she had covered even a fraction of the distance, she came to a dead stop and hit the ground. It was almost as if she had hit a brick wall. Standing on wobbly legs, she turned toward the Lords. High Lord Brennen stood over the Major's body, eyes closed, and arms out-stretched to Roxanne. Snake stood beside him with actual pain in her eyes. *I'm sorry. We just didn't know how else to bring you back. Gabe and I just couldn't reach you.*

Torn between anger and confusion, Roxanne glanced over her shoulder at the now advancing enemy. They were moving at a full run. It became rapidly apparent that she had been heading toward certain death. Shaking her head, Roxie ran at a full retreat to join her comrades. *You can stop feeling guilty, now, Snake. You just saved my life.*

Snake shook her head, and thought to herself, *Yeah, but at what cost?* But, there was no time for remorse now. There were people to protect. *Besides, remorse goes against my cynical nature.*

"Yo! Snake. Would you please help me here."

Snake snapped into focus. *Fuck. How could I be so stupid.* She had been thinking too hard instead of paying attention to her environment. In her line of work, that was a deadly mistake. "Sure, Roxie."

Sheathing her sword, Snake bent down and grabbed ahold of Major Elway's legs, while Roxanne cradled his head and torso against her chest. Snake could see pain pulsating in her friend's eyes as she held her dead lover. It couldn't be easy to loose someone who had been so close to you. As if on a secret command, Gabe's face appeared in her tattered mind. She pushed it away. *When did I stop feeling cold?* She could not afford to let her old emotions restore themselves. She had lived on anger and fury for so long, she didn't know any other way. Looking across at her friend, and down at the lifeless form in her arms, she wasn't sure she wanted to.

Carefully and quickly, the two warriors carried the Major right up to the edge of the forest and laid him at the feet of the Lords. Pain and sadness filled the air around them, but there was no time for tears or comfort. The very ground was shaking with the thunderous roar of the charging enemy horde. So, instead of mourning the dead, they prepared to avenge him.

Lord Earin, covered in sweat and exhausted, pulled the Major's sword from his hand and stepped forward to join the line of defenders. He had to; his guilt was the strongest. He knew that Major Elway had died defending the Lords, but that was not the real concern. His true guilt came from the great feelings of jealousy he had had for the relationship between the Major and Roxanne; a relationship he had envied and longed to destroy. But, now, seeing the pain and fury in Roxanne's face, he would have given the land to bring the Major back to life. Instead, he held the sword in honor, and prepared to defend a memory.

Standing in an ice cold state, Commander Gabriel calmly waited for the first troll to cross into the battle zone. There was nothing but a black calm all around him. He had moved through all the stages of pain and rage quickly; not even bothering to experience them all. Instead, he leaped into an emotional state that was like an old friend. It was the same state of darkness that had consumed him when his daughter died. As visions of her dead form mixed with the sight of the Major's lifeless body, a single thought pulsed in Gabriel's mind, *No one survives.*

There they stood, all the defenders of the land. Each held his own private suffering and guilt deep inside. All the world balanced precariously on the edge of oblivion... and then there was nothing.

****

Chapter 11

At first, there was nothing; nothing solid, nothing tangible. Then, slowly, Roxanne's vision began to clear and she could make out the shadows of her friends standing beside her. She tried to lift her arm, but it hung lifeless at her side. She wanted to rub her eyes, clear her head, and shout out at the others, but she could not move. Then she remembered where she had been, and she thought to herself, *Am I dead?*

The last thing she expected was an answer. *No, you have a long life to live.*

Knowing she should expect the unexpected here, but still confused as hell, she called out to the voice in her head. *Where am I?*

The entrance.

Irritation swept through her body as deja-vu hit. *At least, there aren't any green lights this time.*

Are you in need of light?

No, I'm in need of answers.

Then simply ask.

Roxanne struggled to contain all of the smart-ass remarks that tried to rush forward in response. *You said I'm at the entrance. The entrance to what?*

The Silver Forest.

And, you are one of the fairies?

Correct.

Are my friends here as well?

Yes.

All of them?

All that came with you.

Roxanne swallowed hard and bit down on her next question. *Even Major Elway.*

The voice seemed to have a new sadness in it as it answered. *Especially Major Elway. He was a very brave man.*

How long are we going to be stuck in limbo?

You will remain at the entrance until we can determine the purity of your souls.

Great. We could be here awhile.

"On the contrary, Chosen One," the voice left her mind and entered the beautiful creature that now stood before her, "It won't take any time at all."

Roxanne gasped in awe as the realm of the Silver Forest materialized before her. It, and it's inhabitants were unlike anything she had ever seen. The trees glimmered as though they were not quite real, yet they had the appearance of solid silver. Each leaf sparkled with the softness of fresh dew and was totally separate from those around it. A light breeze drifted through the branches, carrying the smell of freshly sprinkled babypowder, and playing a melodic game of tag with the dancing leaves. The grass beneath her feet was a pale purple and felt as soft as a new down pillow. Small, fury creatures scampered along the tree-tops and chased each other around the trunks. An ice-blue lake shimmered in the center of it all; cooling her with its very presence.

But, all that splendor was muffled by the beauty of the fairy who hovered before her. His eyes seemed to engulf the whole of his slender face. The pupils were like two deep, dark pools of black gold surrounded by an ever-changing mixture of blue, silver, and gold paints that slowly flowed in and out of one another. His skin was so pale white that it bordered on transparent. Long locks of turquoise hair with purple high-lights were draped gently across his shoulders. And, his dainty figure stayed ever so slightly above the ground. Wrapped in a silky white robe, he was angelic. Roxanne stood in awe.

A smile played across his smooth face. "You will find that we are not that different, Chosen One."

Not this, again. Roxie snapped back into the here and now. "You can, and should, call me Roxanne."

"Ah, that is right. Lord Earin mentioned that you are uncomfortable with titles."

She smiled, "Let's just say it's not me." *It's not even a relative of mine.*

"There is much we have to learn about you, Roxanne. But,

218

that will come in time. For the time being, you require rest and food. If you follow me, I will take you to both."

Looking around at her peaceful surroundings, Roxanne found herself overwhelmed with questions.

"Whoa. Slow down. First things first. Not that I don't want or appreciate your help, but there are a few things I need to get straight. First, who are you?"

A flash of thought crossed his eyes, "I am known as Perigyn."

"Nice to meet you. Second, where are my friends?"

"At the entrance."

Now, she was confused. As she stood there, all alone, the beauty of the world began to fade. She was nothing without those she had learned to love and defend. These were people she had laughed with, fought with, and killed for. She wasn't about to take another step without them.

"I'm only going to ask once, and I truly hope there is a very good reason for that, or I may just have to decline your invitation, why are my friends still there?"

Instead of the scorn or fear she had anticipated, Perigyn's face filled with something that resembled pride. *That's another one for their side, 'cause I'm really confused here.*

"There is no need for confusion. You have just shown, again, the purity of your soul, and the reason that you were the first through the entrance. The other's will be along as their souls allow; you had the least hidden in the depths of your soul."

Roxie smiled, "And I thought I was sooo deep."

When, for the first time since they'd met, confusion crossed Perigyn's face, Roxanne felt relief. *And, all is right with the world.*

"Now, would you care to follow me to food and rest?"

Roxanne hesitated, wishfully eyeing the shimmering lake. "Actually, would you mind if I cleaned myself up first?"

Perigyn followed her longing gaze. "Yes, of course. Swim freely in the lake. The sediment at the bottom will cleanse you well. But, please be careful not to hurt any of the life within the lake. All life in the Forest is sacred and holds meaning."

Well, no duh. "I never doubted that for a second."

Motioning toward the water, Perigyn floated off on his own mission. Roxie watched him go; wonder and fascination still fresh on her face. Somehow, she had the sneaky suspicion that he could answer all of those questions that had plagued her for so long. She tore her gaze from him and looked at the welcoming lake. But, now was not the time.

Instead, Roxie dragged her tired body to the edge of the cool waters, stripped off her tattered clothing, and dove in. Total elation touched her every sense as the layers of blood, sweat, and dirt came peeling off her aching body. Like a jubilant child, she dove under the mildly warm waters again and again, running her fingers through her hair in an effort to get it clean. *Thank the maker; this oil bath is going to feel so good.* She smiled. *When in doubt, amuse yourself.*

After a few minutes of pointless frolicking, Roxie decided to put the sediment to use. She found a place to stand, grabbed a handful of the mud-like stuff, and gingerly rubbed it in her hands. Instantly, the ground-in dirt disappeared. *Cool.* She rubbed vigorously, now. Then, she shoved her hands into the water to rinse them. They came out sparkling clean and cut-free. *Now, **that** is amazing.* She overcame her amazement and thrust both hands into the precious mud, smearing it all over her body. Miraculously, bruises, cuts, and scraps vanished. And, for the first time in months, Roxanne felt refreshed.

Invigorated, she swam to the edge and climbed out. The fairies had replaced her war-torn clothes with some fresh, silk garments. They were light and delicate, and made her feel beautiful. *Thank God I didn't have to put those blood stained rags back on.* With that one simple thought, Roxie's life came crashing back to reality. She was not a royal guest in a far-off palace; she was a warrior in the middle of a costly war; she was a woman with far too many dead friends to mourn; and, right now, she was all alone. With a heavy sigh, she sheathed her sword and headed after Perigyn. Now was the time for those questions.

****

Snake waited patiently- it was something she was good at, to

220

say the least. She had quickly discovered that movement was impossible, and all her attempts at contacting Gabe and Roxie were futile. In short, she was stuck. She wasn't sure why, but she had an idea of where. She was either dead or in some lovely type of fairy induced limbo. Either way, she knew how to wait. A slight tugging at her mind wakened her senses.

Gabe? Roxie?

The voice that entered her head was foreign. *They are quit safe, as are you.*

Her immediate reaction was distrust. No one belonged in her head without permission.

Oh, but you did let me in.

Snake allowed herself a mental shrug. *Well, you got me there. I take it you are one of the fairies, come to comfort me.*

Yes, I am a fairy... come to welcome you.

I hope this isn't the whole thing. If it is, you've got a lot of explaining to do.

This is the entrance to the Silver Forest.

Oh, great. A waiting room. How long am I going to be motionless?

Until we can determine the purity of your soul.

Snake cringed. *And, just how are you going to do that?* She had a lot to hide; a past that she didn't care to explain or share.

"We already have," came the newly bodied reply.

As soon as she realized that she could move, Snake took a defensive stance, placing her hand on the hilt of her sword. Then, she scanned the area for a possible threat. What she saw, blew her mind. She was confronted with all the beauty of a world she did not think could possibly exist. Confusion clouded her mind as all of the truths she had formed about the world fell apart. There was no evil, anywhere.

In an effort to anchor herself in the new reality, Snake centered all of her attention on the dainty figure before her. She was small, pale, and beautiful. Her bright purple eyes took up most of her tiny face, with pupils that were large and deep enough to swim in. Snake gazed into those eyes; there was a hidden strength in them. She felt her senses returning to their normal level. *Adapt. That's all. It's just different. Adapt.*

Taking a casual stance, she asked, "And, how did you figure me out?"

The gentle person before her suddenly became very sad.

"I'm very sorry; we all are."

Snake's stomach turned. Nothing made her sicker than pity. And, nothing made her madder than invasion of her privacy. *I'm gonna be sick.*

"Look, it's my life and I'm not sorry. I'm not making any excuses for it either. So, just keep your pity to yourself."

The doll-like fairy shook her head of silver hair, "You learned to hate so young, but you have not forgotten how to love."

Pushing Gabe's visage from her mind, Snake leaned forward and whispered, "Don't be so sure."

In response, the little person merely smiled, "I am called Sophiana, Chosen One."

Snake shook her head, "And, I am always called Snake... always."

"I know."

Pulling her bottom lip between her teeth, Snake contemplated this intriguing creature. She was just too nice to exist. In her long, hard life, Snake had learned to trust no one, but that wasn't the case here. She found herself accepting Sophiana at face value without the hairs on the back of her neck standing on end. *Next thing you know, I'll say something nice to a stranger.* She opened her mouth, then closed it. *Not bloody likely.* Instead, she phrased another thought.

"Where is everybody?"

"Ah, your friends. They are all in the main hall, resting and eating. You will be the last to join them."

"Why does that not surprise me?"

"You have a well protected heart, Snake. One that was hard to uncover, and harder to decipher."

"It's like that for a reason."

"So I was made aware. Would you care to follow me to the others?"

Snake glanced at the shimmering lake she had seen earlier, "I'd rather clean-up first."

Sophiana smiled yet another beaming smile, "Head North when you are through, and you will find us waiting."

I'm sure I will. Snake thought with a mental cringe. *You are entirely too happy.*

I know that, too. Came the gentle reply.

****

High Lord Brennen sat back and closed his eyes and smiled. It was the first time in months that he had actually relaxed with his eyes closed, and the first time in days that he had actually closed them. But, here, he was at home. He was sitting in a room he knew and loved, the main dining hall. He had been given the seat at the head of the long, wooden table, which sat in the center of the great hall. He opened his eyes and took in everything around him.

A huge picture window faced him from the far end of the room. It was ablaze with bright colors depicting a scene of union between all the species- something the fairies longed to see. The walls were a sparkling white and stretched a long way up to join with a vaulted ceiling. With all the space on the inside, this room could have been outside. Lord Brennen was well aware of how the fairies hated to be confined.

The table itself sat nearly a hundred people and was covered with an awesome assortment of food and beverage. And, all up and down the table, his friends ate greedily, consuming the much needed nourishment. He smiled- another thing he hadn't done in a long while. There was peace here so far away from the war that was raging in the Land he had vowed to protect. His desire to stay here was greater now than it had been those long, many years ago when he was required to leave. He sat back and remembered those times. They were long ago but stayed forever fresh on his mind. And, for now, he allowed himself the comfort of those memories.

Lord Earin glanced down the table to the High Lord. What he saw brought a smile to his face. The High Lord was calmly sitting with his eyes closed and a smile firmly attached to his face. It had been forever and a day since he had seen that sight.

At least, here, Lord Brennen could forget. The Major's dead form crossed his mental field of vision... But, he could not.

"Trouble, my friend?"

Lord Earin turned to see the sparkling eyes of Lord Ambrose.

"Just remembering, just remembering."

The chubby, little Lord attempted an even larger smile, a hard task for an eternal optimist, "Now is not the time for grieving. Now is the time for rejoicing in those few joys left in our world."

Lord Earin shook his head, "I just can't let go of the Major," He glanced down the table to Roxanne, "He was just so important to us all."

"She doesn't blame you, you know. You are the only one who blames you."

Both Lords turned in shock at the new voice to enter the conversation. Their jaws dropped to see Snake standing there behind them. In her new clothes, with all the blood and muck removed, she was stunning.

Lord Ambrose was the first to recover. "And why on earth would she blame him?"

Snake's ice-blue eyes pierced Lord Earin's soul as she spoke. And, although she addressed Ambrose, she never took her eyes off of Earin.

"Because, Lord Earin has deep feelings for the Chosen One, and she and the Major had an intimate relationship. So, he feels guilty for secretly wanting to come between them. All of which is all rather asinine, since no one is responsible for another's fate, and our lovely Chosen One has a special relationship with all those around her."

Snake had spoken in an even, nearly disinterested tone throughout her whole speech. It was as though the entire situation was more of an annoyance than anything. It was something she said because she had to, not because she wanted to.

"Now, Snake," piped in the cheery voice of Lord Ambrose, "it is natural for people to assume guilt for bad things that occur around them, especially those who are responsible for guidance."

Snake shifted her gaze to the smiling Lord, desperately attempting to rebuild her emotional walls of ice, "Some of us accept the things we cannot change or control."

Lord Ambrose shook his head, "No. Some of us are just better at redirecting our feelings to eliminate guilt. But, anger is not a healthy substitute."

Snake's eyes closed until they were nothing more than blue slits in her face, as she stared at Ambrose. She wanted to burn him into the back of his chair with the force of her anger and pain, but she couldn't. He was not to blame for her life. Instead, she turned her back to them and walked away. However, a single thought forced her to stop.

Without turning, she said, over her shoulder, "But it keeps me alive."

And, then she was gone.

For a moment, the two Lords sat in silent contemplation; each with his own thoughts with which to do battle. Lord Earin felt suddenly and completely exposed. *Am I really that transparent? Can Roxanne see it, too.* He shuddered at the very thought. While he knew he needed her friendship and love, he did not want her sympathy; she had too much to deal with already. No, his pain had to remain his own.

"That's utter nonsense, you know?"

"Wh-what?" came Lord Earin's stuttered response to the voice of his friend.

"We only overcome our feelings of grief and pain if we share them with those we trust. If you hide them, you will make yourself like Snake."

Lord Ambrose was entirely too insightful for his own good. He could read your thoughts and interpret them almost before you knew you had them. Earin smiled a timid smile at his friend and stood.

"Once again, you are absolutely right. Now, if you will excuse me, I must go talk to my dear friend, Roxanne."

Lord Ambrose watched with contentment in his eyes as Lord Earin made his way across the long chamber. All of his years of life experience had given him the ability to take very accurate guesses at the future and to know how people will act in any given situation. He had been well aware of Lord Earin's feelings, long before Snake's input, (he just had a more sensitive way of handling things). He also knew that Roxanne cared more deeply for Earin than she did for most others. Their's was a unique and rare relationship, that he suspected would really bloom with all the pressures of war removed. *Be happy, my friends.*

Roxanne and Commander Gabriel were in the middle of a heated conversation with Perigyn when Lord Earin approached. He held back in an effort not to disturb them.

"All I'm asking is, if you have the power to resist him, why can't you do something to destroy him?"

Perigyn responded to Roxanne without hesitation, "That is not our way. That is totally contrary to our very beings. If we were to behave in a destructive manner, we would find ourselves on an irreversible path to darkness."

Commander Gabriel leaned back nonchalantly in his chair and took a bite out of a piece of fruit. He had a pensive look upon his face. After a brief moment of contemplation, he said, "What about the Lords?"

Perigyn hesitated, but answered honestly, "They are lesser creatures, and, so, they have become defenders."

Now, the Commander leaned forward like a panther ready to strike, "I'm not arguing that they aren't. What I mean is, are they on an irreversible journey into darkness?"

"They must battle constantly to remain as they are: somewhere between complete purity of soul and darkness. They forever walk a tiny path that is covered with obstacles of every kind. Once they alter that path, they are forced to work with constant effort to regain their footing, or they become as the Three Sisters who gave birth to the greatest evil of all time."

Now, Roxanne, her beautiful eyes gleaming, jumped back into the fray, "But, it is possible for them to regain that path and walk that line again?"

"Yes, or we would not have let them into the Forest. Although some of their deeds are dark, their hearts struggle for purity."

"You are referring to our use of black magic, of course."

Roxanne and the Commander both spun in their chairs to see

226

Lord Earin standing behind them.

I didn't even hear him coming.

Me neither, Rox. That's scary.

Remind me not to let my guard down, even in here.

You mean, especially in here. These guys know too much.

Great Gabe. Now you sound like a bad gangster flick.

"That is precisely what I am referring to. The use of the dark magic was a horrible deed done for honorable purposes. That is something that you may be able to bring yourselves back from a single time, but never again. The more you taste the power, the more consuming it becomes."

Roxanne couldn't help herself. *Once you start down the dark path, forever will it dominate your destiny.*

Stop it.

Luke, mind what you have learned.

Stop it.

Save you it can.

I said stop it.

She glanced over at the pleading eyes of the unwary Commander.

Okay, okay. Party pooper.

Lord Earin took a seat next to Roxanne. Her soft scent touched his nostrils like an old friend, and the feel of her presence caressed him like an old lover. He wanted to reach out to her, take her in his arms... He had been a Lord for so long that he had forgotten what true, physical love felt like. Before he drove himself insane, he turned his attention back to the peaceful fairy.

"But, we have returned to the path and vowed to never use the black spells again." There was a pleading in Lord Earin's voice.

Perigyn let out a minute sigh, "That is the beauty of the Lords. You can save yourselves from darkness as long as you remain a strong, unified whole."

Roxanne felt a warm peace settle across her when Lord Earin took his place by her side. It was good to be with her old friend, again. But, she did not consider this the time or place for reminiscing. There were too many other issues she needed to cover.

"But, the question remains, if the Lords can walk that line, why can't you? Afterall, you guys are infinitely more powerful, right?" asked Roxanne.

"That, is the reason we cannot. Our power is that much stronger and that much harder to maintain. We would be too easily swayed by the ease of the dark way. And, in the end, our arrogance would be our downfall. If we went so far as to use destructive rather than creative magic, we might consider ourselves powerful enough to control it; and, so, we would use more and more, all the while believing we were in control. Until, one day, when it is far too late, we realize that we have been consumed by that we tried to control."

"But you control yourselves now."

"Oh no, dear Roxanne, we are consumed by our magic; it just happens to be a delicate kind."

Roxanne frowned, "So, what you are saying is, the most powerful beings of right can do little more than watch while the fate of their very land hangs in the balance."

"By taking the smallest aggressive action, we would alter this land into a place not worth saving."

Roxanne through her hands into the air, "I give. You win."

Gabriel sat quietly, staring intently into nothing. He appeared to be daydreaming, but his mind was on fire with a myriad of questions and answers. He sensed Roxanne's frustration, which mixed with his own to add fuel to an already fuming fire in his soul. A fire that had started the moment his trusted companion had died. He knew they weren't to blame, but he couldn't help but lay some of the responsibility with the fairies. Why had they taken so long to act?

With his arms folded across his chest, Gabriel began to speak ever so gently, "Well, here we all are, now. Safe and cozy. We went through hell to get here, but we still made it... almost all of us. So, now what?"

Perigyn responded with caution in his voice, "Now, you rest."

"No, I mean what happens after this? You helped us out once, but you have made it clear that you can't do anything else.

So, what are we going to do when we leave this place? We can't stay forever, and those ghouls will be waiting for us as we exit."

Perigyn smiled another of those increasingly irritating smiles at the Commander, "You will use the other exit."

"You mean a back door? Correct me if I'm wrong, but isn't this forest a hundred leagues across?"

"That will be of no concern to you or your men."

Roxanne cringed, "I hate to tell you this, but marching a hundred leagues will definately concern my men."

"It is all very simple. There is a portal that allows you to cross from one side of the forest to the other in mere moments, and that is how you will get to the Betrayer before his troops can make their way home."

Lord Earin thought long and hard, back to his brief stay in the Silver Forest as a training Lord. His memories were fuzzy, but became more precise each passing second. In a flash, it returned to him.

"The lake! All we have to do is cross the lake."

Perigyn nodded, "So, you see, it will not be as bad as you had feared. Now, you must rest. We have much to do before you leave."

Then, he simply floated away. There was no good-bye or explanation, just a silent retreat. *Fairies are so odd,* thought Roxie. *But, then again, so am I.* She shrugged her shoulders and turned to Lord Earin.

"What's up, Doc?"

It was so comforting to hear himself called "Doc" again. Sometimes it's the small things that matter.

Earin shot an anxious glance toward the Commander, "Roxanne, there is something I must talk to you about."

Gabe didn't need to be hit over the head on this one; his presense was not wanted. He debated pushing the issue, but decided against it.

"Well, you two kids have fun. There are some things I need to take care of with the General, and I should find out whether or not anyone has seen Snake."

"Snake has arrived. She was speaking with Lord Ambrose and myself earlier."

"You didn't happen to see where she went, did you?"

Lord Earin frowned, "I never do."

The Commander shrugged, "Well, at least she's herself, again."

Gabe, let me know when you come across her.

And, you let me know if Lord Earin fills you in on anything important. Okay?

It's a deal.

Lord Earin was thrilled that the Commander had left without a fight. He could be an impossible man when he wanted to. And, these issues were things he didn't want to share with anyone except Roxanne, and he wasn't even sure he wanted to deal with her. His chest began to pound.

"Okay, Doc. Mind telling me what's got you so jumpy?"

Then, there he was, facing this auburn-haired beauty, and scared to death. There was so much on his mind; so much to tell her. He didn't know where to start. He tried the beginning.

"It is very peaceful here. No battles, no swords, no death." Roxanne opened her mouth, as though to speak, but Earin cut her off. "Yet, even here, even now, I cannot overcome the loss of Major Elway... and the responsibility I feel for his death."

Roxanne felt a sudden sinking in the pit of her stomach. This conversation was about to take a turn she wasn't sure she could handle. While she missed Elway, and was eager for someone to blame, she didn't want it to be Earin. She also wasn't sure she had the strength to comfort him, or to absorb the emotional out-pourings that were on their way. *I get more like Snake each day... That's not necessarily a good thing.*

"We all feel responsible in some way," she responded. "It's a part of who we are."

Lord Earin nodded, "But, I can't help but carry a secret guilt all my own. Snake tells me it is unfounded, but..."

"Wait, wait, wait. You talked to Snake about this, and she listened."

Earin grinned a tiny grin, "Well, it was more like she tolerated me and set me straight."

Roxanne relaxed a little bit, "That's more like it."

"The fact of the matter is, I envied the relationship you had with the Major. I know it's wrong to have those feelings, but I did. I'm a Lord and should be above such things, but it's been so long since I've felt anything beyond guilt, and even longer since I've had any feelings for a woman, and you are so kind and giving, and I need your company to be happy, and my whole world is falling apart, and now I'm babbling."

Now, Roxanne smiled a simple smile, "Yes, you are, but it's okay. Now, allow me to retort. No duh."

Lord Earin promptly issued one of his ever-famous confused looks. Roxanne couldn't help it, she burst out in laughter. After all was said and done, they were right back where they started; a little worn around the edges, but back at the beginning. Even with all the heart-ache around them, they were still just two people fumbling through a relationship.

"Roxanne, I don't understand you."

"You never did."

"True."

"What I mean is this: Of course you were jealous of the Major and myself, you are a man and my friend; it's like a law of nature. And, of course you feel guilty, because you wanted that relationship to end. But, what you aren't aware of is the fact that Major Elway felt threatened by our friendship. He would never say it, but I could feel it. What it all boils down to is you are human. And, we all just want to be loved. You are no more responsible for Elway's death than Sage is."

Despite all of his newly discovered relief, Earin remained serious, "I noticed that you didn't excuse yourself from blame." *You aren't the only perceptive person in these woods.*

Roxanne attempted to shrug off her deep guilt, "Yeah, well, I was born with a guilty conscience."

Earin shook his head, "Not good enough. You are not to blame. You had no control over his actions or the actions of those around him."

"I just keep thinking that I should have done something, anything to prevent this from happening."

"We all did what we could do."

That was the truth, and Roxanne knew it, but, for some reason, she couldn't make it stick in her mind. Where they had been was a terrible place, what they had been through was a horrible thing, but the were not to blame for the death of a friend. Still... the pain was unbearable. She leaned over and took Earin's hand in her own.

"Are we still on for that date?"

"What are..."

"You know, the one where we meet under the tree when all this is over to work out a true friendship?"

Lord Earin could feel the pressure of Roxanne's heartbeat through her palm. He felt his quickening. All he wanted in the whole world was literally in the palm of his hand, but he could not take it... not yet. His conflicting emotions threatened to overpower him. But, with all the restraint of a Lord of the land, he held onto his sanity for just a little longer.

"Of course we are still on," he said as he withdrew his hand in an attempt to calm himself. "Now, let's go check on the others."

Roxanne sighed at her emptiness and anger. For the first time since she had arrived in the land, she couldn't find something to enjoy. There was no light at the end of the tunnel to make her happy. Which was crazy, considering that she was in the center of heaven right now. *Yeah, but how long is this going to be here?* She felt that eternal optimism of her's slipping away into total oblivion. *What is wrong with me?* She knew the answer to that before she ever asked herself. She had known people would die, but she thought this would be like the movies where the "good-guy" leaders never die and the good-guys always win. With Elway gone, she began to question their chances at victory. They were out-numbered, out-positioned, and out-connived. *What we really need is a nasty, sneaky plan.*

"Roxanne? Are you okay?"

Roxie looked into Earin's concerned eyes. "I'm fine, Doc. Let's go see the others."

****

General Sabastian looked intently at the maps he had strewn about the table infront of him. They were no better than his own. Somehow, he had hoped that the fairy maps would contain a

232

magical power to show him some miraculous advantage; he had, of course, been sadly mistaken. *Well, what did you expect Old Man?* His eyes scanned the maps again. *A miracle.*

"Find anything useful, boss?"

The General kept his eyes on the maps as he answered his right hand man, "Not a damn thing. Even if we do come out ahead of this horde, there is no guarantee we will be able to find our way into the caverns, or whether or not there will be more troops waiting, or even that the Betrayer will still be there."

Now he raised his heavy head and looked for answers in the eyes of Commander Gabriel. Gabe shrugged his shoulders.

"We could always send a recon team out beforehand to see what they can find."

"Yeah, but I'm not sure Snake would be so hot on that idea. As a matter of fact, I haven't even seen her around."

For a brief moment, the Commander remembered his entrance experience, and how painful it had been. The fairies were worse than the Lords with their mind probs; they had gotten in. A shiver ran down his spin as he attempted to imagine what it must have been like for Snake, with all of her deep-seeded secrets.

Pushing all of that emotional crap aside, "Oh, she's around, Lord Earin talked to her. She just doesn't want to be. And, you're right; she definately would not be thrilled with that idea."

The giant of a man sighed, "Still, we need to find a way into the Betrayer's lair."

"We could always follow them," said a soft, yet commanding voice.

Both men looked up into the face of Lord Anjalina; oh, how she had changed. Her fire red hair now possessed gentle streaks of grey, the lines around her eyes had deepened, and the gleam of her green eyes was dulled by silver flecks. Despite all the aging, she looked refreshed and hopeful. It was as though she had found a new source of energy to draw from. The General suspected it was the same for all the Lords as they returned to their roots, and the source of their knowledge and power.

While the General pondered the plight of the Lords, the Commander jumped onto Lord Anjalina's idea, "Great. We could find the caverns that way, and maybe even get into them, but we would still find ourselves face to face with thousands of trolls with nasty tempers."

Unlike her normal response, Lord Anjalina remained calm and smiled smugly, "Not necessarily. Consider this: The Betrayer knows where we are right at this moment. He also knows that we have to get out, and once that happens, that we will head straight for him. Now, there are certain things he's going to be forced to do to prepare for this."

As much as he hated to admit it, Gabe saw the logic in what she was saying and where she was going.

"I see. He will have to leave some men behind, move others to cover the perimeter of the forest, and then pull some home to protect himself. Thus, splitting up these thousands into smaller groups we might be able to handle."

Anjalina nodded. "So, if we can beat them to the other side of the forest, we might just be able to tail a smaller group of them home, while avoiding the others."

Now Gabe smiled, "Tactically simple, yet mortally dangerous. Just as all good plans should be."

General Sabastian followed the discussion, all the while reviewing all possible scenarios of that chosen path. Even though there were a thousand and one things that could, and probably would, go wrong. This was the best option to have been presented, yet. It appeared they would have no other choice. With all the skill of a true military genius, the General did the only thing he could, he stole the best idea of the day.

"Okay, Commander, gather the troops so that we can get operations in motion to execute this plan. And, make sure we find Snake for this meeting."

The Commander put on one of his "'aint I just the best thing that's ever happened to you" smiles and nodded, "You got it boss."

As he watched the Commander walk away, General Sabastian felt a new kind of hope. *I guess the fairies are good for something.* Suddenly, another thought caught up with him, he hadn't seen a fairy in hours. He began to wonder where they had all gone, and what they might be up to. It went against everything he was to not have control over all elements around him. *Hell, I don't even know how to find one if I need one.*

Not to worry, dear General, we will find you.

The General shook the uninvited voice from his head. *That's what I'm afraid of.*

There as no response; he hadn't expected one. He had a feeling that his immediate distrust of all things he didn't understand was unfounded here, but he couldn't change years of conditioning. Instead, he shrugged and headed back to the main dining hall to join his friends. *This 'aint over yet.*

****

Hours had passed since the Lords and their troops had disappeared into the Silver Forest, but Mongrel had not moved. He was far too terrified to draw any attention to himself, and his master was still standing directly behind him in deep thought. Mongrel's legs ached, and his body trembled in fear, but he did not move.

When the Forest opened up to swallow all of the others, Mongrel knew his own death was coming. At first he had dropped to the ground in panic. But, the death blow never came. Slowly, he had climbed back to his feet and turned to face his master. His shadowy form hovered just above the ground, red eyes barely visible, and no other movement perceptible. Mongrel knew he had to be thinking of how to kill him, and, so, he waited.

The sudden and unexpected sound of the Betrayer's voice nearly stopped the knarled little man's heart.

"This is most unexpected. But, perhaps it is fortunate for us. Encouraged by the fact that he was still alive, Mongrel braved a single question, "How so, my Master?"

The fiery red eyes of the Betrayer burned into Mongrel's face, "You are still so naive. The Lords have used a portion of my magic; they have each accepted a part of me into their beings. And, now, they have been accepted into the heart of the Land. Corruption is the only option."

Knowing that this simple thought was the only one that

might spare him, and not caring whether or not it was true, Mongrel jumped on it.

"You are, as always, correct my Lord. This is definitely advantageous for us."

Thinking for a few more seconds, the Betrayer issued another command, "Call a small portion of the guard home to us, order a battalion to stand guard where they are, and spread the remainder around the perimeter of the forest. And, Mongrel, if they escape this time, you will pay the price."

Watching his Master disappear into the caverns, Mongrel swallowed hard and turned to his duties. Working with sweat dripping into his eyes, a single thought entered his panicked mind. *Maybe that would be the best thing he could do for me.*

****

Gabe wandered through the forest, admiring the beauty, and scanning the tree branches. He suspected that attempting to contact Snake mentally would have been an exercise in futility, so, he opted for the more direct approach of good old-fashioned recon... which was quickly becoming an exercise in futility. *Well, at least it's peaceful out here.* The silver leaves swayed gently in the warm, spring-like breeze. Small furry things scampered about. Birds sang... *God, I feel like I'm in the middle of a tampon commercial.*

Why must you continually make no sense whatsoever?

Gabe looked up in the direction of the mental intrusion to see Snake sitting on the branch above his head, legs pulled into her chest, and bottom lip pulled between her teeth. Her freshly washed hair shimmered in the sunlight, and her skin shone with a healthy glow. They way she looked right at that moment melted his heart for the last time, and he knew it. It was all over; there was no longer anything he could do. So, he took a deep breath and admitted to himself that he was in love.

Mustering all of his strength, Gabe plastered a cocky grin to his face and responded, "I make perfect sense. You just don't understand it."

Snake sighed in response and dropped to the ground. She

had a feeling her presence was about to be requested. As she came eye to eye with the Commander, she also came face to face with an inner realization; one that scared the hell out of her. With all of her might, she shoved those unfamiliar feelings back into the pit of her stomach. But, with the sun shining on his soft, brown hair, and the depth of his soul-searching eyes it was a nearly impossible task. Panic seized her as she felt herself slipping. At the last moment, her wall resurfaced and she was able to blame her feelings on time and place. *Damn fairy magic.*

With the same false bravado as the Commander, she asked, "So, I guess you've come to get me."

In more ways than one. "Well, it's just that we've still got this whole war thing going on, and we thought it would be helpful to have all of the leaders around for the tactical planning."

Snake folded her arms and lifted an eyebrow, "Whenever you're through..."

All he wanted to do at that moment was grab ahold of her and take her in his arms, but he knew that was impossible. She would never allow that, not now, and, maybe not ever. Although he had no idea what had happened to make her that way, he was certain that Snake was slipping back into her ice-cold self.

"Okay, okay. Would you kindly follow me back to the main hall?"

Snake dropped her arms, "No. But, I'll lead you there."

As he watched her turn to go, Gabe couldn't help but notice the perfect curves of her body, and the tight muscle definition of those curves. This time a real smile crossed his lips. *Now, there goes one woman I don't mind taking orders from.* With a slightly less protected heart, the Commander returned to his duties.

****

High Lord Brennen looked out over the table at all the anxious faces. Once again, he found himself on the brink of leading all of his friends into the face of death. And, once again, he felt overwhelmed with guilt and sorrow. He did not want this; he would have given anything to stop what was about to happen. And, as he looked into their eyes, he cursed himself for failing the first time. *If only I hadn't failed.*

You did not fail.

It was soothing to hear Shylark's voice.

But, he has returned.

Evil is a strong force. It does not die an easy death.

And, if we win, will he be gone for good, or will we have to destroy him again.

Shylark's mental voice was completely firm. *We will destroy him as many times as it takes.*

The resolve in his mentor's voice left no questions in his mind. This was something they had to do, and it was something they would do, now. Taking a deep breath, the High Lord of the Land addressed his friends:

"It has been a long time since we all began this journey together, and it will be longer still until we reach this journey's end. However, as we stand on the brink of our final push forward, we need to take a look around us at those we love, and remember why it must be done. This must be done so that the people in this room will have a chance to live again; this must be done so that all of those innocent people in our land can stay alive; and, it must be done so that those who have died will not have died in vain."

He paused as images of Major Elway passed through his mind. "The fact remains that, if we fail to try, we will be responsible for the deaths of thousands. But, if we make every honest attempt, even if we fail, we will have done all the damage to evil that we can. And, I will fight until I die, if it takes, to destroy the evil that threatens our land. As long as I am alive, the Betrayer will never control more than his deep, dank caverns."

General Sabastian was inspired by the newfound strength of his dear friend. He had been certain that, at one point, the High Lord had given up on life. But, now, he stood like the oak he had always been. The General stood to join him.

"I swear my allegiance to you and the Land, and I vow that, as long as I'm alive, I will never surrender to the forces of evil."

High Lord Brennen smiled at his friend in thanks for his support. This simple act fostered his growing hope in success. For the first time since this war had begun, the High Lord started to believe that he might actually live through it. It was a comforting thought. A sudden warming covered his body.

It is comforting for us all, my Lord.

Thank you, Lord Ambrose. Now, we can begin.

Then, one by one, every member of the war party silently stood, offering his or her support, once again, to this deadly endeavor. All, except Snake. She merely sat back in her seat, arms folded across her chest, and bottom lip pulled between her teeth. However, this could not dampen the High Lord's spirits.

"Thank you all. Now, please be seated as General Sabastian goes over his plan."

As they all took their seats, and the General began, Roxanne took it upon herself to deal with Snake.

Knock, knock.

What?

Way to show no support. What's up with that?

I've never been the kind to support any cause. Now, leave me alone.

What is your problem? You've completely cut yourself off from the rest of the world.

I don't like the rest of the world.

Fair enough, but you are suppose to be my teacher and my friend.

Look, I just have a lot on my mind. There are some things I need to work out right now.

Fairies got to you, too, didn't they?

Anger seized Snake's cold heart. *They entered an area that was off-limits. I'm just trying to put the blocks back.*

Pain and sympathy flowed through Roxanne. She masked those feelings when she responded to Snake. *Look, I'm not even going to ask. All I'm asking is that you try not to disappear. After all, I have a tendency to get lost on my own.*

After a brief pause, Snake's cynical voice entered her head. *'Aint that the truth. Okay, I won't completely disappear. But, I need some time to fix some parts of my life.*

Alrighty then. Just remember who your friends are and that they need you.

There was no response to that; she hadn't expected one.

Snake was using all of her strength to try and come to terms with her past being exposed. She really didn't have the energy to deal with the emotional baggage that comes with friends. Roxanne let it go and turned all of her attention to the discussion at hand.

"With the Betrayer's troops broken apart, we should be able to successfully handle the single group that we follow into his lair."

Roxanne stared into the General's stern face as he finished what he was saying. She couldn't believe what she was hearing. She looked around for Gabe, hoping his reaction would be a sane one. To her dismay, it seemed quite content with this plan.

Okay, tell me what's up.

Tactically simple and mortally dangerous, just as all good plans should be.

Look, Commander, this is just suicidal.

Look, Chosen One, this is the best plan we've got.

It's the only plan we've got.

My point exactly. Now let's get back to business at hand.

Let's...

Roxanne leaned back in her chair, put her feet up, folded her hands behind her head, and started asking questions, "Do we have any way of knowing what movements are being made by the enemy?"

General Sabastian took a deep breath. He had known these questions would come, he just expected the would come from another source.

"No. We can't scout their movements until we leave the forest."

"And, if we come out on top of the enemy?"

"We will send a small recon force out first to check out the situation."

Now, Snake felt obligated to join the discussion, "Gee, and who are we sending for that job?"

Commander Gabriel leapt to the rescue, "Why, the best man for the job, of course. Who, by the way, just happens to be you."

Nice try, but I'm not flattered.

Come on... You're a little flattered.

"And, if I refuse?"

The General frowned, "Then we send a slightly less qualified person."

Snake cringed at the obvious disappointment in the General's voice, "I'll go... but you knew that."

"And what happens if the enemy isn't cooperating? Then what?" asked Roxanne, returning to her list of questions.

"Then, we regroup."

No back-up plan, Commander?

Like I said, it's the best plan we've got.

Oh, that makes me feel so much better.

Roxanne sat back and attempted a Commander Gabriel grin, "I love this plan. I'm excited to be a part of it. Let's do it."

All around the room, chuckles of relief broke-out. Apparently, the apprehension of the Chosen One had been shared by quite a few others. The General shook his head. *And why not? These are not mindless followers. These are the leaders and future hope of the land.* Resuming his in control stance at the head of the table, General Sabastian started the final round of this war.

"I realize that some of you may doubt this plan, but it is the best offense we have, and we are going to use it. Now, break into your teams for your assignments, and get some rest, we start in the morning."

Lord Earin glanced around the room at the faces of the leaders. Roxanne was resolved, the General stern, the High Lord remained calm, Lord Anjalina looked very anxious, Snake was hidden in the shadows, and the Commander had a "'aint I clever" grin plastered to his face. Every possible personality was reflected in this group of world leaders, and those personalities clashed in every way possible. Earin suspected that that clash was what had got them this far alive. He hoped it would get them even farther.

Roxanne stood, and, before he really knew he was doing it, Lord Earin reached out and grabbed her hand, almost in a panic. She turned and smiled down at him.

"Sor-ry," he stammered.

"Hey, we're gonna make it. All of us. I promise."

As soon as she said it, she regretted it. Now, she was bound by her word to try and keep them all alive. *Like you haven't already been attempting the whole Wonder Woman thing.* Lord Earin released her hand and she moved away from the table, trying to keep all of her emotions in check and in perspective. After all, she had a team of men to prepare and a world to protect. *A woman's job is never done.* Her weak attempt at amusing herself remained just that as she transformed into a leader and vowed to never look into the eyes of another dead lover.

****

Perigyn glided across the soft forest floor with a look of determination on his face. The task that lay before him was going to be difficult, but he had accepted it with a happy heart. He knew that this would be one of the only chances to learn from the Last of the Chosen, and perhaps the only chance to reach her. She was an integral part of all that had happened and was about to happen, and she had no idea what that meant. He was about to enlighten her... he hoped.

Crossing a small valley and cresting the tiny hill, he came upon the raven-haired beauty exactly where he thought he would. She was kneeling on the ground infront of a small mound of freshly placed rocks; Major Elway's place of burial. He approached as silently as possible, so as not to disturb her in this private moment.

However, he could not have disturbed her if he wanted to; she was far too absorbed in what she was doing. As she stared at the cold, hard rocks, her mind traced the remains of memories and feelings. All the moments they had shared played across her mind in vivid detail; from their first suicide mission together, through the love-making, right down to that split second before he lay dead at her feet. Her body trembled as tears ran down her face and soaked her shirt. This was more pain than she could bear. She picked up a small stone and threw it at the burial mound.

"Why the hell did you have to die?! What the fuck were you thinking? If you wanted attention, you could have just asked... I

242

always knew you were suicidal and crazy. Why did you have to prove me right?"

The tears rolled down her face like a raging river as she yelled at the grave. She wanted answers; she wanted comfort; and, most of all, she wanted revenge.

"It's not fair," she sobbed. "The good guys aren't suppose to die. We're suppose to walk on water."

Perigyn spoke softly, "Do not despair, Roxanne. He did not die in vain."

She didn't even bother to whirl around. Nothing much surprised her anymore.

"There's nothing nice about death. All death is despair."

"Did you think he would live forever?"

She sighed, "Yes, as a matter of fact, I did. Death was not an option."

The gentle fairy moved forward and placed his hand on her shoulder. Instantly, he felt the strength of her pain and the fire of her fury. She was an emotional time-bomb. A small amount of fear penetrated his heart as he felt her anger surge. She was dangerously close to crossing that line, and he had to stop her at all cost. Removing his hand, he stepped back and inhaled power from the life-force of the forest.

"May I join you?" Perigyn asked.

Roxanne nodded, "It's a free country."

Confusion flashed across the fairy's face as he sat on the grass beside the Last of the Chosen.

"Lord Earin warned me that you have a tendency to confuse those around you."

This comment put a tiny smile on her face. A slight chuckle even escaped her lips.

"Yeah, I'm like that," said Roxanne. "Now, tell me what's on your mind."

Perigyn spoke cautiously, "I have many questions about you."

Roxanne furrowed her brow, "I thought you guys already checked me out on my way in?"

Perigyn nodded, "That is true in some respects."

"In some respects?"

"The truth is, we can only see certain things about people. We can see whether or not they have something in their past that is hidden, and, usually because that is what most of their mind is concentrating on, we can see what they are hiding. In that manner, we determine whether or not the individual is honest, and, if they are hiding something, what that is and how it affects their souls. So, you see, you had nothing hidden, so we know very little about you."

For some unknown reason, Roxanne felt suddenly relieved. *They don't know everything about me.* Relief quickly gave way to amusement. She didn't have anything to feel relief about; her life was an open book. She had tried to be mysterious once, but she couldn't keep a straight face. Honesty was one of her greatest flaws, right up there with kindness.

"So, what is it that you all-knowing types would like to know about little-ole-me?"

"We want to know what you intend to do."

It was Roxie's turn for confusion, "What do you mean? I intend to help defeat the Betrayer and return the Land to it's original brilliance, just like everyone else."

"Are you certain?"

Roxanne was beginning to get annoyed, "Of course I'm sure. What the hell is that suppose to mean? Look, if there is something you are getting at, I wish you'd get there... it would be most helpful."

Now, it was completely apparent to Perigyn that Lord Earin did, in fact, understand this woman. She was straight-forward and honest. She also expected the same from those around her. He decided to go that direction, as Lord Earin's words rang through his head: *Besides, her reaction might just surprise you.*

"I am sorry. Of course I shall be direct with you. You are have a stronger connection to your amulet than the others, and, therefore, a stronger connection to the Betrayer. He has already made contact with you through your dreams, and it was his right-hand man that delivered you your pendant. We are concerned about his ability to influence you."

For a second Roxanne stared at him through tear-stained eyes, then she started laughing. Perigyn was taken aback. He certainly hadn't said anything he considered to be humorous. Was the Last of the Chosen going mad?

Roxanne stifled her laughter, "I'm sorry. Don't look so concerned; I'm not going insane. I just find it amusing that's all. You basically asked me if I'm a spy. Kinda like, 'Hey, you're not an evil spy or anything, are you?' The answer is: No. I'm not a spy."

Perigyn shook his head, "I do not understand you."

"Of course you don't. I don't even understand me. The fact remains, however, that the Betrayer doesn't understand me either. And, I have no idea what his motives might be for the things he has done. The only influence he has over me is to anger me beyond belief. If I could kill him myself, I would do it with my bare hands."

The flustered fairy contemplated the woman before him and her words. He could see no reason to fear her, and he could not feel any reason not to believe her. With the breeze playing in her long, dark hair, she looked like a fated warrior princess. He did not know what he should do, so he tried honesty.

"You are more important than you can possibly realize. We, the fairies, have long been aware of your presence. We have also known that you would come to our land someday. And, we know that the Betrayer can only be destroyed by you."

Roxanne attempted to lighten the situation, "Good, then we all know there's nothing to worry about, don't we?"

Perigyn dropped his head, as though he was searching for answers in his lap. When he lifted his eyes to her's, there was no hint of humor; there was only absolute seriousness and fear.

"No, Chosen One, we do not. The prophesy of your coming is split. It says that only you may save the land, and only you can damn it."

****

Chapter 12

Roxanne's carefully reconstructed reality came crashing down around her head, which, consequently, was spinning. That they had known about a third Chosen One was fine; that they had known it was her was unnerving. That she was prophesied to either save or damn the Land was beyond the realm of reality as she understood it. *This is not happening. I am not ready for this kind of responsibility. I just want to be one of the pawns.* She pushed the palms of her hands against her closed eyes and tried to get a grip on things around her. *Okay. Think. Think. What does this mean?* Then, a thought came crashing in out of the darkness.

Meekly, she asked, "Does the Betrayer know about this?"

Perigyn answered the only way he could, "Based on his actions, he must."

She nodded, "Why else would he hand over the necklace?" Another terrible thought jumped into her head, "And if I die before the final battle?"

Perigyn closed his eyes, "Then the fate of the Land remains unbalanced."

She didn't like the sound of that. This was getting to be more than she could handle. She had always planned on getting out of this thing alive, but, now, the world depended on it. For a moment there was fear, then panic, then... There comes a time in people's lives when complete clarity sets in; when they become completely calm; and, when the path before them is all too clear. For Roxanne, that time was now. She had no doubt in her mind of the course of action she had to take.   With complete resolve she faced her destiny.

Calmly now, she addressed her newest companion, "The Betrayer must believe that he can control me, or he never would have risked giving me the pendant."

Perigyn became very pensive, "Not necessarily. He might have known that, without you as a player, this game for control was destined to remain at a stand-still. For him, it may have been worth the risk."

That explanation rang hollow on Roxanne's ears. "You and I both find that one hard to swallow. He must think he has some sort of control. I just wonder why."

Perigyn wondered why, himself. The Last of the Chosen had no hidden darkness and no hidden past. She was straightforward, kind, and giving. Her only downfall at the moment was her extreme anger, but that was directed toward the Betrayer and not the world in general. As far as his mental eye could see, she was full of beauty and honesty. So, why did Shylark worry? What could he see that the rest of the fairies could not? And, what was it that he was suppose to keep young Roxanne from doing?

Sitting and staring into each other's eye, Roxanne could see the wheels turning in Perigyn's mind. For a moment she was afraid that he could see into her soul and read her plan. She could not afford for that to happen. As a matter of fact, she could not afford to let anyone know what she intended to do; the entire success of her plan rested on its secrecy. That meant something else as well. *I'm going to have to get rid of Sage.* She turned toward the main hall where he now waited diligently. *This could be harder than I thought.*

"I know that you must feel confused and angry, Chosen One. But, do not despair, for we have won before."

Roxanne's face came to life with a half-Snake, half-Gabe grin, "I told you already, call me Roxanne. Now, let's get back to the others and get this party started."

The bewildered fairy shook his head, "I just don't understand you."

Roxanne threw an arm around his shoulder as they both stood to go, "And the worst part is, you probably never will."

****

The stars that shined in the night sky seemed particularly bright to Roxanne. *Yeah, a little too bright.* But, Mother Nature could not be helped. Moving her refreshed body silently through the forest, she could not believe what she was doing. She couldn't believe that it had been only two days since Major Elway died, and only two days since she had come to the realization of what she had to do, as well. *But two days can be a lifetime in this place. I wonder just how far the Betrayer's troops can move in two days.*

That thought halted her progress for a moment, as the insanity of what she was about to attempt hit her in the face. What if the Betrayer's troops were waiting on the outside? What if she found herself in the middle of a trap? But, her semi-logic quickly returned. *So what. It can' be any worse than marching off to have lunch with the head dude himself.* That was, after all, exactly what she was doing. At the fateful moment when her destiny had been revealed to her, Roxie had been totally aware that the actions she was now taking were the only option; there was no other way.

So, deep into the night on the eve of their departure, she had sent Sage to sleep with the rest of the pages, to protect them, of course, slipped into some black clothes and her gear, and quietly snuck out into the night. She knew she had to get out of the forest before the others waked if she was going to achieve her goal. And, there was always the threat of Snake coming after her, but she knew she had to face Him, and, what's more, she knew how.

A slight movement to her right sent her diving to the ground. She pushed herself into the grass in an attempt to disappear, and waited. Staring into the darkness of the forest, she could barely see. *What the hell happened to all those bright stars from earlier?!* She inhaled deeply and slowly in an effort to calm herself. It didn't work. She couldn't see a damn thing, so she remained still and stared intently into the forest.

Just when she had convinced that she was paranoid and driving herself to an early grave, she caught the movement again. *You see? Just because I'm paranoid, doesn't mean people aren't out to get me.* She peered out into the forest. A shadowy figure was making its way toward her. She slid her hand along the ground until the hilt of her sword was firmly in her grip. Ready to strike, she waited. Her pulse quickened and her head pounded. There was something important she was forgetting; something on the tip of her brain.

What am I missing? Think, dammit! What's not right here? The shadow became an outline as it got closer to her hiding spot. Whoever it was would be on top of her in a matter of seconds. *I hope he's not an ugly one.* Instantly, she knew what she was missing. There were no enemy troops here. She was in the middle of the Silver Forest. Anyone she came into contact with would be friendly. *Great. How am I going to explain this?* She released her vice-like grip on her sword and pushed herself to her feet with an excuse forming in her brain. She was absolutely unprepared for what happened next.

At the exact second that she came to her feet, everything in nature aligned. The stars caught the glow of the moonbeams. The burst of the light from the sky above broke through a clearing in the trees. Roxanne's eyes opened wide to take in the scene. And, Major Elway stepped into the light.

"It's impossible," slipped through Roxanne's mostly closed lips as her senses reeled.

The Major smiled a warm greeting. It was a smile Roxanne had seen many a night before he had climbed into bed next to her, or on top of her, whatever the case might have been. She felt like her head was tearing in two, and tears escaped onto her cheeks. It was torture to see him so real, because she knew it could not be him. But, she was wrong.

"Hey, what's with all the tears? Don't tell me the mighty warrior princess has emotions."

It was his voice. There was no mistaking it in her ears. She fell to her knees in confusion.

"No need to bow... but, as long as your down there."

Now, she was certain it was him. *He never did have any class.*

She shook her head from side to side, "Stop it. Just stop it. This is not possible. It's just not possible."

Realizing that his effort to put her at ease had misfired, the Major softened his approach. He reached out with his hand and lightly touched her long, beautiful hair. *God, I miss you already.* However, it was a failed comfort for them both, as he no longer held solid form and could not really touch her. Quickly he withdrew his hand and knelt infront of her.

"It's not that bad, you know."

Roxanne lifted her sobbing head only to realize that she could see right through his face.

"What?" she stammered.

"Being a ghost," he smiled. "It's not that bad."

She reigned in her emotions as she stared at him. Uncontrollable crying was not going to help.

"How is this possible?"

He furrowed his brow. "I'm not really sure. The last thing I remember is throwing myself, like an idiot, between the High Lord and some arrows, then I was all of a sudden hanging out with a bunch of dead friends. It was too weird..." here he trailed off for a moment, but he caught himself dreaming. "Anyway, after a few minutes, someone said I had some unfinished business I should take care of, and the next thing I know, I'm in the middle of this forest walking straight for you."

"That's it," she teased, in an effort to establish normalcy.

"What do you mean, "That's it"?"

"I just expected something a little more grand, a little less fuzzy."

His eyes lit up with the fire she loved as he spoke, "I come back from the dead to say hi after being horribly murdered, and you want something a little more grand?! You are impossible."

Suddenly, she heard laughter. It took several seconds for her to realize that it was coming from her.

She gazed into his eyes, "You always could make me laugh, you know."

"If memory serves, that wasn't all I could make you do."

She sighed, "Always had an over-inflated opinion of yourself, too."

He chuckled, "Who you callin' over-inflated?"

Roxie raised an eyebrow, "Death has changed you. You use to take that as a compliment."

They laughed together for awhile before they got trapped in each other's eyes. As they stared at each other, they both imagined, for a short time, that he was still alive, and that this was a night like any other. However, when Roxie reached for his hand, reality stepped right back into the picture, and she found herself holding hands with the air. Elway was dead.

Roxie made an effort to fill the awkward silence, "So, did you come back to apologize for dying on me?"

Something between sadness and concern filled Elway's eyes, "No. I came back to try and stop you."

She was taken aback, "Stop me from what?"

"Come on, Rox. What you're about to do is suicide, and we both know it."

"No we don't. Besides, it's the only option I've got left."

"Marching into the Betrayer's lair to take him on one on one is not an option."

Fire shot from her eyes, "Oh, and throwing yourself infront of a bunch of arrows is?"

As soon as she said it, she wished she hadn't. All her life, she had had a nasty habit of saying the most hurtful thing possible in the heat of an argument. The Major had gone silent.

"I'm sorry," mumbled Roxanne, "I really didn't mean it. I just didn't know what else to say."

Elway shrugged his shoulders, "Hey, don't sweat it. It can't kill me, right?"

"Great. Now I feel even worse."

He smiled a weak smile, "Good."

"Look, I'm going. That's all there is to it."

"But you have no idea what the Betrayer is capable of doing. He could murder you, or even cast some mind control spell on you in order to use you as a weapon."

"Not if he doesn't know I'm a bad guy."

The Major looked completely confused, "Come again?"

Roxie grinned slyly, "It's your best friends that make your worst enemies."

That was all the clarification he needed, "Oh my God, you are crazy. There is no way he would fall for that."

"I think he already has. Look, it was his guy that gave me the necklace. He has been invading my dreams since I got here with promises of control. And, he has me backed into a corner. So, what do you suppose he will believe when I'm heading straight for him and no one else on our side has any clue as to my whereabouts."

The Major shook his head, "I just don't know..."

"Come on," she urged, "it's tactically simple and mortally dangerous, just like..."

"... all good plans should be," he finished. "I still don't like it."

"Truth be told, I'm not particularly thrilled with the idea myself. But, I can't see any other way around this thing."

Major Elway sighed and laid a spectral hand on Roxanne's shoulder, "I know I can't stop you, you always were impossible that way, so, please be careful. God knows I'd love to hold you again, but not if it costs you your life."

"Trust me. I have no idea what I'm doing."

He rolled his eyes, "Thanks. That makes me feel so much better."

A light tugging on his spirit told Elway that it was time to go. He looked intently at the beautiful woman that stood before him, memorizing every little detail about her. He could feel himself being pulled away as he hurried to take in every inch of her. He didn't want to be torn from her again. Panic filled him. In a last desperate attempt at contact he cried out to her.

"I love you," and then he was gone.

Elway's final words to her lingered in Roxanne's ears as he faded out like Obi Wan Kanobi. A single remaining tear made its way down her flushed cheek.

"I know," she muttered in return, "I know."

For a few seconds, she remained on her knees, staring after her vanished lover, and contemplating what had just happened. But, she didn't have time for all that now. She had to get out of the forest and on her way before the other's had a chance to catch up to her. There was no more time left for being a woman and a lover; she had to be a warrior.

Swiftly and with purpose, Roxanne made her way to the crystal waters of the Silver Forest's lake where she knew a boat would be waiting. This boat was meant to used by the troops in the morning to get them to the other side of the forest. She wasn't sure how or even if it worked, but she climbed on board anyway. She walked to the front of the boat and examined it.

There were no controls of any kind; no steering wheel, no paddles, no nothing. *Not exactly the Queen Mary, now is she?* As far as she could tell, there was no way to control this boat or to set it in motion. It really wasn't much more than a large wooden raft with seats. Frustration began to rise from the pit of her stomach. *Just how the hell am I suppose to get this thing started?*

Almost as if it had heard her mental plea, the boat suddenly lurched forward, sending Roxanne reeling to the bottom.

"What the hell was that?"

Uneasily, she climbed to her feet and looked out over the edge of the boat. She was shocked to find that the boat was skidding along over the water at what appeared to be a deadly high speed. It was even stranger to discover that there was no wind. Her hair wasn't blowing, her face wasn't being slapped by water, and she wasn't struggling to stand. Yet, to look across the shimmering water, it seemed like she was moving hundreds of miles an hour. *Magic is so cool.*

Assured that she would not figure out how the whole thing worked, Roxanne plopped down on one on the long wooden benches running along the edge of the boat, pulled her legs into her chest, nestled her head on her knees, and wondered. She thought longingly about her friends, and wondered if she'd ever see them again. She thought of poor Sage, and wondered if he'd ever forgive her for sneaking out on him. And, she thought about her little brother... Quickly, she pushed his face from her mind and concentrated on her journey ahead. There was no turning back from her task. *And so it begins.* Firm in her resolve, she moved on.

And, back on shore, Shylark smiled and held the anchor firmly in his hands.

****

Sage hurried down the corridor of the main living hall. He was man with a purpose. He didn't see much of anything as he rushed forward; he ran right past fairies, soldiers, and pages with a single goal in mind. *I've got to find the General.* A flicker of sunlight through the bottom of a nearby stain glass window caught his attention, and, for a moment, he joined those around him in reality. Panic seized him. There wasn't much time left. He had to find the General.

Sage was running now, despite the danger. He just wasn't closing the gap fast enough to make up for all the time he had lost to Roxanne already. *Roxanne.* His heart filled with a mixture of anger and shame. *How could you do this? Why wasn't I there to stop you?* When he had first arrived at her chambers, only to find them empty, he had assumed she was bathing or preparing for battle. So, he returned to his quarters, packed up his gear, and prepared to leave. But, when he went back to find Roxanne and she still wasn't there, he started to worry. After scanning the bed chambers, he came across a simple note: *Sage, Went to get the bad guys. Will explain when next we meet. -Roxie.*

As soon as he read it, he cursed himself for his idealness and ran out the door.

Now, with the note clutched firmly in his fist, the frantic page stumbled headlong into Lord Earin.

Lord Earin placed his hands on Sage's shoulders and held him at arm's length, "Easy there, young one. Why the hurry?"

Frustration seized the dutiful page as he struggled between his desire to move on and his duty to stay.

"I must find the General, my Lord."

"Can it wait, or did Roxanne send you?"

The mention of her name sent a spasm of panic through his body, "I must find the General, now."

Lord Earin saw the terror in Sage's eyes and felt the panic in his soul. Calmly, he dropped to his knees and looked the young man in the eyes. With all the gentleness of a loving parent, he questioned Sage.

"Now, relax and tell me what has you so disturbed. Then, we will go together to the General and handle this problem."

Sage could see that he wasn't going anywhere until he explained himself. He could also tell that he was being unreasonable. He cursed himself for letting fear and indecision get the better of him. He had been trained better than that.

Taking a deep breath, Sage said, "Roxanne is gone. She left only this note," he handed his precious cargo to Lord Earin, "and

I suspect she left somewhere in the night. I think she has been gone for hours."

Lord Earin's eyes opened wide and his jaw dropped open as he read the note in his hands. He slumped back on his haunches and the phrase, "Oh dear God," escaped from his lips. *She's gone insane.*

A tugging at his robes pulled him to the here and now.

"Lord Earin, Lord Earin. We must go."

He shook his head and looked into Sage's pleading eyes. Immediately, he took command of himself, climbed to his feet, and started forward. "Indeed, we must."

****

Snake sat back in her chair, arms folded across her chest and bottom lip between her teeth, and listened intently to the discussion between Sage and the General. It was insane. She glanced at the faces around the room. Everyone, from fairies to soldiers, had gone completely silent. It was as if time had stopped the minute Sage had announced that Roxanne was gone. Now, the General queried the scared little page carefully, searching for any possible clue to help him understand this situation. Snake felt a slight tugging at her mind.

What's up, Commander?

Did Roxie say anything to you about this?

If she had, do you think I'd be sitting here right now?

You got a point there, judge. Any idea what's going on?

I'm not sure, but I suspect that Shylark had something to do with it.

The Commander's mental voice was taken aback. *Shylark? What could he have to do with it?*

Snake answered with a mental shrug. *I don't know. It's just a feeling I get when I look at him.*

The Commander looked over at the head fairy; the most powerful being in the Land. He was calmly hovering above the ground next to the High Lord and the General. That he was different from the rest of the fairies was obvious. He was the only one with facial hair- a long, flowing silver beard- and his

256

face was the only one that held any age. The Commander suspected it was Shylark's great knowledge that had aged him. After all, you couldn't know everything about the universe without some scarring.

Gabe stared intently at the "Papa Smurf" of the fairy world for a few more seconds, but still he couldn't see any signs of deception. *Maybe Snake's going crazy.*

Maybe you've just lost your touch.

Shit! Didn't mean to broadcast that. Regardless, I don't see anything.

Snake scanned Shylark's face, again. There it was, in his ancient eyes. There was that something that assured her she was not crazy. *Well, no more than usual.*

It's something in his eyes, Gabe.

Even in her mental voice, it sent a tingle down his spine to hear her call him by his name. Like a dutiful child, he looked at Shylark's shining golden eyes, again. All he could see was power; pure, proud, and calm power.

I just don't see anything that I shouldn't.

Snake considered cursing him for not having women's intuition, but forced herself to admit that that much was not his fault.

He's too calm, almost relaxed... No, I'd say he's down- right content.

Okay, I can see that. But, isn't that the way an all-powerful being is supposed to look?

Not if everything he knows is about to come crashing down around his head.

You have a point. So, what should we do?

We wait.

That last statement had a final sound to it, so Gabe chose not to pursue that avenue of information any further. It was apparent that Snake didn't have any secret information. It was also apparent that she had a distinct distrust of Shylark. She sat in the corner with her steely blue eyes fixed on him as though he might disappear at any moment. The Commander focused on Shylark yet again, thinking Snake had finally lost her mind. Then, out of nowhere, and for only a fraction of a second, a slight grin passed

Shylark's lips and disappeared into his face.

Sudden realization overcame the Commander, and he turned to look at Snake. She calmly nodded; no words were needed. Something was definitely rotten in Denmark.

"Why would she want to go after him alone? What makes her think she can do it? Does she believe she can succeed where many have failed?" asked a shaken Lord Anjalina. So much of her hope had rested on the missing Chosen One.

General Sabastian turned to the beautiful lady lord with firm determination in his face, "She must, or she would not have gone." Then, he addressed the entire company, "Whatever Roxanne's motivation may be is of little use to us here. What is important are the facts. She has gone to face the Betrayer, she has a full night's head-start, and she must be found. Therefore, we will assemble a team to forge ahead and recover..."

"No," came an unexpected voice from the back.

The General frowned at the interruption, but he did not dare dismiss Snake in this matter.

"And, why not, might I ask?"

Snake leaned forward across the table for effect, "Because we don't have enough men to send a group off looking for her."

General Sabastian folded his huge arms across his massive chest, "Then what do you propose? Do we just let her go?"

"Not exactly," smiled the smug lady of ice.

"Not exactly? Then, would you mind enlightening the rest of us as to *exactly* what you mean?"

Snake remained calm, "I'll go after her by myself."

Hands went up all over the room, accompanied by sounds of exasperation. This was getting to be ridiculous.

"Great. Now they've both got delusions of grandeur. First, Roxanne thinks she can take on the Betrayer single-handedly, and, now, Snake thinks she can stop her!" was the out-cry from Lord Earin.

Snake let Lord Earin slide because she knew it was only frustration and fear that ruled him. When he calmed down, he would see that this was the best option. Who better to track her than the one that trained her? Patiently, she waited for the General to restore order. He never got that chance. Instead,

Snake was rescued by the two people she trusted the least.

"Be calm, my friend. The Chosen One has a point."

All eyes turned to Shylark as he spoke.

"There is no one better suited for this task than Snake. She has all the training and necessary skills."

"Without her, it may be impossible to find Roxanne," added High Lord Brennen, "and we cannot spare any additional men."

Smiling, and staring directly at Snake, Shylark spoke again, "Besides, who better to track her than the one that trained her?"

Shock rippled through Snake's body. He had known her thoughts; he had to. That last act was a deliberate act to emphasize a point. Slowly, she steadied her breathing and brought her heart beat back under control. *You just startled me, old man. It won't happen twice.* Staring right back into Shylark's eyes, she hit him anyway she could. *The more you attempt to know me, the better I understand you.* With that, she was her old self again.

"Well, you heard 'em. Straight from the mouths of the men in charge..."

The General tugged at his beard in deep concentration. He hated the way Snake did things. She was continually pissing him off, but she was right, as were Brennen and Shylark. There was no other good way around things. He was going to have to give up two of the Chosen and two of his best leaders all at once, but only one by choice. *And, what happens if they don't come back?* He shook that thought from his head.

"Okay. Snake goes after Roxanne, and the rest of us carry on as planned, unless there are some further objections."

The General scanned the room with an evil eye. Lord Earin was fuming, Lord Anjalina looked desperate, Brennen and Shylark were communicating on a private level, and the Commander was about to burst. "And, I'll be damned before I'll let you go, too, Commander," added the General.

Gabe put his hands up in mock defense, "The thought never even crossed my mind." He knew better.

"Good," said the General. So did he.

A tiny voice from below called for the General's attention, "What about me, General? I'd like to go with Snake."

A constricting pain seized Snake's heart. *Oh no you don't. I will not be responsible for the life of this child.*

General Sabastian put a firm hand on Sage's shoulder, "No, we need you here. We are going to be short in the leader department, and I'm going to need trusted and skilled people to ease communication problems. You're one of the best we've got; I need you here."

That much was the truth. The General needed good pages like Sage around to help, but that wasn't the real reason he kept the desperate child here. The General kept him to protect him and Snake from each other. Sage would take up too much of her energy, and she would scare the poor boy to death.

"Well, if there is nothing else, I'll be leaving. All I need is a point in the right direction," Snake stated as she stood to leave.

At about that time, Shylark and the High Lord finished their mental "pow-wow," and halted the lady of ice.

"There is something you need to know before you start your journey."

Snake turned all her attention to High Lord Brennen, "Well, let's at least make it quick. I'm running out of time and patience."

Brennen scowled. Things were so hard, and Snake refused to make them any easier. Against his better judgement, the High Lord blurted out a response.

"Then I'll make this very quick and clear. There is a chance that the Chosen One is in greater danger than simply loosing her life. It was the Betrayer's servant Mongrel that gave her the Chosen pendant, and the Betrayer, himself, has made contact with her through her dreams. He may try to capture and control her, not kill her."

"And you're afraid he could succeed?" asked Snake.

"That's impossible. There is no chance that Roxanne could be made to betray us!" burst forth from a nervous Lord Earin.

Shylark attempted to calm him down, "Dear Lord Earin, we are not suggesting that she would ever purposely betray us. But, the Betrayer has powers that we don't understand, and..."

"No! That's garbage! Have you ever looked into her eyes and asked her why she fights to save us?! Well, have you?!" screamed the Lord as he looked around the room. No one answered. "Well, I have. I have looked into her eyes when all my hope was gone and found it anew in her soul. I have seen her fight against an awesome enemy for people she has no real ties to. She is strong. She can't be turned... she can't."

There was silence in the room as Lord Earin's fury died and he collapsed into a chair. No one seemed to know what to say. Then, his pleas were answered. All eyes were now focused on Lord Anjalina as she spoke. She spoke in a slow, measured tone; never raising her voice, but capturing everyone's attention.

"I have looked into her eyes, and I have seen the purity there. I, too, lost my faith and had it restored by the Chosen. I have felt the power of her soul."

Calmly now, Shylark stepped forward and answered their cries, "We have all been touched by this special child, and she does have an honest and innocent heart. But, let us not forget that the innocent are often the target of the greatest corruption."

Snake put a booted foot on the nearest chair and leaned across her leg, "But, why would he want to corrupt her, and why would he bother to give up a pendant if it was in his position? What is it that you are not telling the rest of us?"

Shylark was not ruffled by Snake's piercing eyes, "I cannot pretend to understand evil. I can only warn you against it. The fact remains that the Chosen One may be in graver danger than you realize."

Pausing momentarily, Snake pulled her bottom lip between her teeth, then spit it out, "I'd better get going, then. It seems I had better stop her before she is turned against us," She turned to the General. "Karlis is a very good point man and a strong leader, Roxie told me that. Watch your back, and don't loose any more leaders."

It wasn't much, but it was something. The General took her hand firmly in his, "Until we meet again. Oh, and try to make it *before* we reach the Betrayer."

"I'll meet you there."

That was enough for Snake. She grabbed her gear and slipped out the door. No one said a word as she disappeared through the door. And, no one said a word when Commander Gabriel followed her out. They knew he'd be back, but they knew he had to go as well. Instead, General Sabastian gathered up his military senses and started issuing commands.

"Well, what are we all standing around for? I need gear packed, troops organized, and boats loaded. Let's go. Oh, and Karlis?"

"Yes, General?"

"You're on point."

"Yes, General."

As he picked up his gear and headed out the door, one thought echoed through Karlis' mind. *Oh, I have got to thank Roxie for this one.*

****

Snake stopped at the edge of the lake and contemplated how to get across it. She couldn't take the boat, because the rest of the troops would need it. And, she wasn't sure swimming it would have the same effect. This wasn't going to be as easy as she had thought. She scanned the shoreline for another possibility. She couldn't seem to find an answer. *That's okay. Maybe Gabe has a solution.* She tossed her flowing hair over her shoulder and called out to the man who was attempting to sneak-up on her.

"Got any idea how I should handle this?"

Gabe wasn't surprised she had heard him coming, but it irritated him a little. Then again, what could he expect from the queen of stealth. He stared at her beautiful figure and was, once again, overwhelmed by her. He knew what he had to do, and he knew she wouldn't like it.

"Sure, just take the boat."

She turned around, "Duh. Then how are the rest of you going to get across?"

Gabe grinned, "We'll cross that bridge when we come to it."

"Ha, ha. Very funny."

"No really, stop and think about it. Roxie had to take the boat to get out of here, but here it is right where we left it."

Snake nodded, "It must know how to get back here. Well, thanks."

Gabe grabbed Snake by the arm as she went to get in the

boat. He was not about to let her just disappear, again. There was something that had to be said; he hoped he had the guts to go through with it.

But, Snake didn't want to give him the chance.

"Look, Commander, I've wasted all the time I can afford..."

"So, waste a little more. There is something I need to say to you..."

"Really, Commander, I don't have time for this."

"... and you are going to hear me out. Before it's too late, I want you to know how I feel."

Snake began to panic, she couldn't handle this. It was too much for her to hear and feel all at once. She pulled away from his grasp and headed for the boat.

"Please don't do this to me. I can't handle it, now."

"I can't handle it anymore, either. I'm in love with you. No matter how sick that makes both of us, it is the truth. I can't help the way I feel, and I can't go on with it trapped inside. I love you."

Snake was shaking her head, "I'm not hearing this. I'm not ready for this." Even as she said it, she knew it wasn't the truth. The truth was, her heart leapt with excitement at the sound of those words. However, the emotional wall she had spent a lifetime building remained firmly in place, and kept her cold.

"Anyway, I guess you'd better leave before you hit me." Gabe hadn't expected Snake to take this well, but a part of him had hoped the feelings would be returned. *Yeah, and the Betrayer is about to surrender.*

Snake had no idea what to say. For the first time since her childhood, she was at a complete loss for words. So, she climbed into the boat and waited for something to happen. Nothing did. Looking over the edge, she realized the anchor needed to be lifted.

"Help me with this will ya, Gabe?"

That was all it took to restore his faith in himself and her feelings. She had called him Gabe, and that was always her only act of tenderness. He hefted the anchor from the water and handed it to her. Then, like a flash she was gone. As he stood at the water's edge staring after her, he imagined she had returned his feelings. Then he shook his head to clear it. It was only a dream. Standing there, he couldn't even understand why he had just done that. *Well, that accomplished exactly nothing. I'm so glad I did that. That was so fun. Next time I think I'll just pick my nose with a battle ax.* Putting one of his "gee-'aint- I- clever" grin on his face, the Commander pulled himself together and returned to his troops.

Sitting back in the boat, Snake pulled her legs into her chest and her bottom lip between her teeth. She nearly chewed through her lip as she contemplated what had just happened. She had sworn to never let anyone get that close to her, because it left her open to weakness. She wasn't about to let a man have any control in her life... but, she wasn't sure she could stop it. *This is getting ridiculous. I'm stronger than this.* She looked out over the lake. It was time to regain control of herself and face the harshness of reality yet again. But, for just a brief moment, she had been a normal woman in love, and that was something her heart decided to treasure forever.

****

Perigyn watched as the troops disappeared into the shadows of the forest. They were the final hope of the Land, and there were so few of them left. He wondered if they really had a chance against the Betrayer's thousands, and that bothered him. He wasn't use to wondering; he was use to knowing. He glanced at Shylark out of the corner of his eye and was immediately impressed by his calmness. Nothing ever seemed to phase him; it was as if he always knew what was going to happen next. That thought encouraged him to start a conversation with the leader of the fairies.

"Okay, they are gone. Now, please tell me what we are missing."

Shylark smiled a fatherly smile. He knew he couldn't stop the questions from coming, and he knew he couldn't hide the answers. So, he did the only logical thing he could, he told the truth.

"I had you tell her about the prophesy."

Perigyn understood, "And, she was encouraged to take care of that option. But, aren't you afraid of what might happen to her while she is all alone?"

"No," asserted Shylark, "I even helped her leave. She had to go; there is no other way for this to end. My visions have shown me that she will have to be with the Betrayer for the final battle."

"Have you seen the outcome, or whose side she will be on?"

Shylark hesitated for a brief moment, "No. That I cannot see."

Perigyn decided not to pursue that point, "Why did you allow them to send Snake after her? She will probably find her."

Shylark regained his confidence, "The Betrayer must believe that she has acted on her own, or she will be in great danger. Sending Snake after her protects her in more ways than one."

Perigyn shifted his gaze back to the lake and searched for the fading outline of the transport boat; it was no more. By now, they were well on their way to the other side of the forest and that next step in the war. He sighed and put his arm around Shylark's shoulder.

"I hope we are right."

Shylark attempted a comforting smile, "I hope we are, too."

****

Chapter 13

Roxanne cursed herself as she tripped over a piece of root from a nearby tree. *Some tracker I'd make. Can't even walk down the street without tripping over my own feet.* She had been walking all night and her exhaustion was creeping up on her, but she didn't dare stop. She knew they would be sending someone after her, and she suspected it would be Snake. If that was the case, she'd have nothing but time on her side. And, not even a whole lot of that. Snake could cover twice as much ground in half the time, and Roxanne was doing a lousy job of covering her tracks.

Noises behind her froze Roxanne in her tracks. She held her position as she tried to pin down the location of the sound and its source. There was total silence around her. *Maybe I'm loosing my grip on reality.* She strained her senses. Still nothing, but the hair on the back of her neck was standing on end. There had to be a reason for her concern; her instincts had never let her down before. *But, I just don't hear anything... I don't hear anything at all, as a matter of fact.*

Panic ran down her spine as she realized what the problem was. There were no forest sounds and she was in the middle of a forest. She should hear birds, small furry things running around, and the clicks and chirps of little bugs. Instead, the air was still and a dead calm had settled over the whole of the forest. *This is so not right.*

Unable to see anything from where she was standing, Roxanne began to move slowly forward, scanning every inch of the tree- covered landscape around her. Nothing else seemed to be moving; nothing came near her. She started to wonder if she had fallen asleep and this was a nightmare. *This is too weird.* It was as if the rest of the world had just stopped and she was the only thing still moving. She couldn't think of anything else to do, and she wasn't being attacked, so she kept creeping forward with the hair on her neck waving in the breeze.

As she broke through a group of trees, the reason for the sudden death of the world around her became painfully apparent. She had entered the land of the dead. At least, that's what it looked like. All around her there were mountains and mountains of dark, desolate nothing. *Oh my God.* She hand entered a place of desperation and abandonment.

Directly infront of her, rose two separate spikes of rocks that could be called mountains, although they looked more like jagged rocks just piled on top of one another. These spires trailed off on either side of her into rows and mounds of rocks. Off in the distance, she picked out a few forms that were slightly smoother and looked more like mountains, but they were a long ways from where she stood. The most powerful sensation, however, was the distinct feeling of being alone. There wasn't another living thing anywhere in sight in the scene before her.

Standing alone and exposed, Roxanne's mind leapt to thoughts of home... her real home. She suddenly missed her brother, her parents, and even some of her friends. These were the people who had always been there; they had kept her from facing the world alone; they had been her support. Now, at her weakest moment, they were worlds away. She felt like crying. *Am I crazy? I can't do this myself. I haven't got the strength for all of this. I just want to go home and rest.* Even though she thought it, she knew it wasn't entirely true. She was just tired and lonely, and the hardest part still lay ahead.

Roxanne took a deep breath and surveyed the surrounding country just a little closer. *Nope. No change. This is definitely hell.* What she needed was a hint to the Betrayer's location. She didn't have to think long, it was right infront of her. The passageway between the two rocky spires formed a perfect bottleneck. It was a perfect trap.

"Now, if I were the leading evil villain in the world that's where I'd hide."

Gathering all the strength she had left, Roxanne boldly stepped forward and entered the trap. *Well, here goes something.*

****

Mongrel felt truly happy for the first time in his long, miserable existence. He almost ran through the musty corridors of the underground fortress, but he managed to contain his joy and maintain his dignity as he marched the Last of the Chosen to meet his master. She had come, just as he said she would. She was also alone and being pursued by the others. She had come, and she would betray.

Mongrel checked over his shoulder to make sure his prize was still behind him. She was. She walked with a calm, even gait through the corridors, eyes fixed firmly ahead. There was a look of determination upon her tired face, and a hidden strength in her eyes. She was not the same woman he had bestowed the pendant on months before. She was much older and severe than that child, but it was her. Mongrel increased his pace.

Roxanne used all of her self-control to keep calm and remain focused. That wasn't an easy task with the two smelly trolls walking on either side of her and the nasty, knarled man who started it all directly infront of her. Her heart raced and her hands itched for her sword. It was all she could do not to start hacking away at these three repulsive creatures. But, since she was trying to get in the Betrayer's good side, and they had confiscated her weapons, she decided against the Lone Ranger Plan. Instead, she stared ahead and concentrated on breathing.

The temperature had been dropping since they entered the caverns, but now it took a drastic drop. Roxanne cringed. *I hate the cold.* The further in they went, the worse it got. She hoped they would reach their goal before ice formed on her eyelids. She wasn't disappointed. Just a few feet ahead, stood an entranceway to what appeared to be a large chamber. She guessed it was the Betrayer's chamber by the way Mongrel sped up and the two trolls started to sweat. They were at the door now. Holding her breath, Roxanne crossed the threshold.

Majestically, as though he were performing on a grand stage, the dark, robed figure in the corner turned. He moved slowly, so Roxanne could take in every detail of his being. He had a misty appearance, as though he was at once there and only a hallucination. His spectral arms were folded across his chest, and he hovered above the ground like the fairies. His piercing red eyes shone with an evil fire. The very air around him shimmered with a red glow. He was evil.

Yeah, I've seen worse. Maybe she'd read one too many novels or seen one too many horror movies, but Roxanne wasn't impressed. *I know a couple of women back home that would put you to shame... and they can't float.* Her courage was bolstered when she realized that he didn't have fangs and wasn't going to swallow her head whole. However, she put her courage in check to keep her senses sharp. *No sense in getting cocky.*

"Ahhh, Chosen One, so nice of you to finally join us."

When he spoke, his voice was but a whisper. Yet, the entire mountain shook. Dust fell on their heads. Roxanne shook hers to clear it. And, to give herself enough time to decide how to handle things.

"There's nothing *nice* about it. I didn't come here to pay a social call," she said defiantly.

Mongrel flinched and the trolls took a step back. No one ever talked to the Master like that; no one.

An eery grin crept onto the specter's face, "So, you want me to know that you aren't my friend. Well, I don't have any friends. I'm the Evil Lord of the Land, remember?"

Roxanne looked around the cavern, "Yeah, I can see that."

"Tell me then, Chosen One, why are you here?"

Mentally, she took a deep breath and planned her bluff. Lies had never been her strong suit, and she wasn't entirely sure she could pull this one off. *Just another stage production.*

"I'm here because we need each other."

A small chuckle emanated from the dark figure, "Why would I need you?"

Then, for the first time, Roxanne felt herself to really have the upper hand; he had played his only high card.

She smiled, "Let's not play games. I'm not sure why you need me, only you know that, but I am certain that you need me. If you didn't you never would have had dumb and faithful give me the pendant, and you would have killed me before I ever set foot on your front door."

There was no smile now, and his feigned charm was quickly fading, "So, I need you. And, what do I have to offer you that would convince you to betray your friends?"

Roxanne grimaced at the word betray. He had thrown it in there to test her resolve, of that she was certain. She glared at him, swallowed her hatred, and gave him an answer he couldn't refuse.

"You can get me home, and in one piece."

"And the Lords can't?"

"And the Lords can't. They knew how to get me here, but they can't reverse the spell. I'm tired of nearly dying every day. I've got people I want to get back to; a life of my very own. I want to get back, and they can't do that for me. But, you can. You've already sent someone there before. So, I help you win and you send me home. Then, we'll both get what we want, and we'll never have to see each other again."

Roxanne clenched her teeth and held her breath as she stared at the face of her enemy. *Come on you bastard, buy it!* Her heart wanted to pound right out of her chest, but she held it in check just like Snake had taught her. *Snake!* She forced those thoughts from her mind and concentrated on the evil before her. The Betrayer paced back and forth with a spectral hand upon his misty chin. He was obviously mulling over all that she had said. *Well, here goes nothing.*

"Look, I'd like some sort of answer so I know whether or not I should hang-out here or start killing everyone."

The Betrayer stopped cold in his tracks, "You are in no position to make threats."

"Oh, really."

With that, Roxie spun around, grabbed her sword from the idiot troll who had been standing way to close to her, slit his throat, ran through the second troll before he pulled his sword, knocked Mongrel to the ground, and brought her bloody sword to bear on his throat without breaking a sweat. Evil laughter pulled her attention backwards as she held the terrified servant hostage on the ground. Apparently, she had Old Evil One's attention.

"You make a very strong point for yourself. We have an agreement, then. You will help me take control of the Land, and I will send you home."

She stepped back and dropped her sword. Mongrel scrambled to his feet. That was exactly as she had expected.

"Okay, it's a deal. But, remember, I don't like you."

"And, you remember, I will see every last one of your friends dead. Now, Mongrel, show her to her chambers. We will plan for total domination soon, be ready."

No one tried to take her sword from her as Roxanne left the room. And, no one tried to restrain her as she followed Mongrel down yet another corridor. However, as the door closed on her chamber, and she was left alone, she knew one thing for sure- the Betrayer would never let her out of here alive. *Fair is fair. I'm not letting him out alive, either.* With vengeance on her mind, the seasoned warrior prepared for psychological warfare. *Let's finish the game.*

****

Karlis laid flat against the tree branch on which he had perched and carefully monitored the movements of the enemy throngs. They were marching north, as usual. For two days, they hadn't done anything different. They never altered course; never sped up; and, never did anything of real interest. They just marched. *No wonder Snake's a crazy bitch. This would make anyone insane.* It was definitely getting to him. He saw lines of marching trolls in his sleep.

He watched them for a couple more minutes before he had all the fun he could stand an decided to return to base. Sliding out of the tree, he signaled for the rest of his team to join him. Soon, all of the remaining members of the Roxie's elite strike force were gathered around him. Despite all of their losses, their pride and strength remained.

"Are we done napping?" asked Kilmer.

Karlis let out a chuckle of agreement, "Yeah, that's it for now folks. We get to go back and report that the troops are heading north."

"Again. I guess no news is good news."

"That's great, Kilmer. Maybe you should write it down," responded Karlis.

Kilmer responded with a mock bow. Little did they know, he had already written it down, along with a few other handy sayings. Karlis just grinned. This man was one of the best swordsman in the Land, hard and rough around the edges. But, his sensitivity with the ladies was legendary. *You're not as bad as you'd like us all to believe.*

"Well, we've wasted enough time for today. We'll head back to the camp and start long distance rotating sentry duty. Kilmer and Rikman take first shift."

This called for a grander bow from Kilmer, followed by a huge grin and a smart-ass remark, "At your beck and call, my Lord."

Karlis refrained from responding. Instead, he marched his bored team back to base.

Back at the base, soldiers were busy preparing for the day's march. Tents were disappearing into packs, fires were being destroyed, and weapons were being strapped to any and every part of their bodies. It was just another day in paradise. And, in the middle of it all, stood the majestic General Sabastian handing out orders to everyone. He saw the team immediately and motioned them forward.

"What news?" boomed the General.

Karlis shook his head, "Same as before, they are moving north at a constant speed. They don't even look sideways. It's as though they are just mindlessly following some directive and they don't have the brainpower to do anything different."

The General nodded. However, he did not seem content. He folded his arms across his chest and began tugging at his thick, red beard.

"What's on your mind, General?"

General Sabastian kept tugging at his beard. For a moment, Karlis wondered if he had been heard. But, before he could repeat himself, the General voiced his concern.

"They keep marching and we keep following them. It's just all too convenient."

"You suspect a trap?"

The giant man stopped and stared intently at Karlis, who actually felt the desire to cower. "I always suspect a trap. I spend my days looking for them and my nights dreaming about them. That is why I'm still alive."

Despite the great intimidation force of the General, Karlis found his voice, "Has the trailer team reported any movement?"

The General shook his head.

"Well, at least we are not being ambushed from behind."

"There I will agree with you. But there is still the chance that we could be walking into a trap."

Karlis tried to take a calm look at things, "That is always a possibility, but I have seen nothing from his troops to indicate that they are even remotely capable of thinking."

"They aren't the ones to worry about. I can't believe that we could be this close to the Betrayer without him being aware of our presence."

"Maybe he just doesn't know where to look. Besides, why would he risk letting the Lords get any closer to him when he could turn his troops on us now and squash us with the sheer force of his numbers?"

The General seemed to be concentrating on some unknown spot far away, "Yes, why indeed?"

Karlis waited patiently for another sort of response, something to let him know what course of action should be taken. With things where they stood right now, he didn't have a clue. He missed Roxanne. She had always dealt with this end of things, leaving the rest of them to just fight the fight to the best of their abilities. She fought all the other battles. *Roxie?* For the millionth time, he thought there must be more to her leaving than met the eye. She had to have something up her sleeve. He was pretty sure Snake thought that, and he knew the Commander did. He just wished he knew what it was.

"We proceed as planned, for now," boomed the General, pulling Karlis back from his thoughts. "But, we move cautiously. I want to know if any of those trolls even glance sideways."

"Yes, General. Oh, General?"

"What is it?"

Karlis swallowed hard, "Any news from Snake?"

General Sabastian softened, "None. The Commander has been trying to contact her since we left," he motioned to the far side of the camp where the Commander stood staring out into the forest.

Karlis nodded, "You'll let me know if there's any word?"

The bear of a man put a huge hand on Karlis' shoulder, "Immediately."

Without another word, both men returned to their duties and held their pain inside.

Meanwhile, Commander Gabriel stood, unmoving, at the edge of the camp and stared at the trees. *What? Do you expect her to just materialize out of thin air? Why not? She has a thousand times before.* Gabe shook his head. This was getting ridiculous. He spent all of his time searching the trees for any sign of her, all the while knowing she was not there to be found. He was letting his feelings for her interfere with his ability to carry out his duties. This had to stop before he lost his edge. He was acting like a lost puppy. *Come on Gabe. You are a hardened killer. Get a grip.*

That was all he could stand. He was making himself sick to his stomach. Throwing up a half-assed emotional wall built with bricks like "I gave her my heart and she spit on it," the Commander turned away from the forest and back to the war. He was, after all, the damn leader. Even as he marched defiantly from his post and back to the land of the living, a single thought found its way into his resolved mind. *Damn it, Snake! Where are you?*

****

Snake crouched among the leaves of the tree she was hiding in and watched the trolls moving beneath her. There were hundreds of them barreling forward without a sideways glance, or an upward glance for that matter. She had spent the past two days leaping from tree to tree, following the path Roxanne had left and avoiding entanglement with the trolls. And, the path Roxanne had left was a big one. If she had attempted to cover her tracks, she had failed miserably. Snake knew better. She had trained her better than that.

Snake moved to the edge of the branch, checked the trolls,

and leapt into the next tree. Quickly, she turned to see what the trolls were doing. They continued to march straight ahead, never looking up and never stopping. *Idiots!* Snake was making enough noise to wake the dead, but she couldn't get them to even check for birds. *You really can't think for yourselves can you?* She moved down this new branch to a point where she could better survey the ground.

It only took a minute for her to find what she was looking for. *Why, hello there.* Directly beneath her, lay a perfect little path, which pointed like an arrow to Roxanne's whereabouts. *You want me to find you, don't you?* The thought had crossed her mind several times over the past couple of days. Every time she saw a broken branch or a shred of clothing, Snake knew. The very fact that Roxanne had traveled down the edge of the forest instead of straight down the center where troll movements might hide her tracks showed how anxious she was to be found. She was meant to find her friend, she was sure of it. *Listen to me, friend. When did I learn that world. Next thing you know, I'll be spouting love poems.*

As soon as she thought it, she wished she hadn't. Her mind immediately made the leap to Commander Gabriel and the words he had said. *Why did he have to go and ruin a perfectly good lie?* Everything was complicated now. She had been so confused when she left, and it hadn't gotten much better. She had ignored his every attempt to make contact with her. She knew she was being childish, but she had no clue what to say to him. She didn't remember how to be loved... and, she still wasn't sure she wanted to.

She shook some sense back into her head. *Time and place, Snake. Time and place.* This wasn't the right moment to deal with this. Right now she had more important things to deal with. She had to find Roxanne before it was too late. She made the leap into the next tree and looked up. What she saw blew her mind. There were no more large, luscious trees; there were only desolate mountains. There was no mistaking it, she was knocking on the Betrayer's front door. *Looks like it might already be too late.*

Moving as close to exposed air as she could, Snake began to

scan for any possible signs of an entrance. After only a few seconds, she realized she couldn't see anything from where she was. *Well, what did you expect? A big sign that says: Welcome to hell, check your weapons at the door?* Not exactly, but she had hoped for something. The increased rumbling behind her told her she had better come up with something fast; those trolls would be there any moment. Roxanne had to be inside, that meant Snake had to be there as well. *Think! I could always surrender.* As she laughed at herself, the smile quickly turned to a devilish grin. *Of course. How else do I get in?*

Snake reviewed the details of her plan in her mind. It was tactically simple and mortally dangerous, the Commander would be proud. Quickly, she squelched the emotions that were conjured up inside her by the mere thought of him. *I'm going to have to get over this before I loose my edge and my nasty reputation.* She decided to go forward with her plan. Waiting until the trolls were almost upon her, she summoned her strength, and jumped, hoping they wouldn't try to kill her.

****

A sudden pounding on her chamber door sent Roxanne flying for her sword. Only when she had it in hand, did she calm down enough to look around her and get her bearings. It took a couple of seconds for her to remember where she was, but it came back to her. *Oh, that's right, I'm in hell.* The pounding at the door repeated itself. Roxanne cringed.

"Alright already. Hold your horses. I'm coming."

She swung the door open with all her might and was immediately repulsed by the figure of Mongrel standing at the door.

"What do you want?"

Mongrel inched into the room, "The Master wants to see you, now!"

Roxanne bit down on numerous retorts and insults that leapt to mind. Now was not the time and place for the.

"What does he want?"

Mongrel smiled, a feat that made his hideous face even more

unbearable. "It's a surprise."

A sudden chill ran down her spine. *I have a very bad feeling about this.* With no other choice but to move forward, Roxanne followed the little worm back to the main chamber.

Roxanne nearly gaged when she entered the Betrayer's main hall; the smell of rotting flesh overwhelmed her. She threw her hand to her nose and scanned the room for the source of the smell. It wasn't hard to spot. The smell was coming from the corpses of the two trolls she had killed earlier. Now, as they started to decompose, they created a stench that was sickening. Roxanne looked up at the black hole of evil in the room.

"Why don't you have those things removed? They're making me sick."

The Betrayer slowly raised his head from the cauldron he was standing over and leveled his burning red eyes on Roxanne' shielded face.

"I don't remember asking you to speak."

Every fiber of her being stood on end. *Not much of an equal rights advocate, is he?*

"True, but you called me down here for a reason, and if it's anything other than making me sick, you had better get rid of those corpses so I don't pass-out."

The Betrayer eyed her for a couple more seconds, an act that sent most people screaming. Roxanne held her ground, defiantly staring back at him and daring him to respond. This intrigued the Betrayer. He had never been challenged so by another living soul; he decided not to disintegrate the young beauty on the spot. However, it wasn't enough to get him to move the corpses.

"You have greater troubles than a couple of dead trolls," he said as he stirred the giant cauldron.

Roxanne was afraid to ask. Whatever it was, it had the Betrayer entirely too pleased with himself.

"Really? What's that?"

He motioned her forward to the smoking cauldron. Reluctantly, she moved forward. As she peered over he edge, he let his little secret slip.

"We have captured one of your friends snooping around the edge of the forest."

When the smoke cleared, Roxanne found herself gazing into a dark room that looked like a dungeon chamber. The walls were solid stone, only a fraction of light came through a barred window on the door, dirt covered the floor, and in the middle of it all stood a really pissed off Snake. Roxanne felt her heart leap into her throat. It was all she could do to keep her legs from buckling under her weight. *Jesus, Snake. I knew you'd find me, but I never imagined you'd get caught.* Plans whirled around in her head as she attempted to work this one out. This was going to take an impossible amount of maneuvering. She had to get Snake out of there, alive. *Way to put me on the spot.* Entertaining as many ideas as possible, Roxanne looked back at the Betrayer.

"So, what do you want me to do about it? I can't keep them from scouting the forest and looking for us."

The Lord of Darkness suppressed a desire to erupt with anger at this challenging child, "She is not alone. I have checked the forest and found the rest of your forces moving along behind my troops." The Betrayer leaned over Roxanne, bringing his eyes within an inch of her's. "Now, can you give me one good reason why I shouldn't just turn my troops around, wipe-out the army, kill your friend, and eliminate you?"

Roxanne felt the very real force behind those words. This was no joke. That was exactly what he would do if she couldn't think of a way to stop him and make it believable. She felt her heart pounding against her ribcage as he continued to hover over her. Suddenly, her mind finished sorting through the pictures and pieces in her head, and the answer, clumsy as it may have been, appeared. She swallowed hard and tried it out on him.

"I can give you three."

The red eyes that were keeping her in check, narrowed to mere slits as the Betrayer mulled things over, himself. After a few moments, that seemed like forever, he slowly pulled back.

"Well, make your case."

"First, if you turn the the troops around, you can't guarantee that the Lords, who will be the best protected, won't make a b-line right back to the forest, and we already know they can get in. You run the risk of letting them slip right through your fingers only to return and defy you. Second, the fairies, themselves, have powers that are beyond control and understanding. They might be able to use them this close to the forest without ever stepping outside the forest. And third, we both know about the prophesy that says only I can save or damn the land. So, you need me, and don't pretend you don't."

Roxanne paused and let that sink in. Her heart was still pounding. She had no idea how much of that he would believe; she wasn't sure how much of it she did. She had pulled most of it out of thin air. With her heart in her throat, she waited for a sign.

The Betrayer eyed the Last of the Chosen as she made her case. She sounded like someone trying to save her own neck, and she was. But, there was truth behind her worried words. He decided to use his cunning and let her tell him what he should do.

"There are few other options open, Chosen One," he said menacingly.

Roxanne took a deep breath and threw all her cards on the table, "Your best bet is to get them as close as possible before you attack them. And, I think I know just how we can lead them into a trap."

They are cunning. Just how do you think you can trap them without them knowing?"

For the first time since this conversation started, Roxanne smiled a genuine smile, "I use my fellow... my friend, Snake." She had almost let "fellow Chosen One" slip out of her mouth. She wasn't sure whether or not the Betrayer knew who Snake was, but she wasn't going to take any chances.

The Betrayer mimicked Roxanne's grin, "That would be truly evil. Can it be done?"

She swallowed hard, "If it can't, you can do it your way."

The ominous being turned away, relieving Roxanne from his terrible stare. For a moment, there was nothing but a horrible silence. Then, he spoke.

"Do it."

She nearly ran out of the room, grabbing her guide, Mongrel, as she left. But, before she got out the door, one last phrase made its way to her ears.

"I will be watching you."

****

Snake sat in the corner of her cell and concentrated on the door. There had to be a way to get it open. She just wasn't sure what it was. But, she had to find it because she was running out of options. She had already inspected every inch of the walls and ceiling for any sign of a weakness and came up blank. If she couldn't find one in the door, she would be permanently screwed. *Well, it was my bright idea to get caught. Now, I've got to find a way to get un-caught.*

The sound of footsteps in the hallway stopped her mental wondering. All of her senses searched for information. There were two sets of feet coming her way. Odds were one woman and one man with a slight limp. She guessed that one to be Mongrel, and she prayed the other was Roxanne. The footsteps stopped right outside her door and a familiar voice came through the small window.

"You had better wait out here, Mongrel. She won't trust me unless I'm by myself."

Those words stung Snake's ears like a slap in the face. Could it really be as they all had feared? Was Roxanne being controlled by the Betrayer? Fire welled up in her at the thought of yet another betrayal. She looked around the room for some sort of weapon; her heart ached when she realized all she had left was her bare hands. She was so ferrous, she almost missed the subtle tugging on her mind.

I know you can hear me, Snake. I know you can hear me talking to Mongrel. Stop and think.

Roxanne's mental voice was very faint and highly shielded. Snake pushed her fury aside and thought it through. Roxanne would know that she was listening for sounds. She would also know that she would be overheard, and that Snake would not be happy with the information she just received. The most logical conclusion was a set-up. Snake shielded her own thoughts.

Okay. I thought. This had better be good.

"I will wait out here, but I will be listening to every word."

Roxanne laughed at the little man, "Suit yourself. I don't care if you sit out here and take notes. Your Master knows what's going on. Now, if you'll excuse me."

Snake remained calmly fixed in her corner, eyes on the door as it slowly opened. She controlled a thousand different urges as Roxanne stepped into the cell. Roxanne controlled only one; she wanted to grab her friend and run. Both women held their ground.

"So, it's true. You have decided to join the darkside," prompted Snake.

Roxanne took a deep breath and prayed she could handle this the right way, "Look, I'm just trying to get home, but I don't expect you to understand that." *Please, listen carefully to me. This is going to be tricky.*

"Get home, huh? You think that this asshole is going to send you home? Well, I've got some news for you, you might as well unpack because you are about to betray your friends for nothing." *Tricky? Whatever you are trying to pull is going to be impossible. Remember, I'm a cynic. Just why should I trust you, again?*

Again? You never trusted me in the first place. "No, that's not true," Roxanne moved closer and pretended to be whispering. *Do not listen to a word of this. It's all for his sake.* "Look, I was trying to save my own skin, but now I realize I can't, so listen carefully. The Betrayer is going to pull all of his troops in and prepare for a defensive stand. Now is a perfect opportunity to attack." *He is planning to set up a trap; a trap I devised. He is going to catch you in the bottleneck passage.*

Snake eyed Roxanne very closely before she decided to play along. She whispered just loud enough to be heard by Mongrel, "Go on." *Yeah, go on.*

"He's going to bring in those troops that are waiting on the far side of the forest in a couple of days. You need to get his advance troops now, while you still can." *He's already bringing in the rear guard. They will be here within two days.* "If I were you, I'd wait until they enter the passageway between the two spikes so that they will be trapped in an enclosed area." *In case you didn't notice, that's the perfect bottleneck. He intends to trap you there, but I have a plan.*

282

This ought to be good. "Why should I trust you? For all I know, this could be a trap."

Nice cover. "You don't have to trust me. I'm just sitting here, risking my life if I get caught, telling you how it is. Right now the Betrayer believes I'm on his side. If he catches me here, we will both die." *Leave my strike force behind to come in behind his rear guard. Move the Lords to the front. When he catches you in the trap, have the strike force come in from behind.*

"How do I know you aren't setting me up? He probably knows you are here right now," whispered Snake fiercely. *This plan sounds like suicide to me.*

Oh, but the best is yet to come. "Do you really think he would risk letting me talk to you? Look, I've been here too long already. He's going to start looking for me soon. I have to go, but I'll leave the door unlocked. I know this isn't much, but it's all I can do to make up for the damage I've done." *Once the fighting starts, you have got to get the Lords through and inside these caverns. I'll leave the door open. Maybe, with all of us together, we can finally banish the bastard for good.*

Snake leaned into the light, an evil grin upon her face, "If you are lying to me, I will come back and kill you as sure as you are standing here." *Well, it's mortally dangerous but it 'aint tactically simple.*

"I know." *So sue me.*

Roxanne wanted to clasp hands with her friend and let her know that they were still as one. She wanted to make sure she was trusted, but that was impossible right now. She just had to leave and trust in Snake's instincts to tell her the truth. She stepped toward the door and turned to go.

Snake watched the pain and confusion on Roxanne's face. Whatever her motivation, this was obviously the most painful moment of her life. She had always said she liked a challenge, but Snake suspected that this was more than she had in mind. Without knowing why, Snake decided to trust her. She really had no other option. This was all going to be over soon, one way or another, and nothing they could do would stop it. As Roxanne turned her back, Snake gave one last farewell.

"Don't turn your back on someone you aren't positive you

can trust." *Good luck.*

Roxanne controlled the urge to cry, "I never do." *May the force be with you.*

Then she was gone and Snake was alone in her cell once more. A faint voice reached her ears as the footsteps started to move away from the door.

"It better work," growled Mongrel.

"That's for certain," sighed Roxanne.

Snake moved to the door and tried the handle. It was unlocked as promised. Mustering all of her skill and strength, Snake snuck out of her cell and moved forward to try and get trapped. *I can't believe I'm doing this.*

I can.

Snake grinned and melted into her surroundings. *Let the games begin.*

****

Chapter 14

General Sabastian studied the silhouette of his trusted right-hand man as the Commander paced the edge of the forest. As much as he wanted to, he couldn't do a damn thing about it. He let out a heavy sigh. Commander Gabriel just wasn't the same man since the disappearance of his two friends. But, that was to be expected. The necklaces that bonded the three of them was much more than a physical bond. The General knew the legend and he knew the origins of the

pendants. There had to be strong emotional ties that were beyond their control. It seemed unfair that the fate of the land rested on the shoulders of those who were only human. These weren't beings with magic powers, these were mere mortals with emotional problems. This was going to be one hell of a final battle.

Then, without warning, the Commander turned and rushed back into the camp.

"General, gather all of the Lords and the troop leaders. Snake is on her way and she found Roxanne."

****

All eyes were glued on Snake as she finished her report of the events leading up to her return. No one spoke. It was as though know one dared. The story Snake had just recounted chilled them all to the bone. Roxanne had walked into the viper's nest and held his hand in order to make it possible for them to get one last shot at victory. She had risked her life and her very soul to bring them this chance. They had to take it.

Ever dance with the devil in the pale moonlight?

Snake remained stoic as she responded to Gabe's mental question.

What?

Nothing. I just don't like the thought of Roxie being that close to that devil. It has to do some damage.

That's what I'm afraid of.

Clearing his throat and shaking his head, Karlis asked the one question that no one else dared, "I hate to be the one to say this, but are you sure we can trust her?"

All eyes were suddenly upon him. He felt as though he were being dissected by everyone in the tent. And, Lord Earin came out of his chair in fury.

"How can you even ask that?! Haven't you been listening? Roxanne has risked everything so that we can have this chance. We have to take it."

Karlis remained calm, "And if it's a trap?"

Lord Earin leaned forward into Karlis' face, "It's not."

Karlis faced the Lord without flinching, "No one wants to believe that more than I do. She was my friend and mentor. My heart tells me to trust her, but my head tells me no."

High Lord Brennen decided now was the time to intervene, "Ah, but the question is what do your instincts tell you?"

Both men turned to the High Lord and let their battle die. He had a point. They were in a place where logic mattered little and all hope was dying fast. This one glimmer, from someone they all admired and had trusted, was the only they had to go on. Trap or not, the Betrayer's arm was going to be an overwhelming force. The question was not whether they would fight, but when they would fight. Karlis began to search his soul.

"I trust her."

The High Lord smiled a fatherly smile. He had known he could rely on Snake to see things with her gut. She didn't trust people lightly, and she knew human character all too well. As he had watched her tell her story, he had known that she believed in Roxanne... and, so did he.

Snake took on all the questioning stares, "I was there. I talked to her. I looked into her eyes. I know who she is, and I trust her."

Commander Gabriel leaned back in his chair and folded his hands behind his head, "That makes two of us. Besides, we are running out of really good plans anyway."

Lord Earin took his seat, "You all know where I stand. My

trust is in Roxanne."

Maybe I'd be better comforted if he did more thinking with his head and less with his heart.

Can't blame a guy for trying, Snake. She just overpowered him.

Well, we need him here and we need him clear.

Gabe let those words sink in. He couldn't help but feel they were partially directed towards him. She hadn't said a word about their earlier conversation. Truth be told, he was glad. He still needed time to regather his senses and hopefully make a better case. *We'll talk when this is all over... if we can.* He shook that thought from his head. It was that kind of thinking that had put him in this mess. If he could just keep those thoughts out of his head for a few more days, he might make it through the war with Snake still speaking to him.

Lord Anjalina watched as a silent interplay took place between the Chosen. She suspected that they held secrets to the universe in those silent conversations, but she couldn't prove it and they'd never tell. So, she settled for voicing her own opinion.

"I'm with the rest of you, and you all know that each and everyone of us trusts Roxanne. We have to, or we have to give ourselves over to total despair."

Lord Anjalina's words hit home with all the leaders of the land. Karlis cursed himself for ever expressing any doubt. The lady Lord was right. None of them had any doubt, but, still, he felt the question had to be asked. General Sabastian seconded his thoughts.

"Whether or not we all trust her, we have to be made to think this through. We would question anyone in that position; Roxanne is no different. However, if we think this through, it is obvious that this I still the best plan, regardless of where she stands," the General paused to allow any questions. None came.

"From this point on, we are following the plan presented to us by Roxanne through Snake. We leave tonight. Those of you responsible for individual squads need to get them armed and ready to move by sundown. The rest of you, get packed. Oh, and folks, make no mistake, this is the last battle of this war. Win or loose, we are about to see the end."

For a moment, no one moved as the weight of the General's words sat in their ears and on their hearts. Then, everyone moved at once. Karlis headed for the strike team, the Lords went to prepare their spells, and Snake, the Commander, and the General stared at each other as the weight of the world, once again, descended upon their shoulders.

****

Chapter 15

Roxanne choked down the putrid smell of the Betrayer's war room and made her way to the cauldron in the center of the room. She nearly gagged as she walked past the decomposing corpses of the trolls she had killed three days ago. The Betrayer refused to remove them; he seemed to get some sort of sick pleasure out of the reaction their stench drew from Roxanne. She hurried past them, tying a scarf around her mouth and nose to aid breathing. *I guess the Evil High Lord of Darkness must not have a sense of smell.*

Apparently, the Betrayer either couldn't smell his decaying decor or he 'actually enjoyed the scent, because he stood, unfaltering, over the cauldron and grinned an evil grin. Roxanne suppressed an urge to smack it off his face. He motioned her forward.

"It seems your little plan is working. See for yourself."

Roxanne took a deep breath, which she immediately regretted, *Oh, that was brilliant,* and looked into the murky depths of the black waters. What she saw sent chills down her spine. The lead group of the demonic horde was entering the passageway, hundreds of them. They were being followed close behind by the forces of good, by all of her friends. As she watched them start to close the gap, she found herself praying that she hadn't condemned them to death. When she saw the Betrayer's rear guard come up behind them, she was almost certain she had. There were just too many of them. This was about to become impossible. She felt like throwing up, but the stench in the room had nothing to do with it, she couldn't stand the thought of watching her friends die. *Dear God, what have I done?*

"It would appear that you have upheld your end of the bargain. You have delivered all those who stood in my way. I shall now dispose of all my enemies, and I owe it all to you."

Roxanne turned on the Betrayer with fire in her eyes and

fury in her soul. If she could have killed him with her bare hands, she would have done so with pleasure. But, being around him, she had learned that he could not be killed by ordinary physical means. There was going to have to be magic involved. She just hoped the Lords would be alive to provide it.

"Don't start patting yourself on the back yet. They are still alive...besides, I'm not doing this for you. I'm doing this so that I can see my little brother again," as she uttered those words visions of her little brother mixed with pictures of Sage in her head. Silently, she began to pray.

"That is oh so touching, but I don't have a heart. I don't care why you helped me. And, don't worry, they will all be dead soon enough. Then, I can go on to rule my world and you can go back to your miserable existence in yours."

It took every ounce of restraint in her body not to lunge at his throat and tear it open like a wild animal. She wanted him dead more and more with each passing second. She couldn't stand to be this close to pure evil for much longer. *I don't know how Yoda did it all those years. He must have been a Jedi or something. Hah, hah. See that's funny because... Now, I am loosing it.* Roxanne pulled her wandering mind back into check. She could tell she was crossing the edge; she was telling herself really bad jokes. Mongrel's voice snapped her back to attention.

"It won't be long," he drooled. "The fighting has begun."

Roxanne focused all of her attention on the cauldron. The fighting had definitely started. The picture before her was a mess of flashing swords and flying bodies. Both armies were wedged into the passageway and hacking away at one another. Trolls lunged and people countered. Roxanne searched the battlefield for any sign of Snake and Gabe. She couldn't see them, but she had no trouble finding General Sabastian. He stood right in the middle of things, killing trolls by the dozens. With his red hair dancing in the wind and his huge battle ax swinging around his head, he looked like he could destroy them all single-handedly.

She looked past the General toward the frontline where she hoped the Lords would be, and there they were. They were thirteen proud and majestic figures, and they filled Roxanne's tired heart with joy. There was fire in the Land yet. They stood like fierce statues, each doing his part to fight the demonic horde. A flash of rapid movement caught her eye, so she struggled to follow it. It was Snake! Roxanne felt overwhelming relief at the sight of her friend. That meant that she was alive and that the troops were aware of the plan.

Quickly, Roxanne turned her attention to the rear guard. Unfortunately, the Betrayer did as well. What they saw amazed them both. A small strike team, lead by Karlis, had moved in behind the rear guard and was forcing them to turn their attentions rear-ward. The Betrayer became furious.

"What?! That is impossible!" he boomed. But, then he realized it was possible, and he realized how. He turned his fury on Roxanne. "You did this! You have challenged me for the last time! The prophesy be damned, I will put an end to you all, starting with you!"

Roxanne dived beneath the cauldron as a bolt of magic lightening whizzed past her ear. *I have no idea how I'm going to get out of this one.* She knew she couldn't stay down there forever, but, at the moment, she couldn't think of anything better to do. The Betrayer quickly changed her way of thinking. Reaching behind the cauldron, her hit her with a magic spell designed to knock her into oblivion. Only, it didn't.

There was a blast, a flash of light, but, when the smoke cleared, Roxanne remained crouched beneath the cauldron. She couldn't believe her own senses. Quickly, she groped her body to make sure she was all there. She was. Her mind reeled at the thought of what had just happened. She had been attacked with a magic that spelled certain doom, but had failed to leave a scratch on her. As she examined her hands, a fierce gleam caught her eye; it was the pendant shining with a red force. As fast as it could calculate, her mind put two and two together. *Of course. These pendants were forged out of the dark magic to protect the wearers.*

With a new found confidence, she stepped out to face the Betrayer. He was clearly upset at her presence, but he didn't appear shaken.

"So, the pendant retains its protective qualities. Pity, it would have been a painless death."

Roxanne filled with bravado, "So I can't kill you and you can't kill me..."

A chill ran down her spine as he looked into her eyes, "That's where you're wrong. You are still flesh and blood. You can be killed."

Oh yeah, there is that. He raised his hands, then turned his back to her as though he didn't have a care in the world and put all of his attention into the battle. Roxanne knew she was in trouble when the stench in the room doubled. Pulling her sword from her sheath, she turned to face the enemy she knew would be standing there. This was about to get ugly.

****

Snake ran a sword through one more troll, threw a knife through the throat of another, and backhanded a third. *This is getting ridiculous.* She glanced around to make sure the Lords were still standing before she jumped back into the battle. They were all still alive and doing battle with the creatures around them. Most of them wielded magic spells of protection as their weapons, but Lords Anjalina and Earin were swinging swords through the bodies of any trolls they could reach. For the first time ever in her association with them, Snake found some respect for the Lords. *At last, they are doing something other than serving as targets.*

A tiny voice called out to Snake through the roar of the battle. She hacked a couple more trolls to pieces before searching out the source. A panting and bloody Sage appeared at her side with his sword held infront of him.

"Snake," he gasped.

She pulled him into her side where she could protect him from any oncoming attacks. It was the closest thing to a mothering instinct she had.

"Calm down. Catch your breath and tell me what's going on."

Sage took a couple of deep breaths and pressed himself closer to Snake. He didn't have much time. He had to report to her and get back across the battlefield to help coordinate the effort between the main force and the strike team. He took one more breath, but that was all the time he could afford.

"The strike team has started their attack. They are meeting with little resistance. Karlis seems to believe that the trolls are only interested in attacking the main force, and, although he is having little trouble killing them, he can't get them to turn around and engage."

Snake let her brain race through possibilities as she countered yet another attack. All around her was total mayhem. She didn't have time for this. She was here to fight and get the Lords to the Betrayer, not to listen to problems. This was one for the General.

"So, why'd he send you to me?"

The little soldier sliced a troll across the knees and let Snake cut off his head when he hit the ground. Trying to ignore the horror of it all, he concentrated on talking to Snake.

"Karlis said you have a knack for these situations; something about being able to encourage a fight."

Snake shot a glare in the direction of the strike team. *Thanks a lot.* But, it was too late. She was already trying to figure out how to handle this one. *How the hell am I suppose to protect the Lords, kill the bad guys, and save the strike team? Next they'll expect me to move mountains.* Then it came to her, an idea that was painfully complex and completely dangerous, but it just might work.

"I need you to get to the Commander."

Sage looked up at her with questioning eyes, "Why?"

"He'll tell you when you get there. Now, go before it gets any more dangerous."

As the dutiful little page ran off into the throngs of soldiers, Snake carefully placed four more daggers in the hearts of menacing trolls. That little boy was about to be the most important person on the battlefield; she had to get him through alive. She sliced through yet another troll and then headed for the General. He wasn't hard to find.

General Sabastian stood like an island in the middle of a tumultuous sea. The ground around him was soaked with blood and littered with bodies, but he seemed unscathed. Truth be told, he almost looked at home. Snake felt a small amount of comradery for the commanding giant. She too understood what it felt like to be at home in the middle of adversary, but now was not the time to examine souls; now was the time to save some asses.

The General cleared a path when he saw Snake coming. He had no idea what was on her mind, but he knew it was important by the look on her face. She was totally determined.

"General," she said in between thrusts, "did Sage get to you?"

The General sliced through the nearest troll, "No. Should he have."

"Seems," grunted Snake as she countered yet another attack, "that Karlis can't get the enemy troops to turn around and engage him. They are after the main force. I've got an idea on how to change all that, but I need the Commander and a lot of luck."

General Sabastian didn't like the sound of any of that. It seemed that no matter what they did things just got worse and worse by the minute. Still, Snake was pretty clever at times.

"What do you need from me?"

"Time. I've got to talk to the Commander and I don't want to risk getting myself killed."

The General nodded, "You do what you have to and I'll cover you to the best of my ability."

"Thanks."

Snake crouched down with the General at her back and trusted him to cover it as she called out to the Commander.

Gabe?

Anyone ever tell you that your timing sucks?

Kill whoever you are dealing with and then listen to me.

There was a brief pause and Snake imagined the Commander to be killing some nasty, evil troll. She decided to take the pressure off the General by chopping apart one of the many trolls they were facing.

Okay. I'm here and I've got Sage with me. He tells me we've got more problems.

Yeah, well lucky for you I'm so brilliant. I've got a plan.

I don't like the sound of that. Hold one.

Hold one what?

The lack of a voice on the other end told her that he must be busy. She waited and watched the General ax a few more of the ever-approaching enemy.

Hold one second.

Gee thanks, but I figured it out...

Don't you think we had better get to the point?

Fine. Do you have any of those devices that we used to bring down the Betrayer's fortress?

I built a second one just in case the first one failed, but it's not a good idea. These things are powerful enough to bring down the mountains.

Exactly.

Gabe's heart did a leap into his throat as he contemplated what he was hearing. Snake had gone around the bend on this one. Why on earth would she want to bring down these mountains? Cutting the throat of the troll that was baring down on him, the Commander tried to get an explanation from Snake.

You had better tell me what's going through your head and you had better make it good.

We are going to cut ourselves off from the rear guard by moving mountains.

And, we are going to cut-off the strike team and our only avenue of escape.

We bring the strike team through, and we do not need an escape route. Let's be honest here. No matter what the outcome of this war, we are not leaving the same way we came in. It's all or nothing on this one.

You've got a point. Okay, we'll do it. How do I get the device to Karlis?

You're going to have to use Sage. Snake waited for the verbal attack she knew would follow.

Sage!? Are you crazy? He's just a kid.

A kid with a sword and an attitude. A kid who has already made it across the battlefield more than once.

The Commander looked down at the child standing beside him. His chest was heaving and his eyes were wide with wonder. Roxanne would kill him if anything happened to this kid, but it appeared they didn't have much of a choice.

Looks like it's our only option. I'll send him, but we need him back alive to tell us when to duck.

Fine. Whatever it takes.

Yeah, whatever it takes.

With the mental conversation over, the Commander turned all of his attention back to the current desperate situation. *How do I get myself into these places. Oh yeah, I listen to women.* That thought made him smile. If either of the women he was thinking about had heard that, he wouldn't have to worry about the Betrayer killing him. Thrusting and chopping his way to the face of the nearest cliff, the Commander called out to those around him to form a protective line. He pulled Sage along with him.

Moderately safe, Commander Gabriel reached into his pack and pulled out the bomb he had made and handed it to Sage.

"Listen to me very carefully. This has to reach Karlis. Tell him to put it at the base of one of the mountain spikes at the passage entrance. See this here? This is called the fuse. Tell him to get all of his men as far into this side of the battle as possible and then use an arrow to light it. It's risky and they won't have a lot of time. This thing is going to bring the whole mountain down. Do you understand?"

Sage swallowed the panic that welled up inside him, but not before it registered on is face, "I-I understand."

The Commander nodded, "Good. Don't stick around after you deliver it. I need you to get back to me and let me know so that we can duck in time."

Sage shook his head in agreement.

Gabe patted him on the head, "And may the force be with you."

Sage started at the sound of that phrase. Roxanne said that all the time. It was suppose to give him strength. He took the package and headed out with only a farewell glance at the Commander.

As the brave little messenger made his way through the troops, the Commander called out to his men, "That boy gets through alive! Understand? No one lets him die."

"Yes sir!" echoed back from everywhere and the battle raged on.

****

Karlis stared at Sage like he had gone mad. He had sent him after an answer and he had returned with a package and a prayer. Things weren't looking better, they were looking insane. Karlis examined the package carefully, trying to figure out exactly how it worked. If the stories he had heard about the fortress attack were true, this thing was going to level that mountain. *Well, maybe it's not so crazy after all.*

He looked at the kid again, "Any idea how long we will have before it goes off?"

Sage shook his head, "The Commander just said to get everyone as far away as possible before you light it."

Karlis nodded, "That means not long." He contemplated for a few more seconds, but the decision was already made. "Okay. Get back to the Commander and tell him we are going to do it. When he sees the team, duck."

Sage took a deep breath of air and prepared to run back across the endless battlefield. But, Karlis stopped him mid-step.

"Oh, did I forget to tell you that I'm sending a guard with you this time?"

He was only a kid, but his testosterone level was high enough for this to injury his sense of pride, "I can make it by myself."

Karlis smiled, "Oh, you've proven that a million times over, but I'm still sending someone with you."

Sage smiled, too, "Fine. Just tell him to keep up." Then he was gone, running at full speed.

"Shit," mumbled Karlis. "Rikman! Follow that kid. Make sure he makes it to the Commander."

Rikman snapped to attention, "What kid?"

Karlis turned and looked, and, sure enough, he was gone. "He went that way."

Rikman shrugged his shoulders and headed out at full speed in the direction indicated, bowling over enemy soldiers as he went. *Well, a least that's taken care of. Now, on to the fun stuff.* Karlis looked down at the device in his hands and decided that there was no time like the present. If they were really going to bring down the mountains, they had to do it while there were still people left to protect.

"Fall back!" he yelled without worry. He knew the enemy troops wouldn't follow them, they were too busy moving forward. Within seconds, the entire strike team surrounded him.

"Listen up, there has been a change of plans. We are moving up to the front lines as fast as possible."

Kilmer piped up, "What's up?"

"We are going to attempt to cut the rear guard off by bringing the mountain down on top of them. The Commander sent us a device to handle it, but we haven't got a lot of time. So, it's been nice, see you all at the front lines, leave."

They all stared at him without budging. He knew they wouldn't just leave.

"Look, I'm coming. I just have to set up the device before I go. Oh, and I need Kilmer to set it off," said Karlis.

They stared at him for a few more seconds before Kent spoke up, "You heard the man, we gots to go. There are people up front who need some saving. Let's move out."

As the team finally started to go, Kent turned as clenched hands with Karlis and Kilmer each in turn. "Good luck." Then, they were gone and Karlis and Kilmer were left with the duty of getting this party started.

"Okay, there's not a lot of time to go over this, so here it is in a nutshell. I'm going to place this device against the left spike. You and I are going to get as far away as possible. Then, while I cover you, you are going to hit this fuse here with a flaming arrow. Any questions?"

Kilmer couldn't believe what he was hearing. "Yeah. Are you crazy? You want me to hit that mark from across a crowded battlefield, do you know how impossible that is?"

"Are you saying you can't do it?"

Kilmer shook his head, "No. I'm saying we are going to have to be pretty close."

Now, Karlis shook his head, "We don't have a lot of time

once the fuse is lit."

Kilmer put his hand on his friend's shoulder, "I guess we'll just have to run really fast."

That decision made. The two men started their way toward the cliff face. They hacked through every troll that stood in their way until they stood face to face with solid mountain. Karlis found a crevice in the side of the cliff and stuffed the device in, leaving the fuse dangling down to the ground. Kilmer eyed it over for a few minutes before coming to the conclusion that the whole arrow thing just was not going to work. This was not a doable target. There had to be another way. He looked around for answers, but only the obvious came to him.

"I can't hit this from a distance. We are going to have to ignite it from here."

Karlis examined the set-up and looked across the battlefield. The distance was too great and the fuse too short for this to work. But, Kilmer didn't play games. If he said he couldn't hit it, he couldn't hit it. There had to be a way to ignite it without sacrificing themselves. *I'm just as noble as the next guy, but come on.* He looked around for something, anything, but the only thing around was enemy soldiers. *Enemy soldiers?*

"Hey, I have a crazy idea. Why don't we use the bad guys to ignite it?"

Kilmer stared at Karlis, "You're right, that's crazy."

"No really. If we light a few of them on fire, one of them is bound to brush past the fuse, beings how they are all crammed in here so tightly," he said as he sliced through yet another thick torso.

Kilmer surveyed the situation then shrugged his aching shoulders, "What the hell. I've got nothing better to do today."

Neither man asked the obvious question. They both just hoped it would work so that they didn't have to come up with yet another solution. Karlis took a protective stance infront of Kilmer while he went to work starting a fire. That done, he flamed up his arrows, took a deep breath, and started firing them into the bodies of nearby trolls. He aimed for their flammable parts, such as hair and clothing, and waited for the flames to sprout. They did.

Karlis yelled out, "Great. Now, lets get the hell out of here."

"Right," replied Kilmer, "I'm a much better shot from a distance anyway."

The two men took off down the face of the cliff as fast as they could travel. Kilmer stopped periodically and fired arrow after arrow over his shoulder until he had no more. As the flames began to rage, Karlis had a thought, *God, I hope this works. There is no way we are getting back through this mess to start all over.* They had covered a good distance and pissed off a lot of trolls. The closer they got to the main force, the harder it was to get through the trolls. And, trolls were starting to fight back. Karlis glanced back for any sign that the fuse had been touched; he saw nothing.

In the end, it wasn't what he saw that was important so much as what he heard. There was nothing but grunts and screams and then... A blast cracked through the air, the ground trembled, trolls collapsed, and rock started to fall from the heavens. Karlis and Kilmer looked at each other, picked themselves up off the ground, and made a mad dash forward. All hell had just broken loose.

Chunks of mountain hit the ground at their heels, crushing trolls and anything else that got in the way. The two men never looked back. They just kept running like they were possessed. The more they ran, the more pieces of mountain fell. For a while, it appeared the plan had worked a little too well. That idea was confirmed when Karlis looked up and saw a rather large piece of the mountain about to descend on his and Kilmer's heads.

"Dive for it!" he yelled, and the two men took a flying leap of faith through the air.

When the last of the debris finished showering their heads and the dust finally settled. They were amazed to find themselves still in one piece. Kilmer shook the dust from his head and looked up to see the General and the Commander standing over he and Karlis with huge grins on their faces.

"Do you want to tell us what the fuck is so funny?" he asked.

The two leaders glanced at each other, "Ah, memories," sighed the General.

"Welcome to our world, guys," added the Commander.

Karlis rolled over, "Are we dead yet?"

"No," moaned Kilmer, "we aren't that lucky."

The General and the Commander offered them a hand up which they readily accepted.

"The good news is the plan worked. The bad news is there are still hundreds of bad guys to kill; but, it's a whole lot easier to fight one side at a time."

"So what you're saying is, we only have one set of trolls left to kill? Well, hell. Let's commence with the ass-whooping," said Kilmer.

Karlis groaned, "Here we go again."

But, before any of them could take a step forward to join the ongoing battle, Snake appeared out of nowhere like always.

"Not so fast, gentlemen. I'm afraid there's a little more to it than just that."

Why must you always spoil our fun?

Entertainment value.

The General eyed the battle as he spoke to Snake, "What's going on, now?"

"I just received word from Roxanne. She needs to be rescued and she needs the Lords to stop the Betrayer. It's not over yet."

Why is it that Roxanne always calls you and not me?

I'm better looking and smarter than you.

Hey! I'm fucking gorgeous.

I know.

The General's heart ached. He knew what had to be done, but he hated to leave his men. There just wasn't enough of him to go around. *I wish I could duplicate myself.* He did a moment of mental tactical calculation, then came to a decision.

"Karlis, Kilmer! You two are in charge of the main force. Keep these trolls busy and contained. Have a guard follow my team to the entrance to keep any trolls from following us in. Snake, the Commander, and I are going to take the Lords inside and put a stop to this once and for all."

Kilmer and Karlis nodded, "Yes sir," they replied in unison.

The General nodded as well. "Commander, Snake, you are with me. Oh, and just one more thing."

"Yes, General?" asked Karlis.

"Don't let anybody die."

The two soldiers took a deep gulp of air, for they knew the General was serious. As he watched Snake, the General, and the Commander disappear, he felt a chill run down his spine. This was really the last chance. *And so it begins... Shit! I've got troops to command.* With that thought on his mind, Karlis pulled his sword, nodded to his friend, and charged forward.

****

The Betrayer watched as an entire spiral crushed half of his army. "NOOO!" he cried in anger and sent another bolt of magic flying toward the battered Chosen One. It bounced off her, reflected by the magic of the pendant. This enraged him even more.

"This is all your fault, all your doing!"

Roxanne sucked in all the air she could, "You... are... the... idiot... who... believed... it," she panted as she battled for her life.

Another bolt of magic came flying through the air. "You will die painfully."

How many more times are you going to do that you moron? The magic blasts weren't dangerous, but they were becoming annoying. Roxanne just didn't have time for them. Ever since the Betrayer had realized that he had been tricked, she had been engaged in mortal combat with every troll in the building. She was sweating, panting, and covered with blood. It wasn't looking too good for her side. In desperation, she called out to her friend, again.

Snake! I hate to do this, but HELP!!!

At that precise second a dagger came flying through the air and planted itself in the heart of one of the trolls she was doing battle with. *Quit your whining. I'm here already.* With that, General Sabastian, Commander Gabriel, and Snake came crashing through the door, swords in hand. Gabriel pushed his way in until he was standing back to back with Roxanne.

"Together again," he said. "How we doing?"

Roxanne picked up her cue, "Same as always."

"That bad, huh?"

The Betrayer's rage filled the whole room, "You shall all pay for this interference!"

The Commander raised an eyebrow, "Who the hell is this guy and what is his problem?"

Roxanne smiled, "Oh, him. Just some guy I met at a party."

Snake and the General stood back to back on the other side of the chamber. They looked like a pair of war-crazed warriors. Both fought with a cool vengeance that gave them complete control over their victims.

"Will you two stop gibbering over there and start fighting?" called Snake.

"Sorry mom," came the unisoned reply.

But the jokes stopped when the Betrayer started laughing. Everyone in the room turned to look at the evil specter. His laughter sent chills throughout the room.

"You can fight until you are all dead, but none of you will ever destroy me. I can wait until you are done."

"What's he talking about?" asked the General.

Roxanne yelled back, "It's true. We can't destroy him."

Then, the Lords stepped into the room and High Lord Brennen spoke.

"But we can."

The appearance of the Lords filled Roxanne with relief and panic. She knew that only they could eliminate the Betrayer, but she also knew that they had no way of protecting themselves from him... not in here anyway. She had to react.

Slashing through the nearest troll and drop-kicking another one, she cleared herself a path to the Lords. With only a split seconds hesitation, Gabe and Snake followed her lead. As though he understood it was a Chosen thing, the General stood his ground and waited. Roxanne stepped boldly infront of the Lords. Snake and Gabe quickly joined her, and the Betrayer sent his magic flying.

What happened next shocked everyone except Roxanne and the Betrayer. They simply stood and glared into each other's eyes as the magic hit the pendants and reflected out into the room, wiping out most of the remaining trolls. Snake and the Commander shook their heads to clear the dust. *What the hell was that?* asked Gabe.

"Very clever, Chosen One," mused the Betrayer. "Very clever indeed. Only now I know who the others are, and you cannot protect the Lords forever."

Oh, I get it. It's another lovely magical property of these damned necklaces.

You got it, Snake. "I will if I have to. You can't stop the three of us."

"Oh really. I have plenty of troops to finish you off. Don't I Mongrel?"

All eyes turned to the twisted little man who was hiding, until now, unnoticed in the corner. He put a nervous hand in the air and mumbled a few indistinguishable words. The waters of the cauldron started to bubble and rumble. Mongrel stepped back as the waters came flowing over the top. As the black ooze spread across the floor, figures began to appear and trolls grew where none had stood. It was definitely a turn for the worst.

General Sabastian decided to put an end to this. With the agility of a panther, speed of a cheetah, and strength of a bear, he charged forward and put an end to Mongrel's miserable existence. As he died, Roxanne thought she detected a smile upon his face, but she couldn't be sure. She felt a pity for him even as he died.

Despite the efforts of the General, it was too late. The damage had been done. The room was crawling with trolls and the fight began anew. With an evil smirk upon his face, the Betrayer stood back and waited for his chance.

After several minutes of intense fighting, Roxanne felt a tugging at her mind. It was Snake.

We can't do this forever. We have to come up with something. Got any bright idea?

Roxanne was at a loss. *Nothing. I've been racking my brain for a way to use these damn pendants.*

The Commander decided to join in. *What about the Lords? How did they handle this last time?*

A flash of memory caught the corner of her mind. *Wait a minute.*

You got something? asked Snake.

Maybe. Last time, Brennen used the necklaces to banish the sisters that were wearing them.

Hello, Roxie. That's not going to be good for me, see, I'm wearing the necklace.

Relax, Gabe. Think this through. What happened when the Betrayer zapped us?

Oh, no. I see where you're going. But what if it doesn't work? We only get one shot at something like that.

Snake put in the final word. *If it doesn't work, we won't be around to know any better. I say we do it. Hell, we've done everything else.*

General Sabastian glanced at the three Chosen. He could tell by their slowed reflexes and the empty looks in their eyes that they were having one of those mental pow-wows of theirs. He hacked apart another troll and groaned. There wasn't time for this.

"I have no idea what the hell the three of you are talking about over there, but you'd better hurry up and come up with something before it doesn't matter to any of us!"

Roxanne snapped to attention. He had a point.

"Okay guys, cover me while I talk to the Lords."

Lord Earin had been so relieved to see Roxanne alive that he almost forgot what was going on around him. Now, as she approached him and the other Lords, he forgot his excitement and concentrated on the reality of the situation. He knew things were about to get shaky.

"Okay, fellows. We have an idea. How long will it take you to conjure up a banishment spell?"

The Commander listened to the first question Roxanne asked the Lords, but that was all the attention he could afford. There were too many other things to occupy his time. Namely, the big, black, evil dude in the corner and the twenty or so trolls running straight at them. He had more important things to do than listen to Roxanne and the Lords plan the final fate of the land. He barely had time to hack apart a couple of trolls before Roxanne was standing at his side.

"You guys ready?" she asked her fellow Chosen.

"Ready as I'll ever be," replied Snake.

"Don't you think we should let the hard-working General in on this?" asked Gabe in an attempt to delay the inevitable.

Roxanne grinned an evil grin, "On my mark," she called over her shoulder. "General!"

General Sabastian turned to see the three Chosen poised and ready to pounce.

"What?"

"Duck!"

That was the last word out of Roxanne's mouth, then she and the others were in motion in one last ditch attempt to end this war. Roxanne charged straight for the Betrayer's heart at full speed. He actually took a step back when he realized she wasn't about to stop. He was so engrossed by her insane movements that he failed to notice the other two Chosen who had flanked him, or that the Lords were totally exposed.

Then, when she was close enough to feel his hot breath, Roxanne stopped and turned around. Like synchronized swimmers, the Lords executed a banishment spell right on target. The Betrayer smiled at their pathetic magic, until he realized that they were not aiming for him; they were aiming for the Chosen. Panic seized his heart, but it was too late for him to do anything. The magic of his mothers' amulets was beyond his control. He covered his head and bowed to the force of his beginnings.

The Chosen stood, eyes closed, teeth clenched and waited for the heat of the pendants to die down. Roxanne did not want to open her eyes; she was afraid of what she might see. She couldn't take it if the Betrayer was still standing there laughing. She kept her eyes closed.

Hey, is he gone yet?

I don't know, Gabe. Why don't you tell me?

I can't look.

Oh, for heavens sake, would the two of you open your eyes.

On Snake's command, they opened their eyes and slowly looked around. They couldn't believe what they saw. All of the trolls were gone, the cauldron was laying in little pieces on the floor, the General was smiling triumphantly in the center of the room, the Lords were hugging each other, and there was absolutely no trace of the Betrayer anywhere. Even the air felt warmer.

"There, that wasn't so bad now, was it?"

Snake and Roxanne both turned slowly to gaze at the Commander in disbelief.

"I'll hold him, while you hit him," Roxie said to Snake.

"Deal."

Gabe ran behind the General for protection.

"Hey, don't hide behind me. I don't want to be in the middle of this. I've fought my battles."

Instead of making another smart-ass remark, the Commander stopped and stared at the Lords. The rest of them took a cue from him and turned to look. There was a warm, green glow surrounding them and the High Lord was crying.

"What the?" asked Gabe.

The General nodded, "They are ready to return to **their** home. It's over."

Roxanne put her hand on their shoulders and started them out the door. "Yes it's over. Now, let's go home."

Then, the tiny group of people who had managed to save the Land, headed home. On her way out the door, Roxanne hesitated and almost turned around to check to make sure the Betrayer was really gone. However, her movie sense got the better of her. *In a horror film, once you've killed the bad guy, never, ever check to see if he's really dead.* Instead, she grasped Lord Earin's hand and skipped out the door. It was over.

****

Roxanne stood on the edge of the Silver Lake and looked down upon Major Elway's grave. For the first time, she was able to smile down upon it. She knew he was gone, but a part of him lived on in her heart, and a part of him had saved the Land. Without him, none of them would be alive today. She kneeled and kissed the ground where he was buried.

"I know it's not much, but it's me."

A sudden breeze blew across the forest. Roxie wiped the hair from her eyes and smiled as the familiar scent of the Major touched her nostrils.

"That's not much either. I guess we're even."

She picked herself up and headed back down the grassy hill. Somehow, the Silver Forest seemed even more brilliant since the demise of the Betrayer. The grass was softer, the air fresher, and the sun brighter. *Or maybe it's just my imagination? Who cares.* It didn't matter. The fact was the fighting was over and a new life had begun for everyone, even the fairies. Roxanne smiled again at the thought of life.

"Roxie! Roxie!" Sage called out to her as he came running up the hill to meet her.

When he reached her, he threw his arms around her waist and buried his head in her chest. Roxanne stroked his soft, blond hair. This little boy was her pride and joy. She knew that someday he'd make one hell of a High Lord.

Sage looked up at Roxanne with soulful eyes, "Don't go."

Her heart broke at his tender words. "I have to," she replied.

"But why? There's no more Betrayer here to worry about."

Roxanne smiled down on him, "Exactly. Now, you are all safe and don't need my protection anymore. But, there are still many dangers back in my own land; dangers I now know I have the strength to face. And," she let her mind drift to her little brother, "there are people who need me."

"I need you."

"No, you don't. You just think you do."

Another voice entered the conversation, "Aren't you gone, yet?"

Roxanne turned on Gabe, "You aren't that lucky."

Snake slinked in behind him and leaned up against a tree. In the three days since the Betrayer's destruction, those two had been inseparable, no matter what they wanted others to think.

"You are planning on coming back, aren't you?"

"Snake, I didn't know you cared."

Snake grinned, "I don't. You've got my knives."

Roxie knew better. No matter what she said, Snake loved her. *That's what you think.* Great, she hadn't meant to broadcast that. *Oh well, you can say what you want.*

Gabe came up and wrapped his arms around her, "Be careful, Roxie. Don't forget us."

Tears welled up in her eyes, "Impossible. Take care of yourself."

Gabe stepped back and Snake stepped forward. After years of fighting all emotions except hate, Snake wasn't sure how she should feel, but she knew she didn't want her friend to go. She placed a single hand on her shoulder and didn't say a word. She still had a long way to go, but that was powerful enough for Roxanne.

Soon, everyone was there, saying good-bye and giving advice. Roxanne laughed, hugged, scolded and cried. But, nothing could prepare her for saying good-bye to Lord Earin.

When all the others had finished, he walked up to her and took her hand in his. "You are my best friend. You are the keeper of my soul. I love you deeper than you'll ever understand. And, I swear, I will always be with you."

That was all she could take. There was nothing else left in her. Laying her head upon his shoulder, she sobbed shamelessly. They held each other for a few minutes before a gentle tugging pulled them apart. Roxanne wiped the tears from her eyes and smiled at Shylark.

"It is time," he said.

She nodded. It was time. All of her good-byes were done. If she didn't go now, she wouldn't have the strength to leave. She looked around at all of her friends, but she couldn't think of a thing to say. She didn't have to; they all understood. And, as she started to fade in a glow of emerald green light, they all knew that they were closing the door on a very special chapter in their lives.

For a few minutes after Roxanne had faded away, no one said a word. But, life goes on.

Sage looked up at High Lord Brennen, "Who will I be page to now?"

The High Lord smiled down on the tiny boy who was all too quickly becoming a man, "You are no longer a page. You have served your time and proved your worth."

Sage felt confused, "Then, what shall I do?"

Shylark put his arm around Sage's shoulder, "You will stay with me and learn to be a Lord."

Sage smiled. *Now, that's a good idea.*

Gabe and Snake watched as the others made their way back to the fairy dwellings. They were all alone, again, and Snake had something on her mind. Gabe looked at her and sighed. They had been inseparable for three days, but they weren't any closer than they had been. That saddened Gabe. He had hoped that, with the war over, things would be different. He had been kidding himself. Neither one of them had mentioned the conversation they had that night a week ago. Neither one of them knew how to handle it. Gabe looked at Snake's soft blonde hair shimmering in the breeze. *Fuck it. Here goes nothin'.*

"Snake, I..."

Before he could finish, Snake had slid up to him and put her hand over his mouth.

"Shhh. Don't say it, okay?"

Gabe gazed into her pleading blue eyes, "Okay."

She could feel his pain, "Look, I've spent a lifetime forgetting how to love. You can't make up for that in such a short time."

Gabe nodded his head; he knew it was true. It still didn't stop his pain and longing. He pulled her close in his arms.

"Don't look so beaten," whispered Snake. "The war is over, and we've got nothing but time on our hands."

He looked into her grinning face and knew that he could teach her to love again. Plastering a "gee-aren't-I-just-God's-gift-to-the-world" grin on his face, Gabe scooped Snake up into his arms. As he took her into the forest, a single thought crossed his mind. *Damn, it's not even sunset.*

****

Epilogue

Roxanne dragged her tired body up the third flight of steps leading to her dorm room and her nice, soft bed. Interdimensional travel always wore her out; it was worse than jet-lag. She turned the corner at the top of the stairs and headed down the long hallway home. This had been one hell of a ride.

She had come to in the parking lot behind the movie theater where Rocky was playing. She had been amazed to find her truck still parked in the parking lot. She had been horrified when she remembered her keys were in her pants pocket and those were back at the castle, (she had come home in fresh clothes provided by the fairies). Fortunately, she always kept a spare key under the hood. When she turned on the radio, she almost fell out of her seat. Only a week had past since she left. She had spent months in the land and time had just eeked by back home.

They probably didn't even know I was gone. Standing infront of her dorm room door, she hoped her roommates hadn't gotten any smarter, it was, after all, one o'clock in the morning. She tried the door. It swung open. *Once a moron, always a moron.*

She looked around the living room. There were dirty dishes, books, and different nail polishes everywhere. On the couch, Vic and her boyfriend were fast asleep. Roxanne stared at them for a minute. *Nope. I didn't miss them at all.* She still had every desire to murder Vic with her bare hands. That thought brought a smile to her face as she realized that, now, she could do it. *Ah, but who's got the energy.*

She decided to skip that for tonight.

Instead, she stumbled down the hall and fell into her nice, soft bed. She barely took the time to slide her sword under the bed before burying her head in the pillow and drifting off into a deep, peaceful sleep.

A shrill screaming jarred Roxanne from her dreamless slumber. Without thinking, she rolled from the bed, snatched her sword, and came up in a crouch. Panting and paranoid, it took her a moment to get her bearings. *Of course, Vic's damn alarm clock.* The clock read six a.m. and it was a Sunday morning. *Oh, you've ticked your last tock.* In a single swing, Roxanne sliced through that annoying piece of metal and ended its reign of terror.

"One demon down," she glanced toward the living room, "and several to go." Once again, she returned to her bed.

This time the sound of heavy footsteps awakened Roxanne's senses. She lay motionless and half asleep. A hand on her shoulder sent her into action. She rolled over, grabbed her assailant by the throat, and threw her onto the bed. This woke her up enough to see that it was only Vic. She plopped back down in bed.

"Jesus, Vic. You startled me."

Victoria was clenching her throat and gasping, "You? What about me? You almost killed me!"

The soldier in her took over, "Quit your whining, you are still alive."

Indignation covered her flustered roommates face, Roxanne ignored it.

"What do you want?"

"Well, a lot of thanks I get. I come in here to see if you are still alive because there is some guy here looking for you, and you try to kill me."

For a sudden and unexplainable reason, Roxie's heart skipped a beat. She tried to remain calm. "What guy?"

Vic tossed her hair, "How do I know? Just some weird guy asking if you were home, yet."

Roxanne leaped to her feet and made a dash for the door. She barely even heard Vic's moaning about her alarm clock. Her mind was on the front door and a promise. When she flung open the door, her heart jumped into her throat and started pounding wildly at the sight of the man she loved, Lord Earin.

Laughing and crying at the same time, she wrapped her arms ound him, "It's good to see ya, Doc."

Holding her as he had always wanted, Earin could think of one thing to say, "I love you."

Roxanne looked him in the eye, "And, I love you."

Then they kissed. The second their lips met, it was magic. Not the kind of magic that saves worlds; it was much stronger than that. This was the kind of magic that saves souls.

When their lips finally parted, Roxanne had to grin, "You'll have a lot to get use to here."

Earin looked down at the daggers hanging around her belt and smiled, "Looks like you will, too."

Taking each other by the hand, the two lovers made a silent commitment to live life together, no matter what the odds. Though the battle with the Betrayer was over, the battle with this reality had just started. And so it begins...

About the Author

K.M. Outten has been writing stories, poems, and books since she learned to write. Of all the dreams she had, being a published author has always been the most important. The second in a family of six children, she discovered what hard work and dedication meant at a very young age. With a fiery determination, she graduated from the University of Arizona while working two jobs. Currently, she is a full-time teacher, a part-time bartender, and a graduate student working on her Master's degree. In her spare time, she writes. She has ten poems published in anthologies through the National Library of Poetry. <u>And So It Begins...</u> is her first novel. She hopes to have books two and three out within the next couple of years, as well as a Ph.D. She is an enthusiastic writer and an avid learner. She currently lives in Tucson, AZ with her husband.

"The greatest advice I can give those around me is: Life is far too short not to live. Remember that the time you have now is the only time you will ever have to do what you dream, so do it."